ORANGEBURG LIBRARY
3 2828 00163 7277

W9-AYD-543

DISCARDED

FEAST YOUR EYES

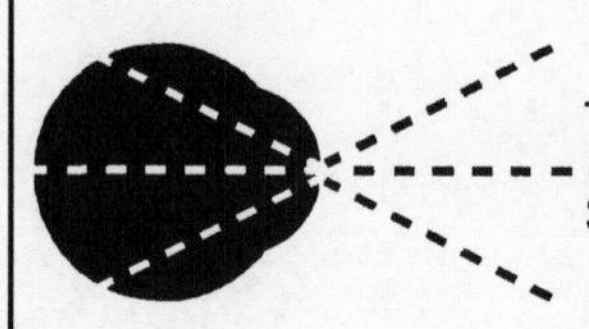

This Large Print Book carries the Seal of Approval of N.A.V.H.

FEAST YOUR EYES

MYLA GOLDBERG

THORNDIKE PRESS
A part of Gale, a Cengage Company

Farmington Hills, Mich • San Francisco • New York • Waterville, Maine
Meriden, Conn • Mason, Ohio • Chicago

Thorndike Press, a part of Gale, a Cengage Company.

Thorndike Press® Large Print Peer Picks.
The text of this Large Print edition is unabridged.
Other aspects of the book may vary from the original edition.
Set in 16 pt. Plantin.

LIBRARY OF CONGRESS CIP DATA ON FILE.
CATALOGUING IN PUBLICATION FOR THIS BOOK
IS AVAILABLE FROM THE LIBRARY OF CONGRESS

ISBN-13: 978-1-4328-6796-6 (hardcover alk. paper)

Published in 2019 by arrangement with Scribner, an imprint of Simon & Schuster, Inc.

Printed in Mexico
1 2 3 4 5 6 7 23 22 21 20 19

To Megan;
to friendship.

I was ten when I saw it, Pops sitting across the breakfast table with his *Daily News* and his cigarette. I looked up from my cornflakes, and there it was, staring at me from the front page: a little kid in her underwear with black bars printed over her eyes and her chest. She was holding out a glass of milk to some woman lying on a bed, and there was a dark spot on the sheet between the woman's legs. The headline above the photo was the same monster size they used when JFK got shot the year before.

Judge Rules . . . MOMMY *IS* SICK

Man, I thought, that girl must have made her mom sick! With a glass of milk! And made her bleed! She had to be real trouble, that girl, because how else do you get your photo on the front page of the newspaper?

On the TV news that night, she was

crossed out just the same, this time sitting on a couch in a beaded necklace. Walter Cronkite said her name was Samantha and her mother was a photographer, Lillian Preston. The pictures in the paper and on TV were from eight photographs that he called "The Samantha Series." They had been on display in a photography show until the gallery got shut down because Samantha was mostly naked in the pictures, not to mention that the photo from the morning paper, which was actually called *Mommy is sick,* had to do with abortion. I didn't know what abortion was, except that it was against the law and some kind of a sin, but that was enough. I grabbed the *Daily News* from the trash bin and stashed it under my bed, and that was how Samantha Preston became a dark goddess to me. Whenever the world went gray, I would pull out *Mommy is sick* and stare at a girl who was ten times worse trouble than I ever was, until I'd start to feel better.

I was twenty before I saw the photo again. I had been in the city a few years, working lousy jobs and going to shows, and my friend Brian and I decided to start a band. As I was looking through one of his crazy scrapbooks, there it was: same picture, same headline. The song came to me right away, like I'd been writing it in my head all that time. When we put out "Mommy Is Sick" as a single, we used a repro of the newspaper clipping for the record sleeve because there was no one to tell us not to. Then we got signed and they told us we had to ask permission for that kind of thing, but it had been ten years and no one we asked even knew who Lillian Preston was, so for the album cover we made our own version: Brian in bed with ketchup between his legs and me in my underwear holding out the milk glass, black grease paint over my eyes and black electrical tape over my B-cups. By the time we were asked to play *Saturday Night Live,* I was performing in that getup only for special occasions, but national live TV is as special as it comes, which is why America saw just half of "Mommy Is Sick" before I ripped off my dress and the network cut to a commercial.

A few days later the phone rang. I picked up and a voice asked, "Are you Frances Pell?"

"Who's this?" I said.

"This is Samantha," said the voice on the phone.

"Samantha who?"

There was a pause, then a click, and then it was too late.

After that Brian and I were touring a lot, doing all the stupid things people do living that kind of a life. Whenever we came back to New York, our manager would drop off a box of band mail that had been sent to the label. To sort through it, Brian and I would spend hours holed up in his apartment drinking Jack and Coke. People sent all kinds of stuff: poetry, drawings, love letters, hate letters. One night I opened a big yellow envelope with my name on it, and inside was a picture of me sitting cross-legged on the hood of a car. I had no memory of anyone taking that photo or of sitting on that car to begin with, which wasn't unusual in those days, but it felt like I'd been spied on. Brian was pissed when I tore the photo in half. He said it was a great shot, but what mattered to me was the invasion of privacy. After Brian grabbed the envelope, he read the note that came with it, then started shaking his head. "Nice job, shithead. You just tore up a photograph by Lillian Preston." When he showed me her name, I wanted to kick my own ass.

For the next twenty-odd years of making music, my Lillian Preston story stayed filed away with everything else I wished I'd done differently, until I got a call from a curator at the Museum of Modern Art. They were planning a Lillian Preston show: would I take a look at the photographs, maybe write something for the catalogue? I figured this would be my chance to thank her. The math in my head told me Lillian Preston was in her fifties, so when I got there, I was looking for a middle-aged person. Waiting for me in the curator's office instead was a woman about my age. I was pretty sure I'd seen her somewhere, but that's a feeling I get all the time. Then she said, "Are you Frances Pell?"

Don't hang up, yelled the voice inside my head. I know who you are.

For the rest of that day, we looked at her mother's photographs. I thought they'd all be naked people, but they weren't, at least not in the usual way. Lillian Preston was mostly a street photographer. She lived her life blending into backgrounds and snapping whoever passed by. For all that, these people aren't strangers. Sometimes it's a look in the eyes, or the way someone is standing, but what's unfamiliar lifts away. The people in Lillian Preston's pictures seem like people I know. Sometimes, looking at a stranger, it feels like I'm looking at myself.

I'll be honest: I didn't always like what I saw. It's hard being jolted like that, time after time, truth after truth, in black and white. But it's also beautiful. These photos — whatever else they may be — are also beautiful. Some of them are from before anyone heard of Lillian Preston or "The Samantha Series," but most are from the years that came after Lillian and her daughter had been threatened, followed, and forced to change their address and phone number. After Lillian had been called brilliant, poetic, brave, visionary, exploitative, criminal, neglectful, selfish, and a bad mother. By 1973, when the Supreme Court finally got around to changing the definition of what was obscene — not to mention rewriting abortion law — Lillian Preston had pretty much stopped showing her pictures to anyone. Luckily, that wasn't the same thing as not making pictures at all.

If you're reading this, you already know all that. You've seen the photographs at the show, or you've looked through the images in the front half of this catalogue, and you've seen all that hard beauty for yourself. So let me tell you something you don't know: aside from the seven thousand rolls of film and hundreds of prints Lillian left behind when she died, separate from the binders of technical notes, were three boxes. Box One held Lillian's twenty-four journals from the summer she split Cleveland at age seventeen to the day cancer killed her at forty. Box Two contained the prints she'd made for this exhibition, plus a letter asking her daughter to bring them to MoMA, in case they might do for her dead what they'd never done for her alive. Box Three had the prints and negatives from "The Samantha Series" and a letter giving her daughter a choice: destroy them, or include them with the prints in Box Two.

Believe it or not, the woman Samantha Jane Preston turned into was going to let some curatorial shirt write about the photographs in this exhibition. "Are you crazy?" I told her. "The only one who can do that is you. You're the one who lived with Lillian, who fought with her, who knew her friends, who went through the whole Samantha thing and came out the other end. Use everything — use her diaries, use her letters, go back and talk to the important people in her life — to show her work in a way that an art-establishment type never could." I got a long stare after that, or what I thought was a long stare until I realized that she'd gone somewhere deep inside herself and I just happened to be standing in front of her. Then, in a quiet voice that was more for herself than anyone else, she said, "It's too late for a lot of things, but I guess it's not too late for that."

And so this catalogue was written by someone whose life was tangled up in these photographs along with the lives of all the people who helped make them, whether they were standing in front of the camera, behind the camera, or somewhere off to the side. Because of that, it's not like any catalogue you've read before. It's personal. It's unprofessional. And when the art-establishment types saw it, they were smart enough to leave it alone.

— Frances Pell, aka "Franny Panic"
New York, 1990

▪ ▪ ▪ ▪

Catalogue of the Exhibition

▪ ▪ ▪ ▪

All works are by Lillian Preston unless otherwise noted and are from the artist's estate.

Greenwich Village, 1953–54

1. *Untitled [Prentice High Camera Club, Cleveland], 1951*
Unknown photographer

Feast your eyes, America. Here she is: America's Worst Mother, America's Bravest Mother, America's Worst Photographer, or America's Greatest Photographer — depending on who's talking — as an anonymous high school junior, sporting the same light blouse/dark skirt combo and fake smile as the other girls. Look for a face with wide-set eyes and bangs at the end of the Camera Club's second row. Lilly Preston, who was never elected to class office or Most or Best anything. Other than Honor Society, this was the only high school club she was in.

Don't blame me for the pencil marks. I never touched my mother's photos. The first circled face is her photography teacher, Mr. Clark. The second is the Camera Club's president, Sam Decker, "the best photographer no one ever heard of." That description, which Lillian added whenever she showed off this picture, was the only time I heard her deploy anything resembling sarcasm.

Apparently my mother started writing Sam when she was a high school senior, at which point he'd already enlisted in the army and was serving in Korea. As far as I know, she never showed anyone else the letters she sent to him, the drafts of which she wrote in her journal. And because I only ever violated her privacy in the usual places — her bedside table, her bureau, beneath her mattress — I never found them. Not that I considered her photo boxes any more sacred than her underwear drawer, but at the time of my rabidly dysfunctional adolescence (not to be confused with my rabidly dysfunctional adulthood), fooling with those boxes would have implied an interest in her photography.

LETTER TO SAM DECKER, JUNE 1953: My Dearest Darling, I did it. After all these months of writing and planning and worrying, getting on that bus was the second-hardest thing I've ever done. The hardest was telling Father that instead of enrolling at Ursuline College, as he and Mother expected, I plan to attend photography classes at the New School. It's funny: since I was little, I knew I was meant to live differently from others, I just wasn't sure how or why. And so I earned decent grades and washed the dishes and ironed my skirts and spoke in turn, which led people to see me as a "good" girl, when really I was just waiting for that different life to reveal itself. Just as I was beginning to worry that waiting was all there would ever be, I picked up a camera — but you know this already. You're the only one who understands when I say that making pictures makes me fully and truly myself.

Thanks so much for the early anniversary present. I know how much we both like to complain about the mail but this time, at least, the army came through because it arrived the week before I left for New York. I don't have pierced ears, but they're such lovely earrings that I may need to change that so I can wear them properly — perhaps in time for our actual anniversary two months from now, especially if you're back by then and we can celebrate together. In the meantime, they make marvelous pins to fasten to my blouse. Whenever I look at them, I imagine I was with you in Kyoto during those five days on leave. It's hard to believe it's only been ten months since my first letter introduced you to a certain Camera Club member who spent her junior year admiring you and your prints without ever saying hello. Even as I rue the distance between here and Korea, I cannot avoid the strange truth of us: had you stayed in Cleveland, I'd never have summoned the courage to make any introductions at all. If you hadn't enlisted, we'd still be strangers, and I would probably be pinning an Ursuline pennant to my bedroom wall.

I won't go into the gory details of Father's reaction after I told him about New York, but when he finally realized he couldn't stop me, he decided he'd rather help than "throw me to the wolves." Never in a million years would I have thought I'd be grateful for his asking the pastor about Christian rooming establishments, but Katharine House is nicer than any hotel I'd have been able to afford, and being around other gals who are also new to the city feels a little less like living with strangers. The only problem is that the quiet girl with bangs who sat in the back row of Camera Club has followed me here. There are days I don't say more than five words between getting out of bed and returning to my room at the end of the day. Luckily, I've got my pictures. I'm taking rolls and rolls of them, and though I haven't developed any yet (the basic amenities here don't include a darkroom), I can see so many of them in my mind that they supply their own sort of company.

2. Young woman with suitcase in the Port Authority Bus Terminal, New York, 1953

Not Lillian. Compare it to the girl in the Camera Club photo and you'll see that Young Woman's nose is too pointy and the hair is too dark, not to mention that the body is all wrong, but I think Lillian still saw herself in the person stepping off that bus. Why? Because even though the station around Young Woman is a big, busy blur, she doesn't seem lost or even alone. One look at her face and you can tell she's exactly where she wants to be.

LETTER TO SAM DECKER, JUNE 1953:
It's silly, but back at home wearing a shirt and coat of Father's on my Saturday photography walks somehow gave me a kind of permission and made me feel less conspicuous. I intended to leave those clothes behind, but in the end I couldn't imagine stalking New York without my

usual camouflage. Every time I put them on, I feel a twinge of guilt, followed by a trace of comfort.

So far I've kept almost completely to the bus station: it's something to do with all those suitcases, and all the faces to whom those suitcases belong. There are so many ways to greet a city! Some people look as if they're waiting for someone, but if you keep watching, you'll see that they're not disappointed when no one comes. That's because they're waiting for the city to meet them, and it always does.

3. Breakfast at Katharine House, New York, 1953

Just look at all those paragons of young womanhood hovering over their cereal bowls. Use a black marker to draw a wimple on each head and — ta-da — instant nunnery. Part of it has to do with the long, narrow wooden tables, but mostly it's the way Lillian captured the sun beaming through those high roominghouse windows, bathing all those bright-eyed girls in churchly light. The one who became her roommate in her first New York apartment is fourth from the bottom right.

PATRICIA STOKES: I'd not been at Katharine House more than a week when Lilly showed up, and immediately I said to myself: this one is worth getting to know. It was easy to see she was the most interesting hat on the stand. While the rest of us were busy reinventing ourselves — which mostly meant a lot of talk and nail lacquer and twisting and pinning our hair overnight to turn us all into Elizabeth Taylor — there was Lilly perched at the other end of the room, wearing a man's shirt, with just a few barrettes to keep her hair out of her face and a camera practically attached to the end of her arm like a second hand. At breakfast she'd set it right beside her prunes and oatmeal like it was the morning paper. She was nice enough if you tried to chat her up, but mostly she just took pictures.

It didn't take long for the rumors to fly. One girl insisted Lilly was a spy for the Reds, another that she was a scout for the Ford Modeling Agency. Well, that got all the aspiring Suzy Parkers in a lather. Suddenly there was a lot of languorous posing on the divans. At that point I didn't know who or what Lilly was, just that she was the only girl besides me not hawking head shots or shorthand.

When I told her about the rumors, I got

treated to her laugh. Lilly laughed like a bicycle pump. Her face turned red and her mouth opened up and you'd brace yourself for something loud, but instead this positively delicate *hsshss* sound would come from between those prim lips of hers; it was the funniest thing. Then it turned out that all those times in the parlor, she hadn't even been taking our pictures! Like every other girl too poor to stay at the Barbizon, Lilly was on a strict budget, so she saved most of her film for walking around. Since she was too shy to actually talk to anyone, she mooned about downstairs taking what she called "practice snaps" with her empty camera just to avoid being alone. I kept that juicy tidbit to myself: I was having too much fun watching the fashion plates flash their profiles every time Lilly walked into a room.

LETTER TO SAM DECKER, JUNE 1953: Father refused me any going-away money, having made it clear that he viewed all those hours I spent working in his office as wages earned under false pretenses. Technically that isn't true: only Father ever described it as "pin money" for my freshman year, but it's equally true that I never corrected him. I suppose, then, that I'm guilty as charged — but to my own mind, what matters is that I never lied about it, even if Father doesn't see the difference!

Some days the disappointment I've caused them is easy to shrug off, and I launch myself into the city feeling equal to anything. Other days (today, for instance) it's a struggle just to leave my room. If I were to go back, Mother would forgive me everything; it wouldn't take long for Father to come around; and I'd attend Ursuline College, and take classes in English or history, with a wall of my room saved for showing off my "little hobby," just like Father and his model planes.

Darling, do you still say my name when you look up at the stars? I can't always find a star in the sky here, but each night I try. My latest letters with my New York address are probably still on their way to you, and it's anyone's guess whether Mother will forward the letters you may have already sent to Cleveland. Once a day I ask at the reception desk for mail, just in case.

My budget doesn't allow for newspapers or magazines, but fortunately there's almost always an abandoned *Times* or *Post* in the sitting room. Even so, there's hardly ever more than one story about

Korea. Usually it's buried in the middle somewhere, and it's never about you, thank goodness. Of course, when *Life* does have something, it's invariably next to an ad for Frigidaires or Philco radios, as if you and everybody else in Korea were no more significant than a household appliance! Really, I think most people want to forget we're at war at all.

We've never discussed what will happen once the war ends, but I'm sure you'll agree it's hardly fitting for the next Robert Capa to stay in Cleveland. If you ask me, there's no finer city than New York for a future *Life* photographer and Pulitzer Prize winner. When you arrive, you'll have the extra advantage of a very friendly face waiting for you at the station.

4. American leg (Patty crossing the street), New York, 1953

LETTER TO WALTER AND DOROTHY PRESTON, JUNE 1953: I have met a nice girl at Katharine House, an aspiring painter called Patricia Stokes who has become my friend. I've even photographed her a few times! After we both find work, we are going to rent an apartment in the neighborhood. I don't know whether I want to go back to working in an office, but there seem to be lots of other suitable opportunities for young women. While I know you and Mother have reservations about the New School, one advantage to their night classes is that I will be able to work and study at the same time. Has any mail arrived for me? I should be at this address for at least another two weeks, so please don't hesitate to forward anything that may come.

Even though I wasn't there (or anywhere) when Lillian took this one, I know exactly how she did it. Lillian was allergic to posed shots, so instead of posing the person, she'd pose the background and wait for someone (in this case, Patricia) to walk in. Lillian called it a spider shot. As far as I was concerned, a longer name would have been better, something full of similar syllables that would take hours to say. Whenever the weather was nice — which for Lillian was anything without rain or snow between 35 and 98 degrees — I spent some serious quality time on benches and stoops while she waited beside her camera for the right person to pass into her perfectly composed frame. My kindergarten teacher thought I was a genius for being able to read chapter books, but by then I'd spent several small lifetimes stuck in places with nothing better to do than try to parse a printed page as Lillian waited beside her web.

Mostly she didn't know who that someone would be until they showed up, but in this case she must have known her roommate's habits and staked out the street corner, waiting for Patricia to strut past the partly burned-out American Legion sign. Without the title's parenthetical bit, this would be just an anonymous pair of cigarette pants, but the name makes those legs feel as personal as a face.

Patricia Stokes must have been a veritable emblem of exotic womanhood to Lillian, considering that it was eight more years before my mother owned a pair of pants. Not that she ever wore them outside the darkroom. After Lillian became the American poster child (or at least the poster child's photographer) for immorality and perversion, some people actually accused her of dressing like a 1950s librarian to mock American decency. For that to be true, she'd have had to put actual thought into her wardrobe, which — going by the skirts and sweater sets — was something she'd stopped doing around age sixteen.

PATRICIA STOKES: Here's why I agreed

to live with Lilly: when I told her I wanted to be an artist, she asked what kind. Back in Wilmington, "artist" always put an end to the conversation. What kind? Now I must *really* be in New York! I found a waitressing job at a place on Madison that served Continental food on good china, hailing distance from some of the art galleries. I was convinced it would take only one regular customer, a wealthy collector intrigued by the terribly attractive waitress who made cryptic references to her work while serving his beef Bourguignon. As you might infer, I was eighteen and not awfully original. Anyhow the shift manager and I got along just fine so when one of the waitresses quit I told him I had a friend. Lilly wasn't experienced, but she was keen to learn. In an abundance of rookie enthusiasm she twisted a corkscrew into a cork without first removing the foil, but as soon as the boss could trust her with a bottle of Bordeaux he started offering her dinner shifts on my nights off. Get this: instead of taking the work like any self-respecting kid desperate to make rent, Lilly told him she'd signed up for evening photography classes starting that fall so he should probably find another girl. Well, that just impressed the hell out of me. It must have impressed our boss, too, because he told Lilly she could work as many dinners as she liked, and he'd schedule her however she needed come September.

5. Bullfrog (boy selling newspapers), New York, 1953

Kids don't show up much in my mother's work until I come along, which — face it — wouldn't have happened if she had been more worldly or if the Pill had appeared in 1954 instead of 1960. But being unplanned isn't the same as being unwanted. For example, the boy in this picture was unplanned. Lillian hadn't set out to photograph a child on that particular day. Still, it's easy to tell that as soon as Lillian saw this kid, she fell in love with everything from the angle of his cap, to the tiny snubbed nose above his gigantic open mouth, to the pieces of broken glass glittering at the bottom edge of the frame.

PATRICIA STOKES: Lilly put the kibosh on a few apartments that had seemed perfectly nice to me. I was beginning to worry that I'd need to find someone less particular if I wanted to escape the Suzy Parkers of Katharine House when Lilly finally found something she liked. The place didn't seem any worse than the ones she had nixed, plus it was only a few blocks from the Village, so I liked it fine enough.

But, oh lord, that apartment. The front door opened directly onto the kitchen, with three more rooms lined up one behind the other, railroad-style, all for forty dollars a month — which was decent even back then, but not for no reason. We were on the second floor, right above a grocery. Between the storefront and everything happening outside, it could be hard to conduct a civilized conversation. Trucks rattled past at terrible hours with deliveries for the meatpacking plants. Every morning, before you could properly even call it that, something I called The Monster started hawking newspapers. I stuffed cotton in my ears, but Lilly used The Monster as her personal rooster to log camera time before her lunch shift uptown.

When she showed me this photo, I thought she was pulling my leg. I'd assumed some burly lumberjack was making all the racket. That boy's talents were seriously underused: he could have been mounted to a police car during a riot or strapped to a lighthouse on a foggy night and done some real public good. I told Lilly she should hang it on the wall between the kitchen windows so that when we were being serenaded, we'd have the face that went with it, to make the mornings a little easier to bear.

LETTER TO SAM DECKER, JULY 1953: It's so challenging to photograph people in a candid way. You can't waste any time thinking, you have to take the picture already knowing exactly what to do. Sometimes I manage it, but most of the time I'm still puzzling things out. I'll be considering composition or light or timing, which inevitably shows up in the print as a kind of distance that reminds anyone who's looking at it they're looking at a photograph. I don't want to make photographs. The way you described it with Capa's work is exactly right: I want to make windows.

6. Getting ready (Patty), New York, 1953
7. Makeup artist on the uptown train, New York, 1953

At this point Lillian had taken so many shots of Patricia that by the time she got on the same train as this woman applying eye shadow, I bet she snapped the shutter without knowing why. To hear Lillian describe it, when she was "locked in," she didn't tell her finger to press the shutter any more than she told her heart to pump blood.

Point being, nothing about the uptown eye-shadow woman calls Lillian's roommate to mind, since the woman in the photo is rounder and shorter and about fifteen years older. But side by side, Makeup Artist and Patricia are twins — or at least cousins, with the same raised brows and parted lips as they put their faces on.

PATRICIA STOKES: For a while I didn't mind it, since Lilly's camera was what drew me to her to begin with. Try to remember, at that point pictures were just things you took for the family album, or for newspapers or magazines. But when I saw what Lilly was doing, I knew I had to start thinking about photography in a new way.

At first it felt kind of glamorous, being followed around like that, but the feeling didn't last long. I could never tell whether Lilly was planning to take my picture until I heard the click. The whole conversation, she'd be looking straight at me. Then her hand would start doing its own thing, like it was possessed. It was creepy, if you really want to know. The worst was when she'd disappear for a while, sneak back into whatever room I happened to be in, and then — click. So in a way, the girls at Katharine House were right: she was a spy. I finally made a rule. Lilly could be in the room with me or she could be in the room with her camera, but she couldn't be in the room with us both.

8. Woman at the window, New York, 1953

It may look like a double exposure or a combination print, but it isn't. Doubters can check the contact sheet, which shows that Lillian got the woman's expression and the outside reflection all at once. I suppose there's no way of knowing what the seamstress at the sewing machine is actually pining for, but the way Lillian caught the reflected cars and people and sidewalks makes it easy to think she wants everything on the other side of that pane of glass.

PATRICIA STOKES: Thinking back, I'd have to say that the lavatory was the beginning of the end. By the time we were moving in, Lilly had a small suitcase full of film she'd shot. When I asked her why she didn't just drop it off at the drugstore, she looked at me like I was telling her to give away her children. Apparently the whole time we'd been apartment shopping, Lilly had been waiting to find a place with a large enough bathtub and reliable hot water — which is how I learned about darkrooms, but if I had known what I was agreeing to, I never would have said yes! In any case, I was too busy deciding what color to paint the living room to notice Lilly's peculiar nesting instincts. She was installing an enlarger over the toilet, which turned our lavatory into some sort of cross between a science experiment and a torture chamber. If you weren't careful, you'd knock your head on the thing when you went to stand up. Then there was that red lightbulb, like something out of a Tennessee Williams play, which made it impossible to check your hair in the mirror. Not that going to the john is terribly complicated, but it's nice to be able to see yourself once in a while.

After Lilly set everything up, she was kind enough to invite me to a demonstration. I could barely fit alongside her and all that equipment, but somehow I managed to cram myself into the corner by the door. Lilly lined the bottom of the bathtub with four metal trays, then attached a hose to the faucet. I vaguely remember her explaining what the different chemicals were, and something else about timing as the image appeared on the paper, but to me the whole thing was magic. Lilly's pictures were just marvelous. Of course they were beautiful, but more than that, they saw through everything that was phony in the world. As consolation, I tried to tell myself that photography was easier than painting: other than pointing the camera in the right direction, you didn't have to *do* anything to make a tree look like a tree. Then I'd stand at my easel, and just the thought of all those perfect photos hanging in the bedroom next to mine made it hard to pick up a paintbrush.

9. Woman in curlers on the Lower East Side, New York, 1953

LETTER TO SAM DECKER, JULY 1953: Every day I wake up thrumming with the feeling that each minute spent inside is an opportunity missed, so I get out as soon as I can. Back home, people carry themselves appropriately in public, which is to say in a way that reveals nothing. Here in New York, with everyone living on top of each other, people do what they want, when and where they want. Almost every day reveals someone showing their true face. I still feel like a tourist, but at least I've put away Father's clothes: around

> here a girl with a camera is about as interesting to people as a fire hydrant. That kind of freedom can feel terribly lonely sometimes, in spite (or perhaps because) of all the people — but it's truly hard only when I'm lying awake at night wondering why I haven't heard from you, or when I'm running low on film. The good news is that I've found a wonderful camera shop that sells bulk film in hundred-foot batches. I bought a bulk film loader and reloadable film cartridges, so now I can make my own rolls for a fraction of the cost, which means I can spend more time shooting and less time waiting for an airmail envelope with my name on it.

That's how *Woman in curlers* became one of 450 shots Lillian took of ladies on their front stoops. Four hundred and fifty middle-aged matrons in housedresses, smoking, reading newspapers, laughing, talking, staring, napping — which, back in Cleveland, would have been as unusual as a giraffe making its way down Fernvale Road. Okay, fine, but ten rolls of them? Well, Patricia had just revoked Lillian's camera privileges, leaving poor Lillian full of unresolved stalker impulses. Plus I think Lillian was hoping that after enough photos, she'd somehow absorb the New York nonchalance that allowed these ladies to lounge outside in their housedresses in a city of seven million strangers.

Curlers is the best of the bunch. The woman is laughing in a way that gives her face a kind of Mona Lisa quality, if Mona Lisa were a wrinkled fiftysomething babushka living on East Second Street. Then there's the off-center thing. The woman stands at the left edge of the picture, her arm and pointing finger taking up the center so that she's gesturing toward something outside the frame. It's like Lillian is trying to tease us with what we can't see.

Then again, what do I know? I wasn't born yet, but by now I've spent so much time studying these pictures that I sometimes forget I'm just guessing. The truth is that when my mother was around to ask, I didn't want to know what was going through her mind. Now that I'm ready, her work is all I have left.

10. Times Square recruit, New York, 1953

LETTER TO SAM DECKER, JULY 1953: Darling, did something happen, or have I somehow upset you? If so, please write and tell me so that I can make amends. In my mind, in my heart, you're already here.

Another spider shot, but this time in the true sense of the word. Lillian would have set up her camera in order to watch future soldiers walking in and out that door, not knowing exactly who she wanted until she saw him. With that hand on his hip and his outstretched leg, this guy could almost pass for Fred Astaire, but then all that bodily joy collides with his face.

If you make a box with your fingers and use it just to frame the guy's top half and the recruitment office door, this becomes a photo about the Korean War. Take your hand away, and there's that dancing body and all of Forty-second Street, complicating things. For better or worse (mostly worse), Lillian never thought of herself as political. As far as she was concerned, she was "just interested in people." *Mommy is sick* was no different in her mind from *Times Square recruit* or any other picture she took, which might lead one to ask Miss Just Interested in People why she'd haunt an army recruitment office at the height of the Korean War to begin with. The thing is, I know exactly what she'd say: because it was July and she hadn't heard from her soldier in a while. Lillian always had reasons for what she did, it's just that her reasons made sense only if the rest of the world wasn't part of the equation.

PATRICIA STOKES: I didn't happen to know any soldiers in Korea, but Lilly claimed hers would be joining her in New York the minute he was discharged, so they could embark upon their "photographic destiny." She made those words sound practically denominational: Our Lady of the Church of Artistic Fate. For a while I thought her soldier might even be a parable she'd cooked up to duck out of hitting the bar scene with me as a sort of social revenge, since I was more outgoing than she was and knew how to dress. Eventually I got it through my thick skull that, really, Lilly hardly ever thought of me at all.

His name was Jim or Tom or Don or something equally dreary. I remember he didn't stand out as wildly handsome. Lilly kept a blurry face pinned to her wall that could have been anyone from the landlord's son to the Duke of Edinburgh. She blushingly explained it was a blowup she'd made from the framed high school club picture beside her bed. I probably said he had nice eyes or something and changed the subject.

11. Reunion, New York, 1953

Lillian's taste in titles tended toward the oppressively literal, which is what makes this one so intriguing. In the grand tradition of *Woman in curlers,* this photo should have been called something like "Couple on park bench." The way his head is lying in her lap suggests, at the very least, two people plenty comfortable with each other rather than two people in the act of reuniting. So, why the poetic title? Just this once, I'm guessing Lillian let her own wishful thinking take over.

> *PATRICIA STOKES:* It was July when the war ended, and absurdly hot, but Lilly said we ought to throw a party anyway. Of course, she didn't actually know anyone, so I invited the upstairs neighbors, some of the other waitresses, and everyone from the Art Students League, and they all piled into our stifling apartment like it was a clown car. I hung some new canvases for the occasion. Lilly even installed a regular lightbulb in the john. An abstract painter I had designs on was there, and a surrealist named Lyle something-or-other who went everywhere with a taxidermy bobcat on a leash.
>
> By the time of the party, Lilly's photo of the boy selling newspapers had been up

for so long that I'd stopped seeing it, but each time I went into the kitchen that night, people asked me about the damn thing. It got so that I was drinking straight bourbon in the living room just to avoid going into the next room for ice. I kept waiting for someone to notice my paintings. Nobody did, so I finally pointed them out to the abstractionist, who said something so terribly polite that I would have felt insulted if it hadn't been so early in the evening and I hadn't been so dead set on having a good time.

That was the only time I ever saw Lilly get loaded. She was smiling, talking everyone's ears off about her photographer-soldier and their bright future. By midnight, I think she was half expecting him to walk through the door — which he didn't, of course, since he was still in Korea, but then weeks passed and Lilly still hadn't heard a word. At first she said how slow the mail was. Then she worried he hadn't been getting her letters, or that her parents hadn't been forwarding his. Well, by the end of August, she was spending all her time in the john in the dark.

One night I brought home a sculptor with tiny hands. It was rather late, and I'd been drinking beer for the past five hours, and the lavatory door was shut. Lilly had me so well trained by this point that I'd gotten used to asking a neighbor, or even using a jar in a pinch; but I wasn't about to knock on a neighbor's door at three a.m., and squatting over an empty Maxwell House can in front of my new friend would have spoiled the mood. So I knocked. Lilly asked for five more minutes, which made the sculptor arch his eyebrows. When I told him my roommate was a photographer, his eyebrows fell and he explained in a disappointed voice that he had thought she was shooting up. It took rather longer than five minutes for Lilly to come out. When she finally did, I ran right in, knocking over I don't know what, but the next morning my white pumps were covered in brown splotches. Look, I told her, stop mooning around waiting for bad news, and find out what happened to your man.

LETTER TO SAM DECKER, SEPTEMBER 1953: Sometimes we're splitting an egg salad sandwich at Horn & Hardart. Sometimes we're heading to the IRT, deciding whether to see a movie or spend a quiet evening at home. Sometimes we're simply on a city street, our arms brushing as we walk. I wish the dreams were grander; then perhaps I wouldn't wake up believing them. Instead the truth hits me each morning like a fall from a third-story window.

The recruitment station looked the same as it had in July, but photographing a place is an entirely different thing from going inside. I was in such a state by the time I stepped through the door that the duty officer had to help me to a chair. He confirmed your absence on the lists of dead, wounded, or missing and was kind enough to explain the difference between an enlisted man and a draftee. I've spent so much time picturing you injured, captured, or buried in an unmarked grave that it didn't feel very different to learn that it will be years before your term of enlistment ends and you are discharged — and still my heart rushes to defend you, insisting that you never lied. The fault is mine: I wasn't paying attention. Before you gave up hope or changed your mind or stopped writing to me for some other reason that I will never know, I failed to notice that among all the pretty words in your pretty letters was never a promise to join me.

When I see men in uniform drinking coffee or running to catch the bus or standing on a corner smoking, my heart still leaps in my chest. Even now, as I write a letter that I will never send.

12. Chair, New York, 1953

The question is, did she stand on that stretch of empty sidewalk watching it burn, or did she happen to stroll by just after the last flame had died out? Either way, the armchair must have been on fire moments before for her to get that one small white plume of smoke rising from its blackened frame. It's easy to forget there aren't people in this picture. Looking at the ruins of that upholstered chair feels like looking at a body, with the scraps of charred fabric scattered on the sidewalk like spatters of blood.

PATRICIA STOKES: By the end of that summer, I'd had it up to *here.* An apartment with a lavatory I couldn't use, a roommate who never wanted to go out or even cook a simple meal — well, that wasn't what I'd signed up for. Lilly's photographs were her real roommates; I was just there to pay half the rent. Then, all of a sudden, Lilly stopped working on her photos. Whenever I was home, she was in her bedroom with the door closed, and it was quiet as church. I figured it was something to do with her soldier, and that if he was dead she would have mentioned it, so I could only assume he was dead to her. Of course I felt bad for her, but I was also just a teensy bit glad to know that not everything always turned up roses for the artistic geniuses of the world. Finally I knocked on her bedroom door. At first I heard nothing. Then I heard the creak of footsteps walking across the floorboards. Next the doorknob turned, and there was Lilly with such dark circles under her eyes that she could have passed for the love child of Peter Lorre. Oh Patty, she said in a quavery voice that I'd never heard before. Sitting on the living room couch, she wept on my shoulder with heaving sobs. As I stroked her hair and patted her arm, I realized the price for Lilly's immense talent was an immense loneliness that I would never have to know.

13. Cynthia Ravitt, New York, 1953

Lillian kept this one in a manila folder beside her copy of Ravitt's *Methods for Better Photography.* She only took it out if she really liked someone. Whenever she showed it, she'd explain in a naughty whisper that Ravitt never knew she was taking it. Then she'd giggle like a kid sneaking a piece of candy.

It's another spider shot. You can tell by how it's framed that Lillian set herself outside the New School and waited for Ravitt to come out. What makes it is how Ravitt leans forward as she walks past the building's facade, totally screwing with all its horizontal lines.

LETTER TO DOROTHY PRESTON, OCTOBER 1953: Thank you for the money. It means so much that you would send it, and of course I will keep the secret of the flour bin. I know you don't approve of what I'm doing any more than Father does, but please know that I would have been miserable doing anything else. It was Father who taught me that the kind of life worth living was one worth working for, even if this wasn't what he had in mind.

For the time being I am still waitressing, though I know you and Father disapprove of that as well. The hours are more flexible than office work, and this allows more freedom for my pictures and my classes. Thanks to your flour bin, next semester I'll be able to enroll in a workshop with the art director of a leading fashion magazine. While I'm enjoying my class with Cynthia Ravitt, it will be good to learn from someone new. Ravitt mostly lectures from her book, which I am already quite familiar with after my time in Camera Club.

Thank you also for the hat and gloves. I'm afraid I don't have a picture of myself to send you, but I promise that I'm taking care of myself, and I will try to send a picture soon.

14. Self-portrait, New York, 1953

As you might guess, this is not the picture that Lillian sent her mother. The photos on the wall behind Lillian's head would have been her favorites. They'd go downhill from there, ending with the ones she didn't like pinned to the wall across from her bed. I saw her do this in every bedroom of every apartment we ever had. I asked once why she didn't hang the best ones where she could wake up to them. She told me that she wanted to be reminded each morning of what she needed to work on, not what she already did well.

If you squint, you can see *American leg, Bullfrog, Woman at the window,* and *Woman in curlers* all here on the "best of" wall, but *Reunion* and *Times Square recruit* aren't there, even though Lillian included them in Box Two. I doubt her opinion of them changed: I just think that in the fall of 1953, they reminded her of someone she was trying to forget.

And, yes, she's naked. As I said before, Lillian was pretty literal. The same way an artist draws from naked models to get a handle on basic anatomy, I think Lillian's portraits were a way for her to study what lay at the core of people — their bodies, but also their fears, hopes, disappointments — to prepare herself for spotting those things out in the world.

Compared to *Mommy is sick, Self-portrait* is pretty tame. There's still a definite look-away-from-the-picture vibe, but it's not coming from where you might think. Lillian is lying on the bed. Her soft, pale body is like something slipped from a shell, and her face — with its crazy mixture of rebellion, invitation, uncertainty, and pride — is the most naked thing about her. Yet somehow, it's not her body or her face but the photographs behind her that make you want to cover your eyes. The way they're arranged on the wall, it's as if Lillian sliced herself open and that's what spurted out.

Pondering what might have been isn't something I waste a whole lot of time on, but it has crossed my mind that if Lillian had never set foot in the Lacuna Gallery, she easily could have spent her life thinking of herself as a street photographer who did nude pics as a hobby. In which case, instead of writing this, I could very well be married with kids and a cocker spaniel named Good Girl in a cushioned suburb farting distance from Manhattan, getting my highlights redone, with all my naked-kiddie photos in a box marked "Miscellaneous" on a shelf next to Lillian's cremains in my climate-controlled two-car garage. I'd be much happier, probably, but also a lot less interesting.

15. The reader, New York, 1953

Once Lillian showed me five prints of this photograph and asked me to pick the best one. When I told her they all looked the same, she made me look again. After a while I pointed to the middle one. Exactly, Lillian agreed, but why? I had no idea. She pointed to the bench the man was sitting on. In the two on the left, she explained, the bench was too light. In the two on the right, it was too dark. In the middle, it was perfect. Sometimes the eye can see what the brain can't put into words.

PATRICIA STOKES: For a little while after the couch episode, Lilly and I were roommates the way I'd always hoped we would be. Not that she approached anyone's ideal of a social butterfly, but for at least a few weeks she wasn't allergic to the notion of visiting a bar. Then her classes began, and the fledgling butterfly returned to her cocoon. Lilly was either at the restaurant, at school, locked inside the john, or out taking pictures. She'd never done anything scarcely resembling her share of the housework, but now she hardly washed her own dishes. In those days I possessed a high tolerance for squalor, but even back then I had certain standards; plus, I was getting bored of being Lilly's personal maid.

Just when I'd reached my limit, I came home from working the dinner shift and Lilly burst from the john like a kid on Christmas morning, holding out a photograph that was still wet. It took ten tries, she explained, but it was finally perfect. She'd made it for me.

I recognized the man straight off. I must have walked past that park bench one hundred times on my way to work, though in typical city fashion, I'd never paid the person sitting on it any more mind than a parking meter. It took Lilly's photo to reveal him to me: the hands holding the book like a dance partner; the face gazing at that page like it's the whole world; the half-smile that says he's on the winning end of some grand secret.

I had seen plenty of Lilly's photos by now, but this one tipped the balance. Back in Delaware, any slob who painted something that wasn't a car or the side of a house was considered an artist, but living with Lilly was different. Not that I wasn't getting a certain amount of praise for my paintings. My professors at the Art Students League said I had promise, and going by what was on some of the other easels, I could tell I was holding my own. But seeing *The reader,* I realized that nobody looking at my work was ever going to feel one crumb of what I felt looking at Lilly's.

Perhaps this explains why, when she gave me the photograph, I didn't exactly dance with thanksgiving. I suppose I must have known she meant it as a sort of peace offering — to apologize, in her own Lilly way, for falling short of anyone's standards for shared living. But by this point, I wasn't feeling terribly forgiving.

Thanks, I'm sure, I said in the voice I saved for men who didn't stand a chance, and was gratified to see a wave of confusion cross Lilly's dopey face.

For one lovely moment, I had instilled in her a particle of artistic self-doubt.

16. Balloon man, New York, 1953
17. Newspaper clipping, "Eyes on Photography," *The New York Times*, December 18, 1953, annotated in red, blue, and black ink

This season's group showing of student work at the New School is a reminder of the form's growing popularity, with one standout worth mentioning. In Lillian Preston's "Balloon man," the spectrum of grays forms a veritable rainbow in a bouquet of sunlit balloons. While the vendor's wares obscure his sitting torso, his threadbare trousers and shabby shoes supply a powerful counterpoint to the humor of his balloon body. The sophisticated grasp of form and technique displayed by Miss Preston shows that she is a photographer to watch.

LETTER TO WALTER AND DOROTHY PRESTON, DECEMBER 1953: You can imagine my surprise when I came to class! I didn't even know the *Times* had a camera editor, much less that he had attended the school show. I begged for the copy, as by that time the paper was already three days old, and it seemed so very important that I send it to you. I took the picture one sunny day in Central Park. There's a zoo there, not nearly as big as Cleveland's but very popular with children, and there are vendors of all sorts on the path leading up to it. I hope the photo arrived safely. If it didn't, I will gladly print you another.

It should have been obvious, since there was only one photograph on display at my grandparents' place, but not until I was settling Grandma Dot's affairs did I realize that the framed photo on her bedroom wall was one of Lillian's. While cleaning out the house on Fernvale Street — which included finally dealing with the three boxes that had been waiting there for me eleven years — I also found the newspaper clipping inside the Bible on Grandma's bedside table. At first I assumed that Lillian had drawn the black circle around her name, afraid her parents would otherwise miss the mention. Then I changed my mind. Next to the black circle was that blue ballpoint arrow; and next to the arrow were the words "Our Daughter" in red, in my grandmother's perfect schoolgirl cursive. Her pride hadn't been appeased until she had made three annotations in three different colors, even for a clipping kept somewhere only she would ever see.

18. Couple standing outside the BMT, New York, 1953

This picture is a Rorschach test: what I see in it depends on my mood. The way the guy is holding her shoulder could be intimate, but then there's the hard look on his face, and that woman! Sometimes I think she's just told him she's in love with someone else and is waiting for him to stop talking so she can swipe his hand off her shoulder and finally leave him. Other times I'm positive her thousand-mile stare comes from listening to the same crappy excuse she always accepts before walking down the station steps to go home with him once again.

PATRICIA STOKES: It started mid-fall. At first, it was nothing terribly momentous, just three or four of the Art League gang swapping the usual gossip. None of us had money, and drinking at home was less expensive than drinking out. Somewhere along the way it became a weekly arrangement, and people started bringing their friends. It wasn't long before word got out that on Thursdays, there was always something doing at the apartment above the grocery at the corner of West Fourteenth and Sixth.

Lilly hated it, of course. After all, she

couldn't very well commandeer the john in an apartment filled with strangers expecting a certain basic level of hospitality. Not that she didn't try, but early on there was an unfortunate incident when someone literally burst down the door, ruining several of Lilly's prints in the bargain. After that, she became scarce, either staying out somewhere or barricading herself in her room.

Thursdays really took off when I started handing out invitations to interesting types I happened to meet: a man sitting with his pet monkey in Union Square; a casting agent; a woman singing opera in front of the Washington Square fountain; a philosopher in red robes standing beside a hotel taxi stand and extolling the virtues of simple living. After I elevated the group beer kitty to a mandatory door donation, I realized that my weekly soirees had more potential than anything else I was doing.

By that December, anyone who saw Lilly and me in that apartment would have taken us for a pair of deaf-mutes, considering how thoroughly we weren't speaking to each other. By this point I had asked her to move out innumerable times in my mind, but I wasn't sure who Lilly knew in the city other than myself. I wasn't at all sure where she would go, if and when I did build up the wherewithal to say the words out loud. At the same time, I was already considering the musicians I could start inviting once her room became available, and how quickly a slightly larger door donation would cover her half of the rent.

Lower East Side, 1954–56

19. Window-shopping on Fifth Avenue, New York, 1954

No one in this picture knows they're being watched: not the dreamy-eyed woman gazing at the smart mannequins, or the smiling man eyeing the dreamy-eyed woman. Lillian wasn't big on themes. She said she took pictures of whatever grabbed her, but around this time there sure are a lot of watched women filling up her contact sheets. The way Deb describes it, Lillian would have had a pretty good reason for that.

DEBORAH BRODSKY: There I am, coming down the stairs, and coming up is a gigantic box with legs. Then the box reaches the landing, and this prim-looking thing steps out from behind it, and that's Lilly. This is February 1954, East Sixth Street — stained walls, cracked tiles, the smells of frying fat and boiled cabbage — and here's this clean-cut girl in a pale blouse with little gold earrings in her little pale ears, looking like she belongs on a nice suburban lawn somewhere. I ask is she lost. She says she's my new neighbor in a voice that reminds me of glass animals. I think to myself: this kid hasn't got a chance.

Down by the entryway, Lilly had a shopping cart filled with her stuff that she'd wheeled over from her old place. I was on my way to the bookshop, but I helped her with a few things before heading out — partly to be nice, partly because I was curious. Lilly had this contraption that looked like a cross between a drill press and an old-fashioned camera, which she called an enlarger. She told me she was a photographer. For the newspapers? I asked, but she just smiled and shook her head. You see, photography didn't register with me. I didn't know anyone who was doing it; that's how ahead of things Lilly was.

I spent that whole day trying to think up reasons for her being there. It wasn't an easy neighborhood back then. It was very, very Polish, and as far as they were concerned, a woman without a man was either a whore or somebody's mistress, which amounted to the same thing. Walking down the street, you'd be invisible or you'd get remarks. You didn't have to speak Polish to know what *kurva* meant, the way they said it. But eighteen bucks a month got you two rooms — a big one with a sink and a bathtub in one corner, the toilet in a closet; and a tiny one that barely had space enough for its own door — with water and heat included. That was why I was there, but I was a poet and just the sort of misfit, self-made orphan that kind of setup would appeal to.

When I got back from the bookshop, I knocked on Lilly's door, just to make sure she hadn't been thrown into some baba's goulash, and out she came into the hallway, grinning ear to ear. The door across from hers had a cloth stuffed under it, and she was pointing at it like she'd found the end of the rainbow. Her neighbor was this Chinese guy, the only other tenant who wasn't a Pole. He'd work through the week, then lock himself in his apartment on weekends. Lilly thought the cloth was there to block out the light. She was going on about her neighbor being a photographer, too, her face lit up like the circus. I didn't have the heart to tell her that he was in there smoking opium. Keeping out the light had nothing to do with it; the cloth was there so that the smell of his little hobby could be kept in.

JOURNAL ENTRY, FEBRUARY 1954: As much as I would like to belong here, this neighborhood has no use for a young single girl who doesn't speak its language. The women merely eye me with suspicion when they look at me at all, but the men are even harder to take. Just the other day one was trailing me — a square-jawed fellow in a stained shirt and work pants — calling after me in what I think was Polish. When I turned around to ask what he wanted, he slowly looked me up and down. "How much?" he asked in perfectly intelligible English. To my complete embarrassment, I blushed. Deb wouldn't have blushed. Deb would have burned holes into the man's chest with her eyes and marched off as if she were leading a parade. I need to be tougher. But it's so hard to be tough when all I want is to be invisible!

20. Washing day, New York, 1954

Lillian thought landscapes were boring. Without people, a picture looked empty to her. That doesn't mean she never took the odd "empty" photo, but whenever she did, a sense of people fills the emptiness. I'm thinking this clothesline was hanging across the ventilation shaft outside her apartment window, because she would have needed to log some quality time looking at it before catching the wind at such a perfect moment. The breeze is filling the man's undershirt, making it easy to imagine the kind of barrel-chested gorilla it's meant for. The stained apron hanging limp beside it on the clothesline gives an ominous feeling, like we've stumbled onto a crime scene one moment too late.

DEBORAH BRODSKY: My first visit to her apartment, Lilly took me into the darkroom and explained how it all worked. It was like watching a conjurer produce doves from thin air. I never got tired of that: whenever I needed to escape my own dramas, I'd go downstairs to Lilly's and knock on the door. If she was in the mood for company, she'd let me in. I'd follow her into the darkroom, standing perfectly still in the dim red light, watching her images rise to the surface.

She'd made her darkroom out of the tiny room. Really it was more of an alcove with a door, no bigger than a walk-in closet.

Mine had my desk, a chair, and a small bookshelf that left me just enough space to slip inside and sit down. Lilly had her enlarger in there, shelves to store her chemicals, and a table for her trays, with a big bucket beneath the table for dumping her used chemicals and a jug for carrying in hot water from the sink in the main room. That didn't leave much space for anything or anyone else, but in the dark, the sense of smallness fell away. Whether I stayed thirty minutes or three hours, I felt better going out than I had going in. Spending time with Lilly in the dark that way felt intimate, like being in bed minus the sex. I could see how easy it would be to devote your life to something like that. Suddenly it was obvious to me that Lilly was doing the same thing with photos that I was doing with poems, Leon and Cass with theater, Judy with paintings, and Renaldo with dancing: we were all seekers and revealers of truth.

LETTER TO WALTER AND DOROTHY PRESTON, FEBRUARY 1954: Perhaps you noticed from the address on the envelope that I've moved. I have learned the only way to work properly is to rent an apartment of my own. Don't worry, my new upstairs neighbor is a woman named Deborah, who has been living on her own for years, so you see, it's really not so unusual! She's been very happy to show me around, so I feel quite comfortable and welcome.

21. Legs, New York, 1954

A basic description of this photo would make it seem boring: half a step stool and the bottom portion of a sitting man. Because of how Lillian framed it, it's not boring. On the left side of the picture, the two legs of the step stool mirror the seated man's legs on the right in a way that's funny, except the joke is made complicated by his tragically skinny ankles and weather-worn hands, which rest on his thighs like lost gloves. More complicated still, the photo somehow makes me feel as much for the stool as for the sitter.

When I was little, I remember Lillian moving orphaned mittens from the middle of sidewalks to the spiked uprights of the iron railings that fronted buildings. She'd tell me she didn't like the idea of them being left alone. Once when I was around sixteen, after one of our endlessly repeating fights, Lillian told me that more than anything else, she had hoped to spare me that lonesome feeling. The way I'd laughed made her flinch, which felt pretty satisfying at the time. No mother can save her child from loneliness, but for a mother like Lillian, it was truly futile.

DEBORAH BRODSKY: When Lilly first moved in, she was pulling lunch shifts six days a week up on Madison. She said she liked it because the tips were good, plus the midday light was lousy for taking pictures anyway, and she and her old roommate, who worked there, too, looked out for each other. When she told me how much she made, I laughed. With that kind of bread, I asked, why live here? At that point I was getting away with ten hours a week at the bookstore, which covered rent, oatmeal, rice and beans, and vegetables from the produce stand on East Second. The rest of my time belonged to me — for wandering, for writing, for working on the magazine. Lilly said she needed the money for film, darkroom chemicals, and paper to print her pictures on. She couldn't afford to think twice before she snapped the shutter. If the picture was there, she had to grab it without worrying if there would be film for tomorrow.

22. *Deb* [Deborah Brodsky], *New York, 1954*

JOURNAL ENTRY, MARCH 1954: When I got back from class last week, I looked so blue that Deb took me out for a chocolate egg cream, and I told her what I've finally admitted to myself: I don't like Mr. Janovic. Once a week, we all gather round while he looks through our portfolios, and it's like a ring of vultures picking at fresh meat. Mr. Janovic is very smart about what makes people want to look at images. His criticisms are almost always correct, but he gives them in such a cutting way! Each week, he seems to take pride in bringing his students to tears. The ones who don't cry make me even sadder because they don't react at all, as if he's turned them to stone.

I didn't bring the photo of Deb to class, though I think it's quite good, because I wanted to spare even her image from that unkind man. I don't regret it one bit. After looking over my photos, Janovic told me to "Carry on," which is the closest he's come to paying a compliment. Still, I felt so poisoned by him that it was several days before I wanted to do anything at all.

Living with Patty taught me the importance of solitude, but I don't know how long I'd have lasted here if Deb hadn't made me her friend. I'm embarrassed to admit I would have avoided someone like Deb back in Cleveland — even assuming anyone like Deb could exist there! — but friendship for Deb is instinctive. Her openness teaches me as much as anything I'm learning in class. I was rather scandalized by her at first, and more than a little disapproving, but that ended the moment I glimpsed myself in the mirror and saw Father staring back.

I'm thinking the whole naked thing also influenced Lillian's decision not to bring the photo to class. After sorting through Box Two, I spent a lot of time looking at this picture of Deb (at her face, anyway), waiting for it to spark memories of someone who apparently knew me from birth through my first fourteen months of life, but nothing caught. When I called to interview her, I used the same fake name I used with everyone: a stab at anonymity that had mixed success, but was a sure bet with Deb, who had last known me when my spoken vocabulary was limited to "hi" and "ball." After the interview, when I came clean about who I was, Deb laughed in a way I'd only ever heard in cartoons. Then she sang "Little

Rabbit Foo Foo" into the phone in a cracked, atonal voice that sent shivers of recognition down my spine.

This is the first nude picture Lillian took of someone else. What I love about it, which is what I love about all of Lillian's portraits, is that it's not posed. I mean, sure, Deb is sitting in a chair in front of a camera, but the whole in-front-of-a-camera thing seems coincidental. Despite the way Deb is sitting — buck naked, feet spread, right arm resting across the chair back, left hand waving a cigarette — you can tell she's not being provocative. Basically, no pun intended, she's just hanging out. I'm sure that part of Deb's comfort has to do with Deb being Deb, but I can vouch for the fact that Lillian really did make you forget you were in front of a camera. Sometimes she did it by talking to you, but other times she did it by fading away, leaving you to do whatever you would have been doing if she hadn't been there. Despite years of being the one she did it to, I'm still not sure how she pulled it off. Rather than it being something she learned, I think it was just part of who she was.

If the nineteen-year-old Deb in this picture seems like a slightly seedy wood sprite, the fifty-four-year-old Deb who invited me to visit her in Arizona was more like a friendly bear. She wears her hair long now, in a messy bun. Her freckled face is lined with over thirty years of bright desert sun and all the things she's done under it. In the portrait, she's looking off to the side, and because of that it's hard to appreciate her eyes, but when I saw them for myself, I knew how she and my mother had stayed friends. Deb Brodsky has the eyes of a loyal hound.

DEBORAH BRODSKY: I think of Lilly's time on East Sixth as a golden era. If someone had told me I would be moving west in two years, I'd have laughed them out of the room. At that point, New York was everything: my cosmos, my dharma, my whole way of life. After years of seeking and struggling, I was enmeshed in this vital, creative clan that was stronger and more loving than my "real" family in Woodmere had ever been. I was too young to think any of it would ever change. Renaldo wasn't using yet, Leon was writing his plays — creating these compelling, complex roles for Cass — and the two of them were on fire with each other, this passionate creative engine. Judy and I were trying each other on for size, and I felt like

I'd discovered a wonderful secret, thought that we'd avoid the usual traps since a man wasn't involved. Lilly didn't fit in with us right away — she looked like she was going to fall over the first time she saw me with Judy — but I could tell she just needed time to shrug off the last bits of Ohio still clinging to her. And once she did — well, it was Renaldo who put it best. She looked like she was on the outside, he said, but she was more inside than us all. Renaldo had a sixth sense for people; it was part of what made him such a beautiful dancer.

The way Lilly sat at the edge of the collective energy made her easy to overlook, but pay attention and you could tell that deep things were going down. The way she watched, she was like a lizard on a rock soaking up the heat, only Lilly was soaking up the people. And this was all before you even saw the camera. Once you did, you realized Lilly existed for that camera, as a living extension of it.

Later, I saw the same thing when she was holding Samantha. It was the first time I thought being a mother could be a positive force, something loving and artistic — though that was an idea I wouldn't do anything with for many years. Anyway, when Lilly first showed up, I was reading every Sunday at the Zenith, and the idea of a journal wasn't something I was just fooling around with in my head anymore. People were starting to submit work: friends from the Zenith scene, friends who read in other places, and friends who weren't reading anywhere and wanted a way to put their words on the wind.

When I saw Lilly's photography, I wanted her images to be part of the mix, but Lilly said no, photos had to be printed on high-quality paper or else they'd be compromised, and I was running a real shoestring operation, without that kind of grease. I was grateful to her for that. Letting the images go kept the magazine a pure voice for poetry, which is what it was meant to be.

As for the portrait, it was all my idea. Asking wasn't Lilly's style. One day when I came to her place, I simply shucked my clothes and told her she could take my picture if she wanted, which I meant as a test and two kinds of invitation. The Lilly who had first moved in downstairs wouldn't have known what to do with something like that, but the Lilly she had become sure did. In moments she'd set up her camera. As for the second kind of invitation, it didn't take me long to realize how silly that was. Art as a means toward another end wouldn't have crossed Lilly's mind, even if she'd been at all curious about women, which I don't think she ever was.

23. Woman on park bench, New York, 1954

Deb's description here is as good as anything I could come up with, since Deb was paying attention and I generally wasn't. First I was too young; then I was too embarrassed; and then I was too busy being absolutely anywhere else.

DEBORAH BRODSKY: I remember one of a woman sitting. She's wearing a little hat and a nice dress, and you can tell she lives in a swank apartment somewhere, only at that moment she's got her shoes off and she's using one foot to massage the other. Her face broadcasts fatigue but also bewilderment, and you can tell she started out life in a place where there weren't little hats and nice dresses. When I asked Lilly how she did it, how she found people in these moments, she looked at me like I'd asked her how to tie a shoe. I wait, she said.

So one day, I followed her to Washington

Square. Sundays it was all guitars and young men singing folk songs, people collecting for righteous causes, and willowy girls wearing macramé belts and dangly earrings. But on Mondays, when Lilly went, the park belonged to everyone. I made sure to stand at a distance so Lilly wouldn't know I was there. In a way, it was like being in the darkroom — I was still watching her conjure an image, only this time we were out in the world, and her images were rising to the surface of the moment instead of the paper.

Lilly would sit for a while in one place; then she'd get up and sit somewhere else. She told me she used a 35mm viewfinder camera because it was small, fast, and quiet; and out in the park, I saw what she meant. She held that camera the way you'd hold a drink at a party when you're busy talking, with a relaxed arm bent at the elbow, always at the same place by her hip. Lilly never looked down, almost as if she'd forgotten the camera was there, but really it was just part of her. She'd taken so many pictures holding it at her hip that she didn't need to look down to use it anymore, the same way any other person doesn't need to look at their hand to open a door.

Even watching her, it took me a while to catch on that she was taking pictures. She would look off into the distance like she was daydreaming, and this was how she'd find what she wanted. If her subject was far away, she'd walk herself into range. She'd pre-focused her camera to a focal range of ten feet. She'd internalized this distance over countless hours of practice. Any time, anywhere, she could tell you what was ten feet away from her at any given moment, and she was always right. This helped her take pictures quickly, without anyone noticing. For each picture, she'd position herself at that same ten-foot distance, always keeping the camera in that one spot at her hip.

The way I'm describing it makes it sound slow, but it happened fast. Next, she would turn her head without turning her body, like she was interested in something else. It seemed so innocent, just a young woman in a quiet moment, but that was when she was really looking. She was doing it the way a bird does, with one eye. The real action wasn't there, though. If you kept watching her face, you'd miss the whole thing, because she never raised her camera to look through the viewfinder. The camera stayed down around where a belt buckle would be, and while she was looking with one eye, she was making small tilts of her wrist, tiny adjustments to compose the shot. That eye and that hand were connected by countless hours of practice, perfect coordination built shot by shot over a small eternity of trial and error. Then the adjustments would stop, and the shutter would click, and if you were looking at her face, you would miss it.

What I noticed about Lilly the day I met her was what worked for her out in the world: she looked like she belonged inside a nice quiet house somewhere. She had what you'd call regular features, everything even and proportionate. She always wore solid colors and knee-length skirts, and people paid her no mind. I admired that about her, because she was doing exactly what she needed to do. Even the rare person who did notice her didn't get bent out of shape. There was no way he could. You couldn't blame Lilly for taking pictures any more than you could blame a pigeon for pecking at a crumb of bread.

24. Kyle, New York, 1954

I saw this photo for the first time on the back of a book when I was fourteen, babysitting for a neighbor. *Rude Poems* by Kyle

Mackinaw was stashed along with the *Kama Sutra: Amorous Man & Sensuous Woman* and *The Function of the Orgasm* beneath some argyle socks in a dresser drawer. I noticed the photo (good-looking, mysterious) without noticing the photo credit. At the time, I'd been more interested in the *Kama Sutra,* which had dirty illustrations. But six years later, Kyle Mackinaw's photograph came back as a poster in the college dorm room of a pale boy named Sebastian who I had designs on. At the time, I'd thought the poster meant Sebastian was literary, but then I read *Rude Poems* and realized it probably meant he was gay.

I had the book half a semester before noticing the name L. Preston in tiny type along the photo's left-hand edge. When I called Lillian in Cleveland to ask her about it, she said she had a copy of *Rude Poems* somewhere. No, Kyle Mackinaw hadn't asked her permission, but she'd given him the photo; and as far as she was concerned, that meant he could do with it what he wanted. I told her about the poster, and she was quiet for a few seconds before telling me that my friend had good taste. When I suggested there might be money in it for her, she laughed. Was I, of all people, encouraging her to take something to court?

I never mentioned it again.

DEBORAH BRODSKY: On Tuesdays, a bunch of us would come together to share whatever we happened to have — beans, greens, beer, bread, grass, a can of anchovies — and we'd eat and drink and talk and get high, and if there were friends of friends passing through, they'd come and tell us where they'd been. Occasionally things got pretty wild. People would pair off in combinations that didn't match the pairs they'd arrived in or that weren't pairs at all. Sometimes this felt like exploring a new way to live, and sometimes it just felt like a bad idea. Lilly wasn't part of that. She didn't drink much, and she didn't smoke, not even cigarettes. On the nights things got tangled, she'd have wandered back to her darkroom long before, but the way she held herself separate wasn't judgment. It was just her being herself.

Sometimes I'd forget Lilly was there, which was exactly what she wanted. She didn't take many pictures. When I asked, she told me she mainly took the camera along for practice. She said it allowed her to focus her eye, but I think it gave her something to do with her hands. Anyway, it was during one of those pre-tangled

Tuesdays that Lilly got Kyle. He'd just breezed in from California, he and Juno shooting across Route 66 in that mustard-colored Cadillac in a hurry for reasons that made sense at the time. This was when Kyle was just starting on *Rude Poems,* though he was already acting like he was famous. Kyle was born big and blustery; he filled up the room. But Lilly caught him. Those big round eyes of his that always saw everything around him are looking inward, and his face is a mixture of fear and pain and hope and wonder at what it sees.

I didn't see the picture until Lilly gave him a copy. Naturally Kyle interpreted it as a romantic gesture and tried to use it to invite himself downstairs to Lilly's place, but that's not what it was about. Lilly is one of the few people I know, gay or straight, who ever declined one of Kyle's propositions. And when *Rude Poems* was published, it was Lilly's photo on the back cover. And of course, like so many iconic images, the people who recognize the photograph never give a moment's thought to the photographer.

25. Man on fire escape, New York, 1954

Lillian never asked for permission to snap a photo, but if she knew the person — like with Kyle — she'd give him a copy. This picture would have been riskier, since she couldn't have known whether or not her neighbor wanted to see himself on his decorated fire escape, practicing tai chi in his undershirt. I wondered how Lillian got the shot until I talked to Deb and realized that she must have leaned over her fire escape. This either means that the two fire escapes were really close together or that my mother risked falling four stories, all because she noticed that when her neighbor stretched his arm, he resembled the ink drawing of a tiger that he'd tied to the rails of his landing.

LETTER TO WALTER AND DOROTHY PRESTON, APRIL 1954: It is time I let you know that even though I won't be taking any more photography classes, I won't be returning home. I'm sorry if you thought New York was temporary. I suppose I knew from the start that I planned to stay.

DEBORAH BRODSKY: We had a heavy talk one night. Lilly's classes were winding down in a month, and she was torn up about what to do next. I told her how, in my one semester at college, I'd felt like my brain was shrinking instead of expanding. She laid down how neither of her New School classes had gone the way she'd expected. She'd come to the city thinking she could learn to be a magazine photographer or a photojournalist, but she'd realized she wasn't interested in making the kind of pictures that magazines and newspapers were after. It was the first time Lilly copped to being an artist.

Somehow it got to be three a.m., but we were too keyed up to sleep, so we decided to hit Ratner's. When we stepped into the hallway, there was her Chinese neighbor, grinning. Beautiful baby, he said from his doorway as he held out the photo. Beautiful baby, this man. It was the first and only time I heard him speak.

26. Charles in Central Park, New York, 1954

JOURNAL ENTRY, APRIL 1954: The first time I saw Charles, I thought he was you. Even though I've said my goodbyes, I still imagine you here, though not as often as I used to. But Charles isn't you, and I almost stopped noticing him, until one day in class, when Janovic was spreading his usual poison, and Charles spoke up.

Charles speaks up often, and unlike some of the other students, he is always worth listening to. "I've had about enough," he told Janovic that day. "Teaching should combine building up with tearing down or there's nothing left, but you're not a teacher. You're brilliant — you may even be a genius — but you're no teacher." Then he left. It made me admire him all over again, and I spent the rest of that week chiding myself for still being the spineless girl from Camera Club. Next week, when Charles wasn't there, I thought it served me right; but the following week after class, there he was, standing outside! Well, I walked straight over and told him how much I admired what he'd said. He told me he was glad I felt that way because the reason he'd come back was to ask if I'd join him for coffee.

The rest, as they say, is history. Charles is already working, and needless to say, it's without any help from Janovic. He's encouraged me to bring my work to MoMA on Portfolio Day; other students have gone without success, but he thinks my luck will be different. He's also invited me to make the rounds of the various art departments, but I doubt any magazine would be interested in my photos, and I'm not keen to take theirs. Speaking of interest, I'm happy to report that I finally understand the fuss about kissing: Charles is quite good at it.

DEBORAH BRODSKY: I only saw the father once, when he wasn't the father yet; he was just Charles from Lilly's photography class, who had impressed her by walking out on the cruelty their teacher was laying down. When Lilly invited Charles to a Tuesday night, he showed up in a coat and tie with a bottle of wine. Right away, he was invited to lose all three by Renaldo as he and a friend of his, wearing matching red tunics, performed a dance with a candle and a painted mirror. Lilly tried to make Charles comfortable — she even gave him her camera to hold — but the two of them didn't stick around. After that, Charles always seemed to have something else going down on Tuesdays. Lilly told me she felt conflicted: she liked him, but not his photos.

I'm betting the picnic basket in the picture is his. Lillian wasn't the type to spring for wicker when a knapsack would do. I saw *Charles in Central Park* for the first time when I was twelve. It was a beautiful fall day, and like a dog whining at the door, Lillian was twitching to get out with her camera. I could come with her, she said, or hang around the neighborhood on my own. I thought both options sucked. If I had a father, I yelled, there would be somebody to do things with me while she was taking her stupid photos; I knew he was out there. When Lillian walked away, I thought she was making for the door. Instead, she came back with the photograph.

Here he is, she said. I was so keyed up I almost ripped the thing from her hand. It's probably true no picture could have scratched my itch, but this one didn't come close. Charles was a perfectly ordinary guy who looked nothing like me (how could he — I look exactly like Lillian). On top of that, Charles's last name was Roberts. By 1967 Charles Roberts could have been anywhere: there were three pages of Robertses in the Brooklyn phone book alone. Even I had to admit there was no chance of a shared custody arrangement in my future.

For a while, I kept Charles under my pillow and imagined myself filling the empty space on his checkered blanket. When he got too ragged to handle, I stuck him inside a book for safekeeping and gave up on that picnic. I'm sure Lillian would have printed me a fresh copy, but a "new" father would have diminished the old one, and the old one was diminished enough.

It would be a simple snapshot if not for the shadows. I didn't notice them at the time (at age twelve, subtlety wasn't my thing), but Charles's shadow overlaps the tree's, making his gray outline look like dangling fruit. This lends the whole thing an erotic undertone that was pretty daring, coming from a girl photographer in 1954.

27. Bow, New York, 1954

Welcome to Lillian's version of landscape photography: woman's wool coat as mountain, her back filling up the bottom two thirds of the picture, a straw hat resting on top like a boulder. The woman inside the coat is probably old: check out the sloping shoulders and the size of the hat's bow, which only a little girl or an old lady could pull off. Not to mention Lillian would have had to stand right behind her to get so much fine-grained texture in the frame, which means this represents a rare violation of Lillian's fixed-focus rule, and that the ears under the hat in question were probably a little hard of hearing. Before I read my mother's journal, I wouldn't have thought twice about the photo's title, but I guess getting laid liberated Lillian's sense of humor.

JOURNAL ENTRY, JUNE 1954: Now that I've spent the night with Charles, the notion of "losing" my virginity seems silly. I've gained much more than I've lost. For example, leaving Charles's apartment this morning, I decided to hail my first taxicab, but what seemed like a fitting occasion on Ninety-sixth Street had become a bad idea by Twenty-third, because I worried that neighbors who saw me arriving home at such an hour and in such a manner would take the taxi for the announcement it was. I had the driver drop me at Eleventh so that I could walk the rest of the way, which was when I came across the old woman in her spectacular hat. Sure enough, once I arrived home wearing yesterday's clothes, Mrs. Dudek peered out her door to give me the hairy eyeball, but it was no different from the baleful look she gives me when I pass her door loaded down with laundry or groceries. It struck me that those who assume the worst of people are predisposed to assume it, just as those who suppose the best are predisposed in that direction. Any given assumption has more to do with its assumer than with the people they're assuming about. This revelation was so liberating that I laughed all the way to Deb's door, and when she wasn't home, I laughed my way back down to the darkroom. There I forgot all about "the great event" (or rather, series of events, the greatness of which improved with repetition) until I finished printing *Bow* and discovered I was half an hour late to meet Charles. I changed into fresh clothes before charging down the stairs to catch the subway. While waiting for the Lexington Avenue line, I realized that the previous night with Charles, my cab ride home, and my emancipation from the Mrs. Dudeks of the world were like taking a personal bow of a completely different sort from the bow I'd just photographed.

Charles is gallant and sincere and very camera-smart. He can size up the look of a magazine in ten minutes and shoot a roll that feels tailor-made for its pages. Some might argue that his passion for photography is purer than mine: for him, the style of a photograph is secondary to the act of taking it, while I'm only interested in making certain kinds of pictures; but I think that passion, properly defined, describes only one of us. Unless he's on assignment, Charles prefers to stay above Fourteenth Street. He's been in New York two years and doesn't think he'll stay. He has gentle hands, brings me a rose every second Sunday, and has told me he wants me to meet his parents. It's funny: the girl I was in Cleveland would have depended on this, but the girl I've become expects more from herself and depends on less.

28. Pennsylvania Station, New York, 1954

If all we saw was the couple, this could be a romantic goodbye. Instead they're huddled against a row of lockers in the middle of the train station, with blurred outlines of passing strangers in the foreground. He's got his back to the escalator; she's facing away from the camera, her foot frozen in a half-step behind her. His profile looks out over the lobby; she's just a head of hair. Because of this, instead of seeming tender, his hand on her back looks like him holding her against her will.

Lillian always swore there was no connection between her photographs and her life, but there's a reason people notice what they do. Knowing what I know, I can't look at this one without thinking of my mother as the woman trapped by that man's arm. Just because Lillian would have hated that idea doesn't make it any less true.

DEBORAH BRODSKY: It was the beginning of September. Judy and I were collating the first issue of *On the Wind,* and it was around two a.m. We had the windows open because summer hadn't let up. To keep the page spreads from blowing around, we had each stack weighted down with a piece of silverware or an ashtray. Judy and I were down to our underwear, partly from the heat and partly from sexiness. Due to that first issue having begun back around the same time we had, we made quite a few of those finished pages unfit for postage, Judy and me and the magazine scattered across the bed, our neat piles all askew, the breeze from the window having its way with things.

I knew from the knock it was Lilly, because it was three soft taps like always. She and I both liked to work late, and she knew she was welcome so long as she saw light under my door. I didn't bother to put anything on, since it was just Lilly, and Judy didn't bother putting anything on because everyone had a crush on Lilly at one point or another. Lilly wasn't holding her camera. What's wrong? I asked. When she said it had been six weeks, I dug her meaning right away.

In those days, if you didn't do it in the first eight weeks, it became much more difficult, and if you hadn't done it after sixteen weeks, you couldn't do it at all. But in the first eight, you could at least go to someone, and if that someone knew what he was doing, chances were pretty good that you wouldn't die. Lilly told me that Charles didn't know, and she thought it would be cruel to tell him, which made sense considering how hard he'd taken it when she'd broken up with him the month before.

I'd never needed an abortion, but Cass had, so the next day I got the number of the person she had used, who was an actual doctor, a Viennese gynecologist who used anesthesia and only charged three hundred dollars, but when Lilly called the number, it was disconnected. The best kind of abortion to get was a therapeutic one, because then it could be done legit in a hospital. For one of those you had to get a shrink to say you needed it for mental health reasons, and none of us had the kind of bread shrinks required. Even if we had, a lot of shrinks wouldn't prescribe them; you never could tell.

Tuesday, I spread the word that a friend of mine needed to know where to go. By Wednesday I had a number. Lilly had to call after five p.m., and then she had to ask for Mike and say she wanted a haircut, and if she said anything different, the person would hang up. It cost five hundred dollars and Lilly only had two hundred. I gave her a hundred and fifty that I'd been saving for the second issue, and Renaldo got a hundred and fifty from a married banker he was seeing. When I gave the money to Lilly, she asked would I come with her, so of course I said yes.

29. River of No Return, *New York, 1954*

The four women standing in front of this movie poster make it impossible to read without the title's help. Obviously, once you violate the art/life connection ban, knowing the photographer's situation at the time changes everything; but even if you're clueless about Lillian's personal history, this one's got power. Four women all with their hair fresh out of hot rollers, all waiting for their dates while twisting their gloves in their hands, four versions of the same black handbag dangling from their wrists. Not one of those women is certain her man is going to show. Marilyn Monroe looks like she's smirking at them from the poster. A different photographer would have had you laughing along with Marilyn, but because this is Lillian's photograph, your eyes dart back and forth, scanning the street, your gloves clenched in your hand.

DEBORAH BRODSKY: The day we took the BMT to Canarsie was the only time I saw Lilly in the world empty-handed. I was a Long Island girl, and Lilly hadn't ever crossed the East River, so heading into Brooklyn felt to both of us like traveling to a foreign country. Then we got there, and except for the Virgin Marys on the front lawns instead of mezuzahs beside the front doors, it was exactly like where I'd grown up in Woodmere. Lots of small brick houses, kids playing kick the can. The familiarity made it feel like one of those dreams where you're back in school and everyone's staring because you're in your underwear. Not that anyone *was* staring, which only added to our paranoia, because we felt conspicuous as hell.

I don't know what we were expecting to find at the address, but it was a regular house like the rest. There were people in the living room, kids running in and out of the kitchen. I sat on the couch beside someone's grandma while a middle-aged guy with a paunch and a comb-over escorted Lilly down a hallway. Ten minutes later, she was back, and I'd never seen her so pale. When we got outside, she handed over the cash. Renaldo's was all there, she told me, but she owed me fifty dollars. I asked was she all right? She was now, she said, and we got back on the BMT. I couldn't tell if she'd decided to marry Charles after all, or if she wanted to find a different doctor. Then Lilly turned and said, He's going to be so awfully disappointed in me; and I could tell by the way she said it that she was talking about her father.

JOURNAL ENTRY, SEPTEMBER 1954: I thought his office was connected to the house, and that Deb and I just happened to arrive at the wrong door. I assumed the man was leading me down the hall toward a proper examination room, but instead he brought me to a large walk-in closet in the back of a cluttered bedroom. Inside the closet was a metal table covered in white towels. Stirrups made from rope with loops at the end hung from the ceiling. The man advised me to keep my shoes on. He told me he wouldn't use anesthesia because it wasn't safe. I had to promise not to scream or his kids would hear. When he held out his hand for the money, I gave him half and got out of there.

30. Self-portrait (nine weeks), New York, 1954

According to my math, Lillian would have taken this about two weeks after the trip to Canarsie. She's wearing the same face she wore whenever she'd made up her mind about something. I hated that face except when I loved it: like the day that face came to my rescue after a front-page photo in the *Daily News* sent me to the principal's office, or every time that face came between me and a nosy reporter.

Without the title, you wouldn't know she's pregnant. She just looks like a strangely fierce naked person, someone you wouldn't want to mess with. But because I know what's coming, I also connect that face with a sense of preparation. At this point, my mother had written home. She had no telephone. If Grandpa Walt wanted to talk to her, there was only one way for him to do it.

> *DEBORAH BRODSKY:* At first I was the only one who didn't think Lilly was crazy, but that was because I'd seen her leaving that hallway. No one I knew had ever been pregnant. Knocked up, sure; but then came the phone calls, and trips to the Viennese gynecologist or to Canarsie.

Cass was more or less back to herself in a few days. Marjory — a sometimes actress, sometimes dancer, and Tuesday regular — had bled for nine days and ended up at the Bellevue emergency room, but eventually she'd come back, too. Only a girl named Dianne had disappeared. Not died, but one Tuesday a few weeks after her abortion, she told me that she hadn't stopped spotting. The week after that, her skin had a greenish look, and her boyfriend was practically hand-feeding her with a spoon. After that, she didn't come around anymore, and I heard she'd gone back to her parents in Morningside Heights.

But Lilly, because she wasn't going anywhere, was going somewhere new. Tuesdays, she still sat on the edge of things with her camera; except now, instead of being invisible, she was more like a two-headed calf. I half expected her to start skipping Tuesdays because of it, but she didn't. Eventually the people who mattered most came around to accepting her decision. It might have been the first time in Lilly's life that she stood out. I could tell it was hard on her, sitting through all those Tuesdays, waiting for people to get used to her big belly, but I think she knew this was something she couldn't do alone.

31. Asleep, New York, 1954

Anyone who isn't Lillian will see this as an obvious time for kids to start showing up in her photos, though technically this is a picture of a large goldfish (party favor? carnival prize?) in a small bowl on a park bench. It seems to be eyeing the sleeping girl on its right with skepticism. Without that sliver of adult along the left-hand edge of the frame, we'd feel afraid, but that bit of full-grown leg means someone's looking out for the small drooling mouth and the dangling arm, those five little fingers hanging just inches above the dirt.

DEBORAH BRODSKY: I was at my desk wrestling with a poem when I heard voices. It was an old building, so I heard voices all the time — through the walls, through the ceiling, through the door — but these were coming up from the floor. Lilly wasn't into hosting, so when I heard a man say, You must, and then, You don't have any choice, followed by the sound of something being knocked over, I was out my door and down those stairs like the place was on fire.

I figured it was Charles. I thought somehow he'd found out or Lilly had decided to tell him; but instead, when Lilly let me in, there was a gray man with wire-rimmed glasses and Lilly's mouth wearing a three-piece suit. He was standing beside a chair that was lying on its back, and he and Lilly were blushing in the same way. After he apologized for disturbing me, Lilly said that this was her father, Walter Preston, but at that point introductions were unnecessary.

Lilly's father had arrived from Penn Station. Lilly explained in a voice like a coiled spring that he had two tickets for the evening train. He wanted to take her to a place in Cincinnati where she could stay until the baby was born, and then give it up for adoption.

She told me she wasn't going, and her eyes reached out to me like hands. Her old man was looking at me, too, their gazes pulling at me from opposite sides of the room.

Walter asked would I talk to her. He was her father, so of course she wouldn't listen to him. He smiled when he said it. Beneath the bad energy I could feel the kindness, could see where Lilly got her interest in people.

I watched as he took in the crooked wooden table with its two chairs, the busted couch we'd scavenged from one of

Leon's plays, furniture Lilly had been so proud to carry past her door. How could she want to give birth to a bastard and raise him in these conditions? he wanted to know. They'd brought her up with a sense of decency, as someone who knew the difference between wrong and right. She'd be disgracing him and her mother, not to mention an innocent child.

He glanced around the apartment and his face went soft. Lilly, he said. It's time to come home.

I *am* home, she said, and her father flinched.

Who did this to her? he wanted to know. She used to be a good, respectable girl; but then Lilly stomped her foot, and two people who had spent their whole lives being polite finally stopped.

No one *did* this to me, she said.

Her father hissed that someone most certainly had.

It was quiet then. In that moment Lilly was ferocious and proud and mighty. She towered over us both.

Father, she said. He wanted to marry me, but I didn't want to marry him.

Those words drained the color from poor Walter Preston's face, until he was as pale as Lilly leaving that house in Canarsie. He put a train ticket on the table.

I don't know who you are, he said to her in a voice gone hollow, but please tell my daughter that I'll be waiting for her. Then he put on his coat and walked out the door.

32. Self-portrait (eighteen weeks), New York, 1954

JOURNAL ENTRY, NOVEMBER 1954: Sometimes I'll forget. I'll be riding the subway or in the darkroom or climbing the stairs and it'll suddenly occur to me, like a new idea, that I'm pregnant. Every time that happens, a warmth starts in my belly where you are and spreads to my chest and arms and down through my legs. It's like we're having a conversation, a very special private conversation.

Lillian took a picture every four weeks for the next five months (I arrived early) and collected them in the only photo album she ever made. On the cover, she painted the words *Book of Samantha.* We looked at the photos a lot when I was little. Whenever we did, she'd compare my size inside her belly to a piece of fruit. In this one, I am a mango. Even during the bad old years, Lillian made a fruit salad on each of my birthdays. No matter what else was happening between us, we'd eat it and not fight. Apples, oranges, and bananas were givens, but we could be behind on rent and Lillian would still somehow manage a peach or a pear, a coconut or a watermelon, an especially impressive feat considering the day of my birth landed, quite untropically, in March.

This brings me back to the difference between being unplanned and being unwanted. By now it should be obvious that I began as both. Thanks to *Mommy is sick,* I knew what an abortion was years before I knew my multiplication tables; yet despite this, I never once wondered about abortion and myself in the same breath. *Why didn't you just abort me?* What kept me from saying that when I was so busy saying so many other vicious things I now regret? And what kept my mother from slinging Canarsie at me in response to my lavish viciousness? It took reading my mother's journal, eleven years after her death, to learn of my own near-elimination inside a walk-in closet in Brooklyn. I don't think Lillian started loving me during the subway trip back from her averted abortion, but clearly something changed between blueberry and mango. From this portrait on, her fierceness has transformed into something radiant and calm. The battle has been fought: love has won.

DEBORAH BRODSKY: Renaldo started bringing Lilly things from the natural foods store — herbal tea, dried beans — and, one Tuesday, two books on natural childbirth and breastfeeding, which Lilly snatched as if she were spring-loaded and read by the window for the rest of the night. Cass knitted Lilly a hat that reminded me of a white angora sweater I'd stopped seeing Cass wearing around the same time. Judy quit lobbying for us to spend equal time at her place and started dropping by Lilly's on the way up to see me.

When Madison Avenue couldn't handle the way Lilly looked in her waitressing uniform, I took her to Barrow Street Books to see John. After she told him she could type, John looked at me and I nodded, and he offered her a gig organizing inventory and typing up mimeograph stencils for the bookshop's mail-order catalog. I'd been working at Barrow Street until the moment John looked at me and I gave him the nod to give Lilly my job, so I knew it was a good place. I also knew that John — who kept banned copies of *Plexus* and *Justine* for customers in a bottom drawer, and whose cot in the bookstore's back room had stored any number of people and materials on their way in or out of town in a hurry — wouldn't care one way or another about Lilly's changing size and shape.

For her maternity wardrobe, she found a bunch of groovy housedresses at the Goodwill that looked borrowed from the babas she'd photographed on their stoops. Lilly was beautiful in those things. As her belly grew, she seemed delicate and powerful all in one, giving off these mighty waves of womanly strength. It felt healthy just being around her. Carrying that baby made her radiate serenity in a way I've only ever seen in Buddhists and Californians.

33. Two girls, New York, 1955

Sisters, going by the matching dresses and waxed-paper-wrapped sandwiches they're eating as they walk. What the title also doesn't say, indicated instead by the words on the plate-glass window behind the girls, is that this doubles as a portrait of Barrow Street Books. It's a place that, like my memories of Deb Brodsky, I must have tucked away somewhere, since John Bosco and his bookstore were two other fixtures of my first fourteen months. By the time I started looking for him, Bosco wasn't around to be interviewed (motorcycle accident, 1974), so there was no chance for another Foo Foo moment, but I've learned he was a very cool guy, not to mention one of the biggest forces to shape my mother's life. Sometimes the people you'd expect to be important drift past like clouds, while the seemingly random types end up changing everything.

DEBORAH BRODSKY: John was the Village's foremost champion of everything modern, from literature to poetry to art. Barrow Street was the first bookstore to carry *On the Wind,* and it was also the first place Dan Minot went with his chapbook collages. The funny thing is I wasn't thinking about that when I brought Lilly there: I just wanted to find her a job. But John also happened to be the perfect person to see her photographs. I remember one evening Lilly burst in, glowing like she was part firefly. John had asked to borrow three of her pictures to show them to his friend, who just happened to be Michael Stromlin from the *Times.* Lilly was so breathless from excitement and from carrying that belly of hers full-tilt up four flights of stairs that for a moment I thought she might give birth early, right there on my floor. A week later, that *Times* editor helped her to get her first show.

JOURNAL ENTRY, JANUARY 1955: We met on Morton at a place I didn't know, a café called Aperçu that actually had a small gallery space in the back just for photographs. I wasn't too keen on the work — still lifes by a West Coast photographer whose name I've already forgotten — but Mr. Stromlin told me that the last show had included work by Granois-Levais and Porter and a lot of others whom Mr. Stromlin (I'm supposed to call him Mike, but I can't manage it) said he preferred to what was up now, which meant we had something in common.

As we found a table, which was tricky since it was a small place and very crowded, Mr. Stromlin told me that the instant John showed him my work, he remembered my name from the New School show. He told me he considered it part of his job to assist promising photographers who "had the stuff." Then he waved, and a tall, elegant man appeared at our table; Mr. Stromlin introduced him as the café owner, Gabriel Wythe. Mr.

Wythe looked at my photos, then turned to Mr. Stromlin and said, "Not uplifting enough for Kleinmann, I dare say, but I think they're clear-headed in the best way." Then Mr. Stromlin said, "Maybe for your next group show?" and Mr. Wythe shrugged. "If I have space. It's hard being the only game in town, as you know, but women are scarce, not to mention ones who shoot like this. May I keep these?" he asked, spreading my photos like a paper fan. My instinct was to grab them back, but Mr. Stromlin gave me a nod, so I said he could, which felt like a gentle mugging. Mr. Wythe asked where he could get in touch, and I told him the bookstore. "I should have known you were a friend of John's," he said, and hurried off, because the whole time he'd been with us, people had been waving him over, though whether they were customers, café staff, or other photographers, I'll never know.

What I do know is that for those five minutes, in that busy place, my shyness disappeared. This would have been more than enough for me, but then Mr. Stromlin went on to explain that he curated photography shows with a public librarian at a small gallery space inside the Hudson Park branch. It wasn't commercial, like

Aperçu, he said, but it was good exposure, and there happened to be an opening in the April schedule. Of course April is when you are due to arrive, but it seems this is the way life happens sometimes, with everything coming all at once!

34. Self-portrait (thirty weeks), New York, 1955.

LETTER TO DOROTHY PRESTON, FEBRUARY 1955: I'm sorry to disappoint you, but everything is exactly as Father described. I won't be coming home or giving up the baby. I plan to stay here, living as I am. Try to understand that I am thriving, and that while I face many challenges, they are the challenges I have chosen. Father mentioned that you almost joined him on his trip. I wish you had! While I don't think you would have approved any more than he did, I think that, unlike Father, you would have seen my happiness and taken some comfort in it. But you were not here with Father, and now you write that until I come around to the "only sensible course," I won't be hearing from you again. Mother, how close did you come to making the trip? Did you pack a bag, then stop at the door? I would have liked to see your face, to hug you one last time, but if you truly mean what you have written, then I guess this is our goodbye.

DEBORAH BRODSKY: That was a crazy time. Lilly was putting in extra shifts at Barrow Street, as well as getting ready for the library show. To do all that, she needed more hours than were in the day, just like me when things were down to the wire with the magazine. It was funny, but she didn't smoke or drink, so when she asked about "some sort of help," I thought she meant an assistant. Which she did, but in the chemical sphere. I gave her a few Dexies and told her how they worked, and after that she became a force of nature in a way that's possible only when you're still nineteen. She traded Tuesday nights for darkroom time, stopped coming up at all, really, so I made sure to go down at least once a day with a sandwich or a piece of fruit. Lilly told me she was pretty sure the *Times* guy hadn't known she was pregnant when he offered her the library gig, since she'd kept on her winter coat. An invitation like that wasn't going to come twice. It wasn't as if she could have told Mr. *New York Times* camera editor: Sorry, I'm about to have a baby, come back again in the spring. If I were her, I would have done the same thing — back then you could drink or smoke or whatever else while you were pregnant and not even your doctor would blink — but I can't help wondering if working double time like that sped up the rest of her, too.

I remember everything exactly. It was 8:35 p.m., March 14. I was reading submissions, and there came Lilly's three knocks, louder than usual. When I opened the door, the bottom half of her dress was soaked through. My water broke, she said, but it's not supposed to do that yet, and now I've ruined two prints that were in the fixing bath.

I ran across the hall to Mrs. Oblacky's. I'd never knocked on her door for anything, but one look at Lilly and Mrs. Oblacky helped me get her down the stairs, no questions asked, then sat with her in front of the building while I ran to hail a cab. After she helped me get Lilly into the backseat, she stood making the sign of the cross from the curb as we sped toward Gouverneur, which was one of the hospitals you could go to if you didn't have any money.

They put Lilly in a wheelchair even though she told them she felt fine. After she finished in Admissions, they said it was time for her to go to Labor and began wheeling her off. I started walking beside her, but the orderly told me to go home. Lilly wants me here! I said. No dice, not even *fathers* are allowed, the orderly announced in a way that made it clear he was unimpressed with us both. As Lilly disappeared down the hallway, she gave me a wave and tried to smile, but I could tell she was scared. More than anything, I wish I'd brought along her copy of *Childbirth Without Fear* so that I could have clocked the orderly with it.

For hours I waited around, pestering the nurses, until one of them put her palm to my cheek. Child, these things take time, she told me. Right now the best thing you can do is go home, get some sleep, and come back in the morning. It was the first kind thing anyone had said to me, and I was so grateful for it that I kissed her hand.

35. Samantha, New York, 1955

JOURNAL ENTRY, MARCH 1955: Well, Squirrel, it wasn't the best of beginnings. Labor was really just a dimly lit room with cots to lie down on. There were five other women when I arrived, all in various stages, screaming, moaning, and crying out in English, Spanish, and what I think was Chinese. Nurses came every so often to measure my dilation and to ask if I wanted anything for the pain. I'd decided on being alert and awake for your arrival, so I kept telling them no, which for some reason they seemed to take personally. The book had talked about breathing, so I tried it. As the pain grew worse, I started to moan and then to swear, surprising myself as much as anyone. I won't repeat what came out of my mouth, but I will say it didn't improve my standing with the nurses.

Finally they said I was dilated enough, and I was wheeled into Delivery. Well, one look at that place and I wanted to go back to my cot in the other room. First they strapped me to a table. Next they placed my feet in stirrups and hoisted my legs above the rest of me. Really, they only could have been less helpful if they'd hung me upside down. Then, just as the doctor said I was crowning, someone placed a mask over my face. I wanted to tear it off, but my arms were tied down, and they were giving me gas, and of course I passed out.

In the split second before the gas knocked me out, I was angrier than I've ever been; but then I woke up, and there you were. According to the nurses, three weeks is not too early after all. As you seem perfectly fine, I'm inclined, this once, to trust them.

There are hardly any pictures between my arrival and the library show, which proves how tired Lillian was. The only other time she went through so little film was right after the Lacuna Gallery show. Even during her two rounds of chemo, she took more pictures.

The reason it looks like I'm lying on a painting is because I'm on top of a table that Judy had painted with a giant bird a month before I was born: by happy coincidence, I happen to fit perfectly between its wings. I didn't see that table again until I visited Deb in Arizona, where I discovered it in her kitchen. When I left her house two weeks later, which was thirteen days longer than I'd been planning to stay, Deb sent the table home with me. She said she'd always thought of herself as its temporary guardian. All I have to do if I ever need her, she says, is knock on that table — that and pick up the phone — and she'll be there. I believe her. It turns out that being there, historically not my strong suit, is something Deb is very good at.

DEBORAH BRODSKY: I don't know whether it was the arrival of that beautiful baby, but suddenly everything seemed fragile. Things had stopped being good between Cass and Leon. First he'd moved out and come back, and then she had, and now they were together again but were both sleeping around. If anyone had asked, I would have said that all was well with me and Judy, but looking back, I think Samantha's arrival kept us together a year longer than we would have lasted otherwise, just because we were both so in love with being her aunts. Once that was gone — well, we broke up about two weeks after Lilly moved out, but that's getting ahead of things.

It was five or six days after Lilly had come home from the hospital. When I got back late from a reading, taped to my door was a note: *I'm bleeding. The baby's asleep. Could you bring Samantha up to your apartment and please look after her until I get back from the hospital?* Lilly's handwriting had always been impeccable, but here it was shaky and jumbled and the look of it, together with the words — all I can say is, in that moment, the world contracted into an incredibly small space.

I couldn't have stared at the note for

more than half a second, but that was all it took. Samantha needed a mother. Maybe just for a night, maybe for longer — maybe a lifetime — but that didn't matter. It wasn't even a question. And thank goodness, before six the next morning Lilly knocked on my door. She'd woken up at midnight with terrible cramps and bleeding. She hadn't known what to do, hadn't been sure she was strong enough to carry the baby up the stairs. So she'd left Samantha sleeping peacefully and stumbled out into the night to find a cab. By the time she'd gotten to Gouverneur, she was terrified by what she'd done, but it was too late.

Luckily, it all went fast. At the hospital, they gave her a shot to stop the bleeding and sent her home, telling her to stay in bed for four days to protect against further hemorrhaging, which was exactly what she did. I'd never seen Lilly stay in one place for so long. Part of it was exhaustion, but part of it was fear. She needed to obey those instructions to the letter because she knew she couldn't go through anything like that again.

In those four days, Lilly and I examined it from all the angles. If she'd taken Samantha with her that night, she might have fallen or passed out, and who knows what would have happened. If she'd made it safely with Samantha to the hospital and they'd needed to admit her — a young unwed mother — it could have been social workers and the baby's "best interests," and (perhaps this seems paranoid now, but remember, this was the 1950s) they might have tried to take Samantha away. Because from the time of Samantha's birth to the day Lilly and Samantha were discharged, those social workers kept making their little visits. I swear they were like circling hawks, telling Lilly how many "good families" were waiting for a healthy baby like hers, practically carrying Samantha away with their eyes. As it was, Lilly had left the baby sleeping peacefully that night, knowing I would be back for her. Perhaps Sam had woken up and cried herself to sleep before I returned, but she came through it just fine.

Lilly and I agreed that she had done the right thing, but it changed the way we looked at the world. We realized this was what it meant to be a woman alone and without money, a single mother. I think that knowledge stuck with us in different ways, perched on our shoulders like an invisible raven. Whenever there was a big decision to be made, there was that bird.

36. Exhibition announcement, "Lillian Preston, Photographer, Little Gallery, Hudson Park Library, April 10–30," 1955, with reproduction of *Pennsylvania Station*

The Hudson Park branch still exists, though when I passed the flyer around, none of its librarians knew what I was talking about. If I'd been old enough to attend the library show, rather than being four weeks old, I could have known what normal was — meaning an exhibition that came and went without a trace — giving me a helpful basis for comparison. As it was, my only experience was the Lacuna Gallery disaster, which left me without a compelling argument to convince my mother to show her work more frequently instead of letting it pile up like she was some kind of photography-world Emily Dickinson, dooming us to a life of food stamps and crappy apartments.

Limited by my experience, I accepted my mother's choices as inevitable and blamed myself. For much of my life, I was convinced that if I'd handled the post-Lacuna world better — the neighbors, the journalists, the newspaper headlines — things might have been different. Feeling responsible made me feel guilty, which made me feel angry, which made me say horrible things, which made me feel guilty, which made me feel angry, which basically describes the grim treadmill of my adolescence. *But!* — my teenage ghost screams from somewhere inside my spleen as I stare at this faded flyer for a gallery show long forgotten — *this library show is proof that Lillian knew enough to choose differently, and if she had chosen differently, then our lives might have been less hard* — but I am not a teenager. Lillian is dead, and it is time for me to give up the habit of blaming my mother.

DEBORAH BRODSKY: The night of the opening, Judy babysat while Cass and I went with Lilly to the gallery. It was the first time she'd left Samantha since that one night, and how different this time was! The whole Tuesday crowd was there, as well as the library people, the *Times* editor, and who knows who else. At first it threw me, seeing photos I'd watched Lilly print in the dark framed like that on a wall. It was like going from seeing Cass in her underwear to seeing her perform onstage: I needed time to recognize what I was looking at. But then something switched inside me, and the strangeness of the moment melted away. I felt like I was back in Lilly's apartment right after she'd returned from the hospital with the baby, except that now, instead of just me, the whole world was crowding around to see what she'd made. For days after the opening, Lilly slept as much as Samantha did, but she'd pulled it off: two births in two months.

JOURNAL ENTRY, APRIL 1955: It occurs to me that it is almost four years exactly since Mr. Clark took the Camera Club on the field trip that changed my life. He'd told us that on the rare occasion the Cleveland Museum showed photography, it filled a narrow hallway leading to the restrooms, but this time the museum had mounted a proper exhibition. When I got there, I saw something that shocked me: photos hanging on gallery walls, complete with their own cards giving the title, the photographer, the year, and all the other details that announce legitimate works of art. I only vaguely remember the images: scenes from Amish country, pastoral landscapes. What remains is a feeling like a rocket launching inside my chest. I promised myself that someday my prints would line the walls of a museum, the card mounted beside each one proclaiming "Lillian Preston, Photographer." Four years ago, that vision felt like the end of a fairy tale. Now I know it marks a beginning.

37. Hot dog vendor on Fifty-third Street, New York, 1955

Funny how Lillian's title neglects to mention that it's the stretch of sidewalk in front of the Museum of Modern Art. Not having studied art or photography in college (surprise, surprise), the *Faces of Our World* show was off my radar, but the date of the photo makes it a safe bet that the line of people stretching across the background and beyond are a few of the 250,000 museum visitors who saw *Faces* between January and May, a period you may or may not have noticed contains the run of a certain other photography show going on fifty blocks south. Did Lillian's MoMA fixation begin then? Possibly. It's also possible I was there when she snapped the shutter on this man's smile, on what was probably one of his better days for selling hot dogs.

> *JOURNAL ENTRY, MAY 1955:* Now I finally know what Mr. Wythe meant that day at Aperçu when he said that my work wasn't uplifting enough for Kleinmann. *Faces* may be the most beautiful photography exhibit anyone has ever made. To experience it is to grasp the enormous potential — of art and of people — to do good in the world. So much so, it was

impossible not to feel the weight of all that potential breathing down my neck! My pictures aren't nearly so pointed. I just want people to see.

I'm tired and hungry practically all the time, but I don't mind because those feelings are connected to you. Without that book from Renaldo, I doubt I could have faced down all the scowling nurses telling me over and over that formula was best during the first bleary days in the hospital when I kept refusing their bottles even though you were hungry, and I was sore, and neither of us knew what we were doing. But now, feeding you is the most soothed I've ever felt, a sense of completeness unlike anything else.

Since you're already six weeks old and the library show has come and gone, it's back to the bookstore. I know I should feel grateful to John for saving my place at Barrow Street, and to Deb for taking such good care of me. Most days I do, but there are also days when I don't see how I can keep going. It was silly to expect so much from a few photographs on a library wall, but still I had been hoping for . . . what? Greater recognition? Strength, I suppose. Something more to sustain me as I continue the work. Instead the Little Gallery show has faded to a distant memory, while you remain very real.

Even though you and photography are practically impossible to reconcile, I can't fathom a world without you both. Some mornings I'm so heavy with dread I can hardly move, but other days like today it's grand to walk west with you through Washington Square. In some ways, a mother with an infant is even more invisible than a woman alone. If anything, people notice the pram that she's pushing and not the camera in her hand.

DEBORAH BRODSKY: Faces was the biggest photography show I'd ever seen — that anyone had seen, really. It took up an entire floor of the museum, with each room dedicated to a different theme, and as I was walking through it, I could see people reckoning with photography in a new way. To go there with Lilly was a trip because of the way she looked at everything. I could tell she was there not just to enjoy the show but to size it up. As far as she was concerned, this was her competition.

Lilly never said it outright, but I think she'd been hoping her library run would catch more eyes. As we were leaving the

Faces show, she told me she could imagine *Window-shopping,* or *Two girls,* or *Asleep* there. Not the others, she said, they were too dark, but those three photographs would be a good fit. It wasn't a question, and it didn't come decked in bravado the way the boys talked about their art: Kyle with his proclamations, Leon with his scorn. The way Lilly said it, it was thoughtful — deferential, even — but also unshakably certain, and I knew that she belonged in that museum. It was just a matter of time.

38. Grocery store, New York, 1955

JOURNAL ENTRY, OCTOBER 1955: Once again I have John to thank, because I wouldn't have met Ken if John hadn't asked me to mind the register while he went to "freshen up." As it was, you were asleep in your pram and John was in the back room getting high when a man about my age walked in. After looking over the shelves, he asked me to recommend something recent, so I handed him the latest issue of *On the Wind.* This got him asking all sorts of questions about poetry that I couldn't answer, so as an excuse, I explained that I was a photographer. That got him asking more questions, but these

I could answer until John reappeared and helped Ken with what he'd really wanted, which was a new novel to read.

When Ken came the next day and asked for me (you were asleep again), John pointed to my usual place at the typewriter in the back, where Ken and I talked as I typed. Just as I was telling him about the lordly line of women I'd caught waiting for the register at the A&P, he asked in the most charmingly nervous way if I wanted to meet him for dinner. I said yes, so long as I could find a babysitter, which really threw him. Then I pointed to you, still conveniently asleep in your pram, and said if that changed his mind, then no hard feelings; but he looked at you and he looked at me, and then he shook his head in an almost puzzled way and said that no, it didn't change a thing.

I don't remember Ken very well, but I grew up with some weirdly specific ideas about fathers that must date back to him: dads put you to bed so that moms can be in the darkroom; dads don't mind eating TV dinners if moms are out taking pictures all day; on weekends, dads cook so moms can catch the golden hour before sunset. In the 1950s, there wasn't even a word like "progressive" to describe dads like that, because dads like that did not exist. But Ken did, at least for a little while.

39. Woman on Mott Street, New York, 1955

This is one of those permanent widows whose husband could have been just as easily dead ten days or ten years. Here's what I wonder: was the guy really so great as all that? Or is wearing black this woman's way of finally getting the world to leave her alone?

DEBORAH BRODSKY: Kenny Lowell was different. The first Tuesday he came, I could tell by the look on his face that he felt the city had given him a present. Not just Lilly but the whole scene: poets and artists scrounging dinner together, telling stories, dancing to Billie Holiday on my tiny turntable. Kenny was in publishing, according to him the only guy in the whole publicity department who read the books. Cass and Leon were history by this point, with shared custody over Tuesday night, so on even-numbered Tuesdays, Kenny and Leon went head-to-head over Woolf, Joyce, Beckett, and Hemingway. Odd-numbered Tuesdays, Kenny talked painting with Judy. All of which is to say, he fit right in.

He was vehement when it came to Lilly. She's brilliant, he insisted as if anyone were arguing, just imagine what she'd do if she had more space and time. Imagine what any of us could do with those, I wanted to say, but that was beside the point. As for Lilly, I could see it was easier for her with Kenny than with Charles. She and Kenny had more in common, and since Kenny wasn't a creative type, Lilly didn't have to wrestle with whether she liked his art. And he was so good to her and so good with Samantha — or at least game, anyway. Like most men, he had no idea what to do with a baby, but unlike the rest, he was willing to hold her and didn't flinch when Lilly took out her breast.

I guess he had an apartment up in the West Fifties, but he was never there. Our neighbors didn't know what to make of him, but Kenny was always saying hello or carrying groceries up the stairs for the babas, so pretty soon they came around. I felt grateful to him — not so grateful as Lilly but grateful all the same — for filling in the void. Because by then it was all falling apart. Judy and I were acting more like dowager roommates than lovers; Leon was talking about joining the merchant marine or making tracks for Morocco; and Renaldo had started using, though I didn't know it yet or at least wasn't ready to connect it to his lashing out at odd moments or disappearing for days at a time. Lilly and Kenny were my last bit of stable ground.

Then one evening, Lilly tap-tap-tapped on my door with this quizzical look on her face, like she was tasting a new food and couldn't decide if she liked it. Kenny had asked her and Sam to move with him to Brooklyn Heights. He'd bought a house as a surprise and taken them there to see it.

He *bought* it? I stuttered.

There was a bedroom for Samantha and space for a proper darkroom, she said in a voice that couldn't quite believe it was true.

But do you even want to move to Brooklyn? I asked.

Lilly had never considered it one way or another, but they'd practically been living together for six months. Her apartment was too small for the three of them, and it was quiet in Brooklyn Heights and full of families. On top of that, she wouldn't have to work at the bookstore: Kenny wanted her to have time for her photography.

What more was there to say? I hugged her, gave her my blessing, and burst into tears as soon as she left.

JOURNAL ENTRY, MAY 1956: Deb threw us a lovely party, and everyone came. Renaldo seemed happy, and Cass and Leon managed to be in the same place at the same time without fighting, which was as grand a present as anything. Cass, Judy, and Deb all found me at separate moments to say how glad they were for me, but their words were practically identical, as if they'd all memorized the same cue card in advance. I suppose their surprise isn't any bigger than mine.

Now Ken and I are back downstairs sitting on my mattress, listening through the ceiling as the party continues without us. This is the last night we will spend in this room. You're asleep in your crib, and I've just finished kissing the bottom edge of Ken's lip, following an angled plane of light cast across his face by the streetlamps outside the window. Kissing Ken feels like a continuation of a conversation, as natural as walking or words. At first his interest scared me a little — he was so eager to meet my friends, to see my work — but it's impossible not to succumb to his intelligence, his enthusiasm, his openness to possibility. I would have been lucky to find Ken at any time, but for the two of us to find him now seems like a particular piece of happy magic.

Brooklyn Heights, 1956–1961

40. Brooklyn Bridge, Brooklyn, 1956

Without the title you wouldn't know, or maybe you would. The crying girl and her mom take up most of the picture, but behind them you can see the bridge cables swooping up and away like the top of a giant spiderweb. An adult face in such extreme distress would signal something big: death, dismemberment, the end of love. But that little girl might just need a snack; or maybe she's freaked out by the decorative bird that looks like it's trying to tear itself off the side of her mom's feathered hat.

I should know. It's a practical guarantee I was with Lillian at the time, though I would have been under two years old, meaning that the experience is buried where memories go before words, to stew and emit their invisible fumes. Going by the hat, let's call it spring. This implies there is a chance the picture comes from our first-ever walk across the bridge, which Kenneth Lowell described in lively detail when I reached him by phone after dialing and hanging up several times.

KENNETH LOWELL: The day I showed Lil the house, I told her a friend of mine in Brooklyn Heights needed me to water his plants while he was away. We could walk across the Brooklyn Bridge and make an afternoon of it. Lil had never been, so I said I would take the stroller to free up her hands, but she explained it was part of her kit. I was amazed what she could do with that thing. Pushing the stroller, the camera resting on the handlebar as she walked, she would stop when she saw something. Then she'd turn to the side to free up her camera hand, bring the camera to waist-level, and snap a shot without ever looking down.

Well, everything about that day was perfect — the weather, the walk, the view — except I was so nervous that my stomach was in agonies the whole slow walk across the East River and down Henry Street. I had been planning to recite a Walt Whitman poem as I opened the front door. I'd thought a marriage proposal might scare Lil off, but even if I was just asking her to move in with me, I wanted to mark the occasion. The problem was, by the time we got to the house, my insides were so knotted up that I didn't have it in me to recite a limerick, not to mention several stanzas by the father of free verse. As soon as I turned the key in the lock, I made a beeline for the john. When I came out, Sam was toddling down the hallway making happy chirping noises, and Lil was in the empty living room, basking in a square of sunlight on the parquet floor. The different shades of honey in her hair matched the grain of the wood. Either your friend has taken a vow of poverty or he's been robbed, she said. I ditched the poem and reached for her hand. I showed her the room where I thought we would sleep, and the bedroom for Sam, and the smallest bedroom, where we could install a sink and board up the window for a darkroom. Once Lil came around to what I was saying, it was like watching a curtain drop away. Her face relaxed. For a moment I saw how hard she had been struggling, and how grateful she was that she would not have to struggle anymore. A different man might have been hoping for a different face, a more passionate one, perhaps; but I was happy because I saw a face that said yes.

41. Batter, Brooklyn, 1956

JOURNAL ENTRY, JUNE 1956: You know, Squirrel, when I first arrived in New York, there were so many interesting people and buildings and cars and bars and bookstores and movie theaters and museums to distract me that I simply underestimated the importance of trees. Our Brooklyn move has made me realize that for three years I have been holding my breath. All these oaks and sycamores make me feel sorry for Manhattan!

Let me just preface by saying: yes, kids played stickball all the time. So, if I were a logic-minded person, I would probably say that there's nothing unusual about Lillian's stickball photo happening to match a stickball-related anecdote of Kenneth's. Except that Kenneth was not remembering just any kid. He was specifically remembering a girl in braids and a Dodgers hat. In Lillian's photo, the head with its braids and hat are all that's visible, since the arms are one big blur. Stillness plus blur equals beautiful, but what makes the picture singularly excellent is the girl's expression. That face is not something we're supposed to see yet. It's a look of total seriousness and concentration, as if, instead of swinging a broom handle, that girl is actually in the middle of removing a tumor from the most delicate part of someone's brain. Her face at that moment is offering a glimpse of the future person she will become, which, considering the odds, is probably not a neurosurgeon. So picture that face on the future version of that girl while removing a splinter from her own child's index finger, or pondering the point in her life when things began to go wrong.

Probably Lillian wasn't going for anything other than the face, but it's possible she also saw what Kenneth saw. For a few years, it seems a future did exist that could have included a version of me in a Dodgers hat and braids, running bases outside that front window. For a few years the three of us — Kenneth, Lillian, and I — were happy.

KENNETH LOWELL: When I first started seeing Lil, Sam was a baby who mostly slept and ate. It was easy not to think about her much, or at least to think about her the way I would think about someone's puppy. But eventually Sam started saying "mama" and "ball." Not long after that she said "Ken." I suppose this would have sent other men running for the door, but on me it had the opposite effect. I realized I could stop being so cautious. I had loved Lil the moment I saw her, but I knew this wasn't mutual. Certainly Lil liked me. It is even fair to say she loved me in her fashion after not too long, but her feelings were slower and more deliberate. This is why I persisted in being careful — that is, until Sam spoke my name and I realized we were not two but three.

I conducted my house hunt in secret. I did not want anyone telling me that I was being hasty or foolish or any of the other obvious things. One day I found myself gazing through the front window of a converted carriage house onto a leafy cul-de-sac. A girl with braids and a Dodgers hat was standing on a chalk outline of home base, and I was certain that I was seeing a future version of Sam, who would play stickball on this street as if she owned it. In that moment, something that once seemed vague and uncertain gained a definite, pleasing shape.

We had been living together only a few months when Sam started calling me Daddy. She was nearly two. I was the man who was living with her mother, the man who was putting her to bed at night and giving her a bath. As far as I was concerned, there was nothing to correct.

42. Packing crates on Fourth Avenue, Brooklyn, 1956

LETTER TO DEBORAH BRODSKY, AUGUST 1956: Ken brags that I'm a pioneer, but desperate is more like it! It's impossible to ride the subway with a stroller. Even if I could somehow manage it, too much time would be lost. After an hour of being strapped in, Sam demands her freedom, and traveling with her to my old haunts would use up half of those precious sixty minutes. Anyway, the biggest question these days is not so much what to photograph but how. Sam is generally accommodating, but of course she's more sensitive to the weather than I am. There are days when, no matter what the weather, she's simply not in the mood.

Enduring two of those days in a row can be difficult. My love for Sam grows daily — a fact that continues to amaze me, since it's already deeper and stronger than anything I've ever known. But if I'm being honest, there are occasions when I do not like her. And these occasions — for instance, when the weather's fine but Sam starts kicking and crying and arching her back when we haven't even been out thirty minutes — inevitably lead to many, many moments when I do not like myself. When

I see other mothers strolling the Promenade with their prams or sitting on park benches, happy to spend their days dandling their children on their knees, discussing whether it's better to let Baby "cry it out" or to ignore the advice of Dr. Spock — then I'm certain there is something wrong with me.

I try to get us outside directly after breakfast and back home by early afternoon, because as much as I wish she would, Sam doesn't nap well in the stroller. And so, each morning I turn on to Court Street and head toward South Brooklyn. Prospect Park is inside the one-hour boundary. I can get as far as Greenwood on the rare day when Sam takes a stroller nap. The farther-flung neighborhoods belong to families who have lived there for generations, but an unfamiliar woman pushing a stroller is never given a sideways look, and if Sam starts to fuss, there is nearly always a neighborhood mother running errands who can point me toward the nearest playground, even if she only speaks Italian. Whether Italian or Irish, Polish or Norwegian, all mothers and children speak sandbox, slide, and seesaw — even, I'll wager, in California. Perhaps one day we'll visit you there.

I wish I could borrow your time zone the way I once borrowed your pep pills! Technically, I know your day doesn't last any longer than mine, but I can't count the times I've looked at my watch and thought longingly of the three hours left in San Francisco, while Brooklyn's day was that much closer to its end. And so I use the night as well. Thankfully, finding a Brooklyn doctor to write me a prescription was as easy as you said it would be, which gained me the darkroom time to develop a portfolio of new work for Mr. Wythe. For a year I'd been hoping to hear from him, but by the time he called, I'd pushed Aperçu so far from my mind that at first I didn't recognize his name! I was rather embarrassed, but Mr. Wythe was nice about it, especially after hearing Sam in the background.

KENNETH LOWELL: Lil was happy to subsist on canned beans for days at a time, so I did most of the cooking. Having lived on my own for several years before meeting Lil, I was perfectly capable of making dinner; plus, my salary was decent enough to spring for a maid once a week.

It was not a conventional arrangement. To be honest, it wasn't how I had pictured myself settling down, but then I hadn't pictured meeting someone like Lil. At work it was general knowledge that I was living with my girlfriend. I got plenty of cat-and-canary grins from the stiffs in my department, not to mention a few dark looks from the secretaries. Everyone thought I was putting one over. Mr. Hardham himself suggested for the sake of appearances that I wear a ring, but I have never been very interested in what other people think of me. From the beginning, I knew that no one else could make the photographs Lil made, while what I was good at — namely, book promotion — was something plenty of other slobs could do just as well. I suppose it did create a hierarchy in my mind.

As for housekeeping, it was obvious to me that Lil was working as hard as I was, so I did not see why she should do things like laundry or dusting, when at the end of my day I certainly had no desire to do them. I suppose that made us unusual, given the times, but honestly it just felt like common sense.

During the week, I did not see much of her: just the few hours between when I came home and Sam went to bed. This is one area where I made concessions for Lil being an artist since, all things being equal, I would have liked more time with her, but it was not as if I hadn't known what I was getting into. By the time I finished putting Sam to bed, Lil would be gone. Sometimes, after reading or watching television, I would join her in the darkroom. That was how I came to understand how many pictures she really took. Working with a fixed focus the way she did was not easy. Plenty of days, Lil chose not to print anything. This meant that the only way to see what she had accomplished was to be with her while she made her contact sheets: one contact sheet per roll of film, thirty-six exposures per roll, two to five contact sheets per day. Do the math and that means anywhere between seventy-two and a hundred and eighty shots. Lil would look at each image through her loupe. If she saw something she liked, she would circle it with a red grease pencil and put the sheet aside. On a good day, she might circle three images. She stored the rejected contact sheets in boxes. Our hallway was half bookshelves, half boxes. The shelves were for my books. The boxes were for the thousands of photos that never made it past the size of a matchbox.

Here's something I remember: one time I climbed those stacked boxes like they were stairs, but when I got to the top of the highest stack, I was too scared to climb down. I wasn't supposed to play on the boxes. I knew if Lillian saw me, she'd be mad. So I stayed up there for hours that were probably just minutes, until my mother started looking for me. I was so frozen with fear that she passed by the first time without seeing me, but when she did find me, she miraculously didn't bawl me out. Instead, she plucked me off the highest box like I was a carnival prize. The packing-crate photo is unconnected to any of this, except that when I see those two kids running across that long pyramid of wooden crates piled up to the second-story window of that Fourth Avenue row house, I want someone to carry them off like they're prizes too.

43. Shopkeeper, Atlantic Avenue, Brooklyn, 1957

By the time I was nine, I'd been dragged up one street and down another on so many of Lillian's photo safaris that I was basically a walking, talking street map. As far as my mother was concerned, I'd earned the right to go anywhere I pleased. Besides, kids back then were always out and about on their own. My mother made sure I had a dime for a pay phone, just in case, but I spent it on sugar, since I knew I wouldn't have to call. Mostly I went to Atlantic Avenue because of shops like this one: the rows and rows of glass jars containing nuts and dried fruits; the men with their dark mustaches and friendly eyes; the burlap sacks overflowing with dried lentils and beans, which were heaven to dive your hand into when no one was looking. The shop in this picture could have been any of several places lining that street, places where a dime could buy a piece of baklava after a few minutes spent fondling the fava beans.

KENNETH LOWELL: The first time Lil and Sam wore out the wheels on the stroller, I bought a new one, but when the same thing happened a second time, Lil told me she would find somewhere to get new wheels put on. Down Atlantic, there was a place near the Middle Eastern bakeries and spice emporiums that was half antique/junk store and half repair shop. It looked small on the outside, but the inside went on forever. There were shelves and shelves of silver shrimp forks, carved ebony buttons, and cracked-glaze vases, candelabra, doorknobs, and zippers. People dropped off lamps that did not turn on or suitcases that had lost their handles, and they left with a peacock feather or a pair of pearl-handled scissors along with their claim receipt, because it was impossible to quit that place empty-handed.

The guy who owned it was our stroller man. Count on him to have the part to fix whatever needed fixing, or at least know where to find one. I could tell when Lil had gone through another set of wheels, because something strange and perfect would be waiting for me when I came home. I still have a pair of hippopotamus bookends and a sandalwood letter opener, but my favorite is an antique penholder in the shape of a tugboat, which Sam gave me for one of my birthdays, and which my daughter made off with when she left for college.

JOURNAL ENTRY, MARCH 1957: You almost broke my camera today. It was my fault: I'd left it on the kitchen table, like always, except you're a little taller now. The strap was hanging over the side, so you walked over and pulled — and when the camera fell off the edge, you fell onto the floor and inadvertently broke its fall with your chubby little legs. Even as you were crying, I felt relieved for the camera. I've decided this does not make me a bad mother. Your bruise will soon heal and be forgotten, but if the camera had hit the floor, it would have been ruined. To reward you for your chance heroism, I treated you to five animal crackers and a sandwich cookie.

I'm afraid you're not the only one deserving a reward. During all my weeks in the darkroom preparing new work for Mr. Wythe, Ken has only seen me in his sleep. Imagine my surprise, then, when I dragged you and me and my portfolio into Manhattan to learn that Mr. Wythe preferred to show the three prints he already had! His explanation: none of the other photographers' work (there are six of them, all men) included children. "A woman and kids," he said. "You see what I mean." I suppose I should be grateful that Mr. Wythe wants my work to be seen on what he deems "equal terms," but I hardly think photographs of children are any less significant or important than photographs of anything else. Especially since the children in my photos aren't the kind you see on the cover of *The Saturday Evening Post.*

What amazes me, now that I've started paying attention, is how differently children inhabit the world. Even though our materials are the same — a tree, a chair, a pile of boxes — we may as well be inhabiting different planets. Mr. Wythe will show what he likes, but to me there's no difference between a photo like *Packing crates* and a photo like *Pennsylvania Station.* Both show what it means to be human.

44. Jehovah's Witness, Brooklyn, 1957
45. Fullerette, Brooklyn, 1958
46. Encyclopedia salesman, Brooklyn, 1958
47. Avon lady, Brooklyn, 1958

KENNETH LOWELL: One day I came home to five-hundred-watt bulbs installed in every room, but Lil was over the moon, and that came as such a relief that I decided not to mind our house being lit like a movie set. The whole winter, ever since Sam's cold, Lil had been depressed. If the new lighting scheme cheered her up, then hunky-dory. At first I thought it was just to brighten things up, but I should have known better. You see, Lil was against anything posed, so for her to be able to shoot at any moment, the conditions had to be perfect. In a row house with windows only in front and behind, that was not going to happen without a lot of help.

JOURNAL ENTRY, JANUARY 1958: You're generally healthy, and this was just a fever and a cough, but I would never take you outside in that condition. When, after four days, you'd returned to normal, it couldn't have been colder than forty-five degrees, sunny, and no wind; but once outside, you shrieked so loudly and suddenly that I thought you'd sat on a pin. As soon as I unbuckled you from your stroller to see what was the matter, you ran to the door of the house and started pounding. I thought we'd left Lomo inside, but your stuffed monkey was right there in the stroller, not that showing it to you made any difference. By this time, Mrs. Yansky had stepped outside to give me the gimlet eye. And so back inside we went, where I couldn't find a pin or any other reason for you to be so upset, other than it was time for our walk and you did not want to go.

In the days that followed, you took off your coat as soon as I put it on (I wish I'd bought you a coat with buttons instead of a zipper), or allowed the coat but wouldn't get into the stroller, or sat in the stroller but wouldn't stop shrieking once I managed to get us outside. All my promises — of hot cocoa, of grilled cheese with chicken soup at the lunch counter, of unlimited readings of *Benjamin Bunny* — did nothing to change your mind. This isn't your fault: you've always been sensitive to cold. Your poor lips turn blue even when you've played in the bath too long. That's why I bought you such fabulously warm clothing, but you also hate the feeling of layers, as you've made quite clear. Though it was only November and winter was just beginning, I had no choice but to wait for warmer weather.

The days became difficult. My exhaustion was similar to what I remembered from the weeks after you were born, but with no physical cause, and no Deb or Judy or Cass to come to my rescue. I have no friends anymore and have only myself to blame: I'm better at being around people than being with them.

Ken's salary allows us a Friday-evening sitter, but even if a morning nanny weren't out of the question, asking would feel ungrateful. Thank you for the house, for the darkroom, for working five days a week while I stay home; would you please take this child off my hands in the mornings, this child you love only out of love for me?

But without my camera walks, I'm a wooden puppet who wakes, eats, mothers, and sleeps as if I am being pulled by invisible strings. When I'm not taking pictures, I feel like I'm treading molasses. I tried sitting with my camera by the window, but a dead-end street in winter is a closed fist.

I don't remember how we passed the time. I don't remember the days as days. There's simply a gray stretch I know I passed through because I'm not inside it anymore. At one point, I heard the sound of crying as I sat paralyzed on the sofa. As I struggled to marshal the energy to stand up and check on you, I realized the sound was coming from my mouth.

One day, the doorbell rang. I opened the door to a clean-cut man in a dark suit. Would I be interested in reading a pamphlet? It was early afternoon, you were napping, and a decent amount of light was coming through the front window. I asked him in and sat him on the recliner in the path of that diffuse light. Photographers aren't vampires — we don't need invitations — but it's one thing to snap a picture in passing and another when your subject is sitting in your living room. Because I was resting the camera on my leg, the poor man didn't realize what I was up to at first. Once he did, he was caught off guard, but he relaxed after I showed him some old prints and promised him a copy of his portrait. For the next twenty minutes, he talked about the greatness of Jehovah while I shot the roll.

I'd never thought much about indoor photography before, but a trip to the photo supply shop solved the problem of light. If Ken hadn't suggested scheduling appointments, I'm sure I'd still be depending on fate for the doorbell to ring. When I explain I won't be buying anything, that sends a few scowling off, but most are happy with the promise of a picture, or confident enough in their abilities to think their sales pitch will change my mind. Even the camera-shy ones become caught up in their work soon enough. I've learned that good salesmen are interchangeable in the best possible way. Looking at the portraits, it's impossible to tell the face of someone extolling Jehovah from someone praising the virtues of Fuller brushes or encyclopedias. The passion to persuade is the same.

48. Cowgirl, Brooklyn, 1958

Salesmen and Bible-thumpers weren't Lillian's only subjects. The title should put to rest any concerns about my well-being as I straddle that vacuum cleaner wearing a shopping bag on my head and an expression like something out of *Rambo.* Given my ferocity, I'm guessing I've just found the man in the black hat. Whatever I'm up to, it's safe to assume I'm seeing something other than the room's armchair and coffee table, which is a testament to both my powers of imagination and my mother's powers of invisibility.

Out of curiosity I went through Lillian's negatives, which she kept in meticulous chronological order, in sleeves attached to their contact sheets. After eleven years in her childhood bedroom on Fernvale Street, those many, many negatives now occupy a rented storage space to spare my mother's legacy from taking up an entire room of my apartment. *Cowgirl* turns out to be one of over three thousand shots Lillian took of me between January and March, after she'd installed those floodlights. It makes sense, math-wise: my mother was used to shooting at least two rolls a day. Though a lot of those early-1958 shots qualify as artful, they're basically variations on Cute Kid, which is why this was the only one that Lillian chose for Box Two. Ultimately, all those thousands of exposures were less about pursuing her art than about preserving her sanity.

KENNETH LOWELL: Toward the end of that winter I knew something was off. When I talked to Lil there was a lag before she answered, like she was at the far end of a long-distance telephone call. This was different from the blue spell before she put in the lights. I could tell she wasn't depressed, just preoccupied; but while Sam required a certain nonnegotiable amount of attention, Lil knew she could rely on me to take care of myself. Finally Lil said she had an idea for a camera, and could she hire a man from the camera store to build it for her? By then I would have bought her a flying elephant if it meant that living together would stop feeling like living alone. She didn't mention the camera project for a long time after that, so I figured she had given it up.

49. Samantha and Kaja, Brooklyn, 1958

I feel like I remember this, but I don't. My "memory" is just a mental snapshot of Lillian's picture of me and Kaja on that metal horse. Real memories come with add-ons. For instance, I know I genuinely remember that playground, because when I see the horse, I can picture the sandbox, which in the summer smelled like pee, and which is not in the photo. Whether or not I remember this particular day, it is still the moment Kaja and I met. And that look on my face? This was a totally normal expression for people first meeting Kaja, whether they were three or thirteen or thirty. Sometimes, upon making Kaja's acquaintance, complete strangers would give her things. I personally witnessed the spontaneous bestowal of free donuts, halvah, packs of gum, pizza slices, and once a brown fedora. This was partly because she was beautiful — how often do you see a caramel-skinned, dark-haired Swede? — but mostly Kaja just gave off a pheromone that made people want to be with her. Colors seemed brighter when she was around. Getting to be her best friend felt like getting to walk on the moon.

JOURNAL ENTRY, APRIL 1958: The weather was warmer but unreliable, so we stayed close to home. When you were through with sitting in the stroller, we went to the playground, where a light-brown-skinned girl was furiously riding your favorite horse. Of course, the girl didn't know I'd promised you a ride on that horse in exchange for all your stroller time while I prowled the Promenade, but instead of fighting over it, the two of you rode together, which had the excellent effect of bending the horse much farther forward and backward on its spring. As I searched the playground for the girl's mother, I was interrupted by a pale blond woman sitting one bench over, who spoke to me in an accent I couldn't place. She was asking about my camera and if I was new to the neighborhood when the girl you'd been sharing a horse with came up to her to ask for apple juice. With a shock, I realized that the mother I'd been looking for and the one I was talking to were one and the same.

At first glance, Grete is not at all like Deb — she's a tall, snub-nosed Swede — but, like Deb, she's a straight talker who doesn't care what the world thinks of her. This is to say that I liked her right away. She, her husband Paul, and Kaja (who isn't older than you, as I first thought, only taller) live on Henry Street, which Grete explained was the only street in the neighborhood where they'd found someone willing to rent to a mixed-race couple. At the end of the afternoon, you and I followed Grete and Kaja back to their apartment, where Grete made no apologies for the clutter, and I felt right at home. Draped across the tables, chairs, and floor were woven pieces, some with figures and others with patterns, all in beautiful colors and finely made. When I asked about the artist, Grete laughed and pointed at the loom in the corner across from where the two of you were jumping on the couch. The blankets, shawls, and rugs were her insomnia projects. Ever since she'd learned to weave as a girl, she told me, she'd sit at her loom when she couldn't sleep. Did that happen a lot? It came and went, she said, but since Paul's newspaper job and their move to Henry Street, it mostly came. Grete laughed to learn I relied on a prescription to create insomnia for myself. When I saw that the radio beside Grete's loom was tuned to WOR, she broke in to Jean Shepherd's opening theme song, and it was my turn to laugh. We each had considered ourselves Shep's only fan, which makes a silly sort of sense considering it's radio for being awake at three a.m., but having that in common gave our meeting added magic.

You didn't want to leave any more than I did when the afternoon was over. Next time, Grete agreed, she and Kaja will come to our house so I can show her my photos while you and Kaja have a turn at destroying our sofa. In the meantime, Grete and I will be connected by a certain voice calling, "Excelsior, you fatheads!" across the airwaves in the smallest hours of the night.

KENNETH LOWELL: Back then, Dexies were a normal thing. These days they're in the same category as cocaine and opium, but understand that doctors used to prescribe Dexedrine to teenage girls for weight loss. My aunt Shirley back in Michigan kept a bottle in her medicine cabinet. And it was an amphetamine, of course, so it worked beautifully. I would wake up at some ugly hour to Lil still in the darkroom, but no matter how briefly she shared our bed on any given night, as soon as Sam started making her morning noises, Lil would pop right up, take her "vitamin," and be ready to start her day.

50. Spit bubble, Brooklyn, 1958

LETTER TO DEBORAH BRODSKY, SEPTEMBER 1958: We seem to be in sync: I'm also working with an idea that's gone in an unexpected direction. While your "simple work poem" has become a sonnet cycle, my cabin fever has led me to invent a new kind of camera. If I'd known my idea would turn into a six-month project, I never would have walked into Montague Photo to begin with! Considering all the time Joe has put in, the price I paid is hardly fair, but he won't take more, insisting "an agreement is an agreement," and that building the camera was the most fun he'd had since the Eisenhower election. All I can say is that I feel incredibly lucky. First, that Ken allowed me something so extravagant — especially when I haven't been giving him any good reason to feel generous — and next, that I found such a perfectly qualified camera technician. Best of all, Joe has finished in time for the cold weather, meaning I can devote this winter to candid indoor shots of Sam and me together, which promises to be much more interesting than what I could expect from a toddler alone.

KENNETH LOWELL: Around the end of that summer, Lil brought home the ugliest camera I had ever seen. It was like something Dr. Frankenstein would have thrown together if Frankenstein had been a photography buff. Lil's pal at the camera shop had grafted bulk-film loaders onto either side of a 35-millimeter camera body, which let Lil shoot a hundred feet of film at a time. Attached to the bottom of the thing was a modified spring-motor drive that could automatically advance the film at four preset intervals. This meant that once Lil got the camera going, it could take a picture every one, two, five, or ten seconds until it ran out of film. With a hundred feet of film, that meant 680 exposures, taken over anywhere between ten minutes to an hour depending on how she set it. It was a pretty expensive way to take pictures, but I figured the money Lil was spending didn't come to much more than what a run-of-the-mill glamour-puss would lay out for clothes, shoes, perfume, and makeup. The important thing was, it made her happy again.

If you look at the contact sheets leading up to this shot, it's pages and pages of Lillian staring at me while I stare at the camera. This goes on for ten contact sheets, thirty-five shots per page. Post-Kenneth, when it was a choice between film or food, Lillian would skip meals. This shot didn't happen until the camera had been going long enough for me to forget about it and start making spit bubbles. Of all the spit-bubble photos, this is the only one that catches a bubble on the verge of popping as it stretches from my open mouth toward Lillian's face like a see-through tongue.

I called the camera Ro-Ro, short for Robot. The tripod was Ro-Ro's legs and the camera lens was its eye, but mostly it wasn't a good name; or maybe it was a good name when I was three, but it didn't age well. As time passed, I suppose it could have become "the indoor camera" or "the winter camera," but it is hard, once something is named, to unname it. A name makes something part of a family. Brothers and sisters and fathers have names. Until the day I told Lillian never to take my picture again, I'd enjoyed being photographed by this camera, but even so, I did not want it to have the status of a brother or sister or father. Lillian, of course, loved Ro-Ro. And because of that, the couch- or refrigerator-type relationship that I would have preferred to have with it was out of the question. This meant that whenever I saw the camera beside the coffee table or standing in a corner, I would think, There's Ro-Ro, reminding me of the father and brother and sister I didn't have.

Every Ro-Ro picture my mother ever exhibited came with the credit, "Camera engineered by Joe Kubiak." Joe earned it. It is a unique and ingenious camera for which he deserves recognition, but really, I'm just as responsible for its creation. If I hadn't made my mother stay inside, she would have been outside, with no reason to invent a new kind of camera at the only time in her life when there was money to build one. While I don't know how much it cost to build Ro-Ro, I'm positive it cost more than new clothes, or dance lessons, or health insurance, which are just a few of the many things (breakfast cereal, cookies) we could not afford after we stopped living with Kenneth Lowell. If there had been no Ro-Ro, there would have been no *Mommy is sick*. Maybe Lillian would have become famous some other way, and maybe that way would have been better. Or maybe she wouldn't have become famous at all.

51. Repairs While You Wait, *Brooklyn, 1959*

She is probably waiting for the bus. Probably she has been waiting for a while, and that is why her stare is so blank and her face is so empty. Her children hang and swing and pull at her dress. She has become a jungle gym for them because she's the only thing around. It's probably a shoe-repair shop behind her, but the window is only half visible. This turns the REPAIRS WHILE YOU WAIT sign into a more general offer, an impossible offer to someone for whom the bus and repairs represent two of many absences perforating her life.

LETTER TO DEBORAH BRODSKY, MARCH 1959: Most of the time being with Ken feels the same as it's been from the first: each of us happy, if in our own way. But then one of us will say something or flash a certain look, and I'll wonder if I've been fooling myself all along. Do you remember when I told you about the Brooklyn house? Sitting at the table Judy had painted, you pinned me with that painfully direct gaze of yours and asked if this was what I really wanted. I didn't say it at the time, Deb, but I was disappointed in you that night. I'd wanted you to be happy for me, and instead I got your stare with a question that seemed silly at best. I thought that you, more than anyone, would know the importance of time and space to work and a partner who understood those things. Your reaction was so unexpected, I even wondered if you were jealous! Now I realize you weren't jealous and that your question wasn't silly at all.

KENNETH LOWELL: Sam had turned four. My brother and I are four years apart, so I suppose that started it. Also around that time, my brother's wife gave birth to number two, and several of my coworkers became fathers for the first or second time. All I know is that when I turned onto our street and saw kids playing stickball, I wasn't just picturing Sam anymore.

It must have been a Saturday night, because Lil was not in the darkroom. Sam was asleep, and Lil was getting herself ready to come to bed when I reached for her arm. Let's get married, I said. I had not been planning to say it, but it felt like the perfect thing at that moment, as if Lil and I were standing at a vista overlooking our future. Lil was unbuttoning an old shirt of mine that she had worn over her blouse to wash the dishes, and I remember the way her long hands poked out from the ends of the rolled-up sleeves. I remember the book beside my bed: I was halfway through *Molloy* and was using a bookmark Sam had colored so thickly with crayon that it was leaving flakes of colored wax on the pages. But mostly I remember the startled look on Lil's face. I want to be Sam's real father, I told her, and the father to all her brothers and sisters to come.

I let go of Lil's arm. My hand was trembling, and I was grinning like I had won the lottery. I'm not a religious man, but it is hard to overstate how predestined this felt, as if every choice in my life had been made in the service of this moment. Then Lil shook her head and smiled in her thoughtful, distant way. I can't have more children, she said. Anticipation had heightened my senses to the point where I could distinguish tiny, almost invisible freckles on the skin near Lil's mouth. She spoke with such certainty that I thought at first there was some medical reason, some condition she had inherited from her mother; but as she continued, I realized it was simply her opinion that one child was enough, which was absurd. I have a brother and a sister, I told her. You told me yourself that your parents tried to have more. I love Sam, I explained, but she is not our child. I want our child. I want Sam to have what I had and what you should have had. If you think about it, nobody chooses to have just one. Lil shrugged. I do, she said. Then she tilted her head to the side to look at me through one eye, the way she did when she was sizing up a photograph. It felt as cold and distant as the gaze of a reptile. I tried explaining again. I told her we could hire a nanny, that the advantage of a job promoting stupid but lucrative books was that it allowed for certain conveniences. And then I explained — because it seemed necessary — that if we hired a nanny, Lil could continue with her photography. Sam's bedroom was large enough to share. I had deliberately given her the biggest one. Nothing would change, I said. Now, instead of looking at me like I was a curiosity, Lil looked at me like I was nuts. Everything would change, she said.

52. Married couple, Brooklyn, 1960

JOURNAL ENTRY, MAY 1960: Seeing as the only other dedicated photography spaces are Little Gallery and Aperçu, I suppose I've run a gauntlet of sorts. Ted Ipplinger is a photographer who works in advertising. If Karen Ipplinger does something besides manage the Picture Shop, she didn't say. The gallery consists of an empty studio apartment on West Seventy-eighth, with a partition down the middle to increase wall space. They were interested in the new work, the Brooklyn photos Mr. Wythe had described. Would I mind coming uptown?

The idea for the gallery — they explained as you turned the glossy pages of a magazine I'd brought to keep you busy — was that regular people would buy photos at affordable prices to decorate the walls of their homes and offices. In this way, photography would begin to gain wider appeal. They had come to Aperçu looking for someone to pair with Harvey Ostrund. Had I heard of Ostrund? I had not.

Ted liked what I'd brought, but Karen wasn't sure. The way they discussed it felt private. "Do you think it's a good fit?" Karen whispered, to which Ted boomed, "It doesn't matter. It's powerful work. It demands our attention." "Yes, but is it too demanding?" in that same breathless whisper. I hadn't planned to photograph the two of them, but the light was too good and their strange conversation too compelling. I felt like a child hiding inside her parents' bedroom late at night. Each time Karen whispered some new concern, Ted grew bolder and she more flushed, until he rose to his feet. "We'll call it *Ostrund and Preston: Two Photographers, Two Views,*" he announced, one arm at his side, the other outstretched, his top shirt button straining. Karen nodded, her body limp, her resistance spent. It's only now that I realize how much their performance depended on an audience. You were too deep into tearing magazine pages into stamp-sized pieces to notice. By the time they'd finished, the floor around you was a carpet of glossy confetti.

Would it have mattered if I'd heard of Ostrund? Would I have then turned down these generous people whose two purchases were the only sales I made? The first half of *Two Views* was taken up by beautifully composed farm scenes — cows and calves, a duck surrounded by pussy willows — all by Harvey Ostrund, the Ansel Adams of animal photography. At the opening, I was flanked by Ken and his artist friend on one side and Grete and Paul, in a rare joint appearance, on the other. Watching reactions shift from Ostrund's end of the gallery to mine was like watching the faces of dinner guests with plates of roast chicken being given a raw egg. Karen Ipplinger was right, of course. People want to come home to something soothing, not the difficult beauty of a stained dress or a chapped lip.

On the day *Two Views* ended, Paul moved out. Grete arrived to help me take the show down in a borrowed convertible, her shirt so wet with tears that I thought she'd been caught in the rain.

KENNETH LOWELL: After our "conversation," I spent a few weeks trying to catch

Lil by surprise, hoping that if we got carried away, nature might take its course, but Lil never let things go beyond a certain point. When I started fantasizing about using force, I knew it was time to stop. Instead of staying home after putting Sam to bed, I started going out. In the years since we had arrived to the neighborhood, Brooklyn Heights had changed. People could now say "the Hicks Street scene" as something other than the punch line to a joke. I started spending time at a bar around the corner from a building where artists rented studio space. I would leave without telling Lil, drink a few highballs, and then come back to see if I'd been missed. Well, I had picked a lousy time to test Lil's powers of observation, since she was working at all hours to prepare for the Picture Shop show.

At the bar I met a cartoonist who drew for the *Voice,* and an abstract painter whose day job was creating steamy covers for pulp novels. The cartoonist told me that if I really wanted to stop wasting my time on Hollywood biographies and self-help manuals, he had a friend over at Gryphon I could talk to. A week later, I was having lunch with the Gryphon man, who said if I was willing to work for half my current pay, he would hire me in a heartbeat. I told him I would have to talk to my wife. I had not meant to use that word, and it was the only time in my five years with Lil that I did.

I invited the cartoonist to Lil's opening on what I thought was a lark, but when he came, I realized how much I had been counting on him showing up. He, Grete, Paul, and I made up Lil's crowd. The rest had come to see Ostrund, who was apparently well established on the West Coast. It was an odd scene. Ostrund's animal photos were so peaceful and composed, each one a perfect little still life, that they made Lil's work seem almost random by comparison. Paul was the only dark-skinned person there. When he beat an early exit, Grete reluctantly followed, which left just myself and my drinking buddy on Lil's side of the room. From his regular barstool the cartoonist always talked a blue streak, but that night at the gallery he was almost grave. I wondered if he wished he had gone back with Paul and Grete or maybe not come at all. Finally, I worked up the nerve to ask him what he thought of Lil's work. Honestly? he said. I think your girlfriend's a genius.

If he had been unimpressed or even

lukewarm, that might have given me the push I needed to go over to Gryphon, and to hell with Lil's photography. Instead he said: your girlfriend's a genius. When I got home, I threw the Gryphon man's business card in the wastepaper basket.

53. Ninth Street, Brooklyn, 1960

This one feels flash-frozen: kids sitting on a mantelpiece that's been yanked from some fireplace and left by the curb; two men carrying what looks like a steamer trunk across the street while a girl in a torn dress throws a ball at them like she means it. Any second, the men are going to start walking again, and the ball will finish its arc. Looking at this photograph makes me feel like I've stumbled into the middle of something unfolding. It makes me feel invisible.

The first rule was quiet. No talking, no singing. Funny noises were definitely not okay; camouflage wasn't camouflage if it attracted attention. If I saw something, I had to keep it to myself. A red motorcycle, a man tap-dancing on the sidewalk, a dog with a missing leg. "Mommy?" "Shh, Mommy's working." Talking when I'm outside still feels like interrupting.

But there were advantages: my comprehensive education in city pigeon behaviors and plumage patterns; my ability to tell time by the sun's reflection off a car; my discovery of *Pippi Longstocking.* Lillian always packed distractions — picture books, a plastic rabbit, a doll with hair and with eyes that closed — but these only got me halfway there or back. I remember bringing *Pippi* along because it was my regular bedtime book and bedtime wasn't enough. At five, I had to limp through each chapter six or seven times before I understood it, but even when only half the words made sense, the story seemed like a friend. Pippi did whatever she wanted, whenever she wanted. She didn't go anyplace she didn't want to go. My first copy got rained on. The second was left at a playground in Gowanus. Eventually, my third copy had only half a front cover and was partly held together with bubble gum. *Pippi* followed me to Cleveland and then to Los Angeles. After that I guess I didn't need her anymore, because by the time I left California, the book was gone for good.

KENNETH LOWELL: By now, I was getting cockeyed at the bar until one or two a.m. and coming to work hungover on a regular basis. Since Lillian did not seem to notice, I had counted on no one else noticing, either, but there I was mistaken. It seemed Mr. Hardham expected us to use the morning to dispatch our more demanding responsibilities in advance of our regular souse at the day's lunch meeting, after which we were supposed to be clearheaded enough to manage the afternoon's litany of telephone calls. My artist pals' drinking regimens were purely recreational and did not extend to three-martini lunches. Also, they could sleep in.

No matter what time I stumbled home, Lil was in the darkroom. One night, instead of going to bed, I lurched over to that inviolable door and heard a man murmuring on the other side. The sound of that voice made me instantly sober, or at least I thought it had, but were that the case, I suppose I would not have slammed my arm into the door. Lil shrieked, and I heard something clatter to the floor. Only then did it occur to me to try turning the knob. As the unlocked door swung open, the man continued to speak, unfazed by my sudden appearance. In the dim red light I saw Lil's terror-stricken face, an overturned tray of developer, and the radio, its dial covered to mask the glow.

In retrospect, I'm thankful that by the time Hardham and Young finally gave me the ax, Gryphon House was still looking for a publicity director. Had that not been the case, I would not have met Catherine. I would not have been the father of Kate and Harrison. And when I think of not having been part of Levin's *Facing North* or *Tillary's The Last Lunge,* I am left feeling almost as empty as when imagining a life without my wife and children.

JOURNAL ENTRY, SEPTEMBER 1960: I'm the only one who benefits from Grete's broken situation, because now you're always keen for our morning excursions. Grete and Kaja's new apartment is an hour's walk away, ninety minutes if we scenically detour through Fort Greene. Knowing Kaja is waiting at our trip's end makes you willing to venture into all kinds of weather. Needless to say, it's a rotten trade.

Twice a month, Grete drops Kaja with Paul in Harlem. "He explains that we cannot be together right now," she told me. "He tells me that he must be part of the community. But really, this is quite funny, because when the Harlem newspaper first hired him, I suggested that we move there, and he said no. You see, it is much more convenient to keep your white wife on one side of the East River and your black girlfriend on the other." She said this while you and Kaja were stacking empty cereal boxes at the other end of the room, and I wanted to rush to Kaja and cover her ears. I don't think Grete did it deliberately: I just think she was too angry and too lonely to care what Kaja heard. This made me question my own resolve. Will my frustration get the better of me? Will Ken's? If anyone's character is to be assassinated, it will be mine. Not because Ken is less well behaved but because my faults are more glaring.

54. Hotel Bossert, Brooklyn, 1961

Daughter or wife? If it weren't the front entrance or such a swank hotel, she might be his mistress (she's young enough), but whoever she is, she clearly knows where her fur-trimmed coat comes from. They're not actually touching, but the way she's positioned behind his arm, it's like he's holding an invisible leash in his kid-skin gloves. Knowing what I know now, I'm guessing Lillian saw a small piece of herself in this couple. Regardless, it's one of the last photos she took in Brooklyn Heights.

Having gone almost thirty years without speaking to Kenneth Lowell, a telephone interview should have been no big deal; or perhaps those three decades were exactly what justified my shaking hands as I dialed. As with Deb, I knew he wouldn't recognize me unless I outed myself, which I didn't think I wanted to do until the moment I did it. He and I agreed to meet for lunch, since we were both in New York. When we saw each other, we traded restaurant-appropriate versions of our lives and talked the way normal people meeting for lunch might talk. Someone could have taken him for my kindly uncle.

Since being made to leave him at age five, I had spent lots of time with the idea of Kenneth, but lunching with my father prototype didn't wreck me the way I'd expected it to. Sitting across a table from Kenneth Lowell was like peeking behind the palace curtain of my own personal Emerald City, except instead of a humbug, I saw a happy older guy with a wife and two grown children, neither of whom was me.

KENNETH LOWELL: I knew something was brewing because when I stepped out of Sam's bedroom that night, Lil was waiting for me, but I figured it had to do with photography or Sam. I was hot to get to the bar, since my pal had landed a contract for a collection of his *Voice* strips, and we were going to celebrate. After the word "pregnant," I was so jazzed that I did not hear what Lil said next. I know I started talking, because Lil had to place her hand on my mouth to get me to stop.

When she told me that she didn't want the baby, I made her repeat it. I suppose I thought if she said it enough times, she would come to her senses and say something else.

I remember getting very angry, very quickly. It was a miracle Sam did not wake up. I told Lil she was perverse for not wanting our child. I called her sick, and cruel, and selfish; I said that if she chose to have the abortion, I never wanted to see her again. We both cried after that, then were very tender with each other. I remember thinking if only I had taken a stronger stance sooner, Sam might have become a big sister years before.

The next morning, Lil kissed me as I left for work. By the time I arrived home, they were gone.

Park Slope, 1961–63

55. Candy store, Brooklyn, 1961

The title's helpful, especially if you're not great at reading reverse lettering off the inside of a storefront window that's partially blocked by slouching twelve- and thirteen-year-olds. The Italian couple who ran this place kept the candy and magazines in the back so the future greasers of South Brooklyn could hang out in front without being tempted to steal anything. I doubt these kids scared Lillian the way they scared me, since she wasn't half their size, but I knew as soon as I saw this store that it would never belong to me. It belonged to those kids the same way the streets belonged to their older brothers, who walked down Seventh Avenue with matching jackets and matching hair. When our own careers in delinquency began, Kaja and I opted for Atlantic Avenue, even though it was a half-hour walk.

We moved to Park Slope when I was

almost six. I remember waking up on the floor beside Kaja's bed and realizing I had peed the sleeping bag, then standing in the bathtub trying to rinse the pee out without making too much noise. I remember Grete bringing me from the bathroom to the kitchen and feeding me pancakes with raspberry jam, even though it was still dark outside. Being angry falls into the much larger category of things I do not remember, but the version in Lillian's journal makes sense. With Kenneth out of the picture, I needed to stick by my mother, or where would I end up? Leaning against a candy store wall looking like I ate kindergartners for breakfast, that's where.

JOURNAL ENTRY, MARCH 1961: When I said we were spending the night at Kaja's, you were thrilled. Since it was your first sleepover, you didn't think to wonder why I was sleeping over, too. I waited until morning to tell you the rest. I was so nervous that I wrote down what I was going to say. Ken and I needed to live apart, I told you, because we wanted different things. "Like what?" you asked. "Children," I said. "Ken wants more children, but I don't. I just want you."

You smiled and said, "That's okay. Daddy

already asked me, and I said you could."
"When did he do that?" I wanted to know.
"A long time ago," you said, and smiled even more. As I tried to explain about having only so much energy and attention and not wanting to divide it any more than I already did, somehow it came out that Ken was not your father. You became very still. "But I always call him Daddy," you said. "Why did he let me call him that if he isn't?" This wasn't a question I was ready for: I'd been too busy thinking of how to put things so that you'd know the separation wasn't your fault.

I said, "Ken loves you so much that to him you are his daughter." But this wouldn't do, and your face grew pale. You looked at your small suitcase and the stuffed monkey sitting on your lap. "Are we ever going back?" you asked. I shook my head, and your stillness became unnerving. All I could do was watch you, waiting to see what would happen next.

You were like a storm cloud bursting. You pounded your fists into the sofa and kicked and thrashed, and after you fell onto the floor, you didn't stop. When I tried to console you, you pushed me away. "Why didn't you tell me?" you raged, your kicks landing on the floor, the furniture, my shins. From the corner of my eye, I saw Grete and Kaja standing frozen in the doorway. Each time I reached out, you fought. Your fury was like nothing I'd ever seen. Only after you thrashed in such a way that your head hit the table did you let me hold you. "He lied!" you sobbed as you clutched at me, burrowing into my chest. "He's not my real daddy, and we are never going back." Your anger tore at you like it was breaking you in half. The only thing that felt worse than being so unprepared was my guilty relief that your rage had shifted away from me.

56. Self-portrait, Brooklyn, 1961

This isn't the first shadow in Lillian's work: there's also that picture of Charles in the park. I could say this proves Lillian's secret sense of connection to my long-lost sperm donor, but I think by the time she took this, she'd forgotten that other portrait almost as completely as she'd forgotten him.

Unlike Charles's photo, all we get here is the dark silhouette of Lillian's head and shoulders centered along the picture's bottom edge. My guess is that she's standing on Ninth, because I remember seeing rails there from the old streetcar route. The way the rails pass through her dark outline at a diagonal makes it seem like her silhouette has fallen onto the tracks and can't get up. Depending on my mood, this feels either funny, like her shadow is a cartoon character, or disturbing, like her shadow is, well, her shadow.

If she'd opted for a boring title like *Ninth Street,* none of this would be an issue, but something called *Self-portrait* begs interpretation. Grete, as Lillian's onetime closest friend, is better equipped for that than I am. I figured she'd be just as hard to find as everybody else, but for kicks I started by trying the old phone number that had lodged in my memory along with assorted jingles, elementary schoolteachers' names, and state birds, dating from when my brain was absorbent and spongy. Grete picked up on the second ring.

GRETE WASHINGTON: One day Lillian arrived at my door and said, I am leaving Ken. It came as a shock, but also I was surprised when Paul left me, so I think that I am not the best judge.

Lillian was very grave that day. I think this was an expression of her fear. I understood immediately why there could not be a second child. You will stay here, I told her, and she began to cry. In the many years of our friendship, I saw Lillian's tears only twice. This time was the first.

The next morning Lillian and I left the girls with a kind neighbor while I borrowed a car from a friend. To pack their things needed most of the day, but we finished before Kenneth returned from work. Kenneth called many times after that. Once he came to the door. I could sense that something was breaking inside him each time he asked to speak to Samantha and Samantha refused. Kenneth thought that Lillian was keeping her from him, but really Lillian was trying very hard to change Samantha's mind. I was watching on the morning Lillian told the truth to Samantha about Kenneth. I saw all the anger inside her. At first that anger turned to Lillian, but then Samantha struck her head on the table. When you need comfort and you are angry at the only person who can comfort you, what can you do? Samantha needed her mother. So I think her heart made a decision.

Kaja and I were living in a one-bedroom parlor flat with tall ceilings. This let us stack Lillian's materials very high. Lillian and I made a line with tape on the floor, and also a rule: no little girls on the box side of the line. It was too dangerous, not just for the girls but also for Lillian's negatives and prints! As for Lillian's camera, I knew she would not feel at home unless it was unpacked. When we set it on its tripod, her face relaxed a little.

I asked among the women where I worked. The first phone number Lillian tried was no good, and I think also the second, but she located an appointment with the third for the end of that week. It was bad timing, but concerning this there is only bad timing. I knew of a woman who did not see someone until she was pregnant for sixteen weeks; after some very frightening things, she entered the hospital, where a doctor removed her uterus. Even if an abortion was performed much sooner, there were many risks. If the hospital became involved, the police would come. The policeman would interrogate you in your hospital bed, and he would demand names. Sometimes in the newspaper there were articles. A mother arrested for finding help for her daughter. A doctor suspended for assisting a young girl. If an heiress or a fashion designer died from an abortion, the newspapers would report this, but not an ordinary woman. Such a plain death was not interesting or important.

The night before her appointment, Lillian gave me a piece of paper with the telephone number of her parents in Cleveland. Before now she never spoke to me of her parents, so I thought they had died. I was to call this number in case something happened, in which case I would also need to tell them about Samantha.

Tell them yourself when you are ready, I told her. Maybe tomorrow, maybe next year; you will have time.

Promise me you will call, she said. Yes, I told her. If it comes to that, of course I will. Then we stared at one another — very silently, very seriously — and that was how we became sisters: not by pricking our fingers and sharing our blood but by sharing our fear.

JOURNAL ENTRY, MARCH 1961: Ken was calling every night. First he would ask if I'd done it yet, and then he'd ask to talk to you. I tried to coax you to the phone every time, but you said you'd only talk to your "real" daddy. "What's a real daddy?" I asked. "The daddy who makes you," you said. "The daddy who makes you breakfast?" I asked. "The daddy who makes you laugh?" Each time, Ken said I'd turned you against him. Then he'd cry into the phone before getting angry again, and then cry some more. Each time I apologized — for you and for me and for everything — until one evening Ken called and I told him the date of the appointment. "That is two days before Sam's sixth birthday," he said, and hung up.

57. Self-portrait, Brooklyn, 1961

The location is the same, but the composition is different: all we get is the shadow of Lillian's decapitated body. Her torso fills the frame, the rail slicing across the base of her neck along the photo's top edge.

JOURNAL ENTRY, MARCH 1961: I went to the service entrance of an apartment building and rang three times. At first no one came. I was afraid I'd written the address wrong or that something had happened. The idea of starting all over again knocked the air out of me. Soon it would be eight weeks, and then no one would take me. I tried the door again. This time a man opened it and led me down a dark hallway to a dark door. When this door opened, I realized its edges had been taped over so that light wouldn't leak into the hallway from the other side.

It was some sort of office, but not for a

doctor. I was led into a room where a second man was waiting. He looked like he was on his way to a dinner party: he smelled like Brylcreem, and he wore a brown suit jacket with a gold tie, a white dress shirt, and metal cuff links shaped like birds. After I gave the first man the money, the second man told me to lie down. There was a wooden table covered in white paper, a tray with cotton gauze, and medical tools beside an ashtray containing a lit cigar.

I lay at one end of the table with my legs dangling over the sides. The cuff-link man hung his jacket on a hook on the door. He told me to relax, but I couldn't. He inserted a speculum. I asked if he was going to use anesthesia, but he shook his head. He picked up what looked like a long pair of scissors. I must have made a noise, because he told me to close my eyes, but of course I couldn't, and anyway the man only used the scissor-thing to pick up a wad of cotton from the tray. He dipped the cotton in a liquid and used it to clean me on the inside. He told me he was doing something "to make the baby come out at home, just like a miscarriage," and if I wasn't going to shut my eyes I should at least shut my mouth. He had rolled up only one shirtsleeve. The cold cuff link at the end of his left arm kept brushing against my thigh while his right cuff link winked at me from the tray.

There was a red rubber tube like a long straw, with what looked like a wire inside it. When the man slid the tube inside me, it felt like being pinched, which didn't hurt too much. Then he pulled the wire out and the tube stayed in, the end of it dangling out from between my legs. Next, more cotton. I suddenly pictured Mother stuffing the Christmas turkey, spooning breadcrumbs into the black hole of its body. This made me giggle in a nervous, terrible way that the man didn't like. "You think this is funny?" he asked as he worked. "You do this for fun?" I shook my head. I was afraid I would throw up if I tried to talk. I looked away from the man and back toward the metal tray. The right cuff link had fallen onto the floor.

When the man was finished packing me with cotton, he told me to sit up and handed me a container of brown pills. I should remove the rubber tube before tomorrow evening, he said, but I needed to take the first penicillin right away, even though it would be a few hours before anything started. "What happens now?" I wanted to know. "Now you go home," he told me. "And on your way, if someone asks what's wrong, you tell them you had too much to drink." He pulled a stick of rouge from his pocket and rubbed it on my cheeks. "So you won't look so pale," he said.

I was worried I'd stain the seat, so I sat on my coat for the taxi ride home. The pain wasn't too bad, and I hoped that having given birth once might somehow spare me the worst of it. The driver kept looking at me but didn't say anything. I wondered how many pale, silent women he'd picked up from that corner. When I thought of the words "make the baby come out at home," I kept picturing that cuff link lying on the floor.

As I rode home with my legs crossed, sitting on a coat I couldn't afford to replace, I wondered how you and I would begin our new life. I was scared, and I was sad — for you, for Ken, for me, and for the family that couldn't be — but I was also relieved. Does that make you angry, Squirrel? Or does it help you to understand?

Part of what made the next few days so frightening was not knowing. The cuff-link man hadn't said anything to prepare me, and even if I'd had a doctor to call, I wouldn't have called him. This wasn't the sort of thing doctors helped with if they wanted to stay doctors. The bleeding started that night and continued for the next two days. It felt like being in labor, only alone and with more blood. As I sat on the toilet, I clenched my teeth to keep the sounds I was making from scaring anyone — even though you were gone during the day, there were still the neighbors to think of — but keeping my mouth shut made it worse. I could feel those sounds trying to come out other openings instead: my nose, my eyes, my ears, between my legs, except that none of those holes were big enough. My muffled sounds combined with the sounds of the blood clots as they hit the water. I told myself not to look, but each time I had to look, and each time it looked like too much blood. I couldn't go to the hospital. I was afraid of what they'd do to me there. Meanwhile, I was leaving a blood trail down the hallway from bedroom to bathroom. In between cramps I mopped it up, to keep from staining Grete's nice floors, and to keep you and Kaja from any unpleasant surprises when you returned home.

GRETE WASHINGTON: I do not like to think of that time. Lillian was in such pain, but she did not make a noise because she did not want to scare the girls. Even so, the pain was written on her face. Sometimes when I was with her, a small sound came from her mouth, and this was like seeing the fin of the shark and knowing the shape that was hidden below.

I told the girls that she was sick. I did not name this sickness, and they did not ask. I told them that until Lillian got better she would need the bedroom for herself, so I slept on the sofa and the girls slept beside me on the living room floor. The first day after Lillian's appointment, I took the girls to the Metropolitan Museum. The second day, I took them to the Natural History Museum. You can pay just a penny in these places, and they will admit you. The girls were too young to enjoy such long trips, but I did my best. On the morning of her birthday, Samantha came into the bedroom so that her mother could sing to her. In the Hall of North American Mammals that afternoon, I saw her walking with a limp. Samantha, does your leg hurt? I asked. Is something wrong with your shoe? I am turning into an orphan, she said. I promised that she was turning into a six-year-old girl with a mother who would feel better very soon. She shook her head. She explained to me that she was half an orphan already. She held out her arm and the limping leg. This half, she said.

That night I sat with Lillian after the girls were asleep. I think it happened today, Lillian said. Did you see it? I asked. No, she said, but so much came out that I can't imagine there's anything left. The pain was so big, she said. Worse than giving birth? I asked. It was probably the same, she said, but because she did not know if things were happening the way they should, she had thought she was dying.

I am sorry I was not with you, I told her. Then you would not have been with Samantha, Lillian said, and that would have been worse. Then I am not sorry, I said. I will buy you some new sheets, she said. Don't be silly, I said, we are sisters, and sisters do not mind such things. People will think I'm too short to be your sister, Lillian said. People think that Kaja is too black to be my daughter, I said. Fuck people, Lillian said.

On the morning of the third day, Lillian left the bedroom and announced that she was better. By the sixth day, I think that she nearly was.

58. Diner, Brooklyn, 1962

You can tell the couple in the front window is married, because otherwise no way would she be fixing his comb-over with her fingers while he eats his soup. I'm not sure what grosses me out more, her need to adjust him in public or his apathy at being publicly adjusted. It's clear that Lillian thought there was something sweet about them. I can see how they might have reminded her of Grandpa Walt and Grandma Dot: not the tacky grooming part, but the married-for-so-long-personal-boundaries-disappear part. My grandparents were the first old married couple I met, leading me to believe that old married couples were like cows or peanut farmers, things that existed only outside New York.

By the time Lillian snapped this one, she had already taken most of the photos that would end up in the Lacuna show, and we'd been living with Grete and Kaja for almost a year. Considering Lillian's total disinterest in housekeeping, it couldn't have been easy on Grete to have us as roommates, but I only remember squabbles between me and Kaja over things like whose turn it was to use the blue china cereal bowl, and our fierce dedication to an endless series of competitions in which Kaja struck me as superior in everything that mattered. Probably I'd been jealous of Kaja from the moment I first saw her riding that playground horse, but my jealousy didn't find its size and shape for years to come.

Different addresses aside, Kaja's parents were still married. According to her mom, it was hard to get divorced in New York, but Kaja was pretty sure Grete still loved him; whereas Kaja believed her dad when he said that he was broke and divorces were expensive. Kaja preferred them split up: Paul did more stuff with her as a sometimes-dad than he'd done as an always-dad. I must have seen Paul a few times when everyone lived in Brooklyn Heights, but back then fathers weren't any more noteworthy than postmen, and I hadn't paid attention. Now when he brought Kaja back from Harlem on odd-numbered Sundays, I took in his wire-rimmed glasses and his skinny striped tie. I saw that he and Kaja had the same eyebrows, the same mouth, and charisma to spare, an aura of glamour that generally belonged to the rich or famous but which Kaja and her father exuded just walking through the apartment door. Seeing Paul on one side of Kaja and Grete on the other, I thought of an ice cream sundae: fudge, caramel, vanilla.

I should have been prepared for moving out. For months Lillian had been waitressing, but I was still shocked when all those months of lunch shifts added up to the first month's rent plus deposit on a place of our own. It was a one-bedroom like Kaja and Grete's, part of a mansion that had been chopped into eight apartments when Park Slope had started going downhill. In our living room, you could see where they'd thrown a wall right through the middle so another family could live on the other half of the first floor. We were far enough from Kaja and Grete that I was zoned for a different school, one Lillian said was supposed to be better. Grete had found a different school for Kaja, too, my mother said, so she and I wouldn't have stayed in the same first-grade class anyway. Plus, she said, don't you want your own bed? I did, but that didn't stop me from crying like we were moving to China and not fifteen blocks away.

GRETE WASHINGTON: Paul did not like Prospect Friends, but he never saw this place, so really it is more correct to say that he did not like the idea of a private Quaker school. He wished for Kaja to receive a strong public education with other black children. This was my preference as well, but such a school did not exist. The public school where Kaja and Samantha started first grade together had many black and Puerto Rican children, but forty children were placed inside each classroom with not enough desks or books. The teacher yelled often, and Kaja was unhappy. I heard this school called bad by many neighbors who sent their children to Catholic school instead. The public school close to Lillian and Samantha's address was considered good. This school was overcrowded also, with not enough desks or books and with teachers who yelled, but the children inside its classrooms were mostly white. At Prospect Friends, the classes were small. The teachers did not yell. There were lessons in music and foreign language and art, and Kaja received a full scholarship. This was perhaps the only time in our life together when her dark skin was a benefit.

LETTER TO DEBORAH BRODSKY, OCTOBER 1962: Since returning to Barrow Street would be impossible unless John could magically take me back at twice the hours, twice the pay, and half the travel time, I assumed that life after Ken would involve working at a camera shop. I'd hoped not to involve Montague Photo, in order to avoid the demotion from customer to employee; but after being turned away everywhere else — including a store with a help-wanted sign in its window — I realized Montague might be my only hope. In a way, I was right. "You see," Joe explained as kindly as he could, "we know you're a girl who knows her stuff, but the customers won't know what to make of you." This saved me a lot of time. Without Joe to set me straight, I don't know how long it might have taken me to notice that the only women working in camera stores were in the photo enlargements decorating the walls.

The manager at Remming's didn't like the gap in my waitressing resumé, but I happened to appear on a day he was short-handed, so he gave me a try. It feels equally strange and familiar to be back at a restaurant. If my younger self and I were somehow to meet, I have a feeling the girl working lunches eight years ago on Madison would admire the photographer I've become but wouldn't know what to make of the woman; and I'd certainly see right through how "modern" that girl was pretending to be. Really, Deb, it's a wonder you had anything to do with me at first, but I'm so grateful that you did.

From home to the restaurant is a forty-minute walk, an hour if I take pictures as I go. Each week, I choose a different route. I use Monday and Tuesday to get to know the streets, and by Wednesday I know what to look for. I noticed the Lacuna Gallery the first Monday I walked down St. John's Place, which is otherwise all grimy brick row houses and stray cats; but I didn't go in until Thursday, when its door burst open and a ball of brown curly hair wearing red cat's-eye glasses came running out to introduce herself. Her name was Nina Pagano, she'd been watching me all week, and she couldn't stand waiting any longer to see if I'd come in.

59. Christmas tree, Brooklyn, 1962

The picture is accurate, since it was usually boys who set Christmas trees on fire, but Kaja and I tried it once. Ambitious girls that we were, we picked a tree doubly taller and wider than ourselves, which had been left at the curb for the garbage truck. To avoid fighting over who got to ignite it once we'd dragged it into the street, we lit our matches at the same time. Back then, setting old Christmas trees on fire was as venerable a tradition as sitting on Santa's lap at Germaine's, but this was the only time I was up close and personal when one caught. The noise and the heat took me by surprise, and for the first of many times in my life I was afraid I'd taken things too far. But the smell was incredible: wet and sweet and so thick and heavy that when I put my nose to my shirt a month later, the scent was strong enough to bring back Kaja's tree-side rendition of Ella Fitzgerald singing "I've Got My Love to Keep Me Warm."

The tree in this picture is bigger than ours was, but then again so are the budding pyromaniacs, their silhouettes black against the blaze.

GRETE WASHINGTON: For more than one year after she gave it to me, I kept the address of Lillian's parents in the drawer beside my bed. At first I told myself this was in the event of some terrible emergency, but in that case I would have written this number into my address book and thrown away the paper long ago. You see, my parents lived almost four thousand miles away in Braås, and while we never got along very nicely, I was sad to think they had not met Kaja and perhaps never would. Such was my thought each time I saw the piece of paper inside my drawer.

This is why on Christmas I wrote to Mr. and Mrs. Walter Preston in Cleveland, Ohio, which was not even five hundred miles away, to share with them Lillian's address and phone number, and to tell them of the lovely seven-year-old girl who happened also to be their granddaughter.

JOURNAL ENTRY, DECEMBER 1962: The phone rang on a Sunday, near seven-thirty. I almost didn't answer because I was helping you into your pajamas, but since the only person who ever called was Grete, and she knew this was your bed-time, I picked up just in case. "Lilly?" a woman's voice said in a quiet, careful way that made me catch my breath. When I said, "Mother?" the voice on the other end began to cry. "Oh, Lilly," your grandmother said. "It is so good to hear your voice." By this time you'd stopped brushing your teeth to stare at my face, which had twisted into an odd combination of alarm and relief.

My first thought was that something had happened to your grandfather, but after your grandmother assured me of every-one's health, she explained that for years she had despaired of finding me, since let-ters sent to my old address on East 6th had come back stamped *Address Unknown.* "Until," she explained, "your friend's Christmas letter arrived like a gift from an angel." I was angry with Grete for a heartbeat, but it was silly to stay that way. Your grandmother and I didn't talk long, phone calls being so awfully expensive. She only asked questions she knew she'd like the answers to, which was anything to do with you. What color eyes and hair did you have? What games did you like? Were you shy? What grade were you in? If she sent a box of oatmeal cookies, should they have raisins or chocolate chips? Could she call again next Sunday and talk to you?

After seven years of just me, you were quite surprised to learn you had grandparents, but you accepted that we had "fallen out of touch" with the grace of any child too young to absorb more than a simple answer to a complicated question. I showed you an old family photo, and your eyes grew wide. "This is your grandmother," I said, pointing to the smiling woman in the flowered dress standing on the white porch of a white house, "and this is your grandfather," pointing to the proud man in the three-piece suit standing beside her. "Who's that?" you asked, pointing to the serious girl in the plaid skirt and knee socks standing between them. "That's me," I said, and your eyes practically fell out of your head. Until that moment, I don't think it had occurred to you that I was once a little girl.

When your grandmother called the following Sunday, you told her your favorite animal (monkeys, of course), your favorite ice cream flavor (Rocky Road), and sang her the chorus of "Hit the Road Jack" before it was time to hang up. Your grandfather didn't come to the phone, but your grandmother passed along his good wishes, which is more than I ever thought we'd receive.

60. Hands (Nina talking), Brooklyn, 1963

Even without the picture, those hands would be hard to forget. Whenever Nina was speaking, which was most of the time, her hands flapped like birds pinned to the ends of her arms, the right-hand bird somehow managing to flap without ever dropping the cigarette it was holding.

In a double whammy of good fortune, I met Nina around the same time that Grandma invited Lillian and I to visit her and Grandpa in the summer. The first time Nina appeared, she brought Chinese takeout. The only restaurant food Lillian brought home was the occasional overdone steak that a customer had sent back. Nina's first appearance in the middle of February with strange flat-bottomed containers filled with chicken chow mein and egg foo young felt like a visit from a skinny, chain-smoking, seasonally dyslexic female Santa Claus of exotic foods.

While she and Lillian looked at photographs, I ate. Nina was around Lillian's age but wasn't married and didn't have kids, so she felt more to me like a big sister. I could tell she laughed at my barf and fart jokes not to be polite but because she thought they were actually funny. This doesn't say much for her sense of humor, but when she called me Sammo, it felt gratifying even before I knew about Groucho or Zeppo. Nina tickled me, and read me stories using funny voices, and always brought Chinese, which never stopped tasting like magic, and from the middle of second grade to the last half of fourth, I loved her.

LETTER TO DEBORAH BRODSKY, FEBRUARY 1963: I didn't know what to make of Nina in the beginning. She's always so terribly excited about things that she comes across as a phony, but stick around and you realize that she means every word. A conversation with her can be exhausting, but her interest in everything combines with her enormous intelligence to make it a pleasant sort of fatigue.

I wasn't sure of her motives at first. She clearly liked the photos, but anyone could see she was lonely. However, one nice thing about Nina is that you can be on the level with her, so I simply asked if she wanted to represent me or be my friend, and she convinced me it was perfectly reasonable for her to be both.

The Lacuna Gallery used to be a tailor's shop. Nina calls the old dressmaker's dummy next to her desk her silent partner, but actually she uses the storefront in exchange for managing the two upstairs apartments. I get the impression that her neighbors on the block appreciate her rather less than I do. Though Nina's opinions about women and art and everything else are pretty strong for South Brooklyn, she would have fit right in with our old Tuesday-night crowd.

Considering everything you've said about San Francisco, it makes perfect sense that the spirit of East Sixth is alive and well on Waller Street. (It's nice of you to invite me to your weekly potluck, by the way, but unless it decides to move east, you shouldn't expect me anytime soon.) I'm so glad the Poetical Theater's production of your poem cycle in the park was a success! I'm glad you miss the snow, and no, I won't send you some. If you want a snowball, you'll just have to come back and make one for yourself.

61. Grete and Kaja in Prospect Park, Brooklyn, 1963

The day Lillian took this one, she wasn't even being a photographer, which is to say that she had her camera, but her finger wasn't tyrannizing the shutter release. People seem impressed that, in the age of three-martini lunches and thirty-five-cent cigarettes, my mother didn't smoke or drink, but if you ask me, she wasn't loftier or purer than anyone else; it was just that a cocktail or a Pall Mall would have gotten in the way. This picture happened on an afternoon when Lillian and Grete were walking Kaja and me back from Mrs. Ardolini's. I've since realized that Mrs. Ardolini got paid to look after children between the end of school and when their parents got off work, but at the time I thought she was just a lady who didn't mind having lots of kids at her place while she smoked Winstons in her green BarcaLounger. Kaja and I had convinced our moms to make a park detour so that we could practice our flying technique on the ratty playground swings. Until recently, we'd been allowed to hit the playground on our own, but that had stopped when the South Brooklyn Boys and the Untouchable Bishops started hashing out their differences with baseball bats and car antennas up and down the park.

The instant Kaja saw the tree, she ran over and started climbing. Unlike me, who had to be lifted onto any limb higher than my waistband, Kaja could climb everything. Lillian caught Kaja balancing on that branch as if confident the air will hold her up. Grete is less convinced, and voilà, Michelangelo's famous ceiling, slightly revised: large white hand almost but not quite touches small dark ankle.

When Nina first came over to discuss a gallery show, she didn't know about the pictures of Lillian and me. My mother's street photos covered all the available kitchen surfaces, along with the steamer trunk we used as a coffee table, and our few chairs and the sofa, leaving us to sit on the floor, eating dinner off our laps. *Grete and Kaja in Prospect Park* was one of ten photos Nina got excited about. If Lillian had known the people in the other nine, she would have asked for their permission, too, but she didn't, so Grete and Kaja were it.

When Grete declined, Kaja started yelling that she wanted to be in the show. The floors of our apartment were old, and the wood was coming away from whatever subfloor it was supposed to be fastened to, so each time Kaja stomped her foot in protest, the room shook a little, like we were sitting on a parquet trampoline. I was so used to Kaja getting everything — grace, charm, a father on alternate weekends, a mother who knew how to cook, a free ride to the cool Quaker school — that I felt too secretly gratified to act offended on her behalf.

> *GRETE WASHINGTON:* Mainly I feared for Kaja's safety. Life in that neighborhood was not easy. Below Third Street was not safe for her, and even the blocks along President were not so good. Of course, there was risk wherever Kaja and I were seen together. Our block was mixed, with whites and Puerto Ricans living as neighbors. People were friendly, and because we were quiet, the people with opinions were quiet also, but maybe you can see why I did not want to call extra attention to us with the photograph.

Please do not think, because of this, that I predicted what would happen. After Nina saw the photographs of Samantha, I also thought what a beautiful idea to include them in the show. You must understand, this was not the MoMA or some other big museum. This was only one small gallery on a small street, where people looking for a tailor still came to the door with suit jackets for mending.

I do not think Nina saw the future any more clearly than I did, but following the exhibition, she thought only of herself. I can explain it this way: no matter where a white mother and her black daughter went, people stared. The stares in Washington Square Park might have been kinder than the stares in South Brooklyn, but a person who stared to make a show of their acceptance used Kaja and myself in the same way as a person who stared to make a show of their contempt. True acceptance does not stare, because true acceptance sees nothing to stare at. To both kinds of people, Kaja and I were a symbol.

I must tell you, it is very tiring to be a symbol. Good symbol or bad, it is tiring all the same. From the moment of her birth, Kaja and I had no choice in this matter, but Lillian and Samantha became a symbol only because Nina turned them into one.

JOURNAL ENTRY, MAY 1963: When I showed Nina our photos later that night, it was as a friend. I wasn't thinking of the Lacuna show. Not because I considered our photos any less important or serious: if anything, I take them more seriously because they belong only to us! Nina, however, can be quite convincing. Though she was passionate on the importance of showing women and girls through female eyes, I was more persuaded by the look that crossed her face before she said a single word.

I put the question to you as neutrally as I could. You're young, but being eight is not like being a baby, as you often remind me, and you're certainly at an age where you can hold and defend your own opinions. When I told you that Nina was interested in showing our photos, your face lit up. "Does that mean I get to be in the show?" you asked, and clapped your hands. Only if you want to be, I explained, which made you laugh. "Why wouldn't I?" you asked. Well, I said, for one thing, it would mean people seeing pictures of you naked. "Mama," you said, rolling your eyes, "I'm only a little girl."

62. Exhibition announcement, "*Brooklyn Lives,* Photographs by Lillian Preston, Lacuna Gallery," 1963, with reproduction of *Diner*

The day after second grade ended, Lillian and I took the subway to Grand Central, where we boarded the Cleveland Limited, an overnight train ride that was the most exciting experience of my eight-year-old life. My seat reclined. There was a car filled with couches and round tables, and a car that was a restaurant, and a car with doors that opened onto little cabins with bunk beds inside. For as long as it was light out, I looked through the window at all the trees and rivers and bridges and houses and roads and cars, a world that, for me, had only technically existed until that moment. I waved maniacally at every kid in every backyard I passed, and some of them waved back. When it got too dark to see out, I played Go Fish with Lillian until way past my bedtime, the rocking rhythm of the rails making it feel like everything was exactly as it was meant to be.

Precocious girl that I was, I shouldn't have been surprised that the grandparents waiting at Union Terminal were not the smooth-skinned, sparkly-eyed specimens from the photograph, but older, cautious-looking types with sagging faces. This, however, did not slow the stampede of my love for the tidy house on Fernvale and those tidy people, especially Grandpa Walt, whose maleness in my maleless world trumped even Grandma Dot's sit-down meals with folded napkins.

When Lillian gave them a copy of the notice for the Lacuna show, my grandparents eyed it like food they weren't sure was safe to eat. Well, isn't this something, Grandma said. Grandpa nodded and added that it was good to have a hobby. I told them they should come, that there were going to be pictures of me. To which Grandma smiled and remarked, How nice, and Lillian said nothing, and that was that.

Not that I was paying much attention: I'd just ridden a train. I was staying in a house with a staircase that led to more of the same house instead of connecting downstairs and upstairs apartments. When Grandma took me grocery shopping — in her *car* — she filled a shopping cart with three times as much food as Lillian and I ever bought at one time. Grandpa taught me how to ride Lillian's old bike, which I was allowed to do *in the street,* which was wide and quiet. When I was done, I could leave the bike on the lawn, and *no one would take it.* Every afternoon at three-thirty, Grandma and I sat at the kitchen table with a piece of homemade apple spice cake to look for birds in the many trees outside her kitchen window. At five, Grandma would start cooking. At six, Grandpa would come home from work. Dinner was at six-fifteen. There was always a tablecloth, meat, and dessert.

We were supposed to stay a week. The morning before the date on our return tickets, Grandma asked if we wanted to stay longer. Lillian said she had to get back to work; plus there was the show to get ready for. Grandma said that even if Lillian had to go, I was welcome to stay if it was all right with her and if I wanted to. My mother said I was too little to ride the train by myself. Grandpa agreed and explained that was why they'd send me home by plane, at which point I was smiling so wide that my face muscles hurt the next day. And that was how I spent my first summer in Ohio.

Everyone being so happy to see each other made it easy to treat our whole eight-year separation as some sort of fluke, what with Grandma touching my head like she couldn't believe I was real, and Grandpa telling knock-knock jokes while I helped him sand and paint his model planes. At no time that summer did I consider the one-sidedness of the Grandma-didn't-know-where-to-send-a-letter scenario. It didn't take a Sherlock to observe that the porch in the old family photo featuring girl Lillian was the same porch that Grandma and I were sitting on to drink lemonade and read the funnies: meaning, Watson, that even though my grandparents hadn't known where to find my mother those many years, my mother had known exactly where to find them.

But why dwell? I was eight. For the first time in my life, I belonged to a family I could count on more than two fingers. Besides, I wasn't the only one not asking questions.

JOURNAL ENTRY, JULY 1963: Your grandfather is thicker around the middle, and he and your grandmother have wrinkles where none were before. Your grandfather wears bifocals now, which he trades for a separate pair of magnifying eyeglasses to work on his planes. The house has been repainted, and there is new carpet in the entry. I was prepared for my room to have been converted into any number of things — a sewing room, a guest room, a second study — so it came as a surprise to find it unchanged. All my books and posters, all the random childhood objects — my souvenir pop bottles, my clay dog, my matching plush kittens — were pristine after ten years of your grandmother's faithful dusting. I was surrounded by signs that time had stood still, yet there you were, asleep on the cot your grandfather had set up beside my childhood bed.

It's almost funny how desperately curious and fearful your grandparents are regarding our New York life. They clearly can't fathom how a woman can raise a child on her own without dying of starvation or embarrassment. While the truth (hard work, stubbornness, overwhelming love for you) might have put them a little at ease, I refused to answer a question they couldn't bring themselves to ask. Luckily, you were an excellent distraction; and once you were asleep, we filled the time discussing the changes in the neighborhood, and the policemen and plumbers and clerks and lawyers who had married my high school girlfriends, until we could make an early show of yawning in order to retreat to our rooms without seeming too eager.

Awkward as it sometimes was for the rest of us, Squirrel, for you it is simple. You love it all — the green and the quiet, the uncluttered rooms and the unchanging schedule — and of course you love your grandparents, who love you back with a ferocity that makes it easier for me to overlook the rest.

Despite my gratitude for the various combinations of kindness and generosity and forgetting that allowed us to visit, I was looking forward to going home when your grandmother made her unexpected offer. As soon as I saw your face, I knew it would be cruel not to let you stay. And why not, when staying mean a mattress with a ruffled bed skirt and matching curtains in a bedroom twice the size of our shared one at home; a grandmother to show you the city; and a grandfather who reads to you from the same Hans Christian Andersen book he once read to me, with the same character voices that made me forget where I was until "The End" brought me back to his lap.

Your absence means darkroom time to print my photos exactly as I'd like for the Lacuna show without relying on my prescription, but the apartment is empty without you. When I look around, I worry that you'll be disappointed with the home you're returning to. Grete teases me about this. She's used to a daughter who travels between two worlds that are no less different for being at opposite ends of a subway line. Grete is right, of course, because each Sunday when you telephone, you ask me questions — Is it hot? When you get back, can we go to Coney Island? Can Kaja sleep over? Is Mr. Fanelli opening up the hydrant with his special key? — that show me all the ways you look forward to coming back. Then there was your excitement describing the shopping trip to Higbee's with your grandmother, and the new dress that you insist on keeping a surprise until the night of the gallery opening. I can't wait to see you in it.

"The Samantha Series"

63. Samantha's tattoo, Brooklyn, 1959

"*Brooklyn Lives,* photographed by Lillian Preston" opened at the Lacuna Gallery on September 14, 1963. My dress was white organdy and taffeta, with a blue embroidered Peter Pan collar, blue embroidered birds on the front, a blue velvet ribbon at the waist, and remains the fanciest piece of clothing I have ever owned. It was a summer dress, and Lillian warned me I would be cold, but I didn't care. I spent that whole evening rubbing my hands up and down my goosebumped arms as I stood at the back wall where my photos were arranged in chronological order, starting with *Samantha's tattoo* and ending with *Sleepwalker.* Grinning like a maniac, I waited for people to ask for my autograph. My mother had told me gallery openings didn't work that way, but I was ready, just in case.

Photographs have an annoying habit of

corroding whatever real memories you have of a moment until the photo is all that's left, but with *Samantha's tattoo* I can still feel the tip of that Magic Marker pressing against my stomach. I'm in my underwear because it's hot. I'm sitting upside down on the couch because that way it's easier for me to draw the monster so it's right side up when I look down at it. It's a big monster because the marker feels so excellently cool and wet on my skin. My belly button is supposed to be it winking. My underwear is supposed to be its hat.

Lillian could have cropped this into a photo of a cute kid doodling on her belly, but that isn't the point. The point is that the couch is a swamp of books, toys, and newspapers, and our makeshift coffee table is a dirty-dish graveyard. The monster I'm scribbling onto my upside-down half-naked self is basically the room's spirit animal. Lillian meant for the shot to be both a little funny and a little alarming, and she succeeded. As I think I mentioned, she wasn't the world's best housekeeper. But even back in the bad old 1950s, crummy housekeeping or letting your kid draw on herself was not against the law.

So there I stood under my photos, waiting to be famous. Grete and Kaja showed up with paper and pen to ask for my John Hancock, but mostly I was bored. Proud but bored. Not many people came. The ones who did mostly stuck by Nina and Lillian, except for a few passersby who looked like they were from the neighborhood. I watched them, trying to figure out what they thought. Nina had told me that anyone who really liked the photos could buy them, giving me ideas about owning a bicycle like the one I'd ridden in Cleveland; but Lillian had advised me not to hold my breath. Still, when one lady stood looking at my pictures for a long time, I decided to make my move.

They're for sale, you know, I said, tugging her arm. She looked down at me, wide-eyed, her nose twitching. Is that *you* in these . . . pictures? she asked. Sure is, lady, I gloated, and you can buy as many as you want.

For a second before walking out, she stared at me, her nostrils flaring like I was a bad smell. After she was gone, Nina sidled over and asked me what I'd said. When I told her, she laughed and said next time to leave the hard sell to her.

During our phone interview, I kept expecting Nina to guess who I was the way Grete did, but she never recognized me. Then again, I wasn't the first person Nina had talked to about herself and Lillian. Nina has cameos in a bunch of documentaries, and her name is in the index of any self-respecting textbook about art history or women's studies or First Amendment issues. Which probably explains why she sounded so self-congratulatory on the phone.

NINA PAGANO: At Pratt I spent my undergraduate years realizing I was talentless, but I partied with the studio-art crowd, and that was all it took for the Vitalists to be born. It was basically eight of us writing manifestos, sharing studio space, and boinking each other in various combinations. Being the historian of the group, I was there to get it all down. If anyone asked, I'd have said we were destroying the barrier between art and viewer; we were placing the goals of the collective above those of the individual. Then, in 1957, we graduated. Lorraine and Eric got hitched, lit out for Vermont, and started raising bees. John embraced the big ugly and started law school, and Susan married him so that she could embrace something big and ugly, too. That left Katherine, Gary, Milt, and me. We all debased ourselves at the same parties and bars; I watched them drag their portfolios to the same Tenth Street galleries. We all knew that Katherine's stuff was the strongest but that Gary talked the better game. Guess who got a show? And then turned his back on everyone except Milt, who went and got a show of his derivative color-bar paintings with Stan Kohl after Katherine's superior color-bar paintings had been nixed? The difference being that Milt had to talk jazz with Stan while matching him drink for drink at the bar, while Katherine had to leave the bar with Stan and go back to his apartment, which Milt did and Katherine did not. Well, that was my limit. Seeing Katherine get shafted made me want to shit on the whole establishment, so that's exactly what I did one night when a bunch of us were passing Milt's second-rate paintings in the Kohl Gallery's window after an otherwise undistinguished night of getting blotto around the corner. It had been the same big talk, big whiskey, and big laughs until I squatted in the middle of the sidewalk and yelled, Number two for number two. As the cold air kissed my bare ass, it got very quiet. After that, it was either leave town or start my own place.

Manhattan, home to the art establishment I'd so eloquently rejected, was obviously out. Not to mention I was so broke that I couldn't have covered a deposit or first and last month at any price. Besides, Brooklyn was my home turf. My pops knew a guy who needed a building manager for a place on St. John's. The location was off the map, natch, but if I showed quality work that people had no chance to dig elsewhere, they'd have to start paying attention. Which they did, didn't they?

I wasn't thinking of it as a women's gallery. Start using labels and you seal yourself into smaller and smaller boxes until it's just you in there. Plus, some see a label as asking for a favor. As in: Oh, Kind Sir, would you please spare a glance for Women's Art, which needs your special attention? Not to say I wasn't showing work by women artists, because I was, but that doesn't mean I had to call it anything. It's not like the Tenth Street places were calling themselves men's art galleries, even though that's exactly what they fucking were.

It wasn't until later that people started calling me a feminist. I've got no beef with that, but things smelled different back then; "feminist" still meant some chick in a long white dress, circa 1918, marching for her right to vote. Remember, *The Feminine Mystique* didn't hit until 1963, and women's lib came on four or five years after that. Now do the math: I opened the Lacuna in 1961. I was an underemployed, overeducated, underappreciated, overconfident art-school pain in the ass who wanted to give her friends a place where they could show their work. It just so happened that those friends were women. When I met Lil, I could see straight off that what she was doing with her camera was the real deal. So, naturally, I made her my friend.

64. The Popsicle eaters, Brooklyn, 1960

Again with the underwear? you ask. Well, again, it was hot. Summers in Brooklyn got pretty ugly, hence those old-timey photos of whole families sleeping on fire escapes, and wide-angle shots of people draped over every grain of sand at Coney Island. Hence children willing to expose their soft child parts to the bruisingly high-pressure water streams of popped fire hydrants. Let me tell you something: it was much easier to lie around in your underthings pressing a dripping Popsicle to your chest between licks, as demonstrated here by me, age five. Naturally, Lillian (camera engineered by Joe

Kubiak) is sitting perfectly straight and dripless, hair neatly brushed, looking like she could be the doyenne of Popsicle etiquette at a finishing school if she happened to be wearing anything more than panties.

LETTER TO DEBORAH BRODSKY, SEPTEMBER 1963: Nina kept handing me cups of Irish coffee and promising that things would pick up, but the sight of Sam grinning beside her portraits did a lot more to temper my disappointment. Back at the Little Gallery eight years ago, in what feels like another life, I accepted Manhattan and Mr. Stromlin's connections and my circle of friends the way a child takes for granted all the pretty presents at her birthday party. By the time I left the Lacuna, only fifteen visitors had come and gone. Nina wanted me to stay through midnight, promising that the Saturday-night art crowd made Brooklyn their last stop, but I decided it was better to risk missing Mr. Stromlin than remain outnumbered by the faces on the wall.

65. Bath, Brooklyn, 1960

It looks like I'm floating. There I lie, arms outstretched, palms up, gazing beatifically at the ceiling, belly and thighs and toes peeking above the water. Depending who you ask, I look like a water nymph or a drowned corpse. Guess which one the newspapers went with? The whiteness of the water is hiding the upside-down cup that's propping up my butt. The water's white because I'd let the soap sit in it for a really long time in order to make "milkshakes." The whiteness of the bathtub almost exactly matches the whiteness of the water, a happy coincidence Lillian wasn't about to pass up.

The first half of opening week was crushingly similar to the first half of any other week. I got up, went to school, then played at Mrs. Ardolini's until Lillian brought me home. It was just like my mother had said: no autographs, no bicycle. Optimist that I was, I kept telling myself it was just a matter of time. In a way that involves yanking optimism into a back alley and kicking its teeth in, I was absolutely right.

Maybe it was the twitchy woman I offended with my sales pitch, or maybe it was someone else, but that Thursday Lillian didn't come for me at Mrs. Ardolini's when she was supposed to. Which was fine, because that meant getting to invent bonus accidents for the Judy Splinters doll Kaja and I were torturing in Mrs. Ardolini's backyard. An hour later Grete came for

Kaja, and Lillian still hadn't shown. As Mrs. Ardolini handed Grete a phone message, she said that I needed to go home with them, something to do with a gallery and a woman named Nina. From the way Grete thanked Mrs. Ardolini and danced us out of there, you'd have thought we were on our way to a ball at the Ritz. Instead, she took us to a stoop a block away. She sat us down on the crumbling steps to read what Mrs. Ardolini had written, but the message didn't say anything Mrs. Ardolini hadn't said already.

I could tell Grete was worried because she asked me and Kaja what we wanted for dinner, something she never did. Chinese, I said even though Grete never did takeout, and I was a big fan of her cooking. Thursdays were Nina nights, and I wanted wonton soup so bad that eating over at Kaja's was actually a letdown. After we'd finished off Grete's meatballs, my mother still hadn't come, so Kaja and I got to watch *The Flintstones.* Next came *Donna Reed,* and after that *My Three Sons,* an unprecedented glut of school-night television that eclipsed thoughts of my mother or Nina until the phone rang and Grete turned off the TV and I learned I'd be sleeping over that night — as well as Friday, Saturday, and Sunday

— because Nina had been arrested, and my mother had been arrested with her.

NINA PAGANO: The whole thing was just bum luck and lousy timing. Lil had dropped by on her way back from work, so we were rapping at my desk when the two cops came in, a pink one and a jowly one. You're a little late, I told them, the party was Saturday. Usually the badges crashed my openings around two or three a.m. to shut things down. Anyway Pink said, You the owner? and I nodded, and then Jowly said, You're under arrest for pandering obscenity and illegal use of a minor.

Well, that just about skinned me. Pandering obscenity and illegal use of a minor? That's dirty-old-man stuff. So I looked at the two cops, and I asked Jowly to repeat himself, which he did, and then I asked him what the hell he was talking about, which probably wasn't the best way to phrase it, but at a moment like that the words choose themselves.

Jowly warned me not to get wise with him. He pointed to the pictures of Lil and Sam and said that I was in a family neighborhood selling dirty pictures. Pink grabbed my wrist and started in with the handcuffs. When I demanded to know what he was doing, he said something clever like, Lady what does it look like I'm doing, at which point Lil, all watercress and cucumber sandwiches, suggested there must be some mistake, which inspired Jowly to ask who she was.

You *made* these? he said when Lil answered, and that was that.

I bet even money it was someone on the block. Not counting the two upstairs tenants who said I was the best super they ever had, I wasn't too popular, especially not with the Suzy Homemakers down the street, who thought I was either a Commie or a dope fiend or both. As I mentioned, there'd been calls to the fuzz before, on nights that went loud and late. One Suzy H went off on me after her paragon of manhood showed up at one of my parties on his way home from the bar and got cozy with the talent. I don't know what that particular Suzy said or did to change things, but afterward the local gentry quit making evening social calls. All of which was a few months before the show.

Once I got over the twist of being handcuffed, it didn't take me long to start feeling righteous. Part of it was having friends who'd done civil disobedience already, so I was hip to that dog-and-pony show, and part of it was the ridiculousness of an art gallery getting busted. But Lil? She was petrified. After they cuffed us, they marched us to the squad car, and the whole block came out to watch. Poor Lil was pale as a slice of Wonder Bread. Oh god oh god, she kept saying, what am I going to do? Like he was doing us a favor, Pink explained that we were going to get booked; then we'd wait for our arraignment. After that we'd post bail, and if it all went real good, we'd be out in time for dinner on Monday.

When Lil heard the word "Monday," I thought she was going to throw up. You got to be kidding me, I told him. That's four days from now! You think judges work weekends? Pink said. I pointed out that it was only Thursday. Like he was talking to a four-year-old, Jowly explained that if we were real lucky, our paperwork would be done by the end of tomorrow so that, come Monday, we'd be ready for the judge.

By this time, Lil was taking really small steps, like her legs had seized up. I was afraid she might faint or fall over. When I told the cops they needed to understand that Lil was a single mom, Jowly shook his head like he couldn't believe it. Lady? he said to her. Can I ask what you thought you were doing?

At first I wasn't sure Lil heard him, but then she looked him straight in the eye. I was making windows, she said.

66. Ice, Brooklyn, 1960

Here's how it usually went: if Lillian and I were doing something that seemed promising, she'd move Ro-Ro to where we were, set it up the way she wanted, then resume whatever we'd been up to. If I was doing something solo, my mother would grab her regular camera from wherever she'd left it, place herself a sofa length away, and start snapping pictures. She never told me to smile or not smile, to look or not look. And she never told me to take off my clothes.

Sometimes I wasn't in the mood for pictures, so I'd stick out my tongue or move outside the frame. Sometimes I'd go stiff as soon as I heard the click of the shutter. But other times I'd call Lillian over myself, because I could see the picture in my head and knew it was a good one. And sometimes I had ulterior motives. When Mom's a photographer, nothing says "I'm sorry" like a good photo op.

For this one, I don't remember what I'd done. Broke something, maybe, or "borrowed" something, or lied about something and gotten caught. Maybe this was the time I busted our only electric fan by sticking pencils into it. Or when I dialed random phone numbers and talked in a made-up accent to whoever answered. I'm not sure if I already knew what the picture would be when I grabbed the ice from the freezer, or whether I figured it out once I came into the living room and saw the patch of sunlight on the floor. Whichever it was, I would already have been naked. I remember making sure to lie down so the rectangle of sun contained my whole body. I remember trying to put the first ice cubes on my ankles, and them falling off, and having to start at my thighs instead. From there, I worked my way up: belly, chest, neck. Once I had those in place, I called for Lillian, then popped an ice cube in my mouth and stuck one on each closed eye before opening up my hands and letting the last two rest on my palms with my arms flat on the floor. The burn of the ice mixed with the warmth of the sun until I couldn't tell cold from hot. I remember the cool wet of the melting cubes pooling on my skin as the sunlight bore down. And I remember knowing from my mother's gasp and the sound of the shutter clicking that whatever my wrong had been, it was forgiven.

JOURNAL ENTRY, SEPTEMBER 1963: By the time we reached the station, my legs had gone wobbly. Nina wanted to help but she was handcuffed, and anyway the officers wouldn't allow it. One held me up as he walked me into the precinct building, while the other walked with Nina. I told them I needed to pick you up from play group in half an hour, but fear had plugged my ears so that my words seemed to seep through layers of thick wool. An officer said he could make one phone call for each of us and handed me and Nina two message slips to write on.

I felt sick, picturing you waiting while all the other mothers came for their children. I had to get word to Grete, but that meant leaving a message with Mrs. Ardolini, and this made me feel sicker. Nina was wonderfully clearheaded and helped me work out what to say. Finally, I wrote, "Dear Mrs. Ardolini, please ask Grete to take Samantha home with Kaja. I am helping Nina with a matter related to the gallery," and handed it to the officer. In Nina's message to her father, she told him everything and asked him to call Grete at home to let her know that we'd been arrested and would be in custody until Monday. This was how I tried to keep the neighborhood from learning your mother was spending the weekend in jail.

For several hours, Nina and I sat inside a holding cell, "awaiting transportation." Nina did her best to comfort me. I remember the weight of her arm on my shoulders and the vague murmur of her voice, but I couldn't hear her over the fear muting my ears, which came and went with the taste of bile in my throat. After vomiting on the floor, I felt a little better. A new officer on duty looked at me with pity until one of the others told him why I was there. "She did what?" I heard him say, and then he didn't look at me anymore.

By the time we were being driven to the jail, I'd stopped feeling nauseated. I kept reminding myself you were safe with Grete. The blockage in my ears had subsided enough for me to hear Nina repeating to me that it was all a mistake and that her father would find us a good lawyer. She used words like "freedom" and "America" and "justice." When I asked, the officer told me without turning his head that we were being taken to the Women's House of Detention.

67. Tea party, Brooklyn, 1960

I don't remember where the clip-on earrings came from (Lillian wasn't the jewelry type), but I do remember how hard they pinched. Any discomfort I deemed trivial, since I thought I looked incredibly sophisticated in them, even when I wasn't wearing anything else but plastic beads. The other visible party guest is my stuffed monkey, looking worse for wear from an accident involving food coloring and Elmer's glue. The anonymous hand at the top of the frame pouring tea from the plastic teapot into my open, upturned mouth is my mother's.

On Friday I went to school in one of Kaja's outfits so I wouldn't be seen wearing Thursday's clothes. I believed Grete when she told me my mother had done nothing wrong and that the police had made a mistake, because that was how it always happened to Bugs Bunny. Kaja told me that when Martin Luther King, Jr., got arrested, everyone knew he was there for righteous reasons, but I didn't want to have to explain anything to anybody. I made sure my face was clean and my hair was brushed. I raised my hand in class, stayed between the lines in my handwriting notebook, showed all my work during math, and didn't whisper or pass notes. I did everything I could not to seem like a girl whose mother was in jail.

I know I felt scared and worried, but what I remember most about that motherless weekend is going with Kaja to her dad's. I don't know if it was Grete's or Paul's idea, but that Saturday morning Kaja told me to roll up my sleeping bag because it was a dad weekend and I was coming. Her dad had promised dinner at the Bombay, popcorn *and* candy when we went to the movies, and pancakes for Sunday breakfast. Once the IND had taken us under the East River and was working its way up the west side of Manhattan, there was a stop where all the remaining white people got off the train, so naturally, I stood up. Then I saw Grete and Kaja still sitting. Hey, Kaja, I whispered, me and your mom are the only white people left. Kaja looked up from her book and grinned. I know, she said.

Harlem had the same brick and brownstone buildings as Brooklyn, some nicer than others, where kids played out front and people sat on stoops; there were newsstands and drugstores and a candy shop and a barber — only here everyone's skin was different shades of brown. Come on, Kaja sang. She started skipping down the street in a way she never did on Seventh Avenue, her face lit up like a candle.

NINA PAGANO: It's funny how you don't see something until you have to. All the times I'd been to the Village, I'd never noticed the prison at Sixth Avenue and Tenth Street, which is weird considering it's bigger and taller than everything else around. Where do they get enough women to fill this thing? I remember wondering as we were brought through the door. It wasn't like women were out robbing banks and killing people. Well, I learned the answer to that question pretty quick.

None of the cops back in Brooklyn had told us what to expect, not that it would have helped. At first, things went the way I figured — fingerprints and mug shots, empty your pockets and your purse — but that changed when they took *everything.* Wallet, hairbrush, chewing gum, tissues, coin purse, lipstick, aspirin; and in Lil's case a few rolls of blank film. They even confiscated the hairpins from Lil's hair. An officer tried to impound my glasses, but I convinced her to let me keep them if she didn't want me walking into walls. I was just grateful Pinky had told Lil to leave her camera at the gallery, because I think they'd have had to kill her in order to bag that.

Next came the showers, which sort of made sense after I saw the shape some of the other women were in. The shower room was like something you'd associate with a high school gym, only without any benches or lockers. They told us to strip. No preamble, no changing room, no privacy. A couple other women were already in there, one looking seriously strung out, the other watching like we were light entertainment. At first Lil just stood there. She deaf? the guard asked. Lil, I said in a low voice, it's okay. Just pretend you're back in tenth grade. Lil nodded and started getting undressed. A guard balled up our clothes and took them away. When we came out of the shower, another guard told us to squat. What for? I asked just as another woman who'd been standing with the guard stood behind me and stuck a finger up my ass. What the fuck? I yelled before she slipped her finger out and told the guard, She clean, boss. Then she went over to Lil, who was pressing herself up against the wall like she was trying to melt into it.

We were each handed a cotton smock to wear and nothing else. Mine ended halfway up my thigh and Lil's went down to her ankles. Then we were brought to another room and told to wait for our medical exams. No one seemed interested in explaining what the hell we needed a medical exam for. We were with a bunch of women now, all in cotton smocks that didn't fit. Most of them were black or Puerto Rican and young. A lot were strung out like the girl in the shower. One kept asking if anyone had a piece of candy, something sweet to keep the DTs away just for a little, but our cotton smocks had no pockets.

When it was my turn the doc asked was I a virgin, then said he was going to check me for VD. I wasn't a hooker or a junkie, I told him. I was there because my art gallery got shut down — but the doc said I had to spread my legs anyway. When I asked why, the guard told me to quit it in a voice I didn't like the sound of. So I did like I was told, and the doc rammed a speculum into me so hard that I screamed. What kind of art do you show at your gallery? he wanted to know. You're hurting me, I yelled. I like art, he said.

68. Mommy is sick, Brooklyn, 1961

Before I opened the last box of my three-box inheritance, I hadn't seen this photograph in twenty-five years. Funny thing is, I thought I had, because that's the way brains work: once you can read, you can no longer open a book and see a jumble of letters; after you get to know someone's face, you can't see her as a stranger.

I had forgotten there weren't any black bars.

For twenty-five years, my memory had been slapping black bars over my eyes and chest in this photo the way I'd seen it in the newspaper when the case first went to trial, and on television when the case went back to trial, and on T-shirts when "Mommy Is Sick" became a punk rock anthem. For twenty-five years I'd been turning my body into a crime scene.

Here's the thing: the original image is beautiful. The grainy, vandalized version that was stamped onto newsprint and TV screens and preshrunk cotton-poly annihilated the spectrum of blacks, whites, and grays that Lillian fine-tuned until the dark stain on the pale sheet so naturally matched the dark eyes in my pale face you'd assume the picture just happened like that, without anyone popping Dexies in order to spend crazy hours dodging and burning the print in the darkroom between putting her kid to bed, and then getting that kid off to school the next morning, and then heading off to waitress for six hours, all so she could run that circle all over again.

Back when Lillian and Nina and I were first going through the photos for the Lacuna, this picture was the only one that took me by surprise. Standing beside that bed at age six, I may or may not have noticed Ro-Ro; but either way, I wasn't thinking photo session, making this one of the few pictures I hadn't known Lillian was taking.

Part two of the surprise came from the picture's location. The eight-year-old examining the photo had forgotten that this terrible, scary morning had occurred before Lillian and I moved into our own apartment. Maybe for reasons of trauma distribution, I'd separated being forced to leave the only father I'd ever known from fearing for my remaining parent's life. And yet there was my mother in Grete's bed; and there was six-year-old me in my underwear, holding out milk in Kaja's favorite drinking glass, the one with rabbits on it; and there was a tennis-ball-sized stain between Lillian's legs as if she had peed the bed, only dark.

That stain was surprise number three: not because I'd forgotten about it but because I'd never seen it before. Ro-Ro, after all, had been positioned above the foot of the bed, angled down. I had been standing near my mother's head, too short to see anything beyond the mattress's facing edge.

You're bleeding, I remember telling Lillian as we looked at the photo. I was having a miscarriage, Lillian said. What's a miscarriage? I asked. For the three seconds preceding her clarifying answer, I'd thought it was a bloody kind of flu.

I'm going to tell you a secret: I hate this picture.

In this, I am not alone. There are many other people who hate this picture; however, those people are not my people. Unlike all the other haters, I do not think this photograph is "immoral," or "pornographic," or "exploitative." I do not think Lillian was "wicked," "depraved," or "an abomination under God." I do not think I was "abused," "neglected," or "manipulated." When I think of all the people who said those things — in newspapers and on TV, in court, and to my mother's face and mine — I want to hurt them, which is progress. For a long time, whenever I thought of those people, I wanted to hurt myself.

My hatred is unique. I hate this picture because I hate my worried expression as I hold the glass. I hate Lillian's weak smile, which is solely for my benefit and only makes things worse. I hate the hollows beneath Lillian's eyes. I hate the matching paleness of her skin and the bedsheet, which makes the stain between her legs even scarier.

This is a sad picture, I told my mother when she showed it to me, and she agreed. She didn't look very good in it, I said. Probably it shouldn't be in the show. Why? my mother wanted to know. Because she didn't look good or because it was sad? Because she was bleeding, I said. People shouldn't see her bleeding: it was yucky and embarrassing. Embarrassing for who? For you? she wanted to know. Yes, I said, but also for her.

My mother didn't answer right away. We kept staring at the photograph.

I'm not embarrassed, she said after we'd looked a little longer. People bleed sometimes. She liked this picture because it showed a difficult part of life in a way that was honest.

As we studied the photograph some more,

I remembered the dead feeling in my stomach that morning, when I realized my mother was too weak to take the glass of milk from my hand. I remembered sitting on the edge of the bed and holding the milk below her mouth. All she had to do was reach up a little with her hand to hold the glass but even then, the milk dribbled from her mouth and onto her chest. This made the deadness in my stomach fill my whole body, so big and deep and dark that for a while I couldn't breathe. Then I remembered how, for the three days my mother had been in Grete's bed, no one — not me, not Kaja, and not Grete — had ever talked about what was happening to her.

Let's put the picture in the show, I said.

JOURNAL ENTRY, SEPTEMBER 1963: One of the women in our holding cell was a beautiful young prostitute named Georgiabelle, who was arrested after the police officer had sex with her. She couldn't understand why I was there. "For real?" she kept asking. "You in here for taking pictures?" There were twenty women in the cell, all of us waiting to be arraigned. A doctor had given me a very rough medical exam and I had bled on my smock, so I tried to remain sitting as much as I could.

Georgiabelle knew a long-timer who had protected her the last time she'd been arrested. By the end of Saturday, she'd used her connections to get me a sanitary belt and napkin. I thanked her so much that she became embarrassed and stayed away.

Occasionally, a guard opened the door to the holding cell and said we could walk down the hall, which had a small window at one end that looked onto Sixth Avenue. It was so strange to see the city through the square hole in that thick brick. Cars passing, children walking home from school, mothers shopping, men on their lunch hour. Sometimes people stood outside, beneath the windows of the prison, calling in. Fathers and mothers and sisters and children. They knew the daily schedule, knew when their loved one would be standing on the other side of that window looking out. "Freddie, that you?" yelled a woman standing beside me. A boy waved from the sidewalk below. "You tell Yolanda to keep her nose clean, you hear? I prob'ly be in here least a month this time, and it's on you to make sure she behave."

Squirrel, the night I was bleeding and had to leave you in your crib to return to the hospital was more frightening than anything I could have imagined. But terrified as I was, I knew that either the bleeding would be stopped or I'd die: one way or another, my fear would end. Separated from everyone and everything I loved, with no idea when I'd be allowed to return, my fear was fathomless.

69. Loose tooth, Brooklyn, 1961

Not a Ro-Ro shot, as you might think. True, the other end of the string attached to my tooth is tied to a door beyond the photo's left edge, which is being closed by an unseen person; but that person is Kaja, not Lillian. And there I am, just left of center, caught mid-flinch: the string leading out of my mouth is taut as a tightrope as the door slams shut.

Once again, my mother went for the wide shot in order to get the doll dangling off the edge of my bed and the clothes dangling off the chair. Everything here is hanging by a thread.

As with *Ice* and *Bath,* people accused my mother of staging my performance, but the slamming-door technique was Kaja's. Kaja had slammed that door at least twice before Lillian discovered us, and after the picture was taken, Kaja slammed many more times before my tooth's liberation. The truth is that I was deeply proud of this picture. At the Lacuna I spent most of my time standing next to it, so there would be no doubt who that brave girl was.

JOURNAL ENTRY, SEPTEMBER 1963: There was nothing to do. We'd been given no pens, no paper, no books. Some women talked. Others cried. Some stared blankly at the wall. A few went into drug withdrawal, and their pain was terrible to see. The guards watched and did nothing. Some women kissed and groped each other. One woman sat down next to me and tried me with her hand. "No!" I yelled very loudly, and she stopped.

The bunks were hard and dirty, with no sheets or pillows. My cot had a cotton blanket, but it smelled and was stained, so I didn't use it. Roaches crawled the area around the toilet and sink. The food was some kind of thin oatmeal or soup and was often cold. By the third day I kept forgetting I wasn't guilty of anything, that I was still waiting to see the judge. When I did remember, I didn't know what to do with the information and fell back into forgetting. My hairpins had been taken away, so my hair hung in tangles. This sounds like a small thing, but it is not.

At some point my hands began to frame things: the lined face of a young addict; the marred skin of her inner arm; the cracked light fixture on the ceiling; the light cast by the sun through the high window on the wall. When one of the women asked me what I was doing, I told her I was taking pictures. "Where your camera at?" she asked, and I tapped my forehead. "Oh, it be like that, huh?" she said and drew circles in the air with her finger while pointing at her head. I smiled. "Would you like me to take your picture?" I asked. "Go ahead, crazy white lady," she said. "I'm feelin' generous today."

70. Sleepwalker, Brooklyn, 1962

The first time I saw this photo, I laughed. According to Lillian, I'd been sleepwalking since we left Brooklyn Heights, but of course, being asleep, I never remembered or got the chance to witness it myself. For once, my mother went in close. My face occupies the whole frame: staring eyes that see nothing, tangled hair, mouth hanging partly open. How often do you get to see something like that?

Kaja's dad lived on a wide street in a building that looked rundown on the outside but inside was all wainscoting with dark wood and gold and green wallpaper that was ancient and water-spotted. There were round push-button wall switches to turn the lights on and off, pressed-tin ceilings, and a footed bathtub below a brown stain in the shape of a dragon. When I said it was the most beautiful apartment I'd ever seen, Paul laughed and said that I needed to get out more. Saturday was Indian food and a science fiction movie, just like Kaja had promised. That night she and I shared the bed instead of sleeping on the floor, because Kaja said sometimes there were rats. Paul sang us a bedtime song that he said was from Ghana. He had a lousy voice, and this made getting sung to weirdly better, since he was singing clearly because he wanted to give us something and not to show off. When he asked us if we needed anything before he turned off the light, I realized that I did.

My mom's in jail, I told him. Paul left the doorway and stood beside the bed. When he spoke, his voice was powerful and gentle at the same time. A lot of people say they want to know the truth, he said, but they aren't strong enough. That's why I respect your mother, Samantha. She can handle what she sees: it's other people who can't.

The next morning was the first time I saw

the word "abortion." Kaja and I were eating Paul's pancakes, which were as thick and fluffy as Grete's were thin. To eat Grete's pancakes, you would spread a layer of jam over the top and then roll them up to take a bite, but Paul's meant maple syrup that oozed out when you pressed down on them with your fork. Would you look at that, Paul said, showing me the Arts section of *The New York Times,* where it read: "PICTURES ON VIEW; Photographer Pushes Boundaries in Brooklyn," by Michael Stromlin.

Upon seeing my mother's name in print, I kept looking down at my feet, surprised to find them still on the floor. Being a precocious reader, I was able to make out most of the words, even if I wasn't sure what all of them meant. After praising Lillian's street photography, Stromlin described "eight troubling but beautiful portraits of the photographer and her daughter in various states of undress that challenge the viewer and prick the conscience . . . one of which, entitled *Mommy is sick,* depicts the photographer bedridden in the days following an illegal abortion."

I read that sentence three times, but it didn't help. First I asked Paul if it was a good review, and he said he thought it was. Next I asked him if an abortion was the same thing as a miscarriage, and he told me they were sometimes related.

Later, on the train back to Brooklyn, I bragged to a man reading the newspaper that my mother was in there. It turned out to be the first and last time this was something I wanted people to know.

NINA PAGANO: My pops was a dockworker — a union longshoreman who'd never been to a museum in his life but who loved me more than I deserved; so I knew he'd come through, and he did. By way of the union, he found a lawyer for our arraignment, a guy who got me and Lil released on our own recognizance and arranged for a trial date that would give us enough time to get our ducks in a row.

The first thing I did when I got out was eat a hamburger. Next I took a long hot shower, and then I called the number the union lawyer had given me for a civil liberties guy named Marcus Sheer. I told him the whole story, from opening the show to me getting hit with possession and distribution and Lil with child endangerment. Marcus Sheer asked whether we had any money. I said no. He said come see him anyway. That was the beginning of *People of the State of New York* v. *Lacuna Gallery.*

PARK SLOPE, 1963–70

71. Self-portrait after leaving jail, Brooklyn, 1963

GRETE WASHINGTON: Lillian spoke of jail only once, years later. I had forgotten the dull look in her eyes, her slow movements, and her uncertainty regarding even simple things; then she showed me this portrait, and I remembered.

In the photograph, her shoulders stoop like an old woman's. Her face belongs to someone who has lost her way. Everything is sharply focused, but not her hands. It feels like a kind of violence to see such blurred hands surrounded by such stillness. To create this portrait, Lillian left the shutter of her camera open for ten seconds while she sat with no breathing or movement; but her hands would not obey. Lillian's hands shook for fourteen days after she was released from jail. All that time, she did not know if the shaking would end.

For fourteen days she could not hold a camera. Her voice trembled as she told me this. Then she put away this picture, and she did not speak of it again.

The Monday after my Harlem weekend, I'd been expecting to walk myself to Mrs. Ardolini's like usual that afternoon. Instead as I stepped outside the school entrance, a woman who looked a lot like my mother started crying my name. Before I knew it, I was swept into the arms of a familiar-smelling coat, but rather than hug back, I froze. I froze because I hadn't been expecting my mother, and because I was being hugged by someone who was crying, which was something my mother never did. Maybe I would have thawed if Lillian had kept at it, and this could have become a bonding moment for us; but she didn't, and it wasn't. Instead, Lillian touched a frozen girl and quickly pulled away. By the time I'd figured out that this familiar-smelling, unfamiliar-acting person was the same person I'd been pining for all weekend, it was too late. The whole thing went something like this:

— Mommy?
— I'm so sorry.
— Mommy, is it really you?

— I didn't mean to scare you.
— Mommy, what happened?
— Let's go home.

So we did. Lillian looked smaller, like in the four days we'd been apart, I had grown or she had shrunk. There was something else I couldn't place until we'd passed the candy store where all the scary kids hung out: my mother was looking down. Normally she was looking for her next shot, but today she was staring at her shoes. She wasn't even holding her camera. And that scared the hell out of me.

JOURNAL ENTRY, SEPTEMBER 1963: It's almost unbearably lovely to prepare your breakfast. To pull a brush through your hair, button the buttons in back of your dress, and tie the bow. But my hands shake, and sometimes I break a milk glass or pull too hard at a tangle or take too long with your clothes. When I sit down to eat, my fork trembles on its way to my mouth, and I stop feeling hungry.

You don't know what to make of me. I'm not the same mother who brought you to school last Thursday. I must believe that this new mother is temporary, because if she isn't, then my time in the Women's House of Detention hasn't ended.

72. Soda jerk, Brooklyn, 1963

Lillian didn't go on a bender with cops the way she did with the babushkas of the Lower East Side. If she had, maybe she would have gotten them out of her system. Instead, they start lurking on the periphery. Take this one: it's the stone-faced counter guy front and center who first nabs you, his wary face all wrong framed by that jaunty bow tie and paper hat. Only then do you notice the cop and the kid in the leather jacket at opposite ends of the counter. The cop is turned toward the kid; the kid is scrutinizing his empty soda glass; and the soda jerk between them is staring his thousand-yard stare, trying not to tip the balance by looking at either one.

Lillian never talked to me about her weekend in jail, but after she'd been home a few days she sat me down to explain why the cops had arrested her and Nina in the first place. Initially I was skeptical; there were plenty of naked statues and paintings in museums, and those hadn't gotten anyone arrested. Lillian explained that museums and galleries were not the same thing, especially not galleries in Brooklyn. Once I accepted that, it was only a matter of time before the obvious question arose: did I break the law, too? My mother assured me that I hadn't. Except I was the one in those pictures, I reminded her. Yes, she said, but I didn't make them; also, I was just a child.

I didn't buy it. Since Lillian had been recently arrested herself, her grasp of the law seemed shaky at best. So I decided to start being careful.

Most of it wasn't dramatic. No jaywalking and no crossing against the light, even if the street was clear. No skipping or running unless other kids already were. I traded my red coat for a less conspicuous dark blue one from the school lost and found. I made sure the coast was clear before heading out the front door. I stopped messing around with the abandoned cars on the blocks between my house and the school. And if I saw a policeman, I ran. This last one wasn't subtle. Lillian and Grete were willing to wait when I spontaneously ducked into a store or changed directions, but Kaja — the third and last person who knew my true motives — was my sole accomplice. Whenever she spotted a cop or a cop car, she'd say "Ofay" low enough for only me to hear, then nod in their direction so I could head the other way. Anyone else who witnessed my disappearances thought I was weird, but I didn't care. As far as I was concerned, being unpopular beat being in jail.

Such premium paranoia was hard to maintain, especially when it became apparent that no policeman had the vaguest interest in me. My hypervigilance aside, the sole difference in the weeks following my mother's return was that Lillian noticed only half of what I said or did, and on Thursdays Nina arrived with so much chow mein that on Fridays I feasted on leftover Chinese for breakfast.

LETTER TO DEBORAH BRODSKY, OCTOBER 1963: Naturally, I agree with Nina. The photographs certainly aren't "obscene" and ought to be shown, though Nina couldn't have helped matters by telling Michael Stromlin the truth about *Mommy is sick.* I didn't swear her to secrecy, so perhaps it's silly to feel she betrayed a confidence, but I feel betrayed all the same!

When I explained this to Nina, she became impatient. Of course she told a *New York Times* critic about *Mommy is sick.* Didn't I understand that was her job? But didn't she understand that I'd been talking to her not as my gallerist but as my friend? Nina claims that if I didn't want people to know the truth about the photo, then I shouldn't have shown it to begin with. In one way, she's right: I do want people to know the truth. But the truth I want them to know is a mother's pain and a child's fear, the love between them, and their loneliness. Now all anyone will see when they look at *Mommy is sick* is a woman who's had an illegal abortion.

The civil rights lawyer Nina found is called Marcus Sheer. He has sad eyes and large hands and works in a dingy office in downtown Manhattan with a window overlooking an alley. I liked him right away. He reminds me of John Bosco, laid-back and tenacious at the same time. Marcus told us straight off in his nonchalant yet no-nonsense way that Nina's charge — intent to sell obscene materials — was more the sort of thing he was used to, though he thought my child-endangerment case was just as promising. The colleague he talked to agreed: these are both pioneering First Amendment cases. If we decide to fight, chances are better than even that we will win. Nina smiled at this, but "better than even" doesn't sound to me like terribly good odds. When I asked Mr. Sheer what happens if we lose, he shrugged. "Then we appeal," he said, "and we keep appealing if we have to, moving up the system until we get somewhere." And if, after all that, we still lose? "That depends," he said. "It could mean a fine; it might mean jail time; or maybe both." When he said that, my hands and feet went cold.

What if I don't fight? I wanted to know. "But Lil, what are the actual chances they'll lock you up?" Nina interrupted, so I repeated myself louder than before. If I preferred, Marcus Sheer explained, I could plead guilty in exchange for time served. Would that be the end of it? There might be a fine, Marcus Sheer said, but he doubted it: I had a clean record and I'd present well in court. And so long as Nina fights, he'll still have his pioneering First Amendment case? "It wouldn't be my case," Marcus corrected me, his voice gentle. "Nina's case is Nina's case, the same way that your case is yours."

Deb, I know that you would fight; you and Nina are alike that way. I try to imagine what I'd do if I weren't a mother, but my imagination fails me. I cannot go back to prison. Does that make me a good mother or a coward?

73. Halloween, Brooklyn, 1963

None of the kids in the picture is me. Lillian went her own way with her camera that night while Kaja and I went ours, me as

Zorro and she as Godzilla. Kaja explained to anyone who would listen that the real *Godzilla* movie was Japanese and didn't star Raymond Burr. I guess because Zorro had been off the air a few seasons, people kept asking how I got the idea for my costume, but I had zero interest in explaining my affinity with a sword-wielding vigilante.

Nina understood right away. Heading over to the Lacuna hadn't been a conscious plan. Kaja and I simply travelled across and down the Park Slope grid. Before I knew it, we were standing at the gallery door with a cluster of other kids as Nina dropped roasted pumpkin seeds into everyone's bags, explaining how we'd need the protein to balance out the sugar if we were in it for the long haul.

Sammo, that you? she said, putting down her pumpkin seeds. She grabbed me around the waist and lifted me up like she'd just arrived at my door on one of our usual Thursdays. She should have known I'd be out there fighting injustice, she told me.

When Nina asked who my friend was and Kaja answered, Louise, in a weird Brooklyn accent, we realized that her mask canceled out the usual rules about where she could and couldn't go. Hence, after Nina's, we worked the forbidden streets into South

Brooklyn's pale heart, Kaja roaring at random Garfield Boys and Butler Gents from behind her Godzilla mask and giggling like a lunatic. Grete was pissed when we were late getting back, but we were too high on sugar and adrenaline to care. Kaja had returned from enemy territory unscathed, and I'd gone the whole night without worrying about beat cops or squad cars.

I'm guessing Lillian snapped *Halloween* after Kaja and I were already back at Grete's place, negotiating candy swaps across the living room floor. The scariest thing about that picture isn't the thin-legged ghost or the cockeyed jack-o'-lantern but the little girl in makeup, fake pearls, and high heels who looks like the understudy for the rundown woman in the faux-leopard coat grimly gripping her small gloved hand.

JOURNAL ENTRY, NOVEMBER 1963: Because I'd already taken off work for my court hearing — hours of waiting for a fifteen-minute transaction in which my lawyer submitted my guilty plea, received my fine, and sent me home — I knew better than to ask for all three days of Nina's trial and resigned myself to attending only the last. Both Nina and Marcus had warned me to be prepared for any outcome, but that didn't stop me from gasping when the judge found her guilty. Nina must have heard me, because she turned and winked. From her face, you would have thought she'd just won. That face should have comforted me: Nina loves a good fight. She'd already told me, guilty or not guilty, that she, Marcus, and I would be going out afterward for celebratory cheesecake at Junior's; but her reaction had no effect on my own anger or shame. The anger I didn't mind, as there was plenty to be angry about, but the shame was a vestige of the Cleveland girl who dogged me despite all my efforts to leave her behind. This bred more shame, in a ridiculous cycle that ended only when I remembered that I would now have to break the news of Nina's verdict to you, which brought me back to my anger.

74. Newsstand, Brooklyn, 1963

There it is: the defining event of that year, smeared across every front page of every newspaper on every rack. A mother is pulling her little boy away by the hand, her face blank as they walk past, as if ignoring all those different versions of PRESIDENT SLAIN will make them disappear. But the kid is looking at the newsstand, and the news vendor is looking at the kid, and in their faces you see everything that kid's mom is trying to wish away.

Two days before Kennedy got shot, Gordy Cardoza told me I was a perv and my mother was a baby killer, which gave me a chance to deploy the back fist strike I'd been practicing with Kaja. She'd been learning karate with her dad ever since he'd stopped making bacon for breakfast and told her he was thinking about changing his last name. Kaja didn't mind about the bacon, since Grete would make it, and she loved karate because now she didn't feel so scared walking around our neighborhood; but the last-name situation presented a dilemma. If she switched with Paul from Washington to Mohammad, Grete would get upset. If she stayed Kaja Washington, it would be like her dad wasn't her dad anymore.

Karate, at least, was straightforward. As we admired our reflections in her bedroom mirror, Kaja asserted that the time for turning the other cheek had passed: she'd heard that at a rally with Paul. I didn't spoil the moment by asking her what it meant. For the same reason, I didn't ask Gordy what he meant by "perv" or "baby killer," since getting someone to explain a put-down before decking him kills the purity of the moment.

I wouldn't have back-fisted Gordy to begin with if Karen Nichols, who at the time was my best friend at school, hadn't asked me if it was true my mom had taken a picture of herself having an abortion. The way Karen said "abortion" sounded much worse than how Paul had said it. Karen made "abortion" sound like a sandwich with rat parts in it. So naturally, I decided Karen was saying a word that sounded like "abortion" but was actually something else. No, I told her, of course my mother hadn't done *that.* Next Karen asked if my mom had taken naked pictures of me. Technically, when I said no to that one, it was not a lie. Technically I was not naked in any of those pictures, since in each one I was wearing underwear — or if not underwear, then at least a string of beads, though I did not explain this to Karen. And because Karen was still my best friend at school, she required nothing more to assure everyone that the source of these rumors — i.e., Gordy — was a liar. My reprieve lasted until that afternoon, when Gordy cornered a bunch of us to explain that his dad was a court reporter who had seen the photos for himself. Which was when I asserted in my fiercest voice that the time for turning the other cheek had passed, and I punched Gordy in the jaw. Because none of the teachers saw it, and because Gordy wasn't going to blab about being hit by a girl — but mostly because two days later President Kennedy was killed, effectively changing the subject — life as I knew it didn't end for another six months, when Nina's appeal reached New York's highest court.

JOURNAL ENTRY, NOVEMBER 1963: Marcus Sheer explained that if *People* v. *Lacuna* loses its intermediate appeal, as he thinks it will, he'll ask the highest state court to hear the case. Naturally, this is why he took the case to begin with. Nina was as excited as I've ever seen her, which is really saying something. She listed all the newspapers and magazines she planned to contact if the appellate court ruled against us, sounding like a little girl writing out her birthday-invitation list. If it came to that, she wanted to know, was I ready to talk to reporters? Of course, I told her; I want to help any way I can. I admire Nina tremendously for what she's doing, but I must admit I was relieved when she finally left. Listening to her makes me tired.

Partly, this comes from breaking with my

prescription. I knew it had become necessary because my temper was rising at the smallest things: you asking to pet the dogs we passed on the walk to school, or a woman holding up the bus to search her purse for the fare. Other times, I'd be standing perfectly still and suddenly feel my heart pounding as if I were running for my life. While my pill vacation has improved my temper and general health, at night I can manage only an hour or two in the darkroom before I have to stop. Each day I fall a little more behind, and the thought of all those undeveloped rolls of film weighs on me.

Just yesterday you said, "Mommy, don't be sad," and petted my arm like I was one of your beloved neighborhood dogs. I guess you'd been talking for a while, because you asked, "Are you sad because of what the kids are saying?" Which kids, I asked, and saying what? "Oh, just stupid Gordy, but he doesn't count." You wouldn't explain, because apparently this was old news. And when I told you I wasn't sad, only sleepy, this seemed to make things all right.

GRETE WASHINGTON: Lillian was anxious what would become of Nina and the gallery if the appeal did not win. She felt badly because she had settled her case, and so there was only one chance in the courts to make things right. I assured Lillian that she should not feel guilt about this. She had made the decision a mother needs to make. Lillian agreed, but this did not change the troubled look in her eyes.

One Thursday, Lillian invited Kaja and myself to her flat for dinner with Nina. When I saw the way that Nina talked about the case, I laughed. Really, I told Lillian, perhaps you are nervous, but you are the only one. No matter if Nina loses in the court or wins, she is having a very good time.

75. Blind man, Brooklyn, 1964

JOURNAL ENTRY, MARCH 1964: I shouldn't have been surprised he knew I was there. Sitting against the wall, his paper begging cup pinned to his coat, the whites of his sightless eyes peeking out between his lashes, he sat taller as I passed. "That's right, lady," he said. "Take my picture. I know I'm pretty today." I had seen him plenty of times before and walked on, but on this day he was different, just as he said.

You're different, too. Now that my court

case is over, you don't look for patrol cars on the way to school, and you've finally given up that horrible blue coat you got from who knows where, which was several sizes too big and made you look like an orphan. For the first time since I was arrested, your smile reaches your eyes.

Change is everywhere. After much hand-wringing, Grete has introduced Kaja to Jim. When we came for our own introduction, you joined the two of them in a game of Parcheesi while Grete fussed in the kitchen, looking happier than she has in a while. "Mommy," you said on our walk home, "why don't you have a boyfriend?" I laughed and told you I was too busy. "Grete is busy," you said, "and she has one." Yes, I agreed, but Grete was lucky enough to meet Jim at the store where she works. Anyway, I told you, it wasn't something I thought about. Between you and my photography, my life feels full. This either satisfied you or convinced you I was hopeless, because after that you changed the subject.

Grete says that since meeting Jim, she's slept like a baby, which must be true because the half-completed piece in her loom has been gathering dust. It's selfish, but listening to Jean Shepherd on the radio isn't as fun now that I know Grete isn't listening, too.

GRETE WASHINGTON: I once did try. Usually I do not meddle, but Lillian's chance to meet people was so small, and Vincent was a friend of Jim's who seemed interesting. Kaja and Samantha played while the four of us talked and drank wine. Vincent asked Lillian many questions about her camera. We made an especially energetic conversation about whether it is right to photograph someone without asking for permission, after Vincent realized in the moment that Lillian with her camera was doing exactly this! Later he asked Lillian for her telephone number. His question confused her. When poor Vincent explained, Lillian's face grew quite red.

I know they did have some dates, because Vincent asked several times if Lillian had mentioned him. I would ask Lillian and learn that she and Vincent had met for lunch or dinner. Finally, I asked after her feelings for him. Lillian explained that she felt about men the way she felt about pistachio nuts: she did not mind to have them around, but she did not go out of her way to find them, and she did not miss them when they were gone. Poor Vincent,

I thought to myself. After that I decided it was better to let Lillian be.

76. Lost child, Brooklyn, 1964

Maybe Lillian and Grete were sitting on a bench in Prospect Park watching me and Kaja dig with sticks when Lillian took this, or maybe it was during one of Lillian's photo walks. Either way, here's the boy, not older than five, alone and crying. Anyone else happening upon a kid like this in a park would stop to ask what was wrong. Once Lillian had gotten that desperate, tear-streaked face on film, she may have tried to help; but first she got the picture.

I'm hoping she took it before the appeals court verdict. I'd like to think that in the month or so after making the papers, even my mother would've thought twice before making a kid her photographic quarry. What I do know is that the date and the weather match. That kid is crying in a park lousy with flowers and butterflies, which means it's spring. Nina had told me that the appeals court date was coming and to keep my fingers crossed, but in my mind the matter had been settled six months ago with my deft handling of the Gordy incident. As far as I was concerned, whatever did or did not happen with the appeal was Nina's deal, not mine. Meaning that until I got to school that May morning, I'd forgotten all about it.

Somebody's father must have been a *Daily News* for breakfast type, because there it was — *Judge Rules . . .* MOMMY *IS* SICK — on the newspaper's front page, slapped across my desk like an invitation to my own funeral.

In a month I'd be done with third grade, and in a week Karen Nichols was having a slumber party to which I was invited. At first I thought a teacher had left the newspaper on my desk by mistake. Then I looked at the picture of the girl standing beside the bed and thought, I know her, which is when I started feeling numb. According to the article, a three-judge panel for New York's highest court had upheld that the photos popularly known as "The Samantha Series" were obscene. The article stated that defendant Nina Pagano had refused to stop reciting the First Amendment after the verdict was read and had been escorted from the courtroom. Afterward her lawyer informed the press that he planned to petition the U.S. Supreme Court to hear the case. Farther down the page I saw my mother's name, but I didn't want to read that part. I just wanted to hide the paper so no one else would see it, except I wasn't sure how to do that because I couldn't move my arms or legs. My body was frozen in my seat, and this bothered me enough that I must not have noticed class starting, or Mrs. Barkley talking to me, because all of a sudden a hand grabbed the newspaper, and there was Mrs. Barkley looking at it like she was looking at a cockroach. I wanted to explain that there'd been a mistake but now, along with not being able to move my arms and legs, I couldn't talk. So instead John Dunahoe said, She's a criminal, Mrs. Barkley, it says so right there, and Gordy Cardoza said, No it don't. It's like how I said before. Her ma's a baby killer; she's just a perv. Then everyone laughed except for Mrs. Barkley, who looked at me like she didn't know who I was. My arms and legs were tingling like they'd fallen asleep, and I couldn't catch my breath. Each time I tried to breathe, I made a high-pitched noise like a guinea pig. There was a buzzing sound in my ears. *zzzKarenzz,* Mrs. Barkley said, *zTakezzzZamanthazzzzTozzzeeNurze,* and Karen Nichols, who until that moment had been my best friend at school, looked at Mrs. Barkley like she'd been asked to touch a turd. The class laughed some more. Mrs. Barkley said something that I couldn't hear through the buzz, but I could tell it was yelling by the size of her open mouth and the redness of her face, also because Karen got up like she'd been pinched. Karen pulled me from my chair. She dragged me hyperventilating to the nurse's office, then left me there without a word. And that was the last time I ever did anything with Karen Nichols.

JOURNAL ENTRY, MAY 1964: By the time I arrived at the school, an hour had passed since the principal's call to the restaurant, and you were falling apart in a way I hadn't seen since the day you learned that Ken was not your father. I thought you were hurt, so I ran over and started looking for blood. You wouldn't tell me what had happened, and I didn't know anything: the principal had said only to come right away. When he showed me the *Daily News* headline, I flinched to see what the newspaper had done to our portrait.

"Miss Preston," the principal said in a voice that didn't hide his opinion. "I've seen a lot in my ten years as an elementary school principal, but this, well, I won't ask you what you were doing taking pictures like this because I suppose it's your right, but to show them in public . . ."

I knew about the verdict. Nina had called

the night before to say they'd be petitioning the U.S. Supreme Court, and to explain when and how they'd learn if the court would hear the case. Possibly she hadn't mentioned the press because she hadn't known. As long as I choose to believe this, I remain recognizable to myself. But if Nina was expecting those newspaper headlines and didn't mention them, that means she stole my only chance to prepare you for what was coming — and if I choose to believe that, then my anger turns me into a stranger. In any case, I was caught completely by surprise. It took me several moments to connect Nina's latest trial with the headline the principal was holding in his hand.

"Let me ask you one thing," he said when at first I said nothing. "Did you ever stop to think what this would do to your daughter?" He viewed my stunned silence through the same broken lens he'd held up to everything else. "That's what I thought," he said.

You didn't want to go back to class, and I wasn't about to make you. We were half a block from home when I saw the man waiting on our stoop. "Miss Preston?" He reached us before I had a chance to think. "Peter Grunloh, *Daily News.* Do you have anything to say about the outcome of yesterday's trial? Does the fact that you took a plea bargain rather than face trial yourself mean you agree with the court's verdict? What were you hoping to accomplish by exhibiting those photos of yourself and your little girl? Is this her? Hey, Samantha, what do you think about —" but by then we'd reached our door. The telephone was ringing. Once I'd locked us inside and closed the curtains I picked up, thinking it was Grete, but it was another reporter. When I hung up, the phone began to ring some more.

"Mommy?" you asked in a small voice. "Why did the newspaper cross me out?" I stroked your hair as we sat on the couch and the telephone rang. I said that you and the picture were both beautiful. I said that laws were sometimes wrong, and that people like Nina went to court to try to fix them. As I said these things, the telephone rang and rang, until I disconnected the handset.

You weren't hungry, so we skipped dinner. You wouldn't change into your pajamas, so I put you to bed in your clothes. Then I stood in the dark of our room, and I watched as you flinched in your sleep.

77. Old woman, Brooklyn, 1964

My memories of the rest of that year are fragments: the moldy smell of the coat closet where I hid during recess; the black-and-white tiles of the girls' bathroom where I hid during lunch; staring at the bedroom wall to avoid seeing my body while Lillian dressed me each morning.

This picture would have come from one of her Saturday walks while I was either at Kaja's or at home, telepathically begging Nina to visit on weekends now that Thursdays had suddenly stopped. Even if I'd known Nina's number, calling wasn't an option, since Lillian had hidden the phone handset. According to Lillian, it wasn't safe for Nina to visit anyway. Reporters were still coming around, and the last thing we needed was another reason to be in the newspaper. I agreed, but there was something weird about the way she said it. When I asked if she was mad at Nina, I knew I'd asked the right question because instead of answering, she asked me why I thought that. Because she was talking in her angry voice, I explained. She was angry at a lot of people right now, she said. But wasn't Nina trying to fix things? I said. My mother agreed that she was.

All I can guess is that Lillian rode the

subway to the end of the line, to some place with factories and warehouses and not many homes. When I see that old lady sitting on that curb with her thick leggings and her men's shoes and her layers of skirts and her dark felt hat too big for her head, her cane at an angle like a broken leg, her elbow resting on her thigh, her cheek resting on her fingers like a little girl waiting for her father to come home, I think: No one is coming for you, old woman. You are a used-up horse, waiting to be glue. And then I think: What kind of person thinks that about a picture? And then I think: What kind of person takes that kind of picture?

JOURNAL ENTRY, MAY 1964: When Nina rang the doorbell later that night, I'd been standing in the dark watching you sleep for so long that the hallway light was blinding. I opened the front door, hardly able to tell who was on the other side. Nina told me she'd come to strategize: if we split the interviews between us, we could do twice as many in half the time. For now it was still a regional story, but assuming the Supreme Court decided to hear the case, it'd be national by early next year. How did I feel about radio and television? With a little practice, she thought I could get comfortable being in front of a camera instead of behind one. She blathered like this for several minutes before realizing I hadn't said a word. "You all right?" she finally asked, at which point I asked why she hadn't told me about the newspapers. "What, today's?" She laughed. "The real story comes when we start talking to the press." I told her they'd printed Sam's picture. "Of course they did!" she said. I told her that I'd brought Sam home from school and she'd cried herself to sleep. "Sounds rough," Nina said. I explained that a reporter had been lying in wait for us outside the apartment. "Oh, yeah?" Nina said, her face lighting up. "Which one?"

This morning you wouldn't get dressed. As I took off yesterday's shirt and tugged your hands into the arms of a fresh one, you closed your eyes. You were limp as I slid yesterday's skirt down your legs and traded it for something clean. You wanted me to take your temperature, so I placed the thermometer under your tongue. I could practically hear you wishing the mercury up, but it didn't budge past normal. You pleaded to come to the restaurant. You'd read in the storeroom; no one would know. Even if I'd let you, there still would have been tomorrow and each day after that, and you can't spend the rest of third grade in Remming's dry storage, nibbling stale bread.

"Mommy," you said as I walked you to school, "Mrs. Mallory just crossed the street with Rusty." I told you it was nothing, but you shook your head. "She saw us," you insisted, your voice full of tears. "She saw us, and she crossed the street because she doesn't want me to pet him anymore." You wouldn't let me walk you all the way to the schoolyard, so I hung back as you entered the front gate, where you remained alone and frozen in place, silently waiting for the morning bell. Squirrel, I wish I could take you with me to the restaurant every morning to read books and eat day-old rolls until the verdict is reversed or third grade is done!

78. Couple on Fifth Avenue, Brooklyn, 1964

At first this one seems pretty straightforward: he's got his right arm across her shoulders, his hand like one of those arcade claws gripping a prize. He's put together, but her coat is unbuttoned and her hair is mussed, like he might have just had her up against the brick wall they're standing in front of. With his tie, pleated slacks, and pomaded hair, he could be on his way to an office. That belted dress could put her on the service side of a department store counter — except that their faces tell you they can't be more than fourteen years old. And there you have it: two middle-aged children, stuck in your head like a sad song.

I made my first post-newspaper-headline visit to the Lacuna on a Saturday when Kaja was with her dad and Lillian was out shooting. I really wanted to see Nina, and my telepathic invitations weren't working. As much as I hated the idea of going outside, being home alone felt worse, so I put on sunglasses and a hat and skulked my way toward St. John's Place, braced for reporters at each corner. On Nina's block, someone had spray-painted an arrow next to a gaping pothole and the words "This Way to China." There was trash up and down the sidewalks, but in front of the gallery, it was clean. I didn't remember the door being silver when I'd come trick-or-treating back in October.

Nothing happened after I knocked, so I rang the buzzer until a voice inside yelled for me to stop. The door opened a crack. Nina must have been surprised to see me, because for a few seconds she was actually speechless. When she finally did talk, she asked how I was doing in a quiet voice that didn't sound like her. Her face was puffy and creased, and her hair stood up all over, and she had black makeup under her eyes. I asked if she was still sleeping. Not anymore, she told me. What time was it, anyway? Next time I needed to check the clock before I headed over and give her at least until eleven. Then she invited me in. Did I like the new door? Every now and then some neighborhood genius spray-painted something clever, and she did a little repainting. But it looked good silver, didn't it?

The walls of the gallery were covered in paintings of naked men lying on couches or leaning against walls or doing handstands, their penises dangling at funny angles. From behind the closed door at the back of the gallery, a man's voice called Nina's name. She called back did he want coffee for the train. Then she turned to me and asked if it was true they were giving me a hard time at school. I nodded. She said she wished she could tell me she was surprised, but the truth was most kids were dopes. I shouldn't tell her niece and nephew this, but I, Sammo, was the undopiest, coolest kid Nina had ever met. Did I play pinochle? Did I want a hangover sandwich?

That was how the card games started.

Some Saturdays Nina wasn't around, but if I knocked and she was there, she'd invite me in, even if she had company. She never offered to teach her company how to play, as she'd taught me that first time, but if he already knew, we'd play pinochle three-handed. If he didn't know, he'd watch us until he realized Nina was serious, and then he'd leave. I'd tell Nina about school and she'd tell me about a painter she was working with, or someone in the neighborhood who was giving her a hard time, or the man she'd just shown the door. We'd crack jokes and eat peanut-butter-and-potato-chip sandwiches on wheat bread as we played, me using a rack Nina made from a broken picture frame because my hands were too small to hold the cards, until it was time for me to put on my hat and sunglasses and walk back home.

LETTER TO DEBORAH BRODSKY, MAY 1964: Ever since the photographs made headlines, Nina has been flooded with offers for them, and at prices that would make life comfortable for a long time. Of course, none of the people who want to buy the photos have actually seen them. They've only seen the censored versions on television and in the newspapers. Even

Nina thinks that selling to these people would be wrong: none of them are interested in art. It's all we've agreed on since this whole thing began — that and Sam's Saturday visits, which are one of the few things that can still make her happy.

In what might be the last conversation Nina and I will ever have, she insisted she didn't understand why I'd stopped fighting for the cause, but regardless of anything that might happen between us, her friendship with Sam was "a separate deal." Next she said something about all great artists suffering hardships of some sort as children, and joked about Sam's fine artistic prospects if I wanted to change my mind about talking to the press now that the case was "hitting the big time." At which point I became so angry that I hung up.

Deb, you're absolutely right: if you'd asked me first, I would have said no. It would be ungrateful not to send my thanks — to you and the Poeticals for adding my name to the benefit, and to all the musicians who played. The money is a help. What was left after covering my own legal expenses, I passed on to the gallery. It's nice of you to say I'm a hero in San Francisco, but the truth is that nothing — not your friendship, or the funds from the

Freedom Concert, or Kyle dedicating his reading to me, or even your beautiful poem — can erase the misery I have brought upon my daughter.

79. Samantha's last portrait, Brooklyn, 1964

Before Lillian and I became popular with the media, one of the best things about our ground-floor apartment was its windows. Not until the end of third grade, when the view became a liability, did I learn the curtains didn't quite close all the way. The gap between them was skinny, just enough to let in a long splinter of sun. One way I liked to pass the time as an eight-year-old shut-in was to stand so that the stripe of light from the crack in the curtains ran from my shoulder to my elbow, creating a glowing bone emanating from deep inside my arm, which I told myself was the beginning of my larger transformation into something better.

Growing up with my mother's camera, I'd stopped noticing or caring what she did with it, only that day she surprised me, or maybe I just surprised myself. I don't know how long she'd been there, but when I heard the click of the shutter, I discovered that my glowing arm bone and I weren't alone. I don't know how to describe what happened next except to say that as I stared at the camera, I concentrated on steering the sunlight up from my arm and into my shoulder, up my neck and into my skull. That's why my face looks the way it does: it is a face willing the light that I am guiding up my arm and into my head to shoot out through my eyeballs and into the camera lens, exploding it into a mess of twisted metal and shattered glass that will never take a picture again.

GRETE WASHINGTON: Ordinarily, if the girls were playing in the bedroom when Lillian arrived, she needed to tell Samantha just a few times to come out, but this time there was only whispering. From the other side of the door, Samantha said, Samantha isn't here. Well, Lillian said, whoever is there, will you please come out? And then the door did open.

Even after twenty-five years, this moment has stayed in my mind.

Samantha was holding a pair of scissors. When you are used to someone's hair hanging past her shoulders, it is quite surprising when it suddenly ends at her chin. I'm Jane, the short-haired girl said. I must admit she looked so different that this new name seemed almost correct.

I do not blame Lillian for what she did next. You cannot blame a person for being herself, but Lillian's reflex was unfortunate, because when Samantha saw her mother reaching for the camera, she stepped back inside the bedroom and closed the door. Samantha? Lillian called.

I'm *Jane,* answered the small angry voice.

Jane, please come out, Lillian said because Jane is Samantha's middle name. Please, Squirrel. It's time to go.

Don't take my picture, said the voice. Lillian tried the door, but it was locked. *Don't* take my picture, the voice repeated.

Please come out, Lillian said. I've put the camera away.

But the voice insisted, Don't take my picture ever again.

Lillian stood quite frozen, staring at the closed door. Squirrel? she said, sounding as if she were no longer certain who stood on the other side.

Promise! cried the voice.

Please . . . Jane, Lillian said. From behind the door, there was a sound. Scissors are quiet, but the sound they make is their own.

Samantha — Jane, stop! Lillian said.

She was pounding at the door.

No more pictures! cried the voice.

Lillian was pale now as she leaned against the door. Sweetheart? she tried. Why don't we —

No! shrieked the voice from the other side, followed again by the soft scissors sound.

Please! Lillian said. Okay, I promise!

Now at last there was silence.

No more? asked the voice.

No more, Lillian answered.

The door opened. Out came a girl with hair cut to her ears and a face that did not know if it had lost or won. And this girl was Jane.

80. Window, Brooklyn, 1964

The boy on the right knows how to behave around an open window. He's got to be six or seven, old enough to have seen grown-ups toss keys out to friends on the street, and he's happy with the view from the inside. But not his brothers. The youngest is sitting on the windowsill, his chubby little toddler legs dangling off it like wet laundry. This would win the prize for Most Disturbing Thing if his slightly older brother — already a fuckup at age four — weren't standing on a narrow molding several feet beneath the window, holding the leftmost window jamb with one hand to keep from falling. And yeah, it's possible the sidewalk is just below, seeing as none of them looks too upset about this, but Lillian framed it so that the photo cuts off right at the four-year-old's feet on that narrow ledge. I can tell myself it's a ground-floor window all I want, if that's the world I'd like to live in. But the truth is, I'll never know.

I have no memory of the day I changed my name. I just remember not answering when Mrs. Barkley took attendance, or when someone sneered, Samantha, in the hallway, because I knew that wasn't me anymore. Not that I told anyone what to call me instead or that anyone asked, which meant to my gigantic relief that people at school stopped calling me anything at all.

GRETE WASHINGTON: Samantha was not eating or sleeping well. Her skin was full of rashes, and she scratched these rashes into scabs. Lillian tried to talk with the teacher, but the teacher blamed Lillian, and so the trouble continued. Tacks were left on Samantha's chair. Red ink was spilled across her desk. Cruel notes were left inside her backpack. Girls pulled up her shirt in the hallways. Samantha suffered nightmares and began to wet the bed. Lillian did not have money to move to a neighborhood with a different public school, but also she had no reason to believe that a different public school would be an improvement.

I spoke with the director at Prospect Friends, and he invited Lillian to see him. After she described her unique situation, he offered a scholarship for Samantha to attend the school starting in September.

Nina continued to speak to journalists about the gallery and the photographs. She also described the inhumane treatment that she and Lillian had received inside the jail. This was the first time that the conditions inside the Women's House of Detention were exposed to the public. An official inquiry was made. Seven years later, that cruel place was shut down and then demolished. A garden now grows where the building once stood, so at least some good thing has come of all this.

JOURNAL ENTRY, JUNE 1964: When I see "Jane" written in black ink across your school notebooks, I still think at first that you've brought home another girl's work by mistake. I named you Jane for your grandmother's sister, a bright-eyed girl who climbed trees and wasn't afraid of snakes and who died of appendicitis before I was born. I wanted that fearlessness for you in case you ever needed it, but I didn't think you would need it so soon.

Your grandmother was frantic when she finally reached me. I'd been dreading her call since the trial made headlines. For the four weeks I kept our phone off the hook, I'd told myself that the news from New York wouldn't travel too far, a delusion that ended the instant I heard your grandmother's voice. She never mentioned the photographs, but from the first, she only asked after you: Were you all right? Could you fly unaccompanied both ways instead of just one? This was how I learned I was no longer welcome to join you this summer. To be honest, I'm glad I won't be going. I haven't got the stomach for your grandfather's disapproval, which I think only his high blood pressure prevented him from sharing over the phone. After spending so much time dreading his judgment, it's almost a relief simply to know for certain that the good graces I'd reclaimed have been revoked.

Part of me wanted to argue: no, you wouldn't fly alone, not there or back. You would not visit Cleveland at all. Your summer plans fill me with mistrust. What will your grandparents say when they have you to themselves? Eight weeks is a long time. Of course, I can't refuse. You'd sleep with your plane ticket if you could, walk the 460 miles if you had to. So I told your grandmother what she wanted to hear, which also happened to be the truth: that you'd be happy to come to Cleveland any way at all.

81. Construction site, Brooklyn, 1964

On the street, Lillian almost never violated her ten-foot fixed-focus rule, so it's weird to see a photo of people at a greater distance. Two girls, around twelve or thirteen, wearing identical cotton smocks that make them look younger, trek across piles of debris in a lot where a building once stood. Because Lillian's lens was set to grab the girls, the rest of the picture is fuzzy in a way that makes it resemble a dream. But a dream of what? Are these girls so charged to get wherever they're going that they refuse to let a field of rubble stand in their way? Or are they ghosting a path through demolished rooms they can picture when they close their eyes?

The day that school let out for summer, I convinced Kaja to meet me at the corner of

Sixth and St. John's. Between my new haircut, my regular Saturday-morning disguise, and Kaja acting as my lookout, I felt as safe as possible under the circumstances. Grete wouldn't have endorsed Kaja's presence in that part of the neighborhood, but it was the middle of the afternoon so we figured it would be okay. Last night's rain had washed the sidewalks clean and taken the stickiness and stink out of the air. No photographers were waiting in ambush, and no one gave Kaja a hard time. It was like the city knew I was leaving for the summer and was doing its best to convince me to stay.

When Kaja and I got to the gallery, Nina was on the phone. I was so used to the dangly-penis paintings that I'd stopped noticing them, but Kaja started giggling right away. I rolled my eyes. I told her that the male as an object of female desire was massively underrepresented in art, an historical oversight that the Lacuna was trying to fix. Luckily, Kaja didn't ask me what I meant, because I hadn't memorized that part of Nina's speech. When Nina hung up, she didn't recognize me with short hair. Then she asked when I'd become the It Girl of South Brooklyn.

In the wake of our scissors standoff, my

mother had found a hairdresser who said she'd turn me into Audrey Hepburn in *Roman Holiday,* but it wasn't until Nina's compliment that I realized my hair might look half-decent. Nina was puzzled when Kaja kept calling me by my new name. Who was Jane? Nina wanted to know. After I explained, I couldn't tell if Nina was disappointed or just sad. Going underground, huh? she said. She knew it might not feel like luck to me, but most artists spent their whole careers trying to get as famous as I was right now.

Kaja laughed. Nina was right, she told me. I was famous, and I wasn't even an artist!

Nina said that some people were artists whether they wanted to be or not.

My stomach twisted around on itself. Nina was smiling like she'd done me a favor, like my life was a present that she'd special ordered. I told Kaja we had to go, but Kaja was in no hurry. She walked to the nearest penis painting and went into a headstand. Now it was like his legs were arms and his ding-dong was a tiny head on a long tiny neck, she shrieked, and fell over. I knew Kaja was gunning for a hangover sandwich and to learn pinochle, like I'd promised, but once she stood back up I grabbed her hand and led her out the door so fast she had no choice but to leave.

LETTER TO DEBORAH BRODSKY, JUNE 1964: I guess it was decent of Mr. Remming to give me any notice, though he let me know it wasn't for my sake but for Jane. (Will I ever get used to that name?) At first the landlady was less accommodating. When the headlines appeared, she said we had to clear out by the end of the week, but I begged on Jane's behalf (there it is again), and the landlady agreed to wait until the school year was over. As payment for this small victory, I'm sure I have her to thank for the social worker who inspected our untidy rooms while marking his clipboard and asking unconvincingly after my well-being. Did I sometimes find it hard to cope as a single mother? Was I ever lonely or depressed? He reminded me of those vultures in the wool skirts at the maternity ward, hungry for a fatherless newborn to cart off to a "good home." I didn't let go of Sam's hand the whole time he was there, afraid he'd take her with him!

Tonight she told me that the same clipboard man had questioned her at school: Had she been forced to pose naked? How many people had been watching? Had she been asked to do other things, not in front of the camera? She told me she didn't mind his questions because it meant getting out of class. Not only had he not seen the photographs, she boasted, but she bet he'd never even been to an art gallery! If I closed my eyes, that voice belonged to someone confident and happy, but when I opened them again, it belonged to a girl trying to comfort her mother even as she wore a ruffled one-piece bathing suit to avoid the sight of her own body in the bath.

Her plane leaves in three days. While I can sense her excitement even in the way she eats her morning cereal, there isn't much difference in my mind between that plane and the clipboard man. Her grandmother has told her that I can't come to Cleveland because her grandfather's high blood pressure limits them to one houseguest at a time. I won't malign her grandparents by expanding upon that answer, and I can only hope that they'll be equally kind to me. But Deb, I do not trust them!

82. Girl, Brooklyn, 1964

The eight weeks I was in Cleveland, Lillian took more pictures than during the rest of that year combined. Most have kids in them, kids who are never by themselves but always alone: take this girl, standing beside the back fender of a parked car as she cries her eyes out, her left hand pressed to her heart like it's falling to pieces. The two kids on either side of her seem unfazed. The one to her left even looks like he's laughing. The girl's dress hangs limp on her skinny body. She's wearing a paper bracelet. Her hair is done up in a braid that's been pinned to her head, revealing one delicate ear.

When I stepped off the airplane in my movie-star haircut and white organdy dress, having drunk three Shirley Temples and been escorted by a stewardess who looked exactly like the one on the complimentary postcard I'd been given along with my junior stewardess pin, what I wanted was last summer all over again. Because I spotted Grandma Dot and Grandpa Walt first, for a split second I was still the granddaughter who was their best wish come true. But my grandparents were old-fashioned types, and in 1964 not many eight-year-old girls had short hair. I'm not sure how much they knew about the photographs, but whatever it was must have been confirmed by what they saw when I stepped off that plane. Instead of seeing last summer in their faces, I saw two different ways to flinch.

Over the next eight weeks, my mother sent

weird rambling letters filled with exclamation points and capital letters about the weather, her new typing job, the new apartment she'd found for us, and her happiness that Kaja and I would be starting fourth grade together at Prospect Friends. She hoped I was having LOTS of fun biking and swimming and playing in the grass, and she COULDN'T WAIT until I was home again. In all those letters, Lillian mentioned my grandparents exactly as often as my grandparents mentioned her, which is to say not once.

GRETE WASHINGTON: I did not see much of Lillian that summer. After she moved into the new flat, she found typing work on Wall Street. Now that Jane was away, Lillian was not interested in our usual Sunday brunches, and to reach her by telephone became quite impossible. Finally, I visited her on a rainy Saturday when I thought that the weather would keep her indoors. I rang her bell many times before she answered. She told me she had been working in the darkroom, where there was no telephone. Inside the new flat, everything was in boxes except for the photography equipment. Lillian planned to unpack before Jane returned from Ohio, but for now she wished to use every minute of Jane's absence. Each weekday provided her eight hours for working and twelve for photography. This became twenty hours for photography on Saturdays and Sundays. I warned Lillian that a person could not exist with only four hours of sleep each night. Using her pills, Lillian had been living this way for five weeks already, so she was quite certain she could continue for three more. This was not healthy, I explained. Lillian thanked me for my visit, then said she must return to her work. She did not wish to waste one minute of the 300 photography hours of summer that remained.

JOURNAL ENTRY, JULY 1964: I tell myself that I am too busy to miss you too terribly because this ALMOST makes it true, since there are really so MANY THINGS going on, for instance our new apartment which is small but comfortable and my new job which PERFECTLY suits my situation, there being no place more anonymous than a typing pool where I am just another ninety-words-per-minute girl (top of my high school typing class) who appears every morning at eight and disappears at four. I walk to Wall Street with my camera, which takes 102 minutes each way, and it is such a PLEASURE after so many years to renew my acquaintance with the Brooklyn Bridge.

Even though I miss you, I do feel a certain THRILL going straight from the front door to the darkroom with NOTHING to stop me in between, especially on weekends, when the only limitation is available light, a LUXURY that I treasure unlike when I was nineteen and took having so much time for granted, but sometimes in this apartment where you have NEVER been, I feel a sudden PANIC that this is all I will EVER have, and that my MEMORIES OF YOU are FIGMENTS or artifacts from an EXTINCT time. When this happens I feel BURIED ALIVE, but I am determined to use every moment of this summer to create a BETTER LIFE for you and me. Nina might THINK such a life will be brought about by the final ruling in *People* v. *Lacuna* but I REFUSE to be defined by THAT verdict.

At the New School people talked about "seeing Kleinmann" as if they KNEW him PERSONALLY, when really they were walking into MoMA on Portfolio Day as nameless NOBODIES with a handful of prints. Perhaps it is my UPBRINGING but

I don't like going anywhere UNINVITED, so maybe this is ONE WAY the terrible events of the last few months have done me some GOOD, because I am doing something I NEVER would have done before.

83. Rope swing, Brooklyn, 1964

Amazing what a background can do. This rope should be attached to a tree branch, with the kid swinging out over a river or a wide, soft lawn. Instead the rope is tied to the metal skeleton of a signpost jutting out from the facade of an abandoned building whose boarded-up windows are covered in scrawl. The kid is caught midswing, dangling kid-height over a barren, hard stretch of sidewalk that ten out of ten doctors would not recommend for breaking a fall. In the world I want to live in, he lands well. In the world I actually inhabit, I give him better than even odds, as long as he drops when he's over the crumbling top step beside the padlocked plywood door. I'm betting that Lillian — picture accomplished — didn't stick around to find out.

Every day that summer, Grandma made me a poached egg and toast with homemade strawberry jam for breakfast, and tomato soup and grilled cheese for lunch. She took me shopping at Higbee's, where she bought me satin headbands and a high-necked bathrobe and a flowered sun hat. She told me how happy it made her that I'd decided to call myself Jane after her sister. And because, by that summer's end, I'd been living in Cleveland for six of the eight weeks that I'd been living as Jane, sometimes I fantasized that Jane had always lived in Cleveland and always would.

GRETE WASHINGTON: One night, very late, Lillian came to my flat with a large envelope. I had been sleeping, but Lillian was not thinking of time. Her eyes were very bright. Her face was too pale. She pulled at her fingers as she spoke. I asked when she had last eaten. She was unsure, so I cooked an egg and filled a glass with water. The egg was gone in four bites, the water in three swallows, while all the time her foot was tapping the floor.

I told her it worried me to see her this way. The pills were not healthy, and she had to stop. Lillian shook her head. In a voice loud enough to stir Kaja in the next room, she told me that her time was running out. I told her that it was very late, the pills had made her excited. I asked her please to talk more softly, but my words had the opposite effect. Lillian began to argue with me in a voice for a noisy bar, not a quiet home in the middle of the night. I asked if it would be better if she went home and returned in the morning. Or if she liked, she could stay here, and I would make a bed for her on the couch.

Lillian accused me of plotting against her: first I would make her stay with me; next I would teach her to cook and introduce her to another of Jim's friends.

I assured her that this was not so, but she started pointing her finger, jabbing it in the air as if she was accusing me of some crime. I had become middling and commonplace, she said. She stomped her foot when she spoke. She refused to live a mediocre life. When she first met me, she and I had scorned convention, but now I embraced it. Everything about me had become boring.

My face must have looked dramatic, because Lillian stopped talking. She apologized and changed back into a person I knew. Yes, she was working too hard, she said, but it could not be helped. The summer was almost over, and this portfolio was the key to a new beginning. When Lillian had looked at the clock, she had been so excited that she had thought it was early afternoon, not early morning, and she knew that her portfolio would not be complete unless she showed it to me.

I could have sent her away. Or, after opening the envelope and seeing so much beauty in combination with so much sadness, I could have told her that she was forgiven. I did neither of these things.

She had done what she set out to do, I told her. The pictures were perfect, and now she must quit the pills. For her health and for Jane, who must never see her like this, but also for our friendship: the time had come to stop.

LETTER TO DEBORAH BRODSKY, AUGUST 1964: My arms and legs are like so much lunch meat wrapped around drinking straws and covered in waxed paper. I can sense each beat of my heart inside my chest, which feels like a jack-o'-lantern that has been scraped out with a dull knife — but Deb, I have done it.

I remember when you'd appear at my door, wild-eyed from not having slept for who knows how long, the latest issue of *On the Wind* pasted up and camera-ready, your fingers sticky with rubber cement. "Celebrate with me," you'd say, and we'd head to Ratner's for borscht and onion rolls. I suppose I could take the IND all the way to Delancey, but even in my current state I know better than to ride the subway at three a.m., and anyway, Ratner's wouldn't be the same without you.

Deb, is it the same for you with poetry? Time, thought, my body with its petty needs and sensations, all fall away. In the darkroom the world disappears. Life is measured not in heartbeats but in the timer's tick. The motions of my hands and arms are automatic: existence is concentrated in the emergence of the image. If shooting is like hitching a ride on the back of the living city, in the darkroom I am riding the current of an invisible slipstream, but the feeling of being carried is the same. In both places, I'm reduced to a mote of pure awareness.

Every part of me is so tired. I'm fatigued down to each small hair of my skin. MoMA's Portfolio Day begins at ten on Wednesday morning, which means that when I take the uptown IRT, you'll still be asleep. Dream a good dream for me, will you?

84. Prospect Park, Brooklyn, 1964

Lillian didn't remember what it was like to be a kid, but unlike other adult amnesiacs, she didn't use that as an excuse to be condescending. She knew kids had the built-in cuteness of baby animals but that real childhood was what went on underneath. The dominant school of cute child photography would have turned these two boys into a platitude: Two Friends with Hard-won Frog. Instead, my mother captured the jealousy of the empty-handed boy as he frowns at that jar, which the victorious boy examines at head height so that his face is replaced by the vague outline of a trapped animal in the jar's murky water. What could have been a childhood cliché becomes complicated. Then again, maybe I'm just reading into things, since that summer I was a lot like that jarred frog.

At the end of my seventh week in Cleveland, my grandmother told me I didn't have to go back. When I asked her what she meant, she said, Back to New York, like it was something we'd been talking about. Because Grandma always seemed to know if I was hungry or hot or tired, it seemed possible that she could read my mind, which made my private Cleveland fantasy suddenly real in a way that was either exciting or terrifying — unless Lillian's secret plan had been for me to stay in Cleveland all along? This thought made my body go hollow. As casually as possible, I asked whose idea it was for me to stay with them. Grandma explained it was something she and my grandfather had been discussing; he would speak to my mother to work it all out. If I close my eyes, I'm still standing in that kitchen. I'm sure your mother means well, my grandmother said, but some people were not meant to raise children.

Hearing those words, I realized I was a child, with a child's view of a world that was complicated and cold in ways I was not equipped to understand. That moment lifted the corner of a veil: I sensed, abruptly and irrevocably, that the simple love I felt for my grandparents was not the love my grandparents and my mother felt for each other.

Grandma talked about how unhappy she knew I had been and how much better I was now, in a good home where I could be properly cared for. Meanwhile, every cell of my body was picturing Lillian in Brooklyn, alone and unloved. I was struck by such intense homesickness that I began to sob, hard enough that weird belching noises came from my mouth. My grandmother interpreted these sounds differently, because she started crying, too, and holding me to her chest, saying things like, You poor darling dear, and All that is behind you, and Your home is with us now. When I turned my head between belches to look, she was smiling.

Grandma's smile didn't waver when I told her I wanted to go back to New York. For a moment she stood very still. Then she nodded and looked at me like she was reading tiny words printed across the skin of my face. Samantha Jane, she said, promise me that if you ever change your mind — whether it's tomorrow or next October, two years from now, or when you're sixteen and a half — that you will call us collect and let us know so we can put you on the first Cleveland plane we can find. Any time of day, any day of the week, any month of the year.

She didn't need to tell me not to tell Lillian. If I told my mother, I knew that I'd never be invited to Cleveland again. So I nodded, and Grandma patted me on the head. Then she started cooking dinner as if the conversation had never happened.

LETTER TO DEBORAH BRODSKY, AUGUST 1964: I knew that someone named

Tsaregorodcev had replaced Kleinmann as chief curator, but in the year since he took over there haven't been any photography shows, so I didn't know what he might like. When I got there, I was pointed toward the museum offices. A secretary told me to leave my portfolio with her: my work would be reviewed by the following day, and I could retrieve it on Friday. I thanked her, left the building, and leaned against a parking meter to keep from falling over. Then I rode back downtown, where I typed memoranda for the next three hours without reading a single word. I'd just entrusted my photographs to a stranger, and Jane wouldn't be home for another six days.

Friday came, and I retraced my steps uptown to the receptionist's desk. When I gave my name, she said that Mr. Tsaregorodcev wished to see me, did I mind waiting? I sat in a chair and tried to ignore the clock as it ticked out the end of my lunch hour. After twenty-three minutes and twenty seconds more, a man with horn-rimmed glasses and a thick mustache appeared in an office doorway. He gestured me in.

"You're quite ambitious, aren't you?" were his first words. My work was spread across his desk. He was younger than I thought he'd be. I must have nodded, because he said, "It shows in your photos. Not in a cheap way. In a very serious, very arresting way. I must admit this wasn't what I thought I'd get when I saw your name. I thought I'd get the famous photos in the flesh, so to speak. But instead . . ." He held up *Prospect Park.* "This is quite forceful. And it's not a setup, is it?" I shook my head. "You're an opportunist, not a manipulator. And yet you manipulate all the same. Who do you work with?" I told him I was a typist. "You're not in the field? Magazines? Fashion?" I shook my head again. "Of course not. You're not malleable. You want things your own way." His gaze was fierce but not cruel. "I'd like to see 'The Samantha Series.' Will you show me?"

I was short with Mr. Tsaregorodcev then. I don't remember what I said, only that it concerned his opportunism in making such a request, and his insensitivity in calling those eight photographs by the name the world used to deform them, a name I had not chosen. Unfortunately, any possible effect of my vehemence was undone by my rising too quickly from my chair and hitting my knee on Mr. Tsaregorodcev's desk. As I blushed violently and limped toward the door with my portfolio he called after me, but I couldn't hear his words above the pounding of the blood pulsing in my ears.

85. MoMA acquisition cover letter, signed by Lyonel Tsaregorodcev, August 28, 1964

Miss Preston — Though, admittedly, I am at the beginning of my tenure here, you are the first person ever to flee my office. I hope you will forgive any inadvertent offense I caused by my request concerning your work. My intention was certainly not to discomfit you.

Your early departure averted the main purpose of our meeting, which the attached document should make clear. Generally, I prefer a more personal approach, but after the customary face-to-face method failed, my office could only locate the phone number of your gallerist, who promised to pass on anything we wished to send. If, as she implied, you might prefer to communicate with us directly rather than through her, please provide contact information to my secretary so that we can reach you regarding future matters concerning the work.

All best,
Lyonel

GRETE WASHINGTON: When Lillian read this letter, she became so pale that I thought she might faint. Instead of falling over, she made a noise like a puppy's bark and jumped into the air. She said, Oh my goodness, many times. She held the letter before her eyes with shaking hands. Thirty dollars for three photographs was not very much money, but this was not important. When Lillian asked if she could give the MoMA my address and telephone number, to protect the privacy of her and Jane, her voice was light. It was the sound of hope.

When I returned from Cleveland, Lillian seemed older and more worn down, as if in the past eight weeks her body had grown a new outer layer made of tired, but when she showed me the letter, she briefly changed back into a mother I recognized. Which photos did MoMA buy? I asked. New ones, my mother told me. She'd only shown the street photos. Anything else was private, she said with such emphasis that the final word flew out like a broken tooth.

Our new subway station was on a busier street about a fifteen-minute walk from the old one, and was surrounded by different constellations of kids, dogs, abandoned cars, and busted hydrants. Trailing New Lillian to New Address, I passed not one familiar face and so did not once flinch or feel the urge to hide. Nobody looked twice at my short hair or saw my mother and shook their head. I realized how crazy Grandma's offer had been. Live in Ohio? Where there were no corner stores, no stoops, no pigeons, and no shaved ice?

New Apartment was four stories up, which I liked, and smaller, which I didn't. There were not quite three rooms: a medium-ish kitchen-dining-living area with just enough space for our couch and steamer trunk; a smallish bedroom; and a walk-in-closet-sized thing that Lillian had turned into a darkroom. Growing up, I hadn't realized that the various half-rooms, nooks, and alcoves appended to our various living arrangements were never coincidental. Time after time my mother traded privacy, square footage, countertops, and a decent bathroom for darkroom space.

Now that I was back from Cleveland, Lillian's 35mm wasn't part of her body anymore, at least not when I was around. I'd see it attached to her hand when she was coming home from work or heading out on weekends, but my mother was a woman of her word: no more 35mm and no more Ro-Ro. I'd like to say this made me feel special, or that it brought us closer, except that without her camera, my mother was twitchy and uncomfortable, like she had an itch she was trying not to scratch. Though she did her best to pretend, she looked lopsided, like her right arm was shorter than it was supposed to be. Of course, just imagining Lillian taking pictures of me made me want to dig a hole and jump in. Between me jumping or my mother jumpy the choice was clear, but that doesn't mean it was fun.

One day as we passed a woman at a pay phone, Lillian made a shape with her hands. I asked what she was doing. She said, What?, like I'd woken her up, but whenever we were together, it was like that: her thumbs and pointer fingers would form a square that she'd hold four inches from her stomach. We were at home and I was sitting on the couch when I looked across the room, and she was doing it again. I ran over and grabbed her hands as they were making the shape. Stop *doing* that, I told her.

September came. I started fourth grade at Prospect Friends as a scholarship kid named

Jane. I wasn't more or less infamous than anybody else. I had a desk next to the only other fourth-grade scholarship kid, the girl who'd been my best friend since before I could eat with a fork. I had a teacher who sang songs on her guitar and who asked to be called Beth as if last names didn't exist. I was still avoiding my reflection but could change clothes without closing my eyes. I'd even stopped wearing a bathing suit in the tub. Things were looking up.

LETTER TO DEBORAH BRODSKY, NOVEMBER 1964: While I've gone off my prescription in the past, this is the first time I've broken with it completely. I don't think Jane notices anything, and I'm sure that Grete does. I was working too intensely this summer to remember what I said or did, but those weeks changed things between us. Grete insists in her new distant way with me that nothing "too serious" happened. If it had been you, you'd have recited a list of my failings, but at least then I'd know! Grete safeguards her wounds.

I can tell Jane is disappointed by the new apartment, but I'm hoping the coziness will make her feel safe again. Of course, the best remedy will be if the

Supreme Court's decision to hear the case means that our photographs will get the verdict they deserve. In one sense, it's already too late: good or bad, no court ruling will change what Jane said to me through Kaja's closed bedroom door. I pretend that framing her with my fingers will hold her image in my mind, but I know that today's memory of her face will fade. Each day I mourn the daughter I cannot keep and each day, over and over, I press that invisible shutter.

86. Duke of everyone, Brooklyn, 1965

It's not as random a title as you might think, though that painted lettering on the sidewalk is easy to miss. When the paint was fresh, those three words were probably a lot more legible, but now they blend in with the dirty concrete so well that without Lillian's title as a hint, your eyes would probably go straight to the brick walls on either side of the empty lot, which bear the outlines of a building that no longer exists. Obviously, I wasn't with Lillian when she took this, or it would have been relegated to the imaginary portfolio she took with her fingers.

My mother wasn't the only one with a vestigial camera reflex. Let's say I spilled the orange juice, or lost my house key, or told Lillian she was a shitty mother. As Samantha, I would have wrapped myself in a curtain, or found some sun to stand in, or grabbed a book to read while sitting upside down on the couch wearing nothing but a knit scarf, called for my mother, and — *snap snap* — instant reconciliation. As Jane, I was out of luck. For homework one night I was supposed to fill in a family tree, which triggered the predictable unpleasantness surrounding my desire for father data and Lillian's inability to provide it. This cascaded into my usual claims of dissatisfaction and my mother's counter-claims of ingratitude, which escalated into animosity (mine) and coldness (Lillian's), culminating in insults (mine), an object thrown (me again), and capped by storming off and slamming the apartment's sole bedroom door (guess who?). There I was in the bedroom, about to reach for one of Lillian's dresses and eyeing my stuffed duck, when I froze. My mother and I were mad at each other, but our primary grievance-diffusing technique was no longer available. So instead, I lay on my bed and listened to Lillian stealth-wash the dinner dishes (the more upset she got, the quieter she became, like some kind of passive-aggressive mime).

Next was the silence that signaled her walking across the living room on little cat feet, followed by the barely audible click of the darkroom door. To say this became the way we settled our differences is both true and false. True, because it's what we were left with; false, because it didn't settle a thing.

GRETE WASHINGTON: When I picked up the telephone, Nina was yelling. I asked her please not to be so loud, but she was too busy shouting that the attorney for New York was a "goddamn, swollen-headed, self-admiring jackass." I thought she was angry until she started to laugh. She explained to me that each lawyer at the Supreme Court may speak for thirty minutes, but that this prosecutor spoke only twenty-eight words before taking his seat. Nina repeated those twenty-eight words to me, which I wrote down for Lillian: "A viewing by this Court of the photographs will demonstrate the factual finding of obscenity is reasonable. The judgment of the New York courts below should be affirmed." Nina was very happy. If the lawyer for New York thought that *People v. Lacuna* was so simple, then surely our side would win.

87. Two men, New York, 1965

For the most part, Lillian didn't photograph men because when you're spending your time in parks, playgrounds, and neighborhood streets, it's women and children you're going to see. In foreign territory like the Financial District, Lillian would have been hard-pressed to find her usual subjects. And so: two men striding down the sidewalk shoulder to shoulder in dark suits. Their neatly barbered heads are turned toward each other at matching downward angles so they can talk and keep sight of their newspapers. Each holds a *New York Post* opened to the same page as they walk, respective college rings glinting identically on respective fingers.

Given the date, it's possible these two are reading about the Supreme Court case my mother thought she was protecting me from. Once she'd realized Nina wasn't feeding me info (our Saturdays became scarcer around then, but when Nina did answer the door we stuck to playing cards), Lillian figured I was safe from what was going down. She might have been right if safe had been something I was interested in, but my mind kept circling the case the way a tongue pokes at a missing tooth. April and May, Kaja and I hit a different newsstand each day on the way home from school to stay on top of the Subject That Dared Not Speak Its Name. Most days there'd be nothing. Some days there'd be one or two stories. The day of the verdict, so many newspapers printed stories that we had to visit eight different newsstands to avoid getting caught, pilfering one or two papers at each one. To give credit where credit is due, Kaja did most of the stealing. After the second newsstand, my emotions had eroded my competence as a thief. Once we'd made the rounds, we hightailed it to a vacant lot at the corner of Seventh and Sterling where, five years before, a plane had crashed into a building, killing six people on the ground and everyone on board. It was there that I read about the U.S. Supreme Court's five-to-four decision in favor of New York in *People of the State of New York* v. *Lacuna Gallery,* affirming that my pictures were not something the decent people of our great nation wanted to see.

JOURNAL ENTRY, MAY 1965: According to Nina, who reached me through Grete, the Supreme Court hadn't ruled on whether the photographs were obscene but on whether the state of New York had the right to decide this for itself. That this had something to do with "contemporary community standards" wasn't helpful, because by that time I was having trouble understanding Nina, my anger having reduced her words to gibberish. Squirrel, I've never been so irate, which surprised me, because I'd convinced myself that no matter the verdict, I wouldn't care! Only now that we've lost do I realize how much I wanted to win. For the past three months I've been imagining you at MoMA, standing proudly beside *Samantha's tattoo* and *Tea party* and *Mommy is sick,* the way you did at the Lacuna. I'm ashamed by my foolishness and at the same time furious that what had passed for hope was foolishness all along.

In my disappointment I wasn't very nice to Nina, but her timing couldn't have been worse. Without stopping to breathe, she suggested we bring the photographs to a place she'd found with the "community standards" to accept what South Brooklyn wouldn't: a San Francisco art gallery that had shown a series of welded sculptures suggesting various sexual positions. Squirrel, I said words to Nina I hadn't said since I'd been in labor at Bellevue. If Deb had overheard me insulting California, there might have been fences to mend; but I think even Deb would have understood, in ways that Nina never will, why I won't give our photographs to some seedy gallery just to see if we can "get away with it" somewhere else. This journey has broken my heart and robbed you of your innocence, but at least it's now a journey that is done.

88. Sidewalk salesman, New York, 1965

The old man with his carefully trimmed beard and his wooden tray of paintbrushes, matchboxes, razors, and playing cards stands at the corner like a Ghost of Christmas Future version of the young businessman with smooth, clean-shaven cheeks and creased trousers who strides past as if the street peddler is a lamppost. It's so easy to imagine an earlier time when the old guy's vest was unstained and his wool fedora was undented, when his unbent body and younger, yet-to-be-defeated eyes breezed past a previous generation of broken-down man in a prior iteration of tattered suit.

For a week after the Supreme Court's verdict, I was afraid someone would thumbtack a clipping to my classroom's current-events bulletin board, but everyone was more interested in the Gemini space mission. At home, I managed to dodge Lillian's attempts to talk about what had happened — Lillian: They're beautiful photographs no matter what anyone says. Me: Uh-huh. Lillian: But we don't have to talk about it if you don't want to. Me: Uh-huh — and in this way became convinced that, as Jane, I'd outgrown the power of those pictures to hurt me.

During my first post-verdict visits with Nina, she seemed crankier and didn't talk as much, but she'd never been a morning person. One Saturday, she said she had good news. Did the Supreme Court change its mind? I asked. Silly Sammo, she said. That wasn't how this country worked. She smiled like she was about to tell me I'd won the lottery, then informed me the Lacuna was moving to Manhattan.

That spring, the gallery was all paintings of oversize body parts: lips, a hand, a knee. At first I didn't recognize the vagina; I'd never looked at one closely, and there was more to it than I'd have guessed. As I focused on unfamiliar anatomy, Nina explained that she'd had it up to here with the small-mindedness of Brooklyn, not to mention the whole U.S. legal system, but at least her efforts hadn't been in vain. A supporter had offered her a new gallery space, somewhere she could show anything she wanted without having to worry about someone calling in the vice squad. Her benefactor owned a building on Broome Street. It was on a block slated for demolition to make way for the Lower Manhattan Expressway, so she could use the storefront gratis and rent the upstairs apartment for a song. Maybe the highway would come through, maybe it wouldn't; all she knew was that she'd set something in motion, and she wasn't about to break the momentum she'd worked so hard to build.

Nina explained in her winningest voice how visiting the new place would be as easy for me as a straight shot into Manhattan on the IND, followed by a short walk. As her sales pitch rolled on, I tried to copy various stoic expressions from various Friday-night boyfriends I'd seen being offered Saturday-morning coffee for the train. Nina tried to send me home with the card rack she'd made me and a peanut-butter-and-potato-chip sandwich, but I tossed them both into the trash on my way out.

LETTER TO DEBORAH BRODSKY, JUNE 1965: When I went to the Lacuna to say goodbye, I thought if Nina apologized for the way things had gone, she and I could try again at being friends. But Deb, it was exactly the opposite! I'd hardly stepped through the gallery door before Nina announced that if she could do it over again, she'd do it exactly the same. As far as she's concerned, it's just a matter of time before New York and the Supreme Court and everyone else sees things the right way, which is her way, and she's willing to keep putting everything on the line until that day arrives. When I asked if she was at least a little sorry for parts of what she did, she actually became sore. "Sorry for what?" she growled. "For defending your art with everything I had? For defending your rights and artists' rights everywhere?" "But Nina," I told her, "you didn't ask if that was what I wanted! You didn't let me choose!" Nina shook her head. "You don't get it," she said. "When something like this happens, you don't choose; you get chosen."

Deb, I do get it. In principle I even agree, but that doesn't mean I forgive her.

89. Ticker tape, New York, 1966

If you're a glass-half-empty type, those white lines look like damage, as if the photograph is a pane of fractured glass or something someone took a key to, like they must have really had it in for all those faces pressed to the windows and done their best to scribble them out. But really, those people are just gazing at the confetti-filled air above a parade.

For the next two years, I was the type of person who would have seen the confetti. Samantha was yesterday's news, and I'd stopped giving cops or magazine stands or even Nina a second thought. When the phone rang every first Sunday of the month, Grandma and I talked as if we were sitting at her kitchen table eating apple spice cake and looking for birds; and between knock-knock jokes, Grandpa quizzed me with spelling words and the times tables. In decent weather, Kaja and I walked around making up stories about the boarded-up buildings or playing hide-and-seek between parked cars. Since Lillian didn't get home from work until at least six-thirty, I was in charge of cooking. This meant I ate a lot of mushy spaghetti with ketchup, but it also meant my mother did the dishes, which seemed like a pretty good deal. Maybe it wasn't the way other kids lived, but for those two years it was close enough.

GRETE WASHINGTON: The MoMA telephoned while I was rolling meatballs. Almost I did not answer because I did not wish to soil the telephone with the meat. Everything was quite confused at first. I had forgotten that Lillian had given Mr. Tsaregorodcev my phone number. Mr. Tsaregorodcev thought he was calling Lillian. When a strange Swedish woman said hello, he apologized and hung up. Thank goodness he called a second time, because I took his number and telephoned Lillian right away. Soon she and Jane arrived with big smiles. I poured two glasses of aquavit and two glasses of cola, and we toasted to Lillian's wonderful news.

LETTER TO DEBORAH BRODSKY, SEPTEMBER 1966: When I learned that *Rope swing* would be shown with other photographs of the "moment," including work by Granois-Levais and Wilson, I went weak in the knees in the best possible way. I explained it to Jane by comparing myself to a musician who gets invited to perform with John, Paul, George, and Ringo. She rolled her eyes and informed me that George was the only Beatle worth anything. Then she asked if this meant she could get a new dress. I explained that my photo was just one in over two hundred and that the opening would go late. There wouldn't be anyone at MoMA to keep an eye on her or to take her home in time for bed. Jane was so surprised to learn she wouldn't be going with me that her jaw literally dropped. At first I thought she was angry, but when she shook herself like a wet puppy and practically danced into Kaja's room to play, I realized that I'd witnessed her liberation. Being told that this photo and this invitation had nothing to do with her severed her remaining ties to the girl she's worked so hard to leave behind.

Deb, you must be wondering if I even received your last letter, but I saved this for last: I'm coming to San Francisco. I wish I could be there for the birth this spring, but by summer I'll have saved enough vacation days for the bus trip there and back, plus four days with you and the baby. I'm happy for you because you sound happy, but as your friend, I must tell you that no matter the circumstances, it is wrong for you to have involved a married man with a family of his own. I know what you're thinking: I didn't know what to make of you and Judy at first, and I ran back downstairs the first time I came to a Tuesday night. But Deb, it doesn't matter how "free" or "open" you say your community is; what you're doing has nothing to do with either of those things! I'm sure my reaction doesn't surprise you. In fact, I bet it's why you waited so long to let me know. But maybe what does surprise you is how none of that changes my love for you, or for the child growing inside you, or how happy I will be to see you both.

90. Woman, Brooklyn, 1967

At first glance, it looks like this woman — bent at the waist in what almost seems like a runner's starting crouch — was cut from another picture and collaged onto this sidewalk so that her back half is emerging from the hedge bordering this apartment building. Except that Lillian didn't go in for collage, and a fashionably hatted, wool-skirted woman in sling-back heels isn't exactly dressed for the fifty-yard dash. All I can figure is that she must have dropped something in that bush — a glove? her inherited notions of femininity? — but with her arms and the lower half of her profile lost to the shrubbery, we'll never know.

It's weird what gets left unsaid. One Sunday in April, a few weeks before the MoMA show, Grandma called like usual, but until I asked to talk to Grandpa, she didn't mention that he was in the hospital. My face must have changed because before

I could reply, Lillian grabbed the phone to ask What? and When? and How? and How long? Grandpa had a heart attack, my mother informed me. Then she handed me back the phone so Grandma could describe the white-breasted nuthatch at the feeder that, she said, was looking forward to my visit that summer because it preferred having a young lady to sing to.

The night of the opening I slept over at Kaja's where, after Jim was asleep, she and I liberated one of his beers and two of Grete's cigarettes and took turns reading aloud from some dirty paperbacks Kaja had found in a shoebox on the floor of her mother's closet. We couldn't understand why Lillian hadn't taken me. Didn't I deserve to go? Eventually, we decided that this was the punishment my mother had fitted to my crime: since I wouldn't let her photograph me anymore, Grete was her date. I prided myself on giving back as good as I got, so if this was Lillian's best attempt at payback, I'd give her my best twelve-year-old rendition of pretending not to care.

I didn't see the MoMA show until Grete took Kaja and me there the week sixth grade ended, a few days before I left for Cleveland and my mother left for San Francisco. Lillian was supposed to come to the museum, too, but at the last minute she decided to get a headache. By that time I was so good at acting like that kind of thing didn't matter, I almost convinced myself it didn't.

GRETE WASHINGTON: Lillian was wearing a blue dress I had not seen, quite charming and old-fashioned. I asked her where she found it, my friend who does not shop for clothes. I laughed when she explained this was her high school prom dress from fourteen years ago. I gave her a shawl I had made, and with this combination she looked almost fashionable.

I had attended openings before, but only in galleries. To enter the MoMA in the evening, when it was closed, was exciting. The museum was crowded. Well-dressed men and women were speaking together like old friends, though Lillian and I did not know a single person. When Lillian began taking pictures, I thought this would be noticed, but in a room where everyone was trying to look important, someone like Lillian was easily overlooked. She was taking so many pictures that her film could not have lasted very long, but having her camera at her fingers was more important to her than having new film inside it.

A woman grasped Lillian's hand. She led

us through several rooms, each more and more crowded, until we reached a man with glasses and a lush mustache. This was Mr. Tsaregorodcev. The room was so filled with people and photographs that it would have been difficult to find Lillian's picture without Mr. Tsaregorodcev's assistance. I knew the photo well, but seeing it in the museum felt like seeing it for the first time. For Lillian, too, I think, because finally, her camera was at rest.

Numerous people wished to speak to her, though not for reasons she liked. When, in the middle of a disappointing conversation, a person complimented the shawl she was wearing, her face became bright. The artist is here, she told them, and pointed to me. Lillian knew I preferred to be called a weaver, but on that night I did not correct her.

When the MoMA made its first exhibition of textiles two years later, Lillian said to me, You see, Grete, this is not a show of weavers at the Museum of Modern Weaving. This is a show of artists at the Museum of Modern Art. Yes, I told her, and that is why there are no shawls or rugs here. If some person did build a museum for shawls and rugs, this would create the problem of bare floors and cold shoulders.

JOURNAL ENTRY, MAY 1967: I knew what I was hoping for but not what to expect. Mr. Tsaregorodcev had warned that people would be "very curious" about me, and true to his word, the whole evening was a series of conversations with those who wanted to schedule a "studio visit" (whatever they imagined, I'm sure it wasn't the alcove off our living room), or to take me to lunch. Those who looked at *Rope swing,* looked just long enough to see that it wasn't a nude portrait. People seemed more interested in staring at me, some of them saying "brave" or "courageous" as if awarding me a medal. In short, the evening was lousy with strangers wanting to see eight photographs that weren't there. I managed not to lose my composure the way I had with Mr. Tsaregorodcev — but Squirrel, it wasn't easy! Thank goodness for Grete, who spent the night at my side murmuring Swedish insults low enough for only me to hear, with a promise to translate them on the train ride home. Meanwhile, I stuck like glue to a spot where I could see my photograph and enjoy the card with my name and the words "Purchase of the Museum of Modern Art."

Sweetheart, you were so cold to me

today that I suspect you wanted to attend the show after all; but think what would've happened if you had! You've been Jane so well for so long, it doesn't occur to you that with me at MoMA, you could only ever be Samantha, your disguise turned from an enchanted coach back into a pumpkin. Would it help to explain this, or is it better not to revisit what belongs to the past? I've made my best guess, but I'll never know.

By the time Mr. Wythe found me that night, I was so unhappy that seeing him was actually a relief. Ever since the show at Aperçu, I've felt that my work fell short of his standards, but in an evening filled with new discomforts, this familiar one was welcome. Ten years had left Mr. Wythe unchanged except for a single streak of silver hair that curled against his forehead like elegant jewelry. "Congratulations, my dear, and condolences," he said in the same tired way he said everything. "You didn't set out to take the world by storm, and now you must contend with the best and worst of it." He liked *Rope swing* very much and wanted to discuss my work, but only after I'd talked to everyone else. Aperçu had closed, but he now had a gallery on Grove Street, the only one in the city devoted to photography since the Ip-plingers had closed Picture Shop and moved to L.A. "Right now you can show your work with anyone," he said, "so you must visit the other galleries before you choose mine." He wanted me to come to him knowing my next show deserved a space dedicated to the form, represented by a gallery that knew photography and not just what was "hot."

I didn't know I was shaking my head until Mr. Wythe stopped talking. Was something wrong? No, I told him, unless he honestly thought he could tell me who I should or shouldn't talk to about my pictures. I wasn't going to waste time with strangers if I could show my work with him — but only if I alone chose the images to exhibit at his gallery, and only if those select images could be viewed or purchased. My new work had to succeed or fail on its own merits: nothing more, nothing less.

We were still surrounded by voices, but as Mr. Wythe stared at me, I didn't hear them. "You're carrying a heavy burden," he finally said. "You want to be taken seriously, but you're afraid of being taken advantage of. I showed your work before because I saw its strength, and that's why I want to show it now."

Squirrel, you know how shy I am, but when I realized what he was saying, I hugged him like a friend. The rest of the evening was easier to endure, knowing that my new work had a new home.

91. Downey Street, San Francisco, 1967

Of all the pictures Lillian took when she visited Deb in San Francisco — featuring the city, the hippies, Deb and her four-month-old son — this is the only one she included in The Box. Logic would dictate that the barefoot boy sitting against the fire hydrant and weaving a yarn God's-eye around two broken twigs belongs to the bearded flute player beside him, but it being the Summer of Love, all bets are off. Though my mother arrived too late for the Be-In or the music festival, during the four days she spent in the Haight before needing to start the three-day bus trip back east, Deb showed her a good time. The letter that reached me in Ohio was written in green ink on the back of a poster for a band called the Purple Clam Bake and described sunny weather, spontaneous concerts, painted people in the park, late-night picnics, and the developmental milestones of Yuma, the weirdest boy name I'd ever heard.

That was a strange summer. With the

Supreme Court case over and my name out of the news, the Quakers had informed my mother that my free ride to Prospect Friends was over. Come September, I'd be back in public school for seventh grade at JHS 23. Lillian was surprised by how well I took the news, but that was only because I had a foolproof plan to stay hitched to the Quaker wagon. At this juncture in my young narcissistic life, I had no reason to believe my grandparents would deny me anything, and — considering the house they lived in — they were obviously rich. I figured I'd spend the first five weeks of my summer visit talking up Prospect Friends and then, in the last week, explain how I'd be able to keep attending only if they covered tuition, thus securing my happy Quaker future.

When I landed, my grandparents were waiting at the gate for me like usual, but Grandpa had more gray hair than before, and he didn't pick me up when he hugged me. We were halfway to the car before I noticed it was Grandma carrying my suitcase. Then Grandpa got in the passenger seat instead of behind the wheel, and Grandma explained in her sunniest voice that Grandpa needed to take things easier than he used to but was otherwise perfectly fine.

Because of his heart Grandpa didn't smoke a pipe anymore, but even worse, Grandma's cooking wasn't as good. When Grandpa complained about his meal tasting bland, Grandma told him that was "salt talk" and that he needed to train his taste buds to appreciate the natural flavors of food. One heart attack was quite enough, she said in a voice I'd never heard her use with him but which got him eating his steamed fish as effectively as it stopped me from sneaking extra cookies from the jar beside the kitchen pantry.

Each night I said one good thing about Prospect Friends at dinner. While Grandma washed up, I went off with Grandpa, who was as crazy for knock-knock jokes and model planes as ever. I put the final phase of my master plan into action four days before my plane trip home. I don't know exactly what I'd been expecting when I popped the question over dessert, but total silence wasn't it. Finally Grandpa asked, in a voice that made Grandma look up from her apple crumble, if my mother had put me up to this, but when I explained that she didn't know, that asking them to pay for school had been my idea, he seemed to calm down.

My face turned bright red when he asked

how much the school cost. I wasn't actually sure. In my fantasy version, I asked, they agreed, and that was that, because when you're rich, price is no object. But in the real version, I asked and then noticed the worn linoleum of the kitchen floor and the towel that Grandma kept beneath the refrigerator to catch the drips. After a quiet that made me want to crawl under the table, Grandpa said how glad he was that I'd asked about school because it meant I knew they'd do anything for me they could. He supposed it must be confusing, coming from a place like Brooklyn, where people didn't have houses and cars, to a place like Cleveland, where they did. He'd worked steady all his life, which had left him and Grandma plenty comfortable and certainly better off than some, but they weren't like the folks in Shaker Heights with their private schools and country clubs and fancy vacations. Why, he wouldn't be surprised if the Shaker Heights folks flew on airplanes a few times a year! As for him and Grandma, they'd never flown themselves, but it was a treat for them to send me that plane ticket every year so that I could. At least I'm pretty sure that's what he said. My memory would probably be clearer if he'd been angry. Instead he was kind and a little wistful, and the sound of all that understanding fogged my brain. If I'm being honest, which is something I try to do now, the embarrassment of learning that my plane ticket was their yearly luxury wasn't the worst thing. In the universe that revolved around my twelve-year-old self, the worst thing was my realization that I'd be attending JHS 23 after all.

LETTER TO DEBORAH BRODSKY, AUGUST 1967: Somehow it didn't surprise me that San Francisco was like one big Tuesday potluck. I felt giddy, walking down a street of people dressing and behaving as they pleased, unworried about being judged. I think I'd always feel like a tourist there, even if I stayed four months instead of four days, but it was a pleasure to be there with two people who belong so wholly to that place as you and Yuma. What a beautiful name for a beautiful boy.

Now that I'm back home and August has arrived, I still don't know what to show with Mr. Wythe. I want to balance old work and new, but I'm not sure what that balance is. Once upon a time, I trusted my instincts; but now, every time I look over a contact sheet or appraise a print, I feel the eyes of the world appraising it with me. I wish I were eighteen again. Unlike other women who yearn for their younger selves, it's not that woman's body I'm after: it's her state of mind!

92. Seventh Avenue, Brooklyn, 1967

Lillian prided herself on grabbing pictures of people who didn't know she was there, so I'm surprised she included this one in The Box. Two of these three people are looking straight at her: one half of the teenage couple making out in the doorway at the left-hand edge, and the beefy girl standing sentry in the middle of the sidewalk, eyeballing the camera like it's a bug and she's a shoe. I almost wonder if my mother was trying to prepare herself for adolescent rage, armed with nothing but a camera for the storm she knew was coming.

After three years of folk songs, hands-on learning, and Quaker meetings, nothing short of electroshock therapy could have prepared me for public junior high. My first day of school, I arrived in the two-tone oxfords and matching purse I'd picked out with Grandma at Higbee's. I knew the outfit was a stupid idea. At JHS 23, new shoes meant hand-me-downs with soles that were still good, and the only people with matching purses were the hookers on Prospect

Park West. But ever since my summer shopping trip, I'd been looking forward to walking into seventh grade wearing the shoe-purse combo, and I wasn't about to let the minor detail of a different school spoil that plan. By lunch, I'd lost track of how many times my feet had been stomped, turning the white part of the oxfords a blackish gray, plus my purse had become the property of a girl named Lina who had sharp nails and a dead tooth. I divided my time between looking out classroom windows while wishing myself back to Kaja at Prospect Friends and testing different versions of cool in the bathroom mirror, trying for a face tough enough to keep away the girl members of the Stone Foxes without scaring off everyone else. It only took me a couple weeks to realize the best way to do that was to start smoking.

For about a year, Kaja and I had been filching the occasional midnight cigarette from her mom, puffing once or twice before letting it burn down, but at JHS 23 that kind of dilettante behavior got called out right away. Sucking down a whole cig didn't stay a hardship for long, though it did mean wanting one more often. This started cutting in to my pocket money, which required fishing for coins behind the sofa cushions or inside Lillian's purse. Conveniently, my mother was spending every moment outside her job worrying about the Biggest Show of Her Career, the one in which she would Show the World the Photographer She Really Was and not the one Nina Had Made Her Out to Be, so she was oblivious to my new habit and the disappearing coins.

As soon as Kaja learned I'd graduated from the occasional sleepover smoke, she upped her game. Grete instantly caught on, but since she was a dedicated smoker whose whole deal was total honesty and openness, she was okay with our smoking as long as we did it with her. As far as I was concerned, this made Grete the best mom ever. Kaja said her mom's perceived coolness was a front: Grete was just desperate to win her favor now that she was spending every weekend with her dad.

Meanwhile, Lillian was so darkroom-obsessed that if she noticed I was spending all my time at Grete and Kaja's, she was either too relieved or too preoccupied to mention it. This lopsided arrangement worked fine until Kaja started hanging out with Jenny Dufresne, who had replaced me as Kaja's desk partner at Prospect Friends. Kaja and I had always made fun of Jenny for wearing monogrammed sweaters. Now

Kaja informed me that Jenny had soul because she was adopted, and that I needed to stop coming over so much on weekday afternoons. However, eating beans from a can while Lillian worked in the darkroom was about as appealing as hanging around after school to see if the Stone Foxes would demand to fight or initiate me, so I kept showing up at Kaja's.

One day Kaja stormed off with Jenny after an argument with me, and Grete came home to find me burning holes in Kaja's favorite shirt with a cigarette. Grete called Lillian, who came over after work so we could all "talk." This didn't go so well. In addition to my anger-management problems, I'd done nothing to discourage Grete's belief that Lillian knew about me and cigarettes, an assumption brought to an abrupt end by my mother's appearance at Grete's door.

LETTER TO DEBORAH BRODSKY, NOVEMBER 1967: I waited until we were home to ask Jane how long she'd been smoking. She rolled her eyes and said, "Gee, Mom, I just started," with such scorn that I'd have crawled under a rock from embarrassment if I weren't so angry. "Is this how you treat people now?" I asked.

Her shoulder twitched in the barest shrug. "Is this how I treat you?" I asked next, which twisted her face into something almost unrecognizable. "You don't treat me like anything," she yelled.

When she told me she was moving to Cleveland, I know I didn't help matters by laughing, but really, it was the last thing I expected. To me, Cleveland was so obviously a cage that I couldn't imagine Jane wanting to climb into it. What did her grandparents think of this idea? I asked, at first skeptical and then astounded when she said they'd promised to send her a plane ticket.

Deb, I was so furious calling my parents' number that it took me three tries. As my shaking finger turned the dial, I wavered between equal certainty that Jane was fibbing and that she was telling the truth. My voice was a model of composure as I asked Mother if Jane's claim was correct. I didn't realize how much I'd been counting on my daughter being a liar until I learned that she wasn't. Mother explained they had made Jane this offer four summers ago. No, she didn't expect I would have known about it: I needed to remember what had been happening then and how worried they'd been. They wouldn't have sent Jane a plane ticket without asking me first. When Jane had called earlier, they'd simply said they were willing to have her — but if Jane was so unhappy and if her school was so unsuitable, perhaps it made sense for her to spend the year with them? That was when my temper erupted and I became my father's daughter. Jane had never heard me, even at my worst moments, use the voice that told Mother if she thought they could so much as begin to discuss such a plan without me, they had even less respect for me than I'd thought. Jane would not be coming. Not only that, they had lost the privilege of being in contact with either of us. By the time I hung up the phone, Jane had locked herself inside the bedroom. I knew it would have been pointless trying to talk to her, and to be honest, I didn't want to. I divided the night between developer, stop bath, and fixer until I was tired enough to fall onto the couch in a dead, dreamless sleep.

93. Central Park, New York, 1967

Lillian's Central Park photo feels like a self-portrait to me even though she's not in it. The family of four standing at the left side of the photo screams out of town. Partly it's the matching wide-brimmed hats on the two boys, and partly it's the way mom, dad, and kids are all standing like they're at a museum or a zoo and not a park, staring at something they'd like to keep at a distance. Meanwhile, the wild-eyed, braless, and shaggy-haired hippies scattered across the park's lawn are acting like the family is invisible or, more to the point, irrelevant. In my mind, I pull back beyond the photo's edge to see my mother standing with her camera, irrelevant twice removed.

Would I have called my grandparents collect if Kaja hadn't dumped me for monogram Jenny? If I hadn't accused Kaja of being a bad daughter and she hadn't accused me of being a worse one? If Kaja hadn't called me a blue-eyed devil? If I hadn't asked her what that even meant, since she and Jenny Dufresne were the ones with blue eyes? If she hadn't told me to leave and never come back? Probably. Sometimes after fighting with Lillian or while smoking beside a dirty brick wall, I could feel myself turning into what had scared my five-year-old self the day I moved to Park Slope and walked into that Seventh Avenue candy store. In some deep animal part of me, I knew if I didn't stop that transformation, I'd be uprooting something basic and important that wouldn't grow back. Cue my grandparents' mothballed offer popping out of the mental box I'd stuck it in. I began picturing myself inside my Cleveland bedroom with its pale green carpet and matching curtains or coming home to the smell of Grandma's pot roast at the end of the afternoon, until not living in Cleveland started feeling like an extra punishment I'd inflicted on myself on top of all my other punishments, earned and otherwise.

In the wake of the Cleveland embargo, I treated Lillian like she was invisible. Mornings, I'd maneuver past her from the bedroom to the bathroom to the kitchen and out the door. I'd been smoking at school long enough to earn a place among the other smokers: afternoons, they hung around a playground whose wooden benches had been burned and whose swings had been slashed, pairs of us taking turns going into the Bohack to knock over grocery displays or switch up labels in the produce section. I liked the smokers because the older ones treated me like a kid sister, and because the Stone Foxes left them alone. Plus, despite growing local tensions since the rumble between whites, blacks, and Puerto Ricans at the high school on Seventh Avenue, the JHS 23 smokers didn't care what color you were as long as you were willing to share, which was very Quaker of them.

When I called to apologize for my behavior, Grete informed me that Kaja had gone to live with her father full-time. In the imaginary conversations I'd been having with Kaja since our fight, I'd already told her about Lillian quashing my plan to leave Brooklyn, so real Kaja's escape to Harlem made it easy to get imaginary Kaja to agree that I was the winner in our long-running worst-mother contest. Competitive though I was, this was not a victory I celebrated. Where Kaja's superior mother had bowed to her wishes, my inferior one had remained unyielding: in losing, Kaja had won. The evening of Lillian's gallery show on Grove Street, I pretended not to notice her putting on her one nice dress, ignored her requests for help with her hair, and feigned absorption in a magazine as she walked out the door.

LETTER TO DEBORAH BRODSKY, APRIL 1968: Thank goodness the burglars kept to the living room and that you and Yuma are all right; though to have your sense of security stolen is the worst theft of all. It breaks my heart picturing you and little Yuma hiding behind your closed bedroom door. Considering the ways the Haight has changed, I don't think it at all "cowardly" of you to want to move. I know you're proud of never asking Yuma's father for anything, but maybe this once you should. I'm sure he'd be glad to help with a security deposit if it meant his son could live somewhere safer.

It should come as no surprise that my first major solo exhibition came and went with as much fanfare as a pigeon crossing the park. The few scattered reviews spent their ink airing the reviewer's opinion on the *New York* v. *Lacuna* verdict, with the expected results. Reviewers in favor of the obscenity ruling deemed the new show "ugly" and "sensationalistic," while those against the ruling called it "honest" and "elegant." I suppose the only way to save my new work from falling under the shadow of the old would be to show it under a false name, but that would be as good as agreeing that the photographer known as Lillian Preston will always and forever be defined by eight photographs taken nearly as many years ago.

According to Mr. Wythe, there were a few sales and several collectors keen to meet me. One in particular, having apparently flown in by private jet, was quite direct about his interest in those eight photographs and his willingness to pay a grand sum to have them. According to Mr. Wythe, this collector left disappointed but undaunted, claiming to be a patient man. I hope, for his sake, that patience truly is its own reward.

Deb, Jane's grandparents apologized for having gone behind my back, and I've decided to let Jane visit them this summer. When I told Jane she could visit Cleveland in July as usual, the joy on her face briefly revealed the child eclipsed by cigarettes and silences, insults and sarcasm. Ultimately, my anger with her or her grandparents has no bearing on their love for each other. I don't trust them, but if they say they won't keep her past the summer, they won't. Jane's grandparents may be judgmental and controlling, but they aren't liars.

I know that if I didn't let Jane go, I'd only lose her some other way, but just because it's the right thing to do doesn't make it easy! If nothing else I'm grateful that, for now at least, she's stopped avoiding me like I'm a piece of ugly, sharp-edged furniture.

94. Old woman, New York, 1968

JOURNAL ENTRY, JULY 1968: Walking to work, I came upon an old woman sitting in front of a restaurant's dark window, her wig squarely in place, her black-stockinged legs crossed at the ankles, the locket against her shapeless dark dress making it look even more like a shroud. Her massive handbag lay on its side like a dead thing as she stared into the distance with the face of someone who knows that what she is waiting for will never come. Only the first of my exposures was any good because my hand started to shake. I felt so certain I was seeing my future that it took every bit of reserve not to grasp that abandoned figure and ask, "Tell me! Does she ever come back?" Looking at that woman birthed the same desperation that filled me earlier this week when I put you on the Cleveland plane. If I want to stop this feeling from coming back, I know something has to change.

Arriving to the house on Fernvale Street, I was ushered in to lemonade and freshly baked chocolate chip cookies. Ever since my grandparents had reneged on the whole "call us anytime and we'll send for you" promise, I'd been mentally honing the righteous indignation I planned to unleash when I saw them; but now I couldn't muster the necessary venom. I wasn't nine anymore. Four years had passed since people across the country were calling me a degenerate. I was simply thirteen and not getting along with my mother. Even I had to admit it wasn't quite the same thing.

My first week in Cleveland, I wrote Kaja a letter about everything that had happened since our fight: my ill-fated phone call to my grandparents, the state of affairs with my mother, my loneliness, my grandmother's flavorless cooking, my grandfather's constant fatigue — and my fear, since Kaja had moved to her father's place before we'd made up, that I would never see my best friend again. Before the end of July, a letter arrived in return. Kaja loved living with her dad and wished she'd done it sooner. She was spending the summer at a Movement school that a friend of her father's had set up in the back of a bookstore, where she was learning about black history and black art, her letter listing a bunch of names I'd never heard of. It was only her and six other kids, and four of those were the teacher's. Because she was the oldest, she got to help teach math and spelling to the younger ones. For the first time, she felt like she was learning about real things and real people. She wished I was there with her. It'd be good for me, plus some of the other kids needed to see that there were a few righteous white people in the world.

Midway through the summer, Lillian wrote to say she'd found a Catholic school with a special fund for "children in need" for which I qualified, thanks to my crap grades at JHS 23 and having a working single mother on food stamps. Being a photographer was a resumé detail my mother kept off that application. I thought it was funny that what had made me valuable to the Quakers would have gotten me blacklisted by the nuns. I briefly considered making a stink about being forced to join the plaid-skirt nation, but if wearing a uniform meant getting to spend eighth grade at my own desk, with my own books, without worrying about getting beaten up, it seemed like a good trade.

Upon returning home in August, Lillian hugged me so hard I could hear her heartbeat. Hearing that steady rhythm, I was flattened by the realization that my stubborn, clueless mother was nothing more than a pile of organs held together inside a flesh sack. I suddenly felt wildly protective of Lillian and privately vowed never to do anything purely for the sake of hurting her. Of course, not hurting someone for harm's sake isn't the same thing as not hurting them at all. Which is to say that I went on to hurt my mother in ways that I continue to regret, even now that she has been dead thirteen years.

95. Cardboard box containing 100 contact sheets marked with variously colored grease pencils, 1968–69

Once when I was little, Lillian let me inside her darkroom to see the trays, the bottles, the enlarger that looked like a miniature deep-sea diving helmet with an old-fashioned camera hanging off it. This was where Mommy worked, she told me. I shouldn't ever come in or I'd ruin her photos. That was it until a few weeks after I started eighth grade. As if talking about going to the store for a carton of milk, Lillian mentioned that if I ever wanted to come into the darkroom, I just had to knock and she'd let me in between stages. She went on about how peaceful it was and how beautiful to watch the images appear. Then, because I hadn't said anything, she stopped. Was that something I might want to see? At first I could only nod because my throat had dried up. Yeah, I said, trying to keep my voice even. Yeah, it was.

I ended up spending a big chunk of that year in the dark. Somehow, being with Lillian in the darkroom was different from being with her anywhere else. Talking with Nina had felt like talking to a big sister, and Grete had always felt like a friend, but it had never been easy in that way with my mother. Because the darkroom didn't have running water, Lillian had to lug in a big container of hot water from the kitchen and then wait for it to cool to the right temperature before mixing the chemicals. She had a thermometer, but she'd been doing this so many years, she knew by touch when the water had cooled to seventy degrees.

Developing film was the first thing I learned. It was straightforward enough that, after Lillian loaded the film onto the metal reel and put it in the tank in the dark, I could hold up my end of a conversation while pouring out developer or adding in stop bath. While the film went between stages, Lillian and I would talk about changes in the neighborhood; or while we were in the kitchen rinsing negatives, she would tell me what it had been like when she first came to New York. Making a test strip, I'd talk about school or Kaja. Naturally, I never mentioned my smoking — which, true to my vow never to hurt my mother for hurt's sake, I now hid — but the darkroom let us be as much of ourselves with each other as we were willing or able to be.

After my mother decided on the best overall exposure for a print, she identified the areas that needed to be darker or lighter. Then she listed which portions of the image she needed to keep covered or uncovered during the exposure and for how long. We kept quiet during this part: Lillian had to concentrate on timing the various sections of the print that needed to be dodged or burned and on the delicate choreography such timing required. If a particular area was in the center of an image, she'd use a piece of cardboard with a hole cut in it, or a cardboard shape attached to a wire that she could wave over the right spot, but mostly she used her hands. As the enlarger projected the negative onto the paper, she gently waved her hands or fingers or cardboard over each designated portion of the image for each preset time. Constant movement kept the outline of whatever she was using — cardboard, fingers — from appearing on the developing print. Watching my mother work in the dim red glow of the darkroom's safe light was like watching a bird that had been awkwardly waddling around on shore finally take to the water and realizing: Oh, that's a swan! The choreography of her hands as she heightened lights and deepened darks was graceful in a way I'd never seen before. As I witnessed that, it wasn't like I stopped being thirteen or her daughter, but those things somehow mattered less. And because they mattered less, there was less to get in the way.

Being at Immaculate Heart was both simpler and more complicated than being at JHS 23. Pretty much everyone else had been learning catechism since kindergarten. My total ignorance of Catholicism's greatest hits, ranging from the Lord's Prayer to the Holy Sacraments, was a constant source of amusement; but I learned that I liked history and biology, and that I was good at memorizing dates and the various divisions of the nervous system. I met a girl named Angie who smoked under the bleachers. She showed me how to blow smoke rings, and I taught her how to slip lipsticks into her purse. When Kaja visited Grete on weekends, she and I would sometimes hang out. I'd tell Kaja about the nuns and the darkroom, and she'd teach me about Mansa Musa and Solomon Northup and all the other stuff she'd been learning at the back of the bookstore. She and Grete were fighting all the time. Her mother kept criticizing the Movement school and everything else in Kaja's new life, and she'd tell me at great length how she and her dad were sick of it. Then I'd say something sympathetic, the way I always did when Kaja groused about Grete, and we'd head to Atlantic Avenue for halvah and Coke.

When Lillian answered the phone toward the end of March and her face went pale at first I thought something had happened to Grandpa. Then she asked me if Kaja had ever talked about leaving New York. Paul had just telephoned Grete to say that he and Kaja had moved to Detroit. I told Lillian everything I knew, which wasn't much. Then my mother handed me the phone, and as Grete wept on the other end of the line, I forced enough air into my lungs to repeat what little there was to say.

GRETE WASHINGTON: I went uptown to Paul's apartment, but it was empty. According to the police, this was not an abduction, because Paul and I were not legally divorced. I made a trip to Detroit the next day. I brought Kaja's favorite spice cookies and also the stuffed bird that she had left behind. I was stupid to think that such a trip would make a difference. After I returned, I did not consider what I was making: I sat at the loom only to stop the trolls in my brain. I tried to live as before. I went to work, I saw my friends. Nothing felt as it should. My first shroud was twenty feet long. All the months of its creation, I slept beside my loom, making for myself a bed of the finished sections. When Lillian saw what I had made, she looked at me with new eyes, eyes that gazed directly at me rather than from slightly above. With a voice of admiration, she told me that this shroud was the most beautiful piece I had ever made. I thanked her. Then I told her to leave. I was trembling with anger, but of course Lillian did not understand. She asked to know if she had said something wrong. Yes, I told her. For years she had looked down on my happiness. But Grete, she told me, she always knew I was more than a simple craftsman. This beautiful work proved that she was right. I told her that I did not want this beautiful work. I did not wish to be considered complex or interesting. I wanted my daughter. Finally, I told her that really she must go before I did something we would both regret.

Every year I weave one shroud, never so long as the first. People cannot buy them, but the gallery displays other things that I am willing to sell. Not tablecloths or shawls. Whether or not I wish to be, I suppose I am an artist now.

96. Bandaged man on Pearl Street, New York, 1969

No self-respecting doctor would have crisscrossed white adhesive tape on a cheek that way. This is a home job, even though a guy wearing a suit like that can afford to see a doctor, which is what makes him so interesting. That and the noble way he's holding his damaged face in profile, like he's posing for a coin. The crazy diagonals of his bandage work against the perpendiculars of the city grid stretching behind him. Cover his face with your hand, and you've got a perfectly ordered streetscape. Take your hand away, and it all goes askew.

I got a letter from Detroit a few weeks after the move, but Kaja was a much better talker than she was a writer, so the letter was short and didn't sound like her. I wrote back, and after that there was nothing. Write to her, my mother said. Write to her, Grete begged the few times I saw her before she and my mother stopped hanging out. Meanwhile I saw Kaja sitting at drugstore counters, and in the passenger seats of cars, and on buses, and running up the block, and walking across the street. For the rest of the 1970s, I saw her in the newspaper or on TV whenever the latest experiment in people's liberation issued a manifesto, or blew something up, or robbed a bank, or got arrested or shot. These days I see her in dreams where I'm my actual age but she's still twelve, like some juvie Peter Pan, daring me to sneak with her through the back door of the RKO or to stuff the latest *Ingenue* down my pants. Then I wake up.

That summer, Grandpa came down to breakfast in his suit; afterward he went to his study instead of his car. This was how I learned he'd taken early retirement and that Grandma was working as a part-time teller at the bank. Doctor's orders, at least the early-retirement part. Grandpa wasn't thrilled about Grandma's bank job, but she said she enjoyed talking to customers and handling money in such a fine-looking place. Grandpa had been coming home from work so tired that he fell asleep at dinner, sometimes so deeply that Grandma had to leave him at the table overnight. He'd always wanted to research his family tree, plus he'd joined a flight club that built model planes with working engines and control lines.

In September, Grete forwarded an invitation from Nina to attend an opening at the new gallery, which Lillian and I both ignored, until one day I noticed it lying beneath a dirty plate and asked my mother how many more pictures before we were ready. Ready for what? she asked. Our next show, I said. By my count, we had at least twenty good images. Lillian smiled like I'd said something funny. She wasn't thinking about that, she said. After her show at the Grove Street gallery, she'd realized the only way to be truly inside the process was not to have an exhibition hanging over her head. She was so happy to be with me in the darkroom, working just for the sake of making good prints. It was liberating to head out with her camera completely free of expectation or doubt. She was enjoying herself far too much to think about when or how or where she'd show her work again.

Over the past year I'd been slowly assembling a show in my mind, populated with prints my mother and I had made together. I'd imagined myself wearing one of Angie's older sister's dresses to the opening, pointing to a framed photograph and saying something like: She took the picture, of course, but I was with her for most of the process and . . .

So maybe in the spring, I said.

Probably not, Lillian said. She wanted to give her work a chance to breathe. When the time came, she'd know.

I'd stopped looking at my mother and was staring at a hole in the fabric of the couch. We'd had that couch for as long as I could remember. The stuffing showed through where the fabric was thin. Where the fabric wasn't thin, it was stained, and wherever you sat on it, it was lumpy. I looked around: everything we owned was run-down and dirty and semi-broken. And nothing my mother might or might not do was going to change that.

As Angie and I passed the Bohack after school the next day, it occurred to me that I could work there. The week after we turned in our applications, the manager started us on the registers. Angie was no good at it, and only boys were allowed to stock shelves, but soon enough I was as fast as the old-timers: seventeen- and eighteen-year-olds who'd been at the grocery store for years but who, like me, had started out in ninth grade by lying about being sixteen. With my earnings and my employee discount, I could afford to buy things like Cheerios and butter and bottled salad dressing. I could take home free steak or pork chops or chicken that was at its sell-by date, which Lillian was perfectly happy to pan-fry until it became a chew toy but which I learned how to properly cook, an event I informed Kaja about via telepathic message, since our pen-and-paper correspondence had dried up. Afternoon shifts meant doing homework after dinner. This cut down on darkroom time, but from the red bell-bottoms I bought with my first paycheck to a life that wasn't all bologna and spaghetti and canned stew, the big difference between making contact sheets with Lillian and working the register at the Bohack was that one changed nothing, and the other changed everything.

JOURNAL ENTRY, NOVEMBER 1969: Squirrel, I've never gone through your backpack or purse or rummaged your drawers. I'll never know if you keep a diary under your pillow. Somehow respect for your privacy, along with your modesty after you became Jane, stopped me from asking questions. After forcing you to face so much, so young, the least I could do was not rush you into discussing something before you felt ready. And so I — who defied generations of prudish Methodists by explaining to you at a young age where babies came from, and why Mama bled once a month — told myself that when your time came, you would come to me.

This afternoon I looked out the window and saw a young woman carrying groceries. A few minutes later, when you arrived from your cashier shift with your Bohack bags (and smelling of the cigarettes you think I don't notice), I realized that the woman I'd just seen was you. At that moment, my mind's outdated images of you were cleared like sleep from the corners of my eyes. I launched into all the motherly questions I'd been saving, even as your face — along with the woman's body I'd somehow managed not to see until now — told me I was too late. You explained that everything had been "taken care of" in the embarrassed voice of a waiter who has spilled the soup, and I realized that I had failed us both.

Do you remember when I'd strap you into your stroller to explore the world? That was what I called it, and when you turned two, "expordewhirl" was one of your first words. I'm not usually nostalgic, but when I close my eyes, I picture you in your green sweater holding Lomo as if the stuffed monkey is your own fuzzy Leica, and I feel like I'm fighting a swift current.

97. Untitled [View from the apartment window], Brooklyn, 1970

From a vantage point of four floors up, it's impossible to tell if these three boys are playing or fighting: all we get are their bodies running down the middle of the street, as viewed from above. The one carrying the leafless sapling twice his size might be making off with a prize or improvising a weapon from what was at hand; the other two could just as easily be his advance guard or targets fleeing his attack. Traditionally, when winter hit, and all the good light came and went while Lillian was stuck behind a Wall Street typewriter, she became even more vigilant about weekend camera time. Hence my surprise one Saturday, when I woke up at my usual late hour to find her sitting on the couch and taking pictures through the window. Lillian asked if I wanted to go over contact sheets with her — like this wasn't something I'd quit months ago, after she'd told me about needing to give her work a chance to breathe — but I was meeting friends at the ice skating rink in the park. Who was I meeting? she wanted to know. Angie, I said, and a few girls from the store. My list was accurate, as far as it went, but left out Danny McAlister. Not because he was a boy, which I didn't think my mother would mind, but because he'd already graduated from high school, which I guessed that she would.

I don't know how many more Saturdays I woke up to my mother taking pictures through the window before it occurred to me to ask if something was wrong. She said she was just a little draggy, and supposed it was one of those colds that can be hard to shake, or maybe the dregs of the flu she'd had over Christmas. In retrospect, this should have triggered an internal alarm, but I had other things on my mind, like whether I should wear my blue skirt or my red pants to the movies, and if growing my hair out would make me look older. Angie thought it would, but Danny liked it short because he preferred a girl who stood out from the crowd.

LETTER TO DEBORAH BRODSKY, MARCH 1970: It's because I can remember being fifteen that Jane makes me feel so old. Fifteen was when I picked up a camera and felt the curtain of my life lifting. That feeling chimes every time an image spreads across a piece of photo paper but now, instead of being fifteen, I'm thirty-five. Before you laugh, I know perfectly well that thirty-five isn't old; but Deb, I'm so tired! I'm sure my tiredness comes partly from being in mourning. The darkroom hasn't felt this lonely since the summer I moved from East Sixth to Brooklyn Heights and left our darkroom hours behind. Having Jane with me reminded me how that small space expands in the right company. I know her new independence won't erase our shared time just as distance hasn't erased yours and mine, but that doesn't mean I'm not sad to see it end.

I thought I was ready for Jane's teenage self. Then I met her boyfriend and felt so dizzy I had to sit down. It's one thing to hear a boy's voice on the phone; it's another to see him at your front door. Jane hadn't told me he was older. He seems nice, but Deb, he's eighteen!

Between any two people, there is always an unbridgeable distance. I used to think basic biology meant that the gulf between me and Jane would be smaller than the one between you and Yuma. Now I know that isn't true. Son or daughter, your flesh can attain a shape so different from anything you could have imagined that the notion it was once inside you feels like a fairy tale.

98. Untitled [Child playing hopscotch], New York, 1970

A few weeks later, Lillian stayed in bed as I got ready for school — Lillian, who only ever took sick days to buy herself more camera time — and at the end of the afternoon, when I came back from Bohack's, she was still there. This went on for about a week before she made a doctor's appointment. Things seemed normal for a while after that. Could I bring home more steak? she wanted to know. The doctor said it would help. Then one Friday I came home to an empty apartment — unusual but not unheard of, since sometimes my mother got sidetracked on her walks home from work.

At this point Danny and I had passed the ten-week mark, which Angie and I agreed was the big time. During our Friday-night home-by-nine-thirty movie dates, Danny and I would start by sharing an armrest during the opening credits, then let our hands wander as we pretended to watch the movie; but after ten weeks of that, I was bored. Enter the Friday I got home from Bohack's and Lillian wasn't there. Looking back, I should have known that my mother took camera detours only in spring, when the light lasted longer, and not on the way home from work in winter, when the light was gone by four. Rather than worry, I got inspired. After putting away the groceries, I changed into my skirt and wrote a note that I was sleeping over at Angie's. I met Danny for a movie and didn't show up at Angie's until after midnight, just as *The Dick Cavett Show* was marking its halfway point with "Glitter and Be Gay." Arriving home the next morning to no Lillian, I figured she was out taking pictures. When the phone rang, I was so sure it would be Danny or Angie that for a second I didn't recognize my mother crying at the other end.

JOURNAL ENTRY, MARCH 1970: After the embarrassment of fainting and being brought to the emergency room like a nineteenth-century woman with the vapors, worrying about you distracted me from the blood draws, and the thick needle at the bottom of my spine, and the odd repeated questions: Had I ever inhaled a lot of benzene? Or swallowed a lot of aspirin? Or taken something called Chloromycetin? I asked if that was the same as Dexies. No, the doctors said as they inserted another, much thinner needle into my arm. My daughter doesn't know where I am, I told them. I called and called, but you didn't answer, and my worry reversed itself. I don't know where my daughter is, I told them. Was there someone I could send to the house, they asked, or a friend of my daughter's I could telephone? I didn't know Angie's telephone number. I even tried calling Grete, though it's been at least a year since we've spoken, but there was no answer there, either. I spent the rest of that night lying awake, dialing our number, and listening to it ring. At one point I dreamed I was gripping your skeleton and awoke to the phone in my hand — so that when I did reach you the next morning and learned you'd been with Angie after all, my relief overshadowed the doctor's diagnosis by the end of the following day. You are safe, and I have leukemia. Between that and its opposite, this is the option I would choose.

99. Untitled [Sleeping hospital patient], New York, 1970

Judging by the angle, Lillian must have been standing beside the bed, gazing down on a roommate, since she couldn't have practiced her usual photography-walk method as a Memorial inpatient. Surrounded by the whiteness of the bedsheets, the sleeping woman's head and one visible hand look like anatomical specimens, carefully laid out for inspection. That, plus Lillian's off-center placement, turns what could have been a peaceful image into something foreboding.

The first few days Lillian was in the hospital didn't feel that different for me, except for not having someone to say goodbye to in the morning, and no one answering back when I said things to the closed darkroom door as I watched television or did homework after Bohack's. My mother explained that since the cancer cells were only in her bone marrow, all she needed were a few transfusions to bring up her red blood cell count, and she'd be released from the hospital. I told her I was fine at home on my own. It sounded like she'd be let out pretty soon and, anyway, I was the one who cooked dinner and bought groceries, but Lillian didn't like that. Angie's mom didn't like me, so staying there was out. When Danny's mom called the hospital to say I was welcome to stay with them, I didn't think my mother would go for it, but she did. Angie said I was probably the only girl in South Brooklyn with permission to live with her boyfriend. She sounded so sure I lived a charmed life that I almost believed it.

By this point, I'd eaten so many times at Danny's house that living there didn't seem like too much of a stretch. The McAlisters said grace before every meal, and there was a crucifix in every room except the bathroom. Mrs. McAlister went to Mass every morning and was a light sleeper besides; after the third night, I gave up on the idea of Danny sneaking out of his room after everyone else was asleep. Mornings, I walked to school with Danny's brother and sister. Afternoons, we'd do homework together at the kitchen table after my Bohack's shift. Friday and Saturday nights, Danny and I had to be back from the movies by nine-thirty or face Mr. McAlister. Ironically this meant that during the two weeks I lived with Danny's family, we fooled around less than before; but our brief opportunities buzzed with the combined electricity of living like boyfriend and girlfriend and brother and sister all at once.

LETTER TO DEBORAH BRODSKY, APRIL 1970: I'd been blaming the aches, breathlessness, and tiredness on some sort of flu, but I should have known from my camera hand that something more was wrong. For the first time, it felt like deadweight. Even after the transfusions, that heavy feeling is still there. Though I haven't stopped taking pictures, snapping the shutter has become an empty reflex, like a hiccup or a sneeze. I know this should upset me, but that would require energy I do not have.

When I told Jane I had leukemia, she asked if I was going to die. I told her that in rare instances leukemia went away, that sometimes it could be staved off; and other times chemotherapy brought remission that lasted years. Deb, I've always prided myself on being honest, but I didn't see the point in giving Jane the numbers. That the majority of leukemics die from infections or pneumonia. That ninety-five percent who undergo chemotherapy die in two years. For the first time in my life, I understand the value of a partial truth.

I can't bring myself to inform my parents yet, but I telephoned Mr. Wythe straight away. Despite my not having been in touch for two years, he immediately wanted to know if there was anything he could do. "Is this how you treat all the girls?" I asked him. "Only the ones I represent," he told me.

100. Untitled [Leukemic woman putting on lipstick], New York, 1970

Because she's awake and her head's in three-quarter view instead of in profile, it takes some looking to realize this is the same hospital patient Lillian caught sleeping, but it makes sense, given the circumstances. I can't help thinking the parallels with *Makeup artist on the uptown train* and *Getting ready* are deliberate, but maybe applying lipstick requires the same absorption no matter whose mouth it is. Lillian never introduced me when I visited, so I don't think they were friends. That means either Lillian took this picture on the sly, or her hospital roommate was too sick to object.

When someone becomes ill in the movies, it's dramatic, but in real life it is incredibly boring. Even the guilt and the fear and the sadness become things you live with, such constant weights that, after a while, you stop feeling anything. I guess because of the way my mother and I lived together and apart, it was easier to forget that she was sick, or maybe I just didn't want to remember. Sometimes I didn't think of it until the afternoon. Sometimes I didn't think of it at all, and I'd jerk awake the next morning with the breath knocked out of me. When I called the hospital, it seemed like Lillian was asleep or getting treatment half the time, and the other half she'd ask about school and I'd ask about her blood cells, and then we'd both dumbly sit there holding the phone. Visiting the hospital after work was out because that meant riding the subway at night, so I'd wait for Saturday to take the train up to Sixty-third in Manhattan, then walk toward the river. It was weirdly clean and quiet up there. Old ladies in fur coats and pinched faces held small dogs and fancy-looking shopping bags as they teetered in and out of stupid-looking stores. I knew I didn't belong, and the old ladies knew that I knew it. I kept hoping one of them would ask what I was doing there so I could yell back that I was going to the hospital to visit my mother who had leukemia, and would they like me better if I was shopping for jeweled hairpins and miniature fruit? Except that none of them ever said anything to me, so each time I had to walk to the hospital without yelling at anyone.

Other than the IV that was feeding good blood cells into her arm, my mother just seemed pale and tired. At first I couldn't help wondering if the doctors were wrong and maybe she only had mono. Then she got a fever. The next time I visited, she told me they needed to put her on antibiotics. She hadn't told my grandparents that she was sick, but now she thought it was time. As she said it, I saw the dullness of her hair and eyes and how the skin of her face looked waxy and weird. I saw the boniness of her finger as it slowly turned the phone dial. I realized everything I'd been telling myself — that she was slowly getting better; that the doctors might have made a mistake — was wrong. Mama, she said in a voice I'd never heard before, speaking a name into the phone that she'd never used. Mama, I have bad news.

Grandma offered to come for a few weeks, but trying to picture my grandmother in South Brooklyn — walking down streets lined with trash and broken glass; passing buildings with boarded-up windows and stoops where junkies hung out; or just staying in the apartment she would hate even if I tried to clean it up — was like trying to picture a unicorn in Prospect Park. Tell Grandma to stay in Cleveland, I told Lillian; things at the McAlisters' were going fine. Next I rode the IRT back to Brooklyn. From the apartment, I called Mrs. McAlister and told her that I had just brought my mother home. Thanks so much for your hospitality, I said. Then I went into the bedroom and closed the door. The air was sour, and the sheets on both beds were stained. There were dishes with old uneaten food on both nightstands and on the floor. I leaned out the window as far as I could. The streetlights were broken, and it was a clear, cloudless night. I counted six stars.

LETTER TO DEBORAH BRODSKY, APRIL 1970: I'm glad to hear about all your changes. Leave it to Kyle to appear with such a perfect opportunity at such a perfect time. You're a natural teacher, and this college sounds very exciting — though I hope you won't think I'm a dummy if I'm still not sure what Transcendental Poetics is. I'm not at all surprised Yuma has settled in so easily. If his three-year-old self is anything like the baby I met, he'll have half the students wrapped around his little finger before the end of the first semester. I only ever glimpsed Arizona in scraps through the window during my cross-country bus trip to see you, but even then I was stunned by its beauty.

I write this using one arm while a tube delivers bright red hemoglobin to the other. Such a happy color in such a gray room, entering my gray body drop by drop, giving me back my desire to look, to read, to eat, to speak. The physical realities of being gravely ill are not a choice you get to make: your body simply gives up on certain things and there's nothing you can do about it. My coming to terms with the larger consequences of this disease has been a very different thing. Against all evidence, I'd continued to insist to myself that my recovery was only a matter of time. If not for Mr. Wythe's visit, I might have continued to think this until it was too late; however, with his help, I've formed a plan for Jane and for the future. While it wasn't easy, and I wish I hadn't needed to, it would have been much worse to risk leaving Jane with nothing.

After all I'd done with Mr. Wythe, telephoning my parents should have been easy, but I cried all the same. I'd always known I would let them back into my life at some point, only I'd pictured it happening in a hazy, distant future sparked by a change in Father's health, not my own.

Grete cried when I told her, which made me cry, too. It felt strangely good to cry together, not for my diagnosis but for our friendship, which we hadn't properly mourned. Jane is to call Grete whenever she likes, Grete's home is her home, sentiments Jane accepted like the echoes they are. And now I'm crying because I'm reading your description of when I was a new mother just home from the hospital, and you arrived at your apartment to the shaky note I'd taped to your door. Deb, I hope your goddaughter won't ever need a second family, but it is a great comfort to know that she has one with you.

101. Untitled [View from hospital roof], New York, 1970

At first Danny was nervous about coming over to my place after work, but I reminded him that we were safe: his mother thought my mother was home with me, and my mother was in the hospital. Besides, I told him, he was doing a good deed, keeping me company. I could tell that Danny sometimes just wanted to watch TV with his arm around my shoulder, talking during commercial breaks about his day at the store, or my day at school, or about what was happening with my mom; but that wasn't what I wanted at all.

By the weekend, the transfusions had given my mother more energy, and the antibiotics had started bringing her fever down. Assuming her blood count stayed good, she would come home by the end of the next week, as soon as the antibiotics were done. To celebrate, she and I rode the elevator to the hospital roof, where benches had been installed inside a sort of chain-link cage that let patients look out over the city without the hospital having to worry about anyone jumping off. Lillian adjusted the focal length of her lens to get a decent shot of the view. As she clicked away with her non-IV hand, I told her about Sister Elaine's eyes tearing up in U.S. History while she recited the Gettysburg Address, and about a man paying for his groceries with only nickels, and it felt almost like Before. Then Lillian turned to me. Listen, she said.

Instead of taking pictures, her camera hand was gripping my arm. It didn't feel like a sick person's hand.

When you're with Danny you have to be careful, she said. Diaphragms don't always work, and even if he says he has rubbers, that doesn't mean he'll put one on.

For a moment it seemed like everything — the clouds, the birds, the cars on the street way down below — was standing still. It couldn't have been quiet, but my mother's voice canceled out the other sounds. My heart started beating like when you're leaving a drugstore with a lipstick stashed in your pocket. A voice inside me said to deny everything, but my mother didn't look angry or disappointed. She didn't even look sick; she looked like a person telling the truth.

Angie's sister knows a clinic where you can get the Pill as long as you're sixteen, I said.

You're fifteen, Lillian said.

Angie's old enough, I said. She'll go for me if I ask.

Good, my mother said, and nodded. Her fingers on my arm weakened. Her face changed back into a sick person's face.

That night I stayed out drinking with Danny and his friends and woke the next morning from a blackout to him on my couch. Danny explained that he had wanted to take me back to his house to sleep it off, but I'd insisted on going home. Given the state I was in, he'd been afraid to leave me alone. He said it was a sign of how much he loved me, him staying the night, because when he went back home that morning there'd be hell to pay.

So don't go, I said. He was eighteen. He could tell his parents he was moving in with his cousin. For as long as my mother was in the hospital, we could be together all the time.

102. Untitled [Doctors conferring outside a curtained bed], New York, 1970

It's a safe bet this is the same hospital roommate, though all we see is her horizontal silhouette cast on the curtains blocking her bed from view. The doctors consulting their clipboards look concerned. As much as I've tried, I can't remember if that bed was empty when I went to visit my mother at Memorial for the last time.

Pretty soon Danny was inviting his friends to the apartment after work, and they'd stay until late. My mother's blood count hadn't stayed good, and one week stretched into two. Mornings, I'd oversleep and the place would be a mess, and my head would be killing me, so I'd stay home to empty ashtrays and wash dishes and clear out empties in time for everyone to come over again after my afternoon cashier shift. Maybe if I'd had Bohack's in the morning, like Danny, I'd have found a way to keep doing everything I was supposed to be doing, but I didn't see the point of being sleep-deprived and hungover just for school, not now that I was living real life. Playing hooky meant not seeing Angie, since she didn't like Danny's friends, but that wasn't a good enough reason to keep going.

Angie kept quiet about it, so it wasn't until

Danny's brother said something that Danny learned I was skipping school. Danny yelled, and that night he grabbed at me and insulted me in front of his friends. After everyone left, I told him I didn't like how he was acting, and he said it was my fault. Living like this was sinful, but I had made him want it, and now he couldn't stop. Each day he wanted me more, but it was lust, not love. I dragged a mattress into the living room, which was all old food and dirty dishes. I lay there thinking about my mother and the life I'd come to hate, trying to remember a time when things had been good. When I arrived at the grocery store the next afternoon, Danny gave me flowers. On break, he told me that as soon as I turned eighteen, we could get married.

Visiting hours were over by the time I arrived at the hospital that night, but the nurses let me see her anyway. Since I'd last been there, I knew everything had changed. My mother's skin was gray and her hair was dull. Her face was choked with pain and exhaustion and fear. She seemed to be using every ounce of her remaining strength to tell me that we were moving to Cleveland. She was going to need chemo: the latest test showed that the cancer was in her blood after all. Treatment was very expensive, and there was also me to think of. Next she started going on about Mr. Wythe: how wonderful he'd been, how grateful she was, and how important it was that she leave me with something. Did I understand? None of it made sense, but her voice was so urgent and her stare so desperate that I nodded and reached for her hand. Mama, I said. I love you so much, she said.

It was late by the time I got back on the subway, but I must have looked too crazy to mess with. Back at the apartment, I told Danny he had to leave. My mother was getting discharged, and she and I were moving to Ohio. After that Danny cried, and I cried, and he was tender with me in all the ways I'd always wanted him to be, but I couldn't feel a thing.

The next day I gave notice at Bohack's and got on the subway to bring my mother home. She was too weak to do any packing, so Danny came over to help while she issued instructions from the couch. The clothes I couldn't take on the plane, I packed into boxes along with all the books and hats and shoes and dishes and records, but the apartment was mostly film. Lillian had always kept her negatives in boxes, so we didn't have to do anything except stack them in one place, but it made me realize how invisible they'd always been, boxes of negatives piled in the corner of the living room, reaching up to the ceiling, lining her side of the bedroom and filling her closet, boxes stacked and pushed together to make night tables beside our beds. Then there were the prints and the darkroom equipment. It was way too much to fit into Danny's brother's Plymouth, but his cousin's uncle was in the moving business, and if we didn't mind waiting, he could use a slow period to borrow a truck. Another of Danny's cousins was in secondhand furniture; Danny would show our stuff to him to see if he couldn't get us something for it instead of pitching it to the curb. It was a long drive and a lot of lifting, my mother said. At the very least, Danny should keep whatever he could make off the furniture and she would pay him for the gas and for his time, but Danny said his reward for driving our stuff to Cleveland would be seeing me.

Packing up the apartment, I wanted to remember the birthdays and bad dreams and funny conversations and wiggly teeth and yelling and laughing and darkroom times before my mother got sick, but instead I saw the life I'd been living with Danny behind my mother's back. I was so mad at those memories for getting in the way that I didn't cry when Danny drove us to the airport in the borrowed Plymouth, or when he kissed me goodbye, or when I looked out the plane window to see New York getting smaller and smaller. I didn't cry until the clouds blotted out even the idea of Bohack's and Immaculate Heart and JHS 23 and PS 542 and Kaja's house and the Brooklyn Bridge. I didn't cry until there was nothing left to see.

CLEVELAND, 1970–76

103. Untitled [Walter Prescott driving], Detroit, 1970

JOURNAL ENTRY, AUGUST 1970: If I'd needed chemotherapy any earlier, I would have wanted to stay in New York; but these last nightmarish months of being truly sick taught me that you and I can't do this on our own. When I asked my doctors if I could be treated in Cleveland, I learned how much I took for granted a city where everything from camera lenses to first-rate leukemia treatment is only a subway ride away. Though the Cleveland Clinic is the top of the line for heart disease, the best leukemia facility in the Midwest is in Detroit; and so three years after I denied your wish, and under circumstances too macabre for anyone to enjoy, you are finally getting to live with your grandparents.

Your grandmother has become careworn

in the predictable ways, but I wasn't prepared for the gray, slow-moving figure beside her. I should have expected it — your grandfather isn't the sort to take early retirement unless he has to — but somehow that hadn't revised my mental picture of a man whose arm I used to hang from like a jungle gym. While I'm glad the hospital transfusions returned some color to my skin, I guess nothing could have prepared your grandparents for the rest of me. Both of them recovered quickly from how thin I've become, but that first look on their faces is something I won't forget.

For most of the three-hour drive west and north, your grandfather kept the radio loud enough to prevent much talking, giving me my first chance since I was seventeen to snap a decent picture of him; but as we neared Detroit, he turned off the music.

"Your mother didn't want me driving you," he told me. "If she had her way, I'd be splitting my waking hours between healthy walks, elevating my feet, and eating carrots, but when I told her I wanted us to talk, even she had to admit it was a good idea." He darted a glance at me before turning back to the road, and his face was soft where I'd been expecting something sharp. "It seems silly now," he said, "but I used to take it personally that at every turn, you seemed to make the choice I'd least approve of. If my heart attack taught me anything, it's that we're all a lot less important than we think. I still don't agree with most of the choices you've made in life, but I've come to see that who you are has precious little to do with me. I love you, Lilly. You're my daughter and I love you, and I'll do anything to help you beat this thing."

Squirrel, so far you've been lucky or canny or sneaky enough to stay in your grandfather's good graces, but that was the most he'd said to me since I'd refused to return to Ohio with him before you were born.

For all that, I didn't answer right away that I loved him back. Maybe that seems spiteful, or maybe your time with Danny has left you old enough to understand. "I love you too" is only ever an echo. I wanted to be sure my words were not just his bouncing back. I waited until the next morning, when he stopped at the hospital before his drive home to you and your grandmother in Cleveland. At first I wasn't sure he'd heard me. I was about to say those three words again when he blinked several times and lifted up his glasses with one hand to dab at his eyes. "It was the glasses that stopped me," he told me. "I've wanted to fly planes since I was a boy, even younger than when you started with cameras, but back then a pilot needed perfect vision. By the time that changed, well, I'd settled into a life — but sometimes I wonder what would have happened if I'd moved us all to Dayton and gone to flight school."

They mean well. They always have. Perhaps you already know that. Maybe you even suspect it of me, but considering my own belated insights, you're allowed to take your time.

The six weeks Lillian was in the hospital getting chemo, we visited Detroit six times. According to her doctors, she had a better than fifty percent chance at remission, and I guess that made my grandparents superstitious. Ordering dinner at the Howard Johnson's where we always stayed, I asked for a hamburger instead of the fried clam strip platter I'd gotten the last two trips, and Grandma flinched. Her voice shook as she asked if I was sure I didn't want the fried clams, since I always seemed to enjoy them so much. Until that moment, I'd thought it was just coincidence that we always stayed in the same room, and that Grandpa always picked the same restaurant booth for us to sit in, and that he always ordered the steak while Grandma got chicken. Now it occurred to me that a better than fifty percent chance of remission meant an almost fifty percent chance of dying. I ordered the fried clams.

For chemo not to kill you before it cured you, it couldn't happen all at once: after being on it for a few days, my mother had to go off it to give her body a chance to recover. I could measure how good or bad a week she'd had by how many film canisters were on her bedside table. She seemed in slightly better shape during recovery phases, but either way, we had to wear face masks and couldn't touch her, since her immune system was shot. The chemo had knocked out her white blood cells along with the cancer cells, it being a poison that couldn't tell the difference.

It seemed significant the city that had been Kaja's home for the last year and a half was now also the location of my mother's leukemia treatment. The first three car trips, I kept my face glued to the window as soon as we hit Detroit's city limits, convinced that spotting Kaja was just a matter of hypervigilance. When that failed, I told Grandpa Kaja's address. He calculated that she lived only five miles from the hospital, and my confidence in fate was restored. Before I'd left Brooklyn, I'd written to say I was moving to Cleveland and that Lillian was sick, but I was still waiting for a reply. The force of my longing when I asked Grandpa if we could make a surprise visit must have been impressive, because as we were leaving Detroit, he told Grandma to make a detour.

Around the hospital were a few nice buildings that might have been mansions once, but toward Kaja's neighborhood, those were replaced by crumbling row houses. After driving down a wide, empty street lined with vacant lots and the occasional building, we turned onto a smaller street with regular houses like the ones in my grandparents' part of Cleveland. People were on sidewalks and porches, and kids rode bicycles like in any other normal neighborhood, except that suddenly my grandparents were locking their car doors and telling me to lock mine. When Grandma started driving slower, I figured we were almost there. Then she said in a scared, shaky voice that she was going to turn around and pulled a U-ey in the middle of the street. Grandpa told me he was sorry, but we needed to go back. What was wrong? I wanted to know. It wasn't my friend they were worried about, Grandpa explained; but in a dark neighborhood like this one, my grandmother continued as if she and my grandfather had merged into one ugly person, it was better to be safe than sorry.

104. Untitled [Dorothy Prescott holding a breakfast tray], Cleveland, 1970

Looking at Grandma Dot's face as she walks through that doorway, I want to stroke the side of her wrinkled cheek, smooth the bent collar of her dress, and tuck the stray strand of hair back behind her left ear. Did my mother transmit her tenderness for this complicated, contradictory person in the moment when she snapped the shutter; or did it happen in the darkroom, as she finessed the print's lines and curves, darks and lights? Then again, maybe those are my own feelings being tapped. For the eleven years between my mother's death and Grandma Dot's, my grandmother scrupulously opened and closed doors and windows to keep the room containing Lillian's three-box legacy and voluminous collection of negatives at the proper temperature. Grandma told me that my mother had left me "some things" I could have when I was ready, but for eleven years I didn't ask what they were, and she didn't say. At first I was too full of sadness and anger, guilt and regret to want to know. Next I told myself I was too busy, because that sounded better than admitting I was afraid. Then Grandma died, and it was time to claim the things whether I felt ready or not. I walked up the stairs of the empty house on Fernvale and into my mother's old room. Seeing those boxes waiting for me was like getting one last message from them both: my mother had left me a way to show her my love, and my grandmother had safeguarded that opportunity, an opportunity I was sure I had squandered.

Two weeks before Lillian was released from the hospital, Danny and his cousin pulled up in front of my grandparents' house. I knew he was coming because he'd said so in his last letter, the fourth I'd received since leaving New York, and the fourth I'd read without writing back. While his cousin stared from inside the cab of the moving truck, Danny came to the door to tell me they wouldn't stay unless I answered the question he'd asked me four times. I looked down at the gold circle sitting on Danny's palm, then back up to his face. My expression must have told him what he needed to know: before I said a word, he walked back to the cab. Less than an hour later, the two of them had transferred all the boxes to my grandparents' garage. They refused my grandmother's offer of dinner and a place to stay the night; instead of heading back the next morning, they would hit the road and drive straight through. As they pulled away, Danny threw something small out the window that arced through the air and landed across the street in a bush. My Brooklyn life seemed like it belonged to another version of myself who still lived in New York, while the Cleveland version of me had been here all along, eating Grandma's food and sleeping between her cool, clean sheets. Somehow I had slipped out of one life and into the other like hopping trains.

LETTER TO DEBORAH BRODSKY, SEPTEMBER 1970: It's so strange to think that after sixteen years, a single phone call, and you've finally "met" my mother. You'll be amused to know she thinks you're lovely; she was surprised Father had formed such a low opinion of you during his one brief visit to New York. Of course, she said, people do change with time, and how remarkable that you and I have remained such good friends over the years. But really, I'm being unfair to her, which shows how much better I'm feeling. Until this week I didn't have the energy to hold an opinion, not to mention a pen. While I acknowledge that the chemotherapy deserves much of the credit for my improvement, your phone calls were crucial medicine. I tried to seem strong when Jane and my parents visited, but whenever the phone rang, it was a relief knowing I could close my eyes and surrender to your voice as you read me a poem, or told me a funny story about Yuma, or held your handset out the window so I could hear the silence of the Sonoran Desert at night.

I'm writing you from my childhood bed. Beside me is a bucket so that I only have to turn my head to vomit, but these days I'm eating more and vomiting less. When I stroke my head, I can feel the hair beginning to grow back. For the past two weeks, Mother has been my cook and my nurse, my laundress and my personal maid. She jokes that I'm a shamming little girl who doesn't want to go to school, but her words are undone by her eyes.

Along with the notebooks and yearbooks and photo albums above my childhood desk is a newer blue scrapbook that I wouldn't have noticed if I weren't stuck in bed. Yesterday I made a foray to my desk to pull it off the shelf. The clippings are chronological, from the first local newspaper articles to the later magazines, with highlighted *TV Guide* listings to document the television news segments. Each clipping has been cut out with immaculate care, centered on its page, and dated in Mother's precise handwriting. When Mother came in and saw the scrapbook open, she asked if I'd made one of my own. On the contrary, I told her. I'd done everything I could to keep Jane and me apart from all that. Well, this one wasn't complete, since it was only Cleveland and the national publications, but it was mine if I wanted it. She'd made it for me.

The world shrinks so much when you're sick! To a person whose life consists of sleep, meals, medicine, and blood tests, your letter may as well describe a distant planet. It's funny, but my first thought was to tell you to move — as if living farther away from all those missile silos would make any difference should the Soviets decide to blow us all to bits. As for how the police treated you, I can name one little boy who must have been thrilled when his mother was released so quickly. I can't imagine that the students who were jailed overnight begrudged you for it. Just because you're no longer a Poetical putting on weekly protest performances in Buena Vista Park doesn't mean you're "playing" at activism any more than you're "playing" at being a poet or a mother, though it's true that life divides us into smaller and smaller pieces as we go, until each piece seems too small to do anything as worthwhile with it as we'd like.

105. Self-portrait without hair, Cleveland, 1970

Even the meticulous blacks, grays, and whites of Lillian's print don't show how, after a month at home, her skin is still that weird orangey chemo color, but the picture is jarring enough as is. A bald woman in a high-necked nightgown sits at a wooden desk chair in a suburban bedroom meant for a teenager, the outline of her skull too visible beneath a face that stares at the camera without expectation, a face resigned to waiting. Lillian had come back a week into the school year and Grandma was the one taking care of her, so I saw my mother only when I wanted to, which wasn't often. After all, I reminded myself whenever I started feeling guilty or neglectful, there was so much studying to do.

I know I did well that fall at St. Margaret's because it was the first and last time I made honor roll, but I can't name my classes or teachers except for Drama with Sister Theresa. I didn't make many friends. By tenth grade, there were too many in-jokes and shared histories, and I figured it was just a matter of time before I moved back to Brooklyn. Besides, the guys my age all looked like boys to me, though sometimes some random blue-chinoed St. Vincent's upperclassman would cross my path, and the smell of English Leather would revive my Brooklyn self. The longer I stayed in Cleveland, the more that self scared me. Studying felt like the opposite of that person, distanced me from Brooklyn and Cleveland at the same time, all those quadratic equations and articles of the Constitution making less room in my brain for everything else.

One day I came home from school, and instead of being in her bedroom, my mother was in the living room. Tears were running down Grandma's cheeks. I wanted to get out of that room so bad, only I couldn't, because my mother was talking to me; but all I could see was her mouth moving. The alarm going off in my head had blocked out the words. Then I heard her say "remission," and I saw that Grandma was smiling as she cried. I walked to the couch. I laid my head in my mother's lap, and she stroked my hair. When I started crying, my mother started crying, too, along with Grandpa, until we were all happy-crying together. Then Lillian explained how half of all leukemia patients got sick again after less than a year, and almost all the rest relapsed after less than two. Remission didn't mean better forever; it just meant better for now. My mother wanted me to know that we weren't going back to Brooklyn, because when — not if — she got sick next, she'd have to do Detroit and chemo and orange skin and barfing and almost fifty percent chance of dying all over again.

After that, I started watching myself like I was the star of my own nature show: "Here is the cancer victim's daughter doing homework; here is the cancer victim's daughter playing cards with the cancer victim's father, who is also ill; here is the cancer victim's daughter going for a walk." Walking was the one thing besides studying that calmed my brain. A few blocks from St. Margaret's was a drugstore and a diner where the girls I wasn't making friends with went after school. A few more streets over was the coffeehouse they avoided because it kept screwy hours and its owner was a weirdo. The pariah café was all tables and chairs and lamps that looked like they'd come from yard sales. After Lillian went into remission, I did my homework there because the furniture reminded me of our Brooklyn apartment. For an hour or so between the end of St. Margaret's and closing time at the café, it was nice to sit somewhere that wasn't school or the guest bedroom. And that's how I ended up meeting the best photographer no one ever heard of.

SAM DECKER: Growing up, the storefront was Anderssen's Shoes. An Anderssen was selling shoes there when my great-grandfather won the building in a poker game, and by my time, an Anderssen was still at it. If someone from back then had told me I'd be running a café there one day, I'd have looked at him slantwise and told him it would always be Anderssen's store on the bottom and Meemaw's apartment on top. Every day after school, I'd rocket those stairs to her waiting for me with a slice of fresh-baked bread. Meemaw wanted a college boy. I would have been first in the family, but I decided the army was my ticket to making it famous in photography. When I was a kid, *Life* magazine was all glossy pics of soldiers in uniform, the storming of the beaches. I wanted to be Robert Capa the way my pals wanted to be Joe DiMaggio. For my ninth birthday, Meemaw got me a subscription so I'd stop tearing out pages at the library. I got a Kodak Brownie the year after that. By fifteen, I'd saved enough for a beat-up secondhand Contax, which was the rig Capa used at Normandy.

I was halfway through high school when Korea came. I kept hoping it'd last long enough for me to join up, and then it did. Meemaw told me over and over how Capa and all the rest went to war as photojournalists, not soldiers. At seventeen, I wasn't about to let that hold me back, even though I should have. Turns out you can't shoot a camera and a gun at the same time, unless you want to do a half-assed job at both.

Sam's Café has never been big with the high school crowd. I just play jazz. I don't serve pop. In winter I close up too soon after school lets out to be any use, and that's fine by me. I'm not running my place for them. Every now and then some kid will come anyways, and that's how it started: with a St. Margaret's girl, sitting in the corner beside the beaded lamp beneath the eight-by-ten of the park bench. I could've sworn I'd seen her before. I figured she belonged to somebody from the neighborhood who knew the score, because whenever I flashed the lights and called, Time, she packed up and headed out without a peep. Then it got to be January. It was maybe three-thirty and I was flashing the lights. She came over and asked me how come. I told her golden hour, same as any other day. She thought for a minute, then asked was I a photographer. That made me wonder if she was local after all. She wasn't, she said, but her mom was, and happened to be a photographer, too. The girl pointed at the walls. Were those all mine? I had to get out to catch the light, but I said we could talk tomorrow. The next day she sat near the counter. She told me she and her mom had moved from Brooklyn. She liked that I did trees and buildings and fences, no people: it was the opposite of what her mom did, but she bet her mom would like my stuff. I explained how the inanimate objects were just backdrop. I take pictures of light, which human subjects are no good for. No one looks at a photograph with a tree in it and wonders about its name or where's it going. That's how I get people to see what I want them to see.

The girl came Monday through Friday, always peppermint tea and raisin toast. Then one weekend she showed up with a lady who was a version of her twenty years down the line. The whole time I was fixing their order, the skin on the back of my neck was prickling. When I turned around, the older one was staring straight at me. I served their drinks like I didn't notice, but the older one, still staring, said, Sam Decker? Well, it's a good thing I'd put down those mugs, or I'd have spilled all over the place. Who's asking? I wanted to know. The older one said, I'm the quiet girl with the bangs.

JOURNAL ENTRY, MARCH 1971: At first I didn't know why I was staring. Then he moved from the counter to where we were sitting, in the same way a certain someone walked from his desk to the front of Mr. Clark's classroom, and I knew. I knew, but I waited because it seemed too strange, even though this was the neighborhood where we'd grown up, in a place called Sam's, its walls covered in photographs. It's funny to think those things didn't come together in my mind until I saw Sam Decker leading with his shoulders as he walked.

When I said his name, your face went blank. Then your mouth dropped open. You'd invited me here because you thought I might like to meet a local photographer. "This is *him*?" you asked, and turned. "You're the guy in my mom's high school photo?" Sam backed away. "I never sent any photos," he said. He moved to the light switch and started flicking the lights. "Closing time," he announced to the room, though it was barely one in the afternoon. "I said closing time," he yelled when his patrons complained it was too early.

Squirrel, he was so old! For almost twenty years, I'd been picturing Sam Decker at seventeen. I'd so completely given up on seeing him again that his memory had turned from something painful into something like a favorite toy from childhood, broken but still on its shelf. When that memory was replaced by this ramshackle man approaching our table, my first instinct was to wish I hadn't come.

After the last of his customers had left, he returned to our table. "I read about you," he said to me. "It was hard just going by the pictures in the papers, but I decided there couldn't be more than one Lilly Preston." He smiled and shook his head. "And here you are. Sitting beneath the blue lamp." Then he nodded at you. "That must make you Samantha."

"My name is Jane," you said, giving me such a fierce look that I could feel its heat beneath my skin. "You named me after him, didn't you?" you accused, pushing your chair from the table. Sweetheart, will you believe me when I say that, until that moment, I didn't realize I had? Meanwhile, you started talking to him as if I weren't there. "She told me she only knew you in high school. She always said my father was some guy named Charles." You practically spat the name.

Sam held up his hands. "I'm not anyone's old man," he said. "Lilly and I just wrote a bunch of times back when I was in Korea, that's all." He turned to me. "Look, I'm sorry. I can probably guess how all that made you feel, but by the time the army was done with me, you wouldn't have wanted to know me anyhow." He stared at my face and his voice became soft. "Eight seventy-four Fernvale Road, East Cleveland, Ohio, 44112." For a split second, he didn't look old. "If it's anything to you," he said, "I've got a darkroom I only use nights. If you're not fixed for a space yet, you can use it days, if you want." Before I could answer, Jane had led me out the door and I was standing on the sidewalk still holding my tea. All of which is to say that I'd have replied to your questions if I'd known the answers, but Squirrel, the truth is that I never really knew Sam at all.

106. Lionel Jr. walking his dog, Cleveland, 1971

SAM DECKER: I didn't think she'd actually take me up on it. I figure a famous photographer like her already has a setup, but apparently she is living with her parents and had been sick without the chance to do much of anything. The very next morning she shows up and orders a chamomile. Even I'm not a big enough jerk to welch on her again all these years later, so I hand over my key. Before I'm done with the next order, she's history. Doesn't reappear until closing time, hands me back the key, and she's gone. It's like this the next few days before it hits me she's as allergic talking to me as I am to her. I start leaving the key inside an empty sugar bowl beside the mugs. Busy mornings, I don't even know she's come until I look in the bowl. Afternoons, she's either waiting until my back is turned, or that key is magically reappearing on its own.

There's no sign of her when I get to my darkroom each night. She doesn't leave her prints lying around, puts everything back the way it was. Meanwhile, the girl hasn't been coming by, so the first time I leave a note just to make sure the kid's all right. The next night, there's a note where I left mine, in handwriting I haven't seen in twenty years. My heart starts pounding like it's mail call after four weeks of night duty on Termite Hill, Lilly's last letter rubbed to pieces in my pocket, the memorized bits looping in my head to block out the sound of the Chinese. It's so real, that feeling. Then it's just me in the darkroom again with Lilly's note, so I pick up a pencil and I write her one back.

LETTER TO DEBORAH BRODSKY, APRIL 1971: It was three weeks before we had a proper conversation, and then we were clumsy because we were so used to paper. The whole building — the storefront plus the apartment above — had belonged to his grandmother, who left it to him. Once he mentioned this "saving" him in a way that made his voice shake, but mostly, we talk about our work. When Sam and I discuss photography, we understand each other in the same bone-deep way that you and I do when we talk about almost anything. When I was seventeen, I confused that feeling for love, but it's more durable than that.

I wouldn't have recognized him from his work. The photographer I'd known liked action: people driving or running or playing or fighting. I remember a shot of two boys duking it out inside a circle of onlookers that's as good as any photograph I've ever taken — except Sam is a different photographer now. I've never been keen on cityscapes, but I like his trash cans and buildings and sidewalks and park benches better than most. They feel alive even though there's nothing in them that's living. Sam insists the life comes from the light. I can practically hear Mr. Wythe calling him the urban answer to the landscape photographers of the Great American West, but Sam isn't interested in the likes of Mr. Wythe, or in showing his work anywhere other than the café. Sam is a different photographer now.

I'm finally working again, which means I've been well enough for long enough to get up each morning without first wondering if I'll be able to get out of bed. To mindlessly dress, eat breakfast, and ride the bus downtown are daily miracles I hope you'll never appreciate. According to the numbers, I know that in the next six months I may get sick again, but the numbers only come to mind every other week when I go downtown for my blood test and booster shot. It's much nicer to measure my health by Jane, who can look me in the eye again because she's no longer afraid of what she'll see.

Jane is so used to taking care of herself that most days I feel more like her roommate than her mother, so I was surprised when she asked my permission to be in the school play. Of course you can be in the play, I said. Did you think I'd say otherwise? No, she told me, but she liked having me there to ask.

The end of the summer after my junior year, Lillian rented the top floor of a house on a street my grandparents thought was too dangerous and didn't like to visit. Next door was Mrs. Bauer, an ancient white lady who, as far as I could tell, never went past her front porch; and downstairs from us were the Osbournes, a black family with a baby and three kids in elementary school. Sandra, Shirley, and Lionel Jr. were always well dressed, their shirts and dresses ironed, their hair perfect, following their mother in a careful line each morning as she walked them to school, Lionel Jr. pulling a stuffed dog behind him on a string. The week we moved in, Mrs. Osbourne came to our door with a sweet-potato pie. My mother returned the tin clean, with the photo of Lionel Jr. After that, those kids weren't shy with us anymore. Our side of the neighborhood was shabbier than my grandparents', but birds built nests in the tree outside my window, and I could smoke. The traffic from I-490 was far enough away to sound like the ocean, and the houses that mysteriously burned down after their owners moved to the suburbs were mostly on the other side of the highway.

A few weeks after we moved, a postcard was waiting for me on Grandma's end table when Lillian and I came for Sunday dinner. On the front was an announcement for a Chambers Brothers show, and on the back was: *Dear Jane, Guess what? We're moving to Liberia! Wish me luck. I'll miss you. Peace, Kaja.* According to my grandparents' *Compton's Pictured Encyclopedia,* Liberia was "an independent Negro republic on the west coast of Africa." I tried to convince myself that the postcard was a good sign; if Kaja wrote once, she'd write again. She'd have to: the postcard didn't include a Liberian address.

When Lillian started going to the coffeehouse in her spare time, I half wondered if I was going to wake up one morning to Sam serving me chamomile in my own kitchen, but that kind of thinking wasn't very serious. Any time that Lillian was spending with Sam in the dark wasn't happening in a bedroom. I'd liked Sam and his café when they'd been personal discoveries, but learning that I'd been named for the guy was enough to make me steer clear until my mother's show there my senior year.

Avoiding the café would have been harder without the school play. Sister Theresa's drama class was filled with girls who'd been putting in their time, slowly rising up the ranks from Bystander to Girl 1, waiting for their shot at meatier roles as upperclassmen. I wouldn't have bothered to audition if Sister Theresa hadn't told me to. Tammy Lyons — who was semi-famous for having landed Aunt Ev in *The Miracle Worker* when she was just a sophomore — informed me not to expect anything more from *Our Town* than People of the Town or, at most, Constable Warren. When I got Emily Webb, Tammy said that Sister Theresa was only taking pity on the new kid, but by senior year, when I beat Tammy out for Abigail in *The Crucible,* she admitted that I deserved it. Being onstage felt like nothing I'd felt before. Once I'd digested a part — not just memorized the words but absorbed them so I didn't have to think about what to say any more than I had to think about how to breathe — being inside the play was like being inside a chrysalis that broke open for the first time every time the curtain went up. I felt a clarity that didn't exist for me anywhere else. I gave myself up to the role, and the rest disappeared — the stage, the audience, the world beyond the play — life fully concentrated and contained in each moment flowing inevitably into the next. When the curtain came down on my final performance of my final year and Tammy whispered, Now what?, I knew I was going to California.

107. Exhibition announcement, "*Life Divided,* Photographs by Lillian Preston, Sam's Café, March 17, 1973," with reproductions of *Untitled* [*Child playing hopscotch*] and *Untitled* [*Leukemic woman putting on lipstick*]

SAM DECKER: I'd never wanted company in the darkroom before. Even back in high school, I'd show up at weird hours just to have things to myself, but one day when Lilly brought the key back, the invitation just popped out. I must have asked on instinct, since it sure wasn't something I'd planned, but when it comes to photography, my instincts have always been good. Everything I've always liked about my solitude — the quiet, the focus, the order — got stronger with Lilly there. My eye got sharper. Nights with Lilly, I was my best working self.

JOURNAL ENTRY, MARCH 1973: Choosing images meant sorting through the Brooklyn prints. Though it felt too silly to say out loud, I was curious to see if the photos might have gotten sick along with me, in some intangible way, so I began with the prints we'd made before I started feeling ill. Seeing all those pictures reminded me how much fun we'd had. I could tell you were a natural the first time we came out of the darkroom and you were astonished that three hours had come and gone. Right away you saw the magic in freezing a passing moment — a playing girl, a crowded sidewalk — to reveal its truths. But for me, the bigger magic was getting to have you and photography at the same time.

It's hard to explain what it's like in the darkroom with Sam. It's not the same as being there with you or with Deb. When Sam and I are working, the quality of the silence between us is electric. At any given moment, I can sense what he's doing; it feeds my own work in ways that are difficult to describe. I quit my pills years ago, but sometimes the two of us stay up all night developing prints, powered only by each other's company — until Sam's clock rings for him to catch the sunrise, and I rush off to be home in time for breakfast with you.

Sam's idea to alternate hospital photos with street shots was so much better than giving a wall to each, I was embarrassed that I hadn't thought of it myself. Combining them this way erases the separation that the outside world imposes between sick and well. But Squirrel, it feels so odd showing portraits of your grandparents when I have none of you! Of all the photos I've taken with my mental camera, moments captured and then stored in my memory, the one I love most is from last spring in the backstage dressing room long after the final curtain call: you are still in your Emily costume, your Emily makeup half removed, your eyes ablaze, your face caught between the world you're leaving and the world you are returning to.

I could tell you were disappointed that none of the prints we made were in the show. You wouldn't admit it, wouldn't even acknowledge the question when I pulled you aside to ask. Since you wouldn't let me explain then, I'll explain now: one day those beautiful images will be seen, but when I discovered that my silly idea about sick photos was correct, this show fell into place. I hadn't noticed I'd stopped writing titles until I looked through the work all at once. My titles only ever supply a general description (a strong image shouldn't need more than that), but when I was sick, even that became a burden.

Selfishly, I'm glad you were there, disappointed or not. Without you to guide your grandparents, I'm sure they would have stayed at that wobbly table in their best church clothes, nervously sipping tea from one of Sam's chipped mugs while darting shy glances at the walls. It was so strange and lovely to see them holding hands as they moved between photographs, these two private people who rarely touch at home and never in public. Thank you.

I know that their willingness to come to the café should have been enough, but I was hoping for more than a polite "nice" from behind their Sunday-church smiles. And so, Squirrel, I suppose this show disappointed you and me both. What I want from your grandparents is as childish and unrealistic as a girl wishing her cat were a pony, but that doesn't stop me from wanting it anyway.

You're cleverer than I was, or maybe you just love your grandparents too much to hurt them the way I did at your age, when I boarded an eastbound bus. Holy Mount is perhaps the one college in Los Angeles they would approve of; but you must have known that, because it was your idea and your plan, presented to them in your politest voice at Sunday dinner. Just because you knew they were the ones you needed to convince, don't be fooled into thinking any of this is easy for me! Being left behind feels very different from leaving.

Holy Mount was the only college in Los Angeles that the St. Margaret's guidance counselor had a catalog for. Besides, my GPA was too erratic to get me into a school anyone had heard of, or to make me scholarship material, so it was a part-time job and what Lillian called "our nest egg," which I assumed was money my grandparents had given her to help us out, though when I thanked them, they swore there was nothing to thank them for.

I kept waiting for someone to point out that Holy Mount meant my being two thousand miles away whenever my mother's cancer came back. My grandparents couldn't have discussed that any more than they could have let me order a hamburger instead of fried clams in the bad old chemo days. I knew that Lillian would never keep me from doing whatever I wanted to do. If anyone was going to bring up those two thousand miles, it would have to be me, and I didn't feel like it. My mother had found a typing job. She was taking pictures and working in the darkroom the way she used to. There was always the chance she'd beaten the odds and wouldn't get sick again, or at least not for a long time. I still think heading out west was the right decision. When the time came to be there for my mother, the problem wasn't the distance between California and Ohio: the problem was me.

108. Father's feet, Cleveland, 1974

The last time I saw him alive, I saw him in his recliner, his feet covered in blankets, so I never knew. Here, the ankles are gone, swallowed by swelling, the toes tiny in comparison. He didn't want me to see that. He wouldn't have wanted anyone to see that, yet he took off the blankets for my mother and let her frame those feet the way another photographer would frame a face. He did it because she asked, and because she was his daughter.

Meanwhile, I was in the land of lemon and orange trees, and people grocery shopping in flip-flops, and finger-sized lizards sunning themselves on curbs. A woman in a halter top and hot pants roller skating down the sidewalk wasn't noticed any more than a man reading a newspaper. It all felt like freedom, like Los Angeles was busy being itself and didn't care what anybody else thought.

Holy Mount had the trees and the basking anoles, but it also had a dress code and course requirements and a dishwashing job after lunch and dinner in the dining hall six days a week. Almost every other student was local, or at least from California, and had a car. My second week there, I bought a secondhand bike. It was lime green with a shopping basket and a banana seat, and riding it reminded me of summers in Cleveland before Grandpa's heart gave out.

Most of the girls in my dorm wore ironed blouses and demure earrings and talked about wanting to get a good husband *and* a good education, like that was something radical. When I complained about spraying spaghetti off plates Monday through Saturday, they joked I could always "go to Clyde," which one of them finally explained was the art school a mile away that hired live models for its life-drawing classes but required posing "in the buff." When I asked if any of them had done it, they looked at me like I was asking if they'd screwed the pope.

The life drawing classes at Clyde School of Art occupied a room that was all dark wood and vaulted ceiling and mullioned window, with fifteen easels arranged in a wide circle. I had to stand still for thirty minutes at a time, while thirteen men and two women drew me from every angle. I went back and forth between feeling like an animal being inspected and feeling like a bowl of fruit. I wasn't crazy about either, not to mention that holding a pose got uncomfortable fast, but it definitely beat washing dishes. Plus, since my body was my instrument, wasn't this the acting equivalent of a musician logging scales? As a model, I had to be in complete control of my arms, my legs, my face; I had to banish my insecurities; I had to empty myself out and become a living lesson in contour and form. Also, I was good at it. In a previous life, in a previous body, I'd done a version of this before.

LETTER TO DEBORAH BRODSKY, APRIL 1974: It was as if he was keeping up appearances for Jane's sake, because as soon as she left for school, he went downhill fast. Mother stuck to their usual routines as if nothing untoward were happening, but she couldn't keep the fear from her eyes. By Jane's Easter visit, Father's feet were too swollen for shoes and he could hardly eat, but his face relaxed whenever she spoke. "Do you still want to be an actress?" he asked. When she nodded, he grinned. "I know better than to get in the way of a Preston girl who knows what she wants," he said, "but for your mother's and grandmother's sakes, I wish California wasn't so far." "What about you, Grandpa?" Jane teased. "Oh, I don't count myself," he said. "When you're in the next room, it's too far for me." Their love for each other is astonishingly uncomplicated. I know how hard that simplicity is on Jane. I know it comes from only showing her grandfather the parts of her he can find easy to love, but I'm jealous anyway. It's hard to describe how she changes. A drawing inward, a slight dimming of her light. She's been doing it for so long I'm not sure she notices anymore, but I'll never get used to watching part of her go away and feeling torn between sadness and awe that she does it so often or so well.

Father went into the hospital two days after Jane flew back to California. He died five days after that. He was only fifty-nine, but being sick for so long had made him seem much older. On my last visit, I held his hand and told him for the second time in my life that I loved him. His eyes were closed, but he squeezed my fingers. I was afraid I wouldn't cry at the funeral because the hospital had felt so final, but when I saw all those people at the church, the tears I thought I'd used up came right back. I'd been expecting a small service, since Father's world had shrunk so much in the past five years, but along with everyone from church, there were his coworkers from the insurance office and his pals from the model-airplane club. People I'd never seen before came up to me like they'd known me all my life. He was so proud, they told me, that I'd worked for a Wall Street firm in the Big Apple. He was so proud, they said, when I bounced back from my illness. Thank you, I told them, thinking of the film in the camera I was holding in my hand, a camera that went unmentioned. Exposed film is all I have of him now. My father has been reduced to imprints of light.

When Mother told me that Father had asked God to take him instead of me, and that my remission helped him to find peace, the way she said it made me stop what I was doing. I asked what she thought about that. "A compassionate God wouldn't make that kind of bargain with a good man, and your father was a good man," she said. She didn't sound sad or angry, just matter-of-fact. This startled me. When Father was alive, it had been easy, or perhaps just convenient, to underestimate her.

I want Mother to have plenty of time to settle into her new life before I think about leaving Cleveland, but the second page of your letter gave me my first real smile since Father's death. Deb, whenever I've pictured myself old (something I've only recently started doing again), I've pictured you nearby. Think of all the darkroom chats, the long walks for poetry and photographs! But there's no reason to wait until we're old. I haven't seen Yuma since he was a baby. From Arizona, Jane in California is just a bus ride away.

As for teaching, a fellow from the Art Institute has invited me to teach in the photography department here. But really, the timing couldn't be better, because this will allow me to come to you and the Desert School with a year of experience under my belt and not just as your friend.

SAM DECKER: I told Lilly I had nothing to do with the guy from the Art Institute, but she kept thanking me anyhow. The only people I know are my customers; I don't bother with anyone else. Sometimes some dope will buttonhole me when I'm out shooting, but no one's got any business talking to me then.

Lilly was plenty nervous, so she decided to practice her lectures on me. Back in Korea, I'd tried making a voice for her in my head whenever I read the letters she sent, but it always ended up sounding like Meemaw. Some of what Lilly was saying now brought back pieces of her old letters. Even then she'd been trying to turn her ideas about photography into something solid. "The palm of the light" is one phrase I remember, as in you've got to put yourself in the palm of the light's hand. When I read that back in Korea, it felt like Lilly was putting words to something that had been inside my own head for a long time, knocking around waiting for a name.

109. Portrait of her absence (closed bedroom door with packed suitcase), Cleveland, 1974

LETTER TO DEBORAH BRODSKY, DECEMBER 1974: I wish I could say Christmas went well, but Jane was distant and distracted the minute she stepped off the plane. Poor Mother thought it meant she hadn't given Jane a warm enough welcome, but all it really means is that Jane has turned into a selfish drip. With Father gone, she doesn't hide her smoking, and while I used to worry about how much of herself she kept hidden, now she seems to be going out of her way to make her grandmother as uncomfortable as possible — or, worse, she isn't thinking of her grandmother at all. Jane waited until she arrived to announce that she'd become a vegetarian, which meant she wouldn't eat most of what Mother had cooked. I've been working steadily since the café show; I was looking forward to asking her into the darkroom with me like old times, until Mother offered to take her shopping and she giggled. "That's okay, Dot," she said, as if her grandmother had made a joke. I realized that this Jane was not someone I wanted to share a darkroom with.

I'd thought I was doing Sam a favor, inviting him to Christmas dinner, but really it was the other way around. What he said about Mother's cooking almost made up for Jane not eating it. He distracted us from Jane's behavior and Father's absence with stories of Christmas with his grandmother when he was growing up. When he sang a Glenn Miller song that he and his meemaw had liked, he even got Mother to join in at "Woo, woo, Chattanooga, there you are."

I tell myself this will pass: Jane is still growing up. This is merely the twenty-year-old version of her wearing an ugly blue coat for most of third grade. Meanwhile, my pride and my irritation are constantly banging into each other. I love my daughter deeply, but right now it's hard to like her very much.

I know I said I'd come in time for spring, but I've already bought a plane ticket to visit Jane in California over Easter, so I think I'd better wait until summer. Also, it would feel lousy telling the Institute on such short notice to find a replacement for the upcoming semester (my fault, I should have said something back in September), and now the chair has asked me to organize an exhibition of student work for the end of the school year.

SAM DECKER: One night when we were setting up the darkroom, Lilly asked if I ever wished I'd had children. I laughed so hard I almost spilled the stop bath. I told her I couldn't think of a time when that would have been possible or anything close to a good idea. Lilly nodded. She said she guessed that was the biggest difference between women and men. I asked how she'd liked it. It had been hard, she said, but it had made her a better photographer. Which one, I wanted to know, being a woman or being a mother? Lilly looked at me the way a teacher looks at a kid who can't spell or tell time. She told me it wasn't a question she knew how to answer: she'd been one for about as long as she'd been the other.

I figured out pretty quickly that Clyde boys and Clyde in general were much more interesting than anything or anyone at Holy Mount. Instead of going out for my school's production of *Tartuffe,* I acted in so many of Clyde's contemporary performance projects — as Snake Queen, as the Ocean, as Enoon the Voice of Us All — that some people thought I was enrolled. One day I came out of a rehearsal to a bunch of students sitting in the solarium, passing around a joint. If she was such a genius, one of them said, then why didn't she do anything after that? Because the system shut her down, said somebody else. Or maybe she and her daughter both got fat, said somebody different.

What are you guys talking about? I said, even though part of me already knew. This was an art school, after all. There were classes with titles like "Issues in Contemporary Photography."

That chick who did the naked photographs of her and her kid, the first one said, who was all over the news back when we were seven or eight. Man, I wish it was still that easy to get famous, he said, and everyone laughed.

The light — not just in the room but in the world — dimmed and then got really bright, like all the electricity in the universe was deciding whether to snuff itself or blow up. Once it got normal again, I suppose I could have walked out of that room or laughed along with everyone else, but neither of those options occurred to me.

She wasn't trying to get famous, I said. Those pictures were personal. They weren't even the sort of thing she usually did.

How would you know? the first one asked.

Because I'm her kid, I said.

110. Skateboarder, Bicknell Hill, Santa Monica, 1975

When I walked into life-drawing class the Tuesday after I'd outed myself in the solarium, twenty people were there in addition to the usual fifteen. Instead of everyone talking to each other like usual, it was quiet. Specifically, it was the quiet before the curtain goes up on a sold-out show that everyone in the audience feels lucky to have nabbed a seat for. The light started doing the same too dim/too bright thing it had done in the solarium, and I felt a little like throwing up, but not in a bad way. I was good at playing the part I was about to play, and I liked having an audience. I went behind the screen, got undressed, then came back out and held poses the way I always did, to the sound of thirty-five pencils drawing in thirty-five sketchbooks.

Back when I was nine, if someone had said, Samantha, the thing making your life a daily misery will one day make you the coolest kid in school, I would have called him a dog-breath dipstick and kneed him in the groin. Under no circumstances would I have imagined a future in which being Samantha Preston would mean free liquor or weed for the asking, a standing invitation to every art party in Los Angeles, and a distinguished-artist boyfriend who liked to eat me for dessert. Leo's whole thing was paintings of animal-headed people working in factories, or actual factory machines with animal-headed people painted onto them. Pretty soon it was the rare evening he wasn't taking me somewhere. Naturally, in a place where everyone went by first names, it wasn't hard to miss that Leo always introduced me as S. Jane Preston, but I liked how it sounded. S. Jane was more sophisticated than Samantha or Jane alone; and if that name meant a dedicated toothbrush in Leo's bathroom and people who looked at me instead of past me when he brought me around, I had no problem with that.

Had my mother visited Los Angeles earlier, she just would have been Jane's mom. Now that I was S. Jane, she was Lillian Preston. I was tormented by the thought that wherever we went, I'd be demoted from headliner to opening act, if I was still written into the program at all. At thirty-five, Leo was much closer to my mother's age than mine. My twenty-year-old self conquered these fears by disappearing on Leo the weekend of Lillian's visit, telling him I'd be out of town, and then carefully dividing the time between photo walks in Santa Monica — which was far enough from Clyde to preclude being seen — and the Holy Mount campus, where I was practically as much a stranger as my mother.

> *JOURNAL ENTRY, APRIL 1975:* When you told me your new friends knew who you "really" were, I didn't know what to think, but from the moment I arrived, you seemed so confident and happy that it felt like my wishes for you, after all these years, had been granted. But Squirrel, if it's true you're so liberated from your past that posing for artists is "no big deal," why am I still not allowed to take your picture or to meet these friends?

Thank you for showing me your city. In the back of my mind, I thought I knew what to expect, but Los Angeles is quite different from San Francisco. There's a hardness beneath its surface that scares me a little, but also an excitement and a sense of freedom, a feeling that important things are happening. I hadn't heard of skateboarding before you took me to Bicknell Hill, but I'll never forget the feeling of watching those boys speeding down that asphalt slope. Passion manifests in such a beautiful variety of forms.

Considering that when I was twenty, I wasn't on speaking terms with my mother, perhaps it's a victory that you tolerated a visit from yours, but you revealed so little of yourself that I couldn't help wondering if you wanted me there at all. Certainly you're old enough to live how you like. What breaks my heart is that you don't think you can — or just don't want to — share the details of that life with me.

111. Sam Decker with an undeveloped film cartridge containing photographs of his friend Private Kevin Conway, Cleveland, 1975

LETTER TO DEBORAH BRODSKY, JUNE 1975: According to Mother, who, since last

Christmas, has made a Sunday habit of asking Sam to dinner and then interrogating me about him once he's gone, Sam hasn't asked me to marry him because I haven't been trying hard enough. When I tell her that Sam and I are simply good friends, she smiles and offers to treat me to a makeover. In truth, I feel closer to Sam in the darkroom than I ever felt to Charles or Ken. It's both wildly different and at the same time exactly what I imagined when I began writing letters to the boy whose photographs I fell in love with at seventeen. I'm no longer in love with Sam's work, and I suppose I was never in love with the man, but what we do in the darkroom goes deeper than either of those.

The portrait wouldn't have happened if Sam hadn't asked me to grab us some pop, then told me where in his refrigerator to find it. The film canister blocked my hand's path. Sam must have known I'd be curious about that single undeveloped roll, but I understood him well enough not to ask questions when I returned with our drinks. Instead I simply handed him the film canister, then snapped the shutter as he spoke.

SAM DECKER: All those years when I wasn't sure where I was or what I was doing, that roll of film stayed in my pocket. Not the best storage conditions, I told Lilly, so that was one reason not to develop it: all the shots would be fogged or faded. But even if the roll was still good, I wouldn't do it. No one needs a picture of Conway dead, especially not me. Broad daylight, the two of us hoofing it back to the battalion from the MLR for our first hot meal in ten days, waxing grandiose over the showers and beds calling our names. Suddenly, there's a whistling sound; I'm knocked off my feet and flat onto my ass. When I stand back up, there's Conway looking the same as before, only on the ground. It's a sunny, peaceful morning. If there wasn't a crater where the Chinese artillery shell had just hit, there'd be no reason to think Conway wasn't getting a jump on all that sleep we'd just been jawing about. He bragged he'd go fourteen hours straight, maybe sixteen. Twenty, I boasted back, maybe twenty-four. I was getting ready to lie down next to him when I saw the medics.

I wouldn't have taken the picture if he'd been anyone else. Up until then I'd been grabbing shots of grunts in the chow line, or writing letters, or playing cards, or sleeping off last night's patrol — because what the hell else would I be taking pictures of? What kind of asshole puts himself in the middle of a war and, instead of trying to do something about the fighting or the bleeding, frames the explosions or the bodies just right to supply the folks back home with some vicarious excitement, some token image to make their lives feel more informed or lucky or safe or whatever else passes for meaning? Forget all that noble gas about bearing witness: anyone who takes war pictures likes doing it. They like it or they wouldn't be there, because there are plenty of better and easier ways to make a buck. None of them are making a difference. Picture or no picture, people will keep killing each other using methods old and new — day after day, year after year, centuries of killing — until one way or another we're all dead, and all the guns and cameras of the world are just so much garbage lying in the dirt. The only thing a war photographer does is make the killing look beautiful. He distorts it into a moment frozen in perfect clarity, when an honest photograph would be messy, blurred, and hard to read. No one wants honesty. No one will frame it or print it on a cover or a front page, because honesty is ugly. And once I realized that, a few days into digging my first foxhole, I didn't want to be a war photographer anymore.

Around the time Lillian was taking Sam's picture, I was cast in my first non-student production, at a theater in Silver Lake. I wouldn't have spent the summer after my sophomore year back in Cleveland no matter what, but the play made it easier to break the news to Lillian and Grandma, who made me swear up and down that I would come home for Christmas. Silver Lake was too far to bike, so Leo taught me to drive, allowing me to conquer the Santa Monica Freeway.

With the excitement of getting my first professional acting gig and my driver's license, I kept forgetting to refill my prescription, so I shouldn't have been surprised when I was a week late. Technically, I knew that the previous five pregnancy-free years were thanks to the little white pill I'd been swallowing nightly. Then again, the unlikelihood that something the size and shape of an aspirin could prevent something so world-altering as a baby made it seem equally plausible that my body wasn't the pregnancy type, a theory replaced by self-accusation as soon as my period didn't come.

I called in sick to rehearsal the day of my clinic appointment. Leo gave me cab fare, since I wasn't supposed to drive after the procedure and he was too busy to go with me. I didn't mind. With Leo there, I might have felt compelled to share my thoughts, and I wasn't in a sharing mood. There were few things I wanted less than a baby, but I couldn't help doing the math: my mother was nineteen when she had me; here I was, twenty and knocked up. What I was doing at that clinic would have canceled me out had Lillian made the same choice. I wasn't sure whether getting an abortion made me a shittier, more selfish person than my mother, or just luckier. By the time the gentle clinic doctor was done with me, I did know that because I wasn't pregnant, I landed a play downtown after the one in Silver Lake; and after that show closed, I got a call from a casting agent, who said the director John Bradshaw had seen my performance and wanted me for his next film.

112. Pages from private journal (No. 24), March 1976

The play I did after Bradshaw finished shooting was having its cast party the same night that Leo was invited to a dinner party at the home of some big-time art collector. Cast parties always went late, Leo told me; I could head there after the dinner was over. Roger Creeland didn't buy single pieces, he bought whole series. Leo said if I cared at all about him or his career, I would come.

I figured it would be a house in the hills or on Mulholland, but Leo started driving north on 101. I squawked when I learned we were in for a three-hour drive to Santa Barbara, but Leo told me to can it. This guy was one of the biggest, richest collectors on the West Coast. When he invited you to dinner, you came.

The collector's house was all glass and white brick at the edge of a cliff. As soon as we arrived, a man with thick white hair and lots of rings kissed my hand and said, Samantha Preston, it is such a great pleasure to meet you. And you must be Leo. Please make yourselves at home. The living room was four times bigger than Leo's apartment. The two walls that weren't glass and sticking out over the cliff were covered in paintings and photographs. The paintings didn't look like the sort of stuff Leo did, and I wondered if Creeland had whole wings of his house devoted to different art styles or what. I recognized a few people from L.A., including one of the painters I sometimes modeled for. I kept trying to ignore that Leo wasn't introducing me as S. Jane, like usual, but as Samantha Preston, the way Roger Creeland had. I'd needed to pee for the last hour in the car, but I stayed with Leo long enough to drink one drink before making for a bathroom.

I was halfway past the wall paintings when I suddenly felt like puking, which was strange since I hadn't eaten anything, and I'd only had the one drink. It took my brain a split second more to realize what my body already knew: I recognized the photographs on the next half of Roger Creeland's living room wall. There were eight of them, all black and white, arranged in a nice straight line leading to the bathroom, the way family photos are displayed in houses where photographs are photographs and not trophies. I walked past each print as if it weren't a hammer to my head. When I locked myself inside Roger Creeland's bathroom, I sat on his Carrara marble floor because my arms and legs weren't working. I was in Mrs. Barkley's class all over again, after eleven years of thinking I was free. I focused on pressing the coolness of the white stone onto my knees and my palms. I stood up. I splashed cold water on my face until I looked mostly normal.

Leo was still working the room. Samantha! he said, there you are. Everyone's asking about you. Babe, I said, I left my bag in your car. Give me your keys and I'll be right back, and I pursed my lips in a promising way.

The longest I'd ever driven before that night was the forty minutes it took to get to the theater in Silver Lake. Three hours later, I threw Leo's car keys through his studio window, grabbed my bike, and stopped at the first motel where it didn't look like I'd get jumped checking in to a room. When I signed the register, Monica Kay was what came out: Monica after the freeway that had brought me to my first real acting gig, and Kay after the friend who'd put on a mask at Halloween and showed to me the power of becoming someone else.

SAM DECKER: I knew it was photography money paying for Lilly's medical bills and Jane's tuition, but I never considered which photographs, and Lilly never said. Sunday at Dorothy's, I was at the sink washing dinner plates when the phone rang. Dot's voice lit up when she said she'd accept the charges. Dot was a nice old lady. She loved Jane the way my meemaw loved me, with about as little to show for it. When she handed the phone to Lilly, the next thing I knew, Lilly was sitting at the kitchen table looking like a bleached-out version of herself. She's gone, Lilly said. I've lost her for good.

JOURNAL ENTRY, MARCH 1976: The question isn't whether I should have sold the photographs — that was a matter of survival — but whether I should have tried harder to tell you. I know what I meant to say all those years ago, the last time you visited me in the hospital before we left New York, but I was so sick then. It's possible I said only part of what I intended, or nothing at all. At the time, I consoled myself with how careful I'd been with Mr. Wythe in setting the terms: the photographs could never be resold, donated, or otherwise placed in anyone else's possession; the purchase was never to be publicized in any way; and the photos could only ever be shown privately in Mr. Creeland's home. I told myself that you were protected. Would things have been different if I hadn't been so sick the night you took the train from Brooklyn? If I'd had the strength to tell you properly? If you had learned the truth at fifteen, would you have reacted the way you have at twenty-one, or would you have found a way to make peace with what I did? In the days after your call, I dialed and redialed the only number I had for you. Finally, a man answered and told me that you were gone.

113. Franny Panic, Agora Ballroom parking lot, Cleveland, 1976

LETTER TO DEBORAH BRODSKY, AUGUST 1976: I hadn't heard of Ms. Panic, but when my students explained about the song, I thought it'd be interesting to go. She's popular enough that I'm sure my students would have gone anyway, but at the club, most of them seemed just as interested in watching me. When I stepped outside for some air, I saw a woman sitting cross-legged on the hood of a car, picking at a scab on her knee like a girl half her age. I didn't realize until I saw that same young woman growling into the microphone that it was Ms. Panic whose picture I'd taken. The song's anger reminded me of you. In our East Seventh Street days, I didn't know myself well enough to say it, but you were someone who knew how to get angry, which was something I both feared and was wild to learn.

I called the school, but Jane isn't enrolled there anymore. There are no Los Angeles listings for Jane or Samantha Preston. Since she and I last spoke nineteen weeks ago, she's called Mother twice. Mother feels guilty about this; I'm just thankful she's still speaking to one of us. No matter what Mother asks, Jane only wants to talk about what birds Mother has seen out the kitchen window. Mother says Jane sounds cheerful enough, but thinks she isn't sleeping well. Jane's calls have come just as Mother was waking up, which means that in California, it was four a.m. It's hard not to fill the spaces in between those lines with worry, but both times Jane called direct and not collect, so she must have a little money. Any small, fleeting glimpse of her is better than nothing at all.

One weekend I was passing around a joint and watching *Saturday Night,* still cracking up over something Dan Aykroyd and John Belushi had done before the last commercial break, when all of a sudden this skinny girl with spiked hair and black makeup across her eyes started singing "Mommy is sick, Mommy is sick," in a voice like her head was on fire. I was watching the same way as everybody else until the guitarist took a solo and the girl put the microphone between her legs and yanked off her dress. Who's that? I asked. I was feeling warm all over partly because I was stoned and partly because underneath her dress, the girl's boobs were barred with black tape. That's Franny Panic, someone said. The girl jerked the microphone back to her mouth and started singing "Mommy is sick," wearing nothing but fishnets and a line of black tape across her chest, before the show cut quick to another commercial. When it came back, the girl was gone and Chevy Chase was making a joke about downtown New York fashions.

I got her civilian name from a copy of *Rolling Stone,* though by the time I called the Manhattan operator and asked for Francis Pell's number, I'd convinced myself that I'd hallucinated the whole thing. This meant when a pissed-off voice said, "Who's this?" into the phone, I was totally unprepared. Samantha, I told her, even though I hadn't spoken that name out loud in twelve years. Suddenly, I realized I didn't know what time it was in L.A., not to mention New York, so when that same pissed-off voice growled, "Samantha who?" it wasn't a question I felt prepared to answer.

When *Under the Fence* came out, Monica

Kay was the name in the credits, finishing something I'd started the night I gave myself that name at the motel. I'd missed so many of my Holy Mount classes by then that I probably would have dropped out anyway. Even if I'd been willing to keep taking "Samantha Series" money to cover my tuition, it seemed stupid to shell out for an education when I was getting paid for one each time I got a part. Not that I was making much, but even before *Under the Fence,* it was usually enough to eat and pay rent. Then came *Parkland* and *No Going Back* and *Fever Dream* and a certain kind of independence.

People who like the kind of movies that got made in the '70s know who I am, but since moving back to New York, I've stuck to plays. I don't like the way movies are done in bits and pieces, with the only real meaning made afterward by the editor in postproduction. Also, I realized pretty quickly after I started in movies that performing for a camera inside a locked room felt too much like hiding, like I was building a relationship and then ducking out on its care and feeding, which felt too painfully familiar. That might not make sense to anyone besides me, but it doesn't need to.

Though I think my grandmother would

have enjoyed seeing me in a play, by the time I was performing back east, travel wasn't an option for her. She never said anything about the movies. This means either she didn't see them or she didn't like them. If I had to guess, I'd say she chose not to see them in order to avoid not liking them. Grandma was a practical person, and by the last decade of her life, our relationship was already complicated enough.

114. Two young women walking and talking, Cleveland, 1976

LETTER TO DEBORAH BRODSKY, OCTOBER 1976: As usual, I'd taken the bus halfway to the Art Institute so I could walk the rest. The two of them couldn't have been older than nineteen. I was content simply to enjoy the energy of their strides and their voices until one of them stopped walking and turned to face her friend. It was clear from their faces that the world around them had fallen away, their lives subsumed by the stream of words flowing between them. They were so intent on each other that I could have taken fifty pictures, but I didn't need to. I sensed the perfection of that first shot in my mind as well as in my hand. And so, happy birthday. Those two don't look anything like us, but it feels like our portrait nonetheless.

Deb, I've been meaning to write you about something for a while, and I think you might know what it is. At first I thought moving to Arizona really was just a matter of honoring previous commitments and tidying loose ends, but it would be dishonest to pretend that the past two years of delays have been accidental. I know joining you in the desert might be all that we've been looking forward to, but what if it isn't? The last time we lived on top of each other, everything about who we were was new and exciting and open to change. This made it easier to overlook our faults, but we've been ourselves for over twenty years now. I'll never pay attention to a newspaper or devote myself to a cause, and you'll never stop following your impulses, no matter where they may lead. We've been able to excuse ourselves these and other perceived failings at a distance, but could we up close? I can already hear you in my mind, because where I hesitate is exactly where you would leap — but Deb, you've got a talent for friends. You make them wherever you go, while I can count the friends I've made in my life on three fingers.

In the ten months or so after I dropped out of school and, in the spirit of self-destruction and self-discovery, gave myself over to everything that everyone associates with Hollywood in the '70s, I didn't telephone Cleveland according to any set schedule. I remember dialing my grandmother around Christmastime from a party at a beach house, using a phone from one of its ten bedrooms so I wouldn't have to call collect. Two months later, I was sitting on a patio with a poolside phone just like the ones in the movies, at a house where I'd spent the night. Though my general recollection of that period is spotty at best, I remember the exact date — Sunday, February 20, 1977 — because as soon as Grandma heard my voice, she told me that my mother was dead. My legs shot straight out in front of me, tipping my chair sideways onto the ground, but I couldn't feel anything, so it didn't hurt. Because Grandma and I were both crying so hard, only half of what we were saying to each other made any sense. When she said I couldn't come to the funeral, I thought she didn't want me there. Very gradually, like a blind person trying to climb a series of barbed-wire fences, I realized it wasn't that I was not invited: I was just horribly and permanently too late.

For an indeterminate period of time after that call ended, I stared at some ants crawling in and out of a crack in a terra-cotta patio tile, until I can only assume someone found me, stood me up, and told me it was time to leave. My mother died on Friday, January 28, 1977. When I called home, she was already twenty-three days gone.

The Last Self-Portraits

115. Self-portrait, Cleveland Clinic, January 28, 1977, 4:22 a.m.

SAM DECKER: No one's always healthy, so sometimes she got sick; except with her, it was more complicated. Once she had to go downtown. For a week they gave her antibiotics and transfusions until she got better again. The final time began the same way, except after a week she wasn't any better, and they told her the cancer was back.

It went fast after that. Dot and I took turns staying with her. Lilly wanted to go home, but the docs wouldn't let her. Instead they started her on chemo along with everything else. Dot was a mess. She wanted to be with Lilly, but she was afraid Jane would call and she'd miss the chance to tell her what was happening. I went around to a bunch of stores until I found one with a telephone answering machine, which was something I'd only ever seen on *The Rockford Files,* a big ugly black box with buttons on it and tape cassettes inside. I hooked it up and helped Dot put a message on it telling Jane everything that was going on. I kept coming over to make sure the thing was working, and to see if Jane had called, but the kid had phoned about three weeks before Lilly got sick so it didn't seem likely.

When Lilly realized she wouldn't be going home, she asked me to bring her the timed-exposure camera. I knew all about how she'd done the portraits of her and Jane, but that contraption hadn't come out of its box since she'd left New York. Boy, was that camera something. Not much in the looks department, but the mechanism was a real beaut. Even though Lilly gave the credit to some guy named Kubiak, it was clear from how she described it that she was the brains behind the gizmo. By this time, she was too weak to work the tripod. I set it up for her, then she adjusted it herself until it was the way she wanted. She had the cable release for it lying next to her on the bed. Every day at visiting hours, I'd check to see if she'd triggered the thing, thinking I could ride her about it, but she never had. She asked if I'd develop the film for her once it was exposed. When I told her that she could develop it herself after she got better, she looked so peeved that I told her I would do it.

One day I'm talking to Lilly when she gasps and her eyes get wide. I'm thinking this is it until she starts crying and saying "Deb" over and over again. Suddenly, a long-haired woman with freckles is bending over the bed. The two of them are hugging and repeating each other's names in a way that sounds like one of those languages where the same word said different ways means a dozen different things.

DEBORAH BRODSKY: Considering the last time I'd seen her was back in '67, it would have been a shock no matter what, but Lilly in that hospital bed wasn't anything I could have prepared myself for. I'd been to a few funerals by that point, so I knew death as a destination, but before Lilly, I didn't know the journey. Lilly hadn't asked me to come. She'd called to tell me she was in the hospital, but she hadn't said, "Deb, I'm dying," and I hadn't come because I thought she was. When she got sick in '70, Yuma was three and the school hadn't been around long enough to feel like family. By the time the second sickness came, Yuma was ten and so used to everyone in the poetics department that I was sure he'd be fine without me for a little while.

As soon as I saw Lilly, I knew. So did she; it was in her eyes, though knowing something isn't the same as being at peace with it. Lilly was forty, and she wasn't ready to die; but if she had to, she was going to die working.

I'd never seen pain like hers up close. It would sweep down like an angry Old Testament god, then stay or leave on a whim. Mornings were her best times, so that's when we would talk. Mostly we told our favorite stories about each other, a lot of deep remembering. After about an hour of this, I'd be as tired as she was. This gnawed at me until I realized we weren't just talking: my brain was building shelves to store all those words in some more archival way, because I was about to be their only custodian.

At one point she asked if I was disappointed in her. Why, I said, for only beating the odds three times over? Ninety-five percent of the people who'd gotten sick when she did were already dead. Was she asking if I was mad that she'd beaten leukemia for five years instead of ten or fifteen? Lilly shook her head. I never came to you, she said. I never met Yuma as a boy. We never taught together like I said we would. She looked so disappointed in herself that I knew I couldn't laugh, even though I wanted to. Lilly, I said, I stopped expecting you to move to Arizona after you first turned me down back in '74. Well, she certainly wasn't expecting that. But Deb, she said as her eyes went big and round, all these years I really thought I was going to do it! I smiled and got her some water. It used to be when a person didn't live up to something, I'd pitch accusations at them and jab at the air like I was fighting invisible dragons. I spent a lot of energy trying to make people in my image and then getting mad when they didn't look the part, but if being a mother and a teacher has taught me anything, it's that you have to work with what's already there. I told Lilly there was a difference between a promise and an aspiration. The whole point of an aspiration is to make yourself reach. The only people who achieve everything they aspire to are lazy or cowards. If one of us had been either of those, we never would have stayed friends.

Day after day, no matter how bad the pain got, Lilly wouldn't let the docs give her anything for it: she wanted to stay present. I pointed out that when the pain took hold of her, she was gone anyway, so she might as well grant herself some relief, but Lilly was afraid that once she started on morphine, she wouldn't be able to stop.

Each day she asked if Jane had called, and each day something inside her clamped down tighter when we told her no. Lying in that bed, she came to look like a marathon runner, her muscles straining, her eyes focused on a distant point, except that she was trying to run away from something instead of toward it. Finally, I had to tell her it was okay to stop. She wasn't a bad mother if she needed to leave without saying goodbye.

116. Self-portrait, Cleveland Clinic, January 28, 1977, 4:43 a.m.

DEBORAH BRODSKY: I'd fallen asleep in a chair by the window like I always did, only this time I woke up to the sound of her camera. The room was silent except for that clicking sound, but inside my head, a congregation of voices suddenly started shouting Lilly's name: some saying Goodbye, some saying Don't go, and some reciting victory poems because she had managed to do this terrible, amazing thing.

She'd picked her time well. It was late. There wouldn't be anyone checking in on her until morning. My chair was positioned by the door in case the night nurse came. As long as that camera was running, I knew Lilly needed me to guard the space. I was desperate to go to the bed, to stroke her face and hold her hand, to do all the things the heart cries for when someone you love is leaving, but any one of those would have ruined the shot. And so I made myself stay exactly where I was.

Lilly was very, very still. Her eyes were open and staring at the camera with such intensity that looking at her felt like staring at a bright light. I was perched at the edge of my seat, every muscle in my body frozen in the act of launching from that chair. I barely breathed or blinked as the camera clicked and the film advanced frame by frame. I sat there and caressed Lilly with my eyes. For each second of each minute of that last holy hour, my muscles strained and the voices in my head shouted and howled and sang, until the film ran out and the clicking stopped.

SAM DECKER: Deb was the one who knew what funeral arrangements Lilly wanted, and who to contact at the Art Institute, and about the boxes she'd left behind — basically all the things Lilly had been hoping to tell Jane, and which, in the end, she told Deb instead. Deb got the newspaper to run an obituary, not one of those paid jobs but the real deal. She made the telephone calls. At the funeral, there was me, Dot, Deb, an old friend of Lilly's from Brooklyn, and a bunch of students and teachers who'd known Lilly from the Art Institute. Afterwards we all went to the café where I'd remounted photos from Lilly's show four years before. Dot was having a pretty hard time. I told her, for what it was worth, she had me now, and I was a stubborn old bastard who wasn't going anywhere. I wish I could have been around for Meemaw the way I was for Dot, but most of life is just timing. It took me five years to get my head together after the army was done with me. By that time, all that was left of Meemaw was the building with the empty storefront where Anderssen's Shoes had been.

117. Self-portrait, Cleveland Clinic, January 28, 1977, 4:57 a.m.

GRETE WASHINGTON: When Lillian left Brooklyn, she was so very ill that saying goodbye felt like the final farewell, but then came her letter to say that the treatment in Detroit was a success. What began as a small piece of hope grew larger, until I did not see its edges anymore. Lillian's return to health did not bring our friendship back to what it once was. Even I, who do not like letting go, knew that this could not come back, but we exchanged letters. I wrote when Paul took Kaja to Liberia, and also when Kaja was accepted to university in Britain. Lillian wrote when Jane went to California and again when Walter died. Our friendship was paler but a friendship still. Then Deborah's phone call came. When Jane was not at the funeral, I cried for them both.

After the service, Deborah and I did not bother with introductions, though meeting face-to-face felt quite strange. Hers were eyes I did not know, and yet I knew so much about the person behind them. I thought of a knot joining two threads, and of the way a vibration will travel from one thread to the other, passing through the knot along the way. Now the knot that had joined Deborah to me was gone.

I asked Deborah if Lillian had been in much pain. She told me that Lillian had died according to her wishes. When Deborah explained about the camera, I laughed, and this made Deborah laugh also. Others near us were puzzled by this, but I could see it bothered Deborah as little as it bothered me. Good for Lillian, I said. I think it *was* good for Lilly, Deborah answered, even though it was very hard. She was always strong, I said. And stubborn, Deborah agreed as she smiled. So many stories were contained in that smile, stories we could share just by this curve we made with our mouths.

Usually, when I speak to Lillian in my mind, it is to tell her about Kaja: about the man she met at King's College whose parents came to Britain from Jamaica after the war; about the children she has had with him and my trips to England to see them; about my recognition that Kaja, like me, has made a home as far away from her parents as she could. Lillian's answers in my mind do not include her voice. I cannot hear her voice anymore, but her eyes remain. Even when we disagreed, Lillian's eyes stayed on my face, as if to remind me that our friendship would always have a place in this world.

118. Self-portrait, Cleveland Clinic, January 28, 1977, 5:04 a.m.

SAM DECKER: The morning after she died, I brought the exposed film back from the hospital, thinking I'd develop it straightaway, but I didn't. For weeks I'd been working in the darkroom without her, waiting for her to get better, and seeing that film on Lilly's shelf made it easier to pretend she'd be coming back. Then came the funeral. I didn't cry until I got to the darkroom, where it was something private between her and me. After that, working got hard. The smallest things left the biggest gaps. The missing sound of her breathing or the floor shifting under her weight. The feeling that if I stepped to the right, I'd brush against her arm. At some point, I started resenting that four-inch-thick roll of undeveloped film. Every time I came into the darkroom, I felt it staring at me, waiting for me to do what Lilly had asked. Maybe I would have felt different if I didn't already have an unfinished job of my own, but Lilly was the only one who knew about the canister I'd been holding on to, and it felt like she was testing me. I took her out of the darkroom and put her in the fridge next to Conway, where I knew she would keep.

One night I'm drinking beers with Conway in a dream and he says, Don't be an asshole, Decker, who else could she trust? You're the only one as fussy as she is. Fine, I told him, but I'm still leaving your roll alone. Why would I give a shit what you do with that? Conway said. I've been dead twenty-three years.

The next night I closed up the coffeehouse at the usual time, but instead of catching the sunset, I went upstairs. First golden hour I'd skipped since I started the place. Over the next eight hours, I made contact sheets for all 680 shots. I was wrong to think it'd be quiet work. Anyone standing outside the darkroom door would've thought I was cracked, but I was just dictating one last letter to the air. I told her when I was arranging the negatives on the photo paper, and when I was placing the paper in the developer. I told her what I missed about her as I put each sheet in the stop bath, and what I remembered about her as I rinsed it and hung it to dry. Inspecting each exposure, I described what was beautiful in each of those last pictures she had taken, and what was difficult to see.

I'd assumed she'd be staring at the camera the whole time, and she was; but

I'd also thought it'd be easy to tell when she died, and it wasn't. For the first 120 shots, Lilly's face is tense the way it had been that whole week because of the pain. After that, she gets a look like when she's trying to explain something about camera technique, only stronger, and that look stays with her for the next 86. Then, starting at frame 207, her face starts to change. The pain and focus are still there, but by frame 229, it's clear you're seeing a record of that pain and focus stored within the face's stillness, and that Lilly has left that face behind.

ACKNOWLEDGMENTS

As I wrote this book, I was inspired by the work and lives of many people, including Berenice Abbott, Diane Arbus, Richard Avedon, Amiri Baraka, Judy Chicago, Louis Faurer, Harold Feinstein, Robert Frank, Helen Gee, Hettie Jones, Leon Levinstein, Helen Levitt, Vivian Maier, Sally Mann, Lisette Model, Alice Neel, Ruth Orkin, Grace Paley, Diane di Prima, and Garry Winogrand. Steven Millhauser's novella *Catalogue of the Exhibition: The Art of Edmund Moorash* (*1810–1846*) introduced me to the enormous potential of the museum catalogue as a way to tell a story. I could build a small habitable cabin of all the books I read for research, but I'm especially thankful for *The Choices We Made,* edited by Angela Bonavoglia, which helped me wrap my post–*Roe* v. *Wade* mind around the pre–*Roe* v. *Wade* era; and for *Hellhole,* by Sara Harris, which detailed conditions inside the New

York City House of Detention for Women in the 1960s. In my various research quests, several people generously allowed me to interview them or otherwise shared their work and knowledge with me: thank you to Jennifer Bernstein, Mary Engel, Harold Feinstein, Chloe Mills, Ruthann Robson, and Charles Spurlin.

Many thanks to the Sustainable Arts Foundation for their ongoing support of artists and writers with families, and for their grant, which provided me a much needed boost in material and immaterial ways.

Thanks to Jin Auh for becoming my ally and my agent, and for fighting for me and this book. Thanks to Kathy Belden for the care, intelligence, and acuity of vision that allowed this book to achieve its final form. Thanks to Wendy Schmalz for twenty years of agenthood and friendship.

Thank you to David Gassaway, Tim Kreider, Anthony Tognazzini, and Ellen and Mark Goldberg for reading. Double thanks to Jason Little, Ellen Twaddell, and Megan Kelso for reading . . . and then reading again.

Thank you to my daughters for expanding my idea of what love is and for teaching me what it means to be a mother. Thank you, Jason, for us.

ABOUT THE AUTHOR

Myla Goldberg is the bestselling author of *The False Friend, Wickett's Remedy,* and *Bee Season,* which was a *New York Times* Notable Book, a winner of the Borders New Voices Prize, a finalist for the Hemingway Foundation/PEN Award, and was adapted to film and widely translated.

The employees of Thorndike Press hope you have enjoyed this Large Print book. All our Thorndike, Wheeler, and Kennebec Large Print titles are designed for easy reading, and all our books are made to last. Other Thorndike Press Large Print books are available at your library, through selected bookstores, or directly from us.

For information about titles, please call:
(800) 223-1244

or visit our website at:
gale.com/thorndike

To share your comments, please write:
Publisher
Thorndike Press
10 Water St., Suite 310
Waterville, ME 04901

The employees of Thorndike Press hope you have enjoyed this Large Print book. All our Thorndike, Wheeler, and Kennebec Large Print titles are designed for easy reading, and all our books are made to last. Other Thorndike Press Large Print books are available at your library, through selected bookstores, or directly from us.

For information about titles, please call:
(800) 223-1244

or visit our website at:
gale.com/thorndike

To share your comments, please write:
Publisher
Thorndike Press
10 Water St., Suite 310
Waterville, ME 04901